P9-DYZ-274

# U is for
# Universal Acclaim...

# U is for Undertow

"No private eye comes close to Sue Grafton's endearing California sleuth, Kinsey Millhone."
—*The New York Times Book Review*

Looking solemn, Michael Sutton arrives in Kinsey Millhone's office with a story to tell. When he was six, he says, he wandered into the woods and saw two men digging a hole. They claimed they were pirates, looking for buried treasure. Now, all these years later, the long-forgotten events have come back to him—and he has pieced them together with news reports from the time, becoming convinced that he witnessed the burial of a kidnapped child.

Kinsey has nearly nothing to go on. Sutton doesn't even know where he was that day—and, she soon discovers, he has a history of what might generously be called an active imagination. Despite her doubts, Kinsey sets out to track down the so-called burial site. And what's found there pulls her into a hidden current of deceit stretching back more than twenty years . . .

"Has this reliable series lost its addictive appeal? Not at all."
—Marilyn Stasio, *The New York Times Book Review*

"Arresting prose . . . [a] brilliantly inventive novel."
—*Richmond Times-Dispatch*

"Makes me wish there were more than twenty-six letters at her disposal."
—Maureen Corrigan, NPR.org

"Her most structurally complex, psychologically potent book to date."
—Sarah Weinman, *Los Angeles Times*

"Kinsey Millhone shows no signs of slowing down . . . ★★★★."
—*People*

*continued . . .*

# Praise for the Kinsey Millhone novels

"A refreshing heroine." —*The Washington Post Book World*

"Millhone is all too human, and her humanity increases with each novel, each investigation . . . An incredibly even and satisfying series, one that keeps the reader interested in the plot—and in the continuing development of Kinsey Millhone."
—*Richmond Times–Dispatch*

"Grafton's prose is lean and her observational skills keen."
—*Chicago Tribune*

"A confident, likable sleuth with a good sense of humor."
—*Orlando Sentinel*

"A long-lived and much-loved series." —*Publishers Weekly*

"A stellar series." —*The Baltimore Sun*

"The spunkiest, funniest, and most engaging private investigator in Santa Teresa, California, not to mention the entire detective novel genre." —*Entertainment Weekly*

"Grafton's alphabet thrillers just keep getting better."
—*USA Today*

"[Graton] has mastered the art of blending new and old in novels that are both surprising and familiar."
—*The San Diego Union Tribune*

"Grafton deserves an A for maintaining her series'. high standard for excellence." —*Library Journal*

"Returning for another visit with the perpetually grumpy, smart-alecky, and utterly dedicated Kinsey is a treat."
—*The Cleveland Plain Dealer*

"Kinsey Millhone is Grafton's best mystery, one that has been unfolding deliciously since the letter 'A.'"
—*San Francisco Chronicle*

"[A] first-class series." —*The New York Times Book Review*

"Book for book, this may be the most satisfying mystery series going." —*The Wall Street Journal*

# IS FOR
# UNDERTOW

## SUE GRAFTON

BERKLEY BOOKS, NEW YORK

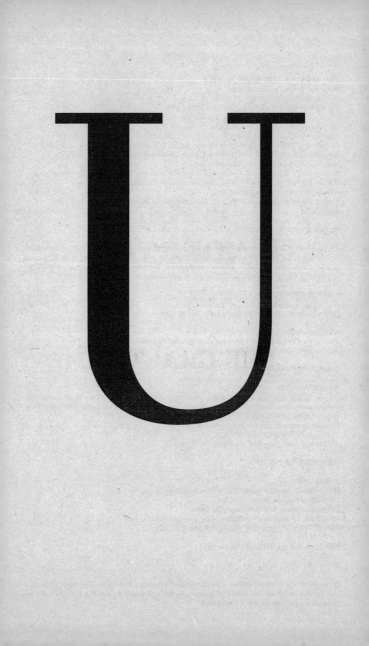

**THE BERKLEY PUBLISHING GROUP**
**Published by the Penguin Group**
**Penguin Group (USA) Inc.**
**375 Hudson Street, New York, New York 10014, USA**
Penguin Group (Canada), 90 Eglinton Avenue East, Suite 700, Toronto, Ontario M4P 2Y3, Canada
(a division of Pearson Penguin Canada Inc.)
Penguin Books Ltd., 80 Strand, London WC2R 0RL, England
Penguin Group Ireland, 25 St. Stephen's Green, Dublin 2, Ireland (a division of Penguin Books Ltd.)
Penguin Group (Australia), 250 Camberwell Road, Camberwell, Victoria 3124, Australia
(a division of Pearson Australia Group Pty. Ltd.)
Penguin Books India Pvt. Ltd., 11 Community Centre, Panchsheel Park, New Delhi—110 017, India
Penguin Group (NZ), 67 Apollo Drive, Rosedale, North Shore 0632, New Zealand
(a division of Pearson New Zealand Ltd.)
Penguin Books (South Africa) (Pty.) Ltd., 24 Sturdee Avenue, Rosebank, Johannesburg 2196,
South Africa

Penguin Books Ltd., Registered Offices: 80 Strand, London WC2R 0RL, England

This is a work of fiction. Names, characters, places, and incidents either are the product of the author's imagination or are used fictitiously, and any resemblance to actual persons, living or dead, business establishments, events, or locales is entirely coincidental. The publisher does not have any control over and does not assume any responsibility for author or third-party websites or their content.

U IS FOR UNDERTOW

A Berkley Book / published by arrangement with the author

PRINTING HISTORY
Marion Wood / G. P. Putnam's Sons hardcover edition / December 2009
Berkley mass-market edition / December 2010

ISBN: 978-0-425-23811-0

BERKLEY®
Berkley Books are published by The Berkley Publishing Group,
a division of Penguin Group (USA) Inc.,
375 Hudson Street, New York, New York 10014.
BERKLEY® is a registered trademark of Penguin Group (USA) Inc.
The "B" design is a trademark of Penguin Group (USA) Inc.

PRINTED IN THE UNITED STATES OF AMERICA

10  9  8  7  6  5  4  3  2  1

For Larry Welch, who left us,
steering a course for ports unknown,
and for Pam, who sails on,
navigating her journey over high seas.
Safe passage to you both.

# ACKNOWLEDGMENTS

The author wishes to acknowledge the invaluable assistance of the following people: Steven Humphrey; Sam Eaton, Eaton and Jones, Attorneys at Law; John Mackall, Attorney at Law, Seed Mackall LLP; Bill Turner, Detective Sergeant (retired), Santa Barbara County Sheriff's Department; Deborah Linden, Chief of Police, San Luis Obispo; Mary Ellen Tiffany, Vice President Business Development, Montecito Bank & Trust; Penny Braniff and Krys Jackson, Hope Ranch Park Homes Association; Special Agent Leane Blevins, Federal Bureau of Investigation, Ventura field office; Lisa Lowseth, DVM; Amy Taylor, Veterinary Technician, Cat Doctors; Susan Burke, Librarian, Laguna Blanca School; Diane Miller, Assistant Dean, Helen Bader School of Social Welfare, University of Wisconsin, Milwaukee; Kevin Frantz; Sally Giloth; Tracy Kanowsky; Suzanne Perkins; Steve Tipton; Kim Showalter; Jamie Clark; Susan Gulbransen; Joanna Barnes; and Sue Parks; along with a special thank-you to Margie and Keith Kirkendall, Patricia L. Erbe, M.D., and Jeffrey Grill, M.D., for the use of their names.

# 1

## Wednesday afternoon, April 6, 1988

What fascinates me about life is that now and then the past rises up and declares itself. Afterward, the sequence of events seems inevitable, but only because cause and effect have been aligned in advance. It's like a pattern of dominoes arranged upright on a tabletop. With the flick of your finger, the first tile topples into the second, which in turn tips into the third, setting in motion a tumbling that goes on and on, each tile knocking over its neighbor until all of them fall down. Sometimes the impetus is pure chance, though I discount the notion of accidents. Fate stitches together elements that seem unrelated on the surface. It's only when the truth emerges you see how the bones are joined and everything connects.

Here's the odd part. In my ten years as a private eye, this was the first case I ever managed to resolve without crossing paths with the bad guys. Except at the end, of course.

My name is Kinsey Millhone. I'm a private detective, female, age thirty-seven, with my thirty-eighth birthday coming up in a month. Having been married and divorced twice, I'm now happily single and expect to remain so for life. I have no children thus far and I don't anticipate bearing any. Not only are my eggs getting old, but my biological clock wound down a long time ago. I suppose there's always room for one of life's little surprises, but that's not the way to bet.

I work solo out of a rented bungalow in Santa Teresa, California, a town of roughly 85,000 souls who generate sufficient crime to occupy the Santa Teresa Police Department, the County Sheriff's Department, the California Highway Patrol, and the twenty-five or so local private investigators like me. Movies and television shows would have you believe a PI's job is dangerous, but nothing could be further from the truth . . . except, of course, on the rare occasions when someone tries to kill me. Then I'm ever so happy my health insurance premiums are paid up. Threat of death aside, the job is largely research, requiring intuition, tenacity, and ingenuity. Most of my clients reach me by referral and their business ranges from background checks to process serving, with countless other matters in between. My office is off the beaten path and I seldom have a client appear unannounced, so when I heard a tapping at the door to my outer office, I got up and peered around the corner to see who it was.

Through the glass I saw a young man pointing at the knob. I'd apparently turned the dead bolt to the locked position when I'd come back from lunch. I let him in, saying, "Sorry about that. I must have locked up after myself without being aware of it."

"You're Ms. Millhone?"

"Yes."

"Michael Sutton," he said, extending his hand. "Do you have time to talk?"

We shook hands. "Sure. Can I offer you a cup of coffee?"

"No, thanks. I'm fine."

I ushered him into my office while I registered his appearance in a series of quick takes. Slim. Lank brown hair with a sheen to it, worn long on top and cut short over his ears. Solemn brown eyes, complexion as clear as a baby's. There was a prep school air about him: deck shoes without socks, sharply creased chinos, and a short-sleeve white dress shirt he wore with a tie. He had the body of a boy: narrow shoulders, narrow hips, and long, smooth arms. He looked young enough to be carded if he tried to buy booze. I couldn't imagine what sort of problem he'd have that would require my services.

I returned to my swivel chair and he settled in the chair on the other side of the desk. I glanced at my calendar, wondering if I'd set up an appointment and promptly forgotten it.

He noticed the visual reference and said, "Detective Phillips at the police department gave me your name and address. I should have called first, but your office was close by. I hope this isn't an inconvenience."

"Not at all," I said. "My first name's Kinsey, which you're welcome to use. You prefer Michael or Mike?"

"Most people call me Sutton. In my kindergarten class, there were two other Michaels so the teacher used our last names to distinguish us. Boorman, Sutton, and Trautwein— like a law firm. We're still friends."

"Where was this?"

"Climp."

I said, "Ah." I should have guessed as much. Climping Academy is the private school in Horton Ravine, K through 12. Tuition starts at twelve grand for the little tykes and rises incrementally through the upper grades. I don't know where it tops out, but you could probably pick up a respectable college education for the same price. All the students enrolled there referred to it as "Climp," as though the proper appellation was just, like, *sooo* beside the point. Watching him, I wondered if my blue-collar roots were as obvious to him as his upper-class status was to me.

We exchanged pleasantries while I waited for him to unload. The advantage of a prearranged appointment is that I begin the first meeting with at least *some* idea what a prospective client has in mind. People skittish about revealing their personal problems to a stranger often find it easier to do by phone. With this kid, I figured we'd have to dance around some before he got down to his business, whatever it was.

He asked how long I'd been a private investigator. This is a question I'm sometimes asked at cocktail parties (on the rare occasion when I'm invited to one). It's the sort of blah-blah-blah conversational gambit I don't much care for. I gave him a rundown of my employment history. I skipped over the two lackluster semesters at the local junior college and started with my graduation from the police academy. I then covered the two years I'd worked for the Santa Teresa PD before I realized how ill suited I was to a life in uniform. I proceeded with a brief account of my subsequent apprenticeship with a local agency, run by Ben Byrd and Morley Shine, two private investigators, who'd trained me in preparation for licensing. I'd had my ups and downs over the years, but I spared him the details since he'd only inquired as a stalling technique. "What about you? Are you a California native?"

"Yes, ma'am. I grew up in Horton Ravine. My family lived on Via Ynez until I went off to college. I lived a couple of other places, but now I'm back."

"You still have family here?"

His hesitation was one of those nearly imperceptible blips that indicates internal editing. "My parents are gone. I have two older brothers, both married with two kids each, and an older sister who's divorced. We're not on good terms. We haven't been for years."

I let that pass without comment, being better acquainted with family estrangement than I cared to admit. "How do you know Cheney Phillips?"

"I don't. I went into the police department, asking to speak to a detective, and he happened to be free. When I told him my situation, he said you might be able to help."

"Well, let's hope so," I said. "Cheney's a good guy. I've known him for years." I shut my mouth then and let a silence descend, a stratagem with remarkable powers to make the other guy talk.

Sutton touched the knot in his tie. "I know you're busy, so I'll get to the point. I hope you'll bear with me. The story might sound weird."

"Weird stories are the best kind, so fire away," I said.

He looked at the floor as he spoke, making eye contact now and then to see if I was following. "I don't know if you saw this, but a couple of weeks ago, there was an article in the newspaper about famous kidnappings: Marion Parker, the twelve-year-old girl who was abducted in 1927; the Lindbergh baby in 'thirty-two; another kid, named Etan Patz. Ordinarily,

I don't read things like that, but what caught my attention was the case here in town . . ."

"You're talking about Mary Claire Fitzhugh—1967."

"You remember her?"

"Sure. I'd just graduated from high school. Little four-year-old girl taken from her parents' home in Horton Ravine. The Fitzhughs agreed to pay the ransom, but the money was never picked up and the child was never seen again."

"Exactly. The thing is, when I saw the name Mary Claire Fitzhugh, I had this flash—something I hadn't thought about for years." He clasped his hands together and squeezed them between his knees. "When I was a little kid, I was playing in the woods and I came across these two guys digging a hole. I remember seeing a bundle on the ground a few feet away. At the time, I didn't understand what I was looking at, but now I believe it was Mary Claire's body and they were burying her."

I said, "You actually saw the child?"

He shook his head. "She was wrapped in a blanket, so I couldn't see her face or anything else."

I studied him with interest. "What makes you think it was Mary Claire? That's a big leap."

"Because I went back and checked the old newspaper accounts and the dates line up."

"What dates?"

"Oh, sorry. I should have mentioned this before. She was kidnapped on July 19, which was a Wednesday. I saw the guys on Friday, July 21, 1967 . . . my birthday, the year I turned six. That's how I made the association. I think she was already dead by then and they were getting rid of the body."

"And this was where?"

"Horton Ravine. I don't know the exact location. My mother had errands to run that day so she dropped me off at some kid's house. I don't remember his name. I guess his mom had agreed to look after me while she was gone. Turns out the other kid woke up with a fever and sore throat. Chicken pox was going around and his mom didn't want me exposed in case that's what it was, so she made him stay in his room while I hung around downstairs. I got bored and asked if I could go outside. She said I could as long as I didn't leave the property.

I remember finding this tree with branches that hung down to make a little room, so I played there for a while, pretending I was a bandit in a cool hideout. I heard voices and when I peeped through the leaves, I saw the two guys walk by with shovels and stuff and I followed them."

"What time of day?"

"Must have been late morning because after I came in again, the kid's mother fed me lunch—a plain lettuce and tomato sandwich, no bacon, and it was made with Miracle Whip. Our family didn't eat Miracle Whip. My mother wouldn't have it in the house. She said it was disgusting compared to real homemade mayonnaise."

"Your mother made *mayonnaise?*"

"The cook did."

"Ah."

"Anyway, Mom always said it was rude to complain, so I ate what I could and left the rest on my plate. The kid's mom hadn't even cut the crusts off the bread."

"There's a shock," I said. "I'm impressed your memory's so clear."

"Not clear enough or I wouldn't be here. I'm pretty sure the two guys I saw were the ones who abducted Mary Claire, but I have no idea where I was. I know I'd never been to the house before and I never went there again."

"Any chance one of your siblings would remember who the kid was?"

"I guess it's possible. Unfortunately, we don't get along. We haven't spoken in years."

"So you said."

"Sorry. I don't mean to repeat myself. The point is, I can't call them up out of a clear blue sky. Even if I did, I doubt they'd talk to me."

"But *I* could ask, couldn't I? That would be the obvious first move if you're serious about this."

He shook his head. "I don't want them involved, especially my sister, Dee. She's difficult. You don't want to mess with her."

"All right. We'll scratch that for now. Maybe the kid's mother was being paid to babysit."

"That wasn't my impression. More like she was doing Mom a favor."

"What about your classmates? Maybe she left you with one of the other moms, like a playdate."

Sutton blinked twice. "That's a possibility I hadn't thought of. I've kept in touch with the other two Michaels, Boorman and Trautwein, but that's the extent of it. I didn't like anybody else in my kindergarten class and they didn't like me."

"It doesn't matter if you *liked* them or not. We're trying to identify the boy."

"I don't remember anyone else."

"It should be easy enough to come up with a list. You must have had class photos. You could go back to the school library and check the 'sixty-seven yearbook."

"I don't want to go back to Climp. I hate the idea."

"It's just a suggestion. So far, we're brainstorming," I said. "Tell me about the two guys. How old would you say?"

"I'm not sure. Older than my brothers, who were ten and twelve at the time, but not as old as my dad."

"Did they see you?"

"Not then. I decided to spy on them, but where they ended up was too far away and I couldn't see what they were doing. I sneaked up on them, crawling through the bushes and crouching behind a big oak. It was hot and they were sweating so they'd taken off their shirts. I guess I wasn't as quiet as I thought because one of them spotted me and they both jumped. They stopped what they were doing and asked what I wanted."

"You actually talked to them?"

"Oh, sure. Absolutely. We had this whole conversation. I thought they were pirates and I was all excited about meeting them."

"Pirates?"

"My mother was reading me *Peter Pan* at bedtime, and I loved the illustrations. The pirates wore bandanas tied around their heads, which is what the two guys had done."

"Beards? Earrings? Eye patches?"

That netted me a smile, but not much of one. He shook his head. "It was the bandanas that reminded me of pirates. I told them I knew that because of *Peter Pan*."

"What'd you talk about?"

"First, I asked 'em if they were pirates for real and they

told me they were. The one guy talked more than the other and when I asked what they were doing, he said they were digging for buried treasure . . ."

As Sutton spoke, I could see him regressing to the little boy he'd been, earnest and easily impressed. He leaned forward in his chair. "I asked if the treasure was gold doubloons, but they said they didn't know because they hadn't found it yet. I asked to see the treasure map and they said they couldn't show me because they were sworn to secrecy. I'd seen the bundle on the ground, over by this tree, and when I asked about it, the first guy said it was a bedroll in case they got tired. I offered to help dig, but he told me the job was only for grown-ups and little kids weren't allowed. And then the other one spoke up and asked where I lived. I told them I lived in a white house, but not on this street, that I was visiting. The first guy asked what my name was. I told him and the other one spoke up again and said he thought he heard someone calling me so I better go, which is what I did. The whole exchange couldn't have taken more than three minutes."

"I don't suppose either of them mentioned their names?"

"No. I probably should have asked, but it didn't occur to me."

"Your recall impresses me. Much of my life at that age is a total blank."

"I hadn't thought about the incident for years, but once the memory was triggered, I was right there again. Just like, *boom*."

I reran the story in my mind, trying to digest the whole of it. "Tell me again why you think there's a connection to Mary Claire. That still seems like a stretch."

"I don't know what else to say. Intuition, I guess."

"What about the kidnapping. How did that go down? I remember the broad strokes, but not the particulars."

"The whole thing was horrible. Those poor people. The ransom note said not to contact the police or the FBI, but Mr. Fitzhugh did it anyway. He thought it was the only way to save her, but he was wrong."

"The first contact was the note?"

Sutton nodded. "Later they phoned and said he had one day to get the money together or else. Mr. Fitzhugh had already called the police and they were the ones who contacted the FBI. The special agent in charge convinced him they'd have a better chance of nabbing the guys if he and his wife appeared to cooperate, so they advised him to do as he was told . . ."

"Twenty-five thousand dollars, wasn't it? Somehow the number sticks in my head."

"Exactly. The kidnappers wanted it in small bills, packed in a gym bag. They called again and told him where he was supposed to leave the money. He stalled. They must have thought there was a tap on the line because they cut the call short."

"So he dropped off the ransom money and the kidnappers didn't show."

"Right. After a day passed, it was clear the FBI had bungled it. They still thought they had a chance, but Mr. Fitzhugh said to hell with them and took matters into his own hands. He notified the newspapers and the radio and TV stations. After the story broke, Mary Claire was all anybody talked about— my parents and everyone else."

"What day was it by then?"

"Sunday. Like I said before, she was kidnapped on Wednesday and I saw them on Friday. The paper didn't carry the story until Sunday."

"Why didn't you speak up?"

"I did. I'd already done that. When my mother came to get me, I told her about the pirates. I felt *guilty*. Like I'd done something wrong."

"How so?"

"I don't know how to pin it down. I believed what they said about digging for treasure. When you're six, things like that make perfect sense, but on some level I was anxious and I wanted reassurance. Instead, Mom got mad. She said I wasn't supposed to talk to strangers and she made me promise I'd never do it again. When we got home, she sent me straight to my room. On Sunday we heard the news about Mary Claire."

"And your mother didn't see the relevance?"

"I guess not. She never mentioned it and I was too scared to bring it up again. She'd already punished me once. I kept my mouth shut so she wouldn't punish me again."

"But it worried you."

"For a while, sure. After that, I put the incident out of my mind. Then I saw Mary Claire's name and it all came back."

"Did you ever see either guy again?"

"I don't think so. Maybe one of them. I'm not sure."

"And where would that have been?"

"I don't remember. I might have made a mistake."

I picked up a pencil and made a mark on the yellow pad lying on my desk. "When you explained this to Cheney, what was his response?"

His shoulder went up in a half-shrug. "He said he'd check the old case notes, but he couldn't do much more because the information I'd given him was too vague. That's when he mentioned you."

"Sounds like he was passing the buck."

"Actually, what he said was you were like a little terrier when it came to flushing out rats."

"Sucking up," I said. Mentally, I was rolling my eyes because Cheney wasn't far off the mark. I liked picking at problems and this was a doozy. "What about the house itself? Think you'd recognize it if you saw it again?"

"I doubt it. Right after I read the article, I drove around the old neighborhood, and even the areas I knew well had changed. Trees were gone, shrubs were overgrown, new houses had gone up. Of course, I didn't cover the whole of Horton Ravine, but I'm not sure it would have made any difference since I don't have a clear image. I think I'd recognize the place in the woods. The house is a blur."

"So twenty-one years later, you're clueless and hoping I can figure out where you were."

"Yes, ma'am."

"You want me to find an unmarked grave, basically a hole."

"Can you do it?"

"I don't know. I've never tried before."

I studied him, chasing the idea around to see where it might go. "It's an interesting proposition. I'll give you that."

I rocked in my swivel chair, listening to the squeak, while I sifted through the story, wondering what I'd missed. There was something more going on, but I couldn't imagine what.

Finally, I said, "What's your stake in the situation? I know it bothers you, but why to this extent?"

"I don't know. I mean, the article talked about how the kidnapping ruined Mrs. Fitzhugh's life. She and her husband divorced and he ended up leaving town. She still has no idea what happened to her little girl. She doesn't even know for sure she's dead. If I can help, it seems like the right thing to do."

"It's going to cost you," I said.

"I figured as much."

"What sort of work do you do?"

"Nothing right now. I lost my job so I'm on unemployment."

"What was the job?"

"I sold advertising for KSPL."

KSPL was the local AM station I sometimes tuned in on my car radio when I was tooling around town. "How long were you there?"

"About a year, maybe a little less."

"What's it mean when you say you 'lost' your job? Were you laid off, downsized, fired, what?"

He hesitated. "The last one."

"Fired."

He nodded.

I waited and when it was clear he had no intention of continuing, I gave him a nudge. "Uh, Sutton, I'd consider it a courtesy if you'd be a bit more forthcoming. Would you care to fill me in?"

He rubbed his palms on his pants. "I said I had a BA from Stanford, but it wasn't really true. I was enrolled and attended classes for a couple of years, but I didn't graduate."

"So you lied on the application?"

"Look, I know I made a mistake . . ."

"That would cover it," I said.

"But I can't do anything about it now. What's done is done and I just have to move on."

I'd heard a host of criminals make the same remark, like boosting cars, robbing banks, and killing folks could be brushed aside, a minor stumble on the path of life. "Have you given any thought to how you're going to pay me out of your unemployment benefits? We're talking about five hundred bucks a day, plus expenses. Assuming I agree to help, which I haven't."

"I have some money set aside. I thought I'd write a check for one day's work and we'd see how it goes from there."

"A *check*?"

A flush tinted his cheeks. "I guess that's not such a hot idea."

"You got that right. What's plan B?"

"If you're going to be here for a while, I could make a quick run to the bank and bring you cash."

I considered the notion. The prime item on my Thursday To Do list was to make a bank deposit and pay bills. I had two reports to write and a few calls to make, but I could shift those to Friday. The job itself might end in folly, but at least when he mentioned "the right thing to do," he didn't turn around and ask me to work for free. I wasn't convinced he was right about what he'd seen, but Cheney must have considered the story credible or he wouldn't have sent him over to me.

"Okay. One day, but that's it. And only if you pay me cash in advance. I'll be here until five o'clock. That should give you plenty of time."

"Great. That's great."

"I don't know how great it is, but it's the best I can do. When you get back, if I happen to be out, you can stick the money through the mail slot. In the meantime, give me a contact number so I'll know how to reach you."

I handed him my yellow pad and watched while he scribbled down his address and telephone number. In return I handed him my business card with my ~~office~~ number and address.

He said, "I really appreciate this. I don't know what I'd have done if you hadn't agreed."

"I'll probably regret it, but what the hell? It's only one day," I said. If I'd been listening closely, I'd have caught the sound of the gods having a great big old tee-hee at my expense.

I said, "You're sure you don't want to make the trip up to Climp? It would save you a few bucks."

"I don't want to. They probably wouldn't talk to me in any event."

"I see." I studied him. "You want to tell me what's going on here? You can't talk to your siblings and now you can't talk to your prep school pals?"

"I already told you I didn't have pals. It has more to do with the administration."

"How come?"

"There were some difficulties. I had a problem."

"Like what, you were expelled?" I love stories about flunking and expulsions. With my history of screwups, those are like fairy tales.

"It's not something I want to get into. It has nothing to do with this." A stubborn note had crept into his voice. "You go up there. They'll let you see yearbooks as easily as me."

"I doubt it. Educational institutions hate handing over information about their students. Especially with the words 'private investigator' thrown into the mix."

"Don't tell 'em you're a PI. Think of something else."

"I didn't even attend Climping Academy so why would I want to see a yearbook? It makes no sense."

He shook his head. "I won't do it. I have my reasons."

"Which you're not about to share."

"Right."

"Okay, fine. It's no skin off my nose. If that's how you want to spend your five hundred bucks, I can live with it. I love driving through Horton Ravine."

I got up, and as we shook hands again, I realized what was bothering me. "One more question."

"What's that?"

"The article came out two weeks ago. Why'd you wait so long before you went to the police?"

He hesitated. "I was nervous. All I have is a hunch. I didn't want the police to write me off as a crank."

"Nuh-uh. That's not all of it. What else?"

He was silent for a moment, color rising in his cheeks again. "What if the guys find out I remembered them? I might have been the only witness and I told them my name. If they're the ones who killed Mary Claire, why wouldn't they kill me?"

# 2

While Sutton and I were chatting, the mail had been delivered. Walking him to the door, I paused to collect the scattering of envelopes the postman had pushed through the slot. Once he'd gone off to the bank, I moved into my office, sorting and separating the stack as I sat down at my desk. Junk, bill, another bill, junk, junk, bill. I came to a square vellum envelope with my name and address written in calligraphy: *Ms. Kinsey Millhone*, with lots of down strokes and flourishes, very lah-di-dah. The postmark was Lompoc, California, and the return address was printed in the center of the back flap. Even without the sender's name in evidence, I knew it was a Kinsey family member, one of numerous kin whose existence I'd first learned about four years before. Until that strange turn of events, I'd prided myself on my loner status. There was a benefit to my being an orphan in the world, explaining as it did (at least to my way of thinking) my difficulties in forming close bonds with others of my species.

Looking at the envelope, I could guess what was coming up—a christening, a wedding, or a cocktail party—some formal affair heralded by expensive embossing on heavy card stock. Whatever the occasion, I was either being informed of, or invited to, an event I didn't give a rat's ass about. At times,

I'm a sentimental little thing, but this wasn't one. I tossed the envelope on my desk, then thought better of it, and threw it in the wastebasket, which was already brimming with trash.

I picked up the phone and punched in the number for Cheney Phillips at the STPD. When he picked up, I said, "Guess who?"

"Hey, Kinsey. What's up?"

"I just had a chat with Michael Sutton and thought I better touch base with you before I did anything else. What's the deal with him?"

"Beats me. That story sounded just screwy enough to be true. What was your impression?"

"I'm not sure. I'm willing to believe he saw two guys digging a hole. What I'm skeptical about is the relevance to Mary Claire Fitzhugh. He says the dates line up because he went back and checked his recollections against the articles in the paper, but that doesn't prove anything. Even if the two events happened at the same time, that doesn't mean they're related."

"Agreed, but his recollections were so specific he pretty much talked me into it."

"Me, too. At least in part," I said. "Did you have a chance to look at the old files?"

"Can't be done. I talked to the chief and he says the case notes are sealed. Once the FBI stepped in, they put everything under lock and key."

"Even after all this time? It's been twenty years."

"Twenty-one to be precise, and the answer is, definitely. You know how it goes. The case is federal and the file's still active. If the details are leaked then any clown off his meds can walk into the department and claim responsibility."

I caught a familiar racket out on the street. "Hang on a sec."

I put my hand over the mouthpiece and listened, picking up the hydraulic grinding, wheeze, and hiss of a garbage truck approaching from down the block. Shit! Garbage day. The week before, I'd forgotten to take out my trash and my waste-baskets were maxed out.

"I gotta go. I'll call you later."

"*Vaya con Dios.*"

I hung up in haste and headed down the hall to the kitch-enette, where I grabbed a plastic bag from a carton under the sink. I did a quick round of the wastebaskets—kitchen, bath-room, and office—shaking trash into the plastic bag until it sagged from the weight. I scurried out the back door, tossed the bag in my trash bin, and rolled it down the walkway on one side of the bungalow. By the time I reached the street, the gar-bage truck was idling at the curb and I just managed to catch the guy before he hopped back on. He paused long enough to add my contribution to the day's haul. As the truck pulled away, I blew him a kiss and was rewarded with a wave.

I returned to my desk, congratulating myself on a job well done. Nothing makes a room look messier than a wastebasket full of trash. As I settled in my swivel chair, I glanced down and spotted the vellum envelope, which had apparently missed the plastic bag and now lay on the floor. I leaned over, picked it up, and stared at it. What was going on? Instead of happily winging its way to the county dump, the damn thing was back. I'm not superstitious by nature, but the envelope, coupled with Michael Sutton's reference to his family estrangement, had set an old train of thought in motion.

I knew how treacherous and frail family bonds could be. My mother had been the eldest of five daughters born to my grandparents Burton Kinsey and Cornelia Straith LaGrand, known since as Grand. My parents had been jettisoned from the bosom of the family when my mother met my father and eloped with him four months later. She was eighteen at the time and came from money, albeit of the small-town sort. My father, Randy Millhone, was thirty-three years old and a mail carrier. In retrospect, it's difficult to say which was worse in Grand's eyes, his advanced age or his occupation. Apparently, she viewed civil servants right up there with ca-reer criminals as undesirable mates for her precious firstborn girl. Rita Cynthia Kinsey first clapped eyes on my father at her coming-out party, where my father was filling in as a waiter for a friend who owned the catering company. Their marriage created a rift in the family that had never healed. My Aunt Gin was the only one of her four sisters who sided with her, and she ended up raising me after my parents were killed in a car wreck when I was five.

You'd think I'd have been pleased to discover the existence of close kin. Instead, I was pissed off, convinced they'd known about me for years and hadn't cared enough to seek me out. I was thirty-four when the first family overtures were made, and I counted their twenty-nine years' silence as evidence of crass indifference for which I blamed Grand. I really didn't have a quarrel with my aunts and cousins. I'd tossed them into the pit with Grand because it was simpler that way. I'll admit it wasn't fair, but I took a certain righteous satisfaction in my wholesale condemnation. For the past two or three years, I'd made a halfhearted attempt to modify my attitude, but it hadn't really worked. I'm a Taurus. I'm stubborn by nature and I had my heels dug in. I shoved the invitation in my shoulder bag. I'd deal with it later.

Sutton returned after twenty minutes with five crisp one-hundred-dollar bills, for which I wrote him a receipt. Once he was gone again, I locked the cash in my office safe. Since I'd be devoting Thursday to Sutton's business, I sat down and did a rough draft of one of the client reports on my To Do list, figuring I might as well get one chore out of the way. By the time I'd finished, it was close to 4:00 and I decided to shut down for the day. One reason I'm self-employed is so I can do as I please without consulting anyone else.

I rescued my car from the semilegal parking spot I'd found earlier. My office is on a narrow side street barely one block long. For the most part, the surrounding blocks are posted No Parking, which means I have to be inventive in finding ways to squeeze my Mustang into any available space. I was due for a parking ticket, but I hadn't gotten one yet.

I drove home along the beach, and within minutes my spirits lifted. Spring in Santa Teresa is marked by early-morning sunshine, which is eradicated almost immediately by dense cloud cover. The marine layer, known as the June Gloom, usually stretches from late May until early August, but that's been changing of late. Here we'd scarcely made it into April and low clouds had already erased the offshore islands. Seabirds wheeled through the fog while sailboats, tacking out of the harbor, disappeared in the mist. In the absence of sunlight, the surf was the color of burnished pewter. Long strands of kelp had washed up on shore. I inhaled the salty essence of damp sand and sea grass. Cars rumbled along the wooden wharf with a sound like distant thunder. It was not quite tourist season, so traffic was light and many of the beach hotels still sported vacancy signs.

I turned left from Cabana onto Bay and left again onto Albanil. I found a length of empty curb across from my apartment and paralleled my way into it. I shut the engine down, locked my car, and crossed the street, passing through the squeaking gate that serves the duel purpose of doorbell and burglar alarm.

Henry Pitts, my landlord, was in the backyard in a T-shirt, shorts, and bare feet. He'd set up a ladder near the house and he was hosing out the rain gutters where a thick, nasty mat of wet leaves had collected over the winter. During the last big rain, small gushers had poured down on the porch outside the kitchen door, drenching anyone who dared to enter or leave.

I crossed the patio and stood there for a while, watching him work. The day was getting chilly and I marveled at his determination to cavort about in so few clothes. "Aren't you going to catch your death of cold?"

Henry had turned eighty-eight on Valentine's Day, and while he's sturdy as a fence post, the fact remains he's getting on in years. "Nope. Cold preserves most things, so why not me?"

"I suppose."

The spray from the hose was creating an area of artificial rain so I stepped back out of range. He turned his hose in the opposite direction, inadvertently watering his neighbor's shrubs. "You're home early," he remarked.

"I gave myself the afternoon off, or what's left of it."

"Hard day?"

I waggled my hand, indicating so-so. "I had a guy walk in and hire me for a day's work. As soon as I said yes, I knew it was dumb."

"Tough job?"

"More pointless than tough. He gave me five hundred dollars in cash and what can I say? I was seduced."

"What's the assignment?"

"It's complicated."

"Oh, good. I like it when you're challenged. I'm just about

done with this. Why don't you stop by for a glass of wine and you can bring me up to speed?"

"I'd like that. There's another issue up for grabs and we can talk about that, too."

"Maybe you should stay for supper so we won't feel rushed. I made corn bread and a pot of beef stew. If you come at five-thirty, I'll have time enough to shower and change clothes."

"Perfect. See you shortly."

Henry is the only person alive I'd talk to about a client, with the possible addition of his sister, Nell, who'd be turning ninety-nine in December. His brothers, Charlie, Lewis, and William, were ninety-six, ninety-one, and ninety respectively, and all were going strong. Any talk about the frailties of the elderly has no bearing on them.

I let myself into the studio and dropped my shoulder bag on a kitchen stool. I moved to the sitting area, turning on a couple of lamps to brighten the room. I went up the spiral staircase to the sleeping loft, where I perched on the edge of the platform bed and pulled off my boots. Most days, my work attire is casual—jeans, a turtleneck, and boots or tennis shoes. I can add a tweed blazer if I feel the need to dress up. Though I'm capable of skirts and panty hose, they're not my first choice. I do own one dress that I'm happy to say is suitable for most occasions. It's black, made of a fabric so wrinkle-resistant, if I rolled it up and stored it in my shoulder bag, you'd never know the difference.

At the end of the day, my clothes hurt and I'm eager to be shed of the restraints. I stripped off my jeans and hung them on a peg. I pulled off my shirt and tossed it over the rail. Once I was downstairs again, I'd retrieve it and add it to the garments waiting in the washing machine. In the meantime, I found a set of clean sweats and my slippers, rejoicing, as I always do, that Henry and I are beyond the need to impress each other. As far as I'm concerned, he's perfect and I suspect he'd say much the same thing about me.

I've been his tenant for the past eight years. At one time, my studio was Henry's single-car garage. He decided he needed a larger one to accommodate his station wagon and his pristine 1932 five-window coupe, so he converted the original garage to a rental unit, which I'd moved into. An unfortunate explosion had flattened my apartment six years before, so Henry had redesigned the floor plan, adding a half-story above the kitchen. On the ground floor I have a living room with a desk and a sofa bed that can accommodate overnight guests. The kitchen is small, a galley-style bump-out off the living room. There's also a bathroom and a combination washer-dryer tucked under the spiral stairs. The whole of it resembles the interior of a small boat, lots of highly polished teak and oak, with a porthole in the front door and nautical blue captain's chairs. The new loft, in addition to a double bed, boasts built-in cubbyholes, as well as a second bathroom with a view that includes a small slice of the Pacific Ocean visible through the trees. Henry had installed a Plexiglas skylight above my bed, so I wake to whatever weather's drifted in during the night.

Between the studio and Henry's house there's a glassed-in passageway where he proofs batches of bread, using a Shaker cradle like an enormous buttered bowl. In his working days, he made his living as a commercial baker, and he still can't resist the satiny feel of newly kneaded dough.

At 5:29 I grabbed my shoulder bag, crossed the flagstone patio, and tapped on the glass pane in Henry's back door. Most of the time he leaves it unlocked, but our unspoken agreement is to respect each other's privacy. Unless my apartment was in flames, he'd never dream of entering without permission. I peered through the glass and saw Henry standing at the sink, filling it with hot water into which he was squeezing a long shot of liquid detergent. He took three steps to the side to open the door and then returned to his task. I could see numerous place settings of tarnished silverware on the counter with a roll of aluminum foil and a clean towel laid out. He'd set an eight-quart pan on the stove and the water had just reached a rolling boil. On the bottom of the pan there was a crumpled section of foil. I watched him add a quarter cup of baking soda, after which he placed the silverware in the bubbling water with the foil.

"Oh yum. A pot of flatware soup."

He smiled. "When I pulled the silver from the canteen, most of it was tarnished. Watch this."

I peered into the boiling water and watched as the foil

turned dark and the tarnish disappeared from all the forks, knives, and spoons. "That doesn't do any harm?"

"Some people think so, but anytime you polish silver, you're removing a thin layer of oxidation. That's a Towle pattern, by the way. Cascade. I inherited service for eighteen from a maiden aunt who died in 1933. The pattern's discontinued, but if I haunt garage sales, I can sometimes find a piece."

"What's the occasion?"

"Silver's meant to be used. I don't know why I hadn't thought of it before. It lends a meal an air of elegance, even when we're eating in here." He poked the silverware with a set of tongs, making sure all the pieces were totally submerged. "I put an open bottle of Chardonnay in the refrigerator for you."

"Thanks. Will you be having some with dinner?"

"As soon as I finish this."

He paused to take a swallow of the Black Jack over ice that constitutes his usual late-afternoon pick-me-up. I retrieved the Chardonnay, took two wineglasses from the cupboard, and filled mine halfway. Henry, meantime, was using the tongs to move the silver from the kettle to the sink of soapy water. After a quick rinse, he laid the freshly polished silver on the waiting towel. I took a second towel from the linen drawer and dried the pieces; I set places for two at the kitchen table, where Henry had laid out freshly ironed cloth napkins and mats.

We postponed our conversation about the job until we'd each eaten two servings of beef stew. Henry crumbled corn bread in his, but I preferred mine on the side with butter and homemade strawberry jam. Am I in love with this man or what? When we finished our meal, Henry put the dishes and silverware in the sink and returned to the table.

Once he was settled, I gave him the *Reader's Digest* condensed version of the story Michael Sutton had related to me. I said, "Where have I heard the name Michael Sutton? Does it mean anything to you?"

"Not offhand. You know what his father does for a living?"

"Not much. He's deceased. Sutton told me both his parents were gone. He's got two brothers and a sister, but they're not on speaking terms. He didn't explain himself and I didn't ask."

"I wonder if his father was the Sutton who served on the city council. This was maybe ten years ago."

"That I don't know. I suspect the reference will come to me, if there is one."

"In the meantime, you have a game plan?"

"I've got some ideas percolating at the back of my brain. I want to see what the papers have to say about the Fitzhugh girl. Sutton might have forgotten something relevant or embellished where he should have left well enough alone."

"You don't trust him?"

"It's not that. I'm worried he's conflating two separate events. I believe he saw two fellows digging a hole. What I question is the connection to Mary Claire's disappearance. He says the dates line up, but that doesn't count for much."

"I guess time will tell. So what's the other one?"

"The other what?"

"You said there was another issue up for grabs."

"Oh, that."

I leaned toward the empty chair where I'd placed my shoulder bag. I retrieved the still-sealed envelope and passed it across the table. "I don't have the nerve to open it. I thought you could peek and tell me what it is."

He put on his reading glasses and studied the front and back of the envelope in the same way I had. He slid a finger under the flap and lifted it, then removed a card with an over-leaf of tissue. Inside, there was a smaller card with a matching envelope, so the recipient could RSVP. "Says, 'The Parsonage. Groundbreaking and Dedication Ceremony, celebrating the removal of the Kinsey Family Homestead to its new location at . . .' blah, blah, blah. May 28, 1988. I believe that's the Saturday of Memorial Day weekend. Four P.M. Cocktails and dinner to follow at the country club. Very nice."

He turned the invitation so it faced me and I could read it for myself. "Big family do," he said. "Doesn't say black tie optional, so that's good news." He picked up the smaller card with its stamped envelope. "They'd appreciate a reply by May 1. Couldn't be easier. The envelope's already stamped so that will save you return postage. Well, now, what do you think of that?"

"This is just not going to go away, is it?" I said. "Why do

they keep harassing me? It's like being nibbled to death by ducklings."

He pulled his reading glasses down low on his nose and looked at me over the rims. "Two contacts a year isn't 'harassment.' This is an invitation to a party. It's not like someone put dog turds on the front seat of your car."

"I barely know these people."

"And you won't if you keep avoiding them."

Reluctantly, I said, "I've dealt with Tasha and she's not so bad. And I'm fond of Aunt Susanna. She's the one who gave me the photograph of my mother and then sent me the family album. I'll admit I was touched by that. So here's what worries me. Am I just being stubborn for the sake of it? What do they call that, 'cutting off your nose to spite your face'? I mean, most families want to be close. I don't. Does that make me wrong?"

"Not at all. You're independent. You prefer being alone."

"True, and I'm pretty sure that's considered the opposite of mental health."

"Why don't you sleep on it and see how it looks in the morning."

# 3

## DEBORAH UNRUH

### April 1963

Deborah Unruh hated the girl on sight. Her son Greg had dropped out of Berkeley in his sophomore year, claiming his academic courses were irrelevant. Since then, he'd hitchhiked across the country, calling home when his funds were low and he needed money wired to the nearest Western Union office. Deborah and Patrick had last seen him the previous fall, and now, without warning, he'd reappeared, driving a big yellow school bus with a girl named Shelly in tow.

She had a gaunt face, a mass of dark tangled hair, large hazel eyes, and barely visible brows. She wore heavy eye makeup, a black turtleneck sweater, and a long gypsy skirt, the hem of which was torn and gray from trailing on the ground. When she wasn't barefoot, she wore black tights and ragged tennis shoes. She had a little boy with her, Shawn, who was six years old. She was quick to tell Deborah the child wasn't Greg's. When Deborah made the mistake of asking about her ex-husband, Shelly told her she had never been married and had no idea who the boy's father was. Her tone implied that only uptight middle-class bores would be concerned with an outdated concept like paternity.

Deborah let the matter pass without comment, but the girl's brazen attitude netted her a black mark in Deborah's eyes.

Greg took their welcome for granted, offering no explanation of why they'd come or how long they meant to stay. Deborah offered them the guest room, but he and Shelly declined. They preferred to sleep in the bus, which they parked out behind the garage.

The vehicle was little more than a shell. They'd removed all the seats and outfitted the interior with beds, a low table and chairs, and a camp stove, though Shelly never lifted a hand when it came to meals. They used a milk crate to hold canned and dried goods and had cardboard boxes for everything else. Shawn slept on a tatty futon behind the driver's seat while Greg and Shelly occupied a double-bed mattress at the rear. An Indian-print bedspread was hung between the two beds for privacy. The bus was left close enough to the pool house that the three could use the toilet and shower out there, not that any of them ever bathed as far as Deborah could tell.

They hadn't been in the house five minutes before the little boy had peeled off his clothes and was running around naked. Deborah knew better than to raise an objection because Shelly was already warbling on about how our bodies were so precious and nothing to be ashamed of. Deborah was appalled. Greg had gone off to college, clean-cut and polite, and here he was back again, promoting this trashy little upstart whose values were equivalent to a slap in the face.

At the first opportunity, Deborah excused herself, went up to the master bedroom, and called Patrick in Los Angeles. He was a sportswear manufacturer and he spent Tuesday morning through Friday afternoon at his plant in Downey. She didn't dare let him come home for the weekend without telling him what was going on. He listened to her description of Shelly, patient and bemused. He made sympathetic noises, but she could tell he thought she was exaggerating.

"Don't say I didn't warn you," she sang.

Patrick's reaction to Shelly was just as swift as hers. He was more analytical than Deborah, less intuitive, but just as quick to recoil. At forty-eight, he had wiry hair, layered gray and white, cut short, wavy over his ears where the hair was slightly longer. His eyes were brown, his eyebrows a washed-out gray. He was color-blind, so Deborah selected his clothes. His everyday attire was chinos and sport coats that she kept in a range of pale browns and grays. His shirts were a crisp white, open at the collar since he refused to wear ties except on the most formal occasions. He was slim and kept fit doing five-mile runs when he was home on weekends. Deborah was four years younger, a honey-blond wash concealing the natural gray. Like Patrick, she was brown-eyed and slender. The two made a handsome pair, like an advertisement for graceful aging. They played golf together on weekends and the occasional tennis doubles match at the country club.

Patrick tolerated "the bus people," as he referred to them, for three days, and he was on the verge of telling them they'd have to move on when Greg announced that Shelly was five months pregnant, expecting in early August, and they needed a place to stay. For one fleeting moment, Deborah wondered if he was telling the truth. Shelly was petite, so slight and bony it was hard to picture her giving birth to a full-term infant. Deborah studied her discreetly. She looked thick through the middle, but that was the sole indication that she was with child. Neither of them seemed embarrassed at her condition and there was no talk of getting married.

Shelly used the occasion to air her views about childbirth. She didn't believe in doctors or hospitals. Childbirth was a natural process and didn't require the services of Western medicine, which was dominated by rich white men whose only goal was to undermine a woman's trust in her body and the freedom to control what happened to it.

That night, Patrick and Deborah had the first quarrel they'd had in years.

Deborah said, "We can't ask them to *leave*. You heard Greg. They don't have anyplace else to stay."

"I don't give a shit. He got himself into this and he can get himself out. What the hell's the matter with him? The girl's an idiot and I won't put up with her, pregnant or not. Is he out of his mind?"

Deborah gestured to him to keep his voice down even though Greg, Shelly, and the boy had retired to the bus. "You know if we kick her out, he'll go, too."

"Good. The sooner the better."

"She'll have that baby in a cornfield."

"If that's what she wants, let her do it. She's in for a rude awakening. Wait 'til she goes into labor and then let's hear about the joys of natural childbirth."

"She's already had one child. I don't see how the process could come as any big surprise."

Deborah let Patrick rant and rave until he ran out of steam, and then she prevailed. She was just as repelled as he was, but this would be their first (and perhaps their only) grandchild. What good would it do to voice their outrage and disappointment when it wouldn't change a thing?

Two weeks passed before Deborah found a moment alone with her son. She'd been working in the kitchen, putting together an eggplant Parmesan that would probably go untouched. Shelly was a vegetarian. Deborah had originally offered to make a tuna casserole, remembering how much Greg had liked them as a child.

Shawn licked his lips, rubbed his tummy, and said, "Yum!"

Shelly put a reproving hand on his shoulder and said, "No, thank you. We don't believe any living creature should have to die so we can eat."

As soon as they left the kitchen, Deborah repeated the sentiment aloud, mimicking her tone. Pious twit! Fortunately, they'd planted Japanese eggplant in the vegetable garden. Deborah had gone out and picked half a dozen, which she'd sliced, salted, and allowed to drain.

With Patrick gone the better part of the week, Deborah was accustomed to cooking for herself and she'd had to wrack her brain coming up with meatless meals in deference to Shelly's moral stance. Deborah sprinkled cheese on top of the casserole and placed it in the refrigerator until it was time to bake it. Washing her hands, she peered out the kitchen window and spotted Greg and Shawn in the backyard. She knocked on the glass, waved to them, and the next thing she knew, the back door opened and in they came.

Greg said, "We're in exile for the afternoon. Shelly's tired and needs a nap."

"I'm happy to have the company. Have a seat," she said.

Greg was clueless when it came to entertaining Shawn. On the occasions when he was left in charge of the boy, he usually brought him into the house and left it up to his mother to provide him with paper and colored pencils or the Tinkertoys she'd had stored in the attic since Greg was his age.

Deborah had wanted to talk to him and now that she had the chance, she wasn't sure how to go about it. She hardly knew what to make of him these days. He was tall, slim, and fair-haired, a younger version of his dad. He'd been a good-hearted kid with an easy disposition. He'd made A's all through school though the good grades hadn't come easily for him. Because he struggled so hard, she thought his achievements had been meaningful to him. Perhaps he'd only excelled out of a desire to please his parents. Until he left for college, there was no sign of rebellion or defiance. He wasn't oppositional and there was nothing in his behavior to suggest he was disenchanted with the life his parents had provided.

Shelly was a revelation. Clearly, this girl embodied attitudes he'd been harboring for years without the means, or perhaps the courage, to express them. Bringing her home, he was sending a message: This is what I want and what I admire. Deborah could only hope he'd realize how far off track he was. She'd tried to be accepting of Shelly, for his sake if nothing else, but everything about the girl was repugnant.

Of course, Shelly didn't approve of Deborah any more than Deborah approved of her. She was smart enough to avoid Patrick altogether, sensing he was an adversary she'd regret taking on. She disdained their lifestyle and made little effort to disguise her animosity. For Deborah, tact and good manners were the ballast that kept social interactions on an even keel. For Shelly, being blunt and abrasive was proof she was being authentic. Without the buffer of mutual courtesy, Deborah was at a loss, and though she hated to admit it, she was afraid of the girl.

Greg went into the refrigerator and found a container of leftover spaghetti with meatballs that he proceeded to eat cold.

Eyeing him, Shawn said, "I'm hungry."

"What about Velveeta," Deborah said with a quick look at Greg. He was responsible for enforcing Shelly's food laws when she wasn't in the room. Deborah had given up trying to make sense of Shelly's rules, which were arbitrary, capricious, and nonnegotiable. Greg shrugged his approval, so Deborah opened the package of Velveeta and handed Shawn a slice. He wandered into the living room, engrossed in pulling off pieces and dropping them in his mouth like a baby bird. He wasn't allowed to watch television, and Deborah hoped he'd find a way to amuse himself without getting into trouble.

She filled the sink with soapy water, tucking in the dirty bowls and utensils before she took a seat at the table. She knew Greg didn't want to have a heart-to-heart talk, but she had him cornered and he seemed resigned.

"I've been thinking about Shelly and I realized I didn't know anything about her family. Where's she from?"

"Los Angeles. Tustin or Irvine, I forget which," he said. "Her family disowned her when she was fifteen and got pregnant with Shawn."

"That's too bad. It must be hard for her."

"Nah. They didn't get along anyway, so it was no big deal. She says they're a bunch of pigs with their heads up their butts."

"I see." She hesitated and then plunged on. "I'm not sure this is the time to bring it up, but your father and I are curious about your plans. I wondered if you wanted to discuss the situation."

"Not particularly. Plans for what?"

"We assumed you'd be looking for a job."

She heard Shawn giggling and she looked over to see him round the corner from the living room, stark naked. He dashed into the kitchen with a certain brash confidence, whooping and leaping to claim their attention. Deborah looked over at him coolly as he shook his bottom at them and galloped away. She could hear his bare feet slapping down the hall as he ran around the house, circling through the living room, dining room, kitchen, the front hall, and back through the living room. Clearly, Greg had learned to block out the child's shrieking, which Shelly, of course, encouraged as freedom of expression.

"A job doing what?"

"You have a family to support. At the bare minimum, you have to have income and a decent place to live."

"What's wrong with the bus? We're doing fine. Unless you begrudge us the parking space."

"Of course we don't *begrudge* you the parking space. Don't be ridiculous. All I'm saying is that once the baby's here, you can't go on living like vagabonds."

"Shelly doesn't want to be tied down. She likes being on the road. Lots of our friends do the same thing and it's groovy. You gotta go with the flow."

"What will you do for money? Babies are expensive. Surely, I don't have to tell you that."

"Mom, would you just cool it with this stuff? I'm twenty-one years old. I don't need your advice. We'll take care of it, okay?"

Deborah let that one roll off her back and tried again. "Could you at least give us an idea how long you plan to stay?"

"Why? You want us out of here?"

Shawn tiptoed into the room, like a cartoon character, with exaggerated steps. Deborah watched him creep up on Greg with his hands out in front of him like claws. He let out a fake roar and gave Greg a swipe. Greg growled and grabbed at him. Shawn screamed with laughter as he galloped toward the dining room. "You can't catch me! You can't catch me. Nah, nah, nah." He stopped and made a face, fingers wiggling at his ears. Off he went again. Deborah absolutely could not stand the child.

She said, "Why are you being so argumentative? That's not like you. I'm trying to get a sense of your intentions if it's not too much to ask."

"Who says I have to have intentions?"

"Fine. You have no plans and no intentions. We do. We're willing to have you stay here until the baby's born, but it can't be permanent."

"Would you get off that stuff? I said we'd take care of it and we'll take care of it."

Deborah stared at him, struck by his refusal to address reality. This was the first time she'd understood how immature he was. He had no idea what he'd gotten himself into. He'd adopted Shelly's worldview, but without foundation or depth. Maybe it was the same form of parroting that had gotten him through school. "I don't understand what you see in her."

"Shelly's cool. She's a free spirit. She isn't all hung up on material things."

"The way we are. Is that what you mean?"

"Mom, you don't have to be so defensive. I didn't say that. Did I say that?"

"You've been looking down your noses at us since the day you walked in. Shelly despises us."

"That's not true."

"Of course it is. Why don't you just admit it?"

"You despise her so why don't you admit *that*? Take a look at yourselves. Dad works to make money so you can buy, buy, buy. His employees scrape out a living at minimum wage and he reaps the profits. Are you proud of it?"

"Yes, I am. And why not? He's worked hard to get where he is. He provides jobs and benefits for hundreds of people who're devoted to him. Most of them have been with him for over fifteen years so they must not feel too downtrodden."

"Shit, have you ever really talked to those guys? Do you have any idea what their lives are like? You pat yourselves on the back for doing good deeds, but what does that amount to? You and your hoity-toity girlfriends have 'charity luncheons,' raising a pittance for whatever tidy little cause has taken your fancy. What difference does it make in the overall scheme of things? None of you put yourselves on the line. You're safe and you're smug and you wouldn't dream of dirtying your hands with the real problems out there."

"I wouldn't be so quick to judge if I were you. You talk about safe and smug. You've had everything handed to you. You blew off your education and now you're playing house, thinking you're a grown-up when you haven't accepted a shred of responsibility for yourself or Shelly or even that poor son of hers. What have you done that makes you think you're superior?"

"I'll tell you what we've done. We're civil rights activists. You didn't know that, did you? Because you never bothered to ask about our beliefs. We've marched in support of Freedom Rides, desegregating bus terminals and restrooms and water fountains in the South . . ."

Deborah was taken aback. "You went to Washington, D.C.?"

"Well, no. There was a rally in San Francisco. There were hundreds of us. You and Dad are sheep. You'd go along with anything just to avoid making waves. You've never stood up for anything . . ."

She could feel a flash of temper. "Watch yourself, Greg. None of your political rhetoric has anything to do with what's going on here so don't muddy the waters. You've dropped a bomb in our laps and we're doing what we can to adjust to the situation. You and Shelly don't have the right to abuse and insult us."

Shawn tore into the kitchen again, running full tilt. Deborah reached out a hand and grabbed him by the upper arm. "Listen here. You stop that! I won't have you screaming and shrieking while we're having a conversation."

Shawn stopped in his tracks. He wasn't accustomed to reprimands. He looked from her to Greg. His face crumpled and he burst into tears, his mouth coming open in a howl so profound there wasn't any sound at first. He clutched his penis for comfort, perhaps realizing for the first time how vulnerable he was without clothes on. Deborah couldn't even bear to look at him. When his tears failed to have the desired effect, he added screams. "I hate you. I want my mama. I want my mama."

Deborah waited for his tantrum to subside, but he just revved it up a notch, the tone of his screams climbing up the scale.

Greg said, "Hey, hey, hey," doing what he could to calm him, trying to reason and explain while Shawn collapsed on the kitchen floor. He lay on his back and kicked his feet hard, catching Deborah's ankle in the process.

"Shit," she said, knowing she'd be bruised for a month.

Shelly appeared in the door, the picture of righteous indignation. Her face was puffy and her hair was matted from sleep. She took one look at Shawn and turned on Deborah. "What did you *do* to him? You have no right. How dare you lay a hand on my child? I won't have you interfering with my discipline."

Adopting a pleasant tone, Deborah said, "What discipline, Shelly? All I did was tell him to stop running around, shrieking, while Greg and I were in the middle of a conversation. That's common courtesy, though I don't expect you to embrace anything as bourgeois as that."

"Bitch!" Shelly grabbed Shawn and lifted him, turning on her heel and hurrying him from the room as though saving him from personal assault. Deborah gave Greg a long, cool look, daring him to take Shelly's part.

"Jesus, Mom. Now look what you've done." He shook his head, aggrieved, got up, and left the house.

For the next hour, Deborah could hear Shelly out in the bus, yelling and weeping. Accusations, recriminations. She leaned forward and laid her cheek on the cool surface of the kitchen table. Dear god, how would she get through the next four months?

# 4

## Thursday morning, April 7, 1988

Thursday, I woke at 6:00 A.M. and pulled on my running shoes for my three-mile jog. I brushed my teeth but left the rest of my "toilette" for the damp morning air. When the weather's hot the run leaves my hair sweaty and when it's cool, as it was that day, the fog makes a mess of it anyway. At the beach, the only people I see are as unkempt and baggy-eyed as I am. I don't jog for the health benefits, which are probably minimal at best. I do the (almost) daily three-mile run for the sake of vanity and peace of mind. I see couples walking or running while they chat or lone individuals with their headsets in place, listening to god knows what. I crave the quiet, which allows me to sort out my thoughts.

Home from my run, I showered, dressed, and grabbed an apple, which I ate in the car. I'd intended to hit the public library first thing, but I put that on hold until I made a visit to Climping Academy. At 10:13, I drove through the two stone pillars that mark the entrance to Horton Ravine. I took the first left, turning onto Via Beatriz, a narrow two-lane road that wound up the hill to the academy, which overlooked a spring-fed lake. The main building was the former residence of a wealthy Englishman named Albert Climping, who arrived in Santa Teresa on his retirement in 1901. Prior to immigrating, he was engaged in the manufacturing of inlet valves and flotation devices for toilets, and while he'd amassed a fortune, the source of his money ruled out acceptance in polite society. At a lawn party, *really*, how *could* one converse with a toilet valve magnate?

If he was aware that the nature of his livelihood forever barred him from hobnobbing with the Horton Ravine elite, he gave no sign of it. He purchased a hilly thirty-five-acre parcel, which had languished, undeveloped, near the Ravine's front entrance. The property boasted a natural spring, but the general location was deemed undesirable because it was too far from the ocean and too close to town. Undismayed by these deficits, Climping brought in heavy equipment and excavated a crater-sized containment pond for the spring water that bubbled up out of the hillside. Having created Climping Lake, he set up an extensive network of water pipes that crisscrossed his land. He flattened the peak on the steepest of two hills and began construction on a fake English manor house, complete with stables, a phony chapel, a barn, and a massive glass conservatory. All the exteriors were clad in a golden sandstone that he had imported from his native Sussex. The interiors featured heavy ancient-looking beams, coffered ceilings, mullioned windows, and rich "twelfth-century" tapestries he had made in Japan. If there had been an architectural board of review in his day, he would *never* have been granted approval for this faux-medieval domicile, which was completely out of place in an area noted for its one-story, Spanish-style homes made of adobe and red tile.

Albert Climping had grown up in poverty with no education to speak of, but he was smart, he was an avid reader, and he had an uncanny understanding of the land. The sweeping views from his hilltop property were astonishing. The Pacific Ocean was visible to the south and the mountains loomed to the north, with the city of Santa Teresa spreading out between the two. During drought years, Climping's acreage was always green, supported by an irrigation system that also allowed him to maintain orchards and vegetable gardens sufficient to sustain him. While his perspicacity was undisputed, his humble origins remained a fatal defect. If Climping thought he could purchase respectability among the carriage trade, he was

sorely mistaken. The ladies were prepared to rebuff any over-
ture he might make. Sadly for them, he had no desire to ingra-
tiate himself and they were left with various biting remarks
growing sour on their tongues.

For the next twenty years, he went about his business, entertaining foreign dignitaries and Washington politicians, men
who appreciated his financial acumen and his lively sense of
humor. When he died, a charter school was established out of
his estate. Climping Academy was richly endowed, and from
the day the doors opened, the well-to-do parents in Horton
Ravine clambered to enroll their kids. Over the years, with the
blessings of the city, additional sandstone-clad buildings were
erected, all in the same imposing architectural style, which set
the school apart from, and above, its competitors.

I pulled into the gravel motor court and found a parking
space in an area screened by boxwood hedges. I locked my
car and walked around to the front entrance, where I climbed a
flight of low stone steps and entered the main building. While
the grand architectural elements were still in evidence, the
interior had been updated and furnished with all the modern
conveniences. I paused to read the school's mission statement,
which had been framed and hung just inside the doorway.
In support of its claims of scholastic excellence, the school
boasted that one hundred percent of Climping graduates went
on to college. I had to read that line twice. One hundred percent? Well, shit. Maybe if I'd attended Climp, I wouldn't have
wasted my education smoking dope with a tatty bunch of
ne'er-do-wells at the public high school.

A class bell rang and students began to spill out into the
corridor. I stood and watched them passing in twos and threes.
I did envy them, but I could feel an old prejudice rising to
the surface. I wanted to believe the offspring of the rich were
snooty and spoiled, but such was not the case. These kids
were friendly, well behaved, and conservatively dressed, no
flip-flops, no cutoffs, and no T-shirts imprinted with offensive
expletives. Some actually smiled at me and a few said hi. They
were disconcertingly *nice*.

On the other hand, why *wouldn't* they be nice when they
sailed through the world with all the advantages? Behind
closed doors, they were probably subject to the same miseries

as everyone else, parents whose alcoholism, financial scandals, divorces, and emotional shenanigans left them as vulnerable as the children of the middle class and the poor. Money couldn't possibly protect them from all of life's woes. On the other hand of my first other hand, whatever their problems, whether inherited or self-generated, their parents could at least afford the best doctors, the best lawyers, and the most exclusive rehabilitation facilities.

I beckoned to a passing student. "Excuse me. Can you tell me where I can find the library?"

She was a good-sized girl, built like an athlete with a sturdy set of bones. Her dark hair was straight and sleek, pulled into a complicated knot at the nape of her neck. When she smiled, her braces gleamed. "Sure. I'm headed in that direction anyway."

"Thanks."

We walked the length of the corridor and turned right. She left me in the hall outside the library while she continued to her next class.

The room I entered must have been the mansion's original library. Shelves of books extended from floor to ceiling on all four walls with a movable platform ladder resting against a brass rail. The panes in the leaded-glass windows were marked by imperfections, lending a shimmering effect to all the outside views. Two groups of students sat in dark green leather chairs arranged around refectory tables. The students were quiet and there wasn't much activity except for the turning of pages and the scribbling of pens.

The librarian was seated at a desk under one of the windows. The name plaque in front of her read LORI CAVALLERO, HEAD LIBRARIAN. She looked up at me expectantly. She set her pen aside, got up, and crossed the room, walking on the balls of her feet to minimize the sound. She appeared to be in her late forties, her dark hair a long, careless tumble around her face. Her mouth was bracketed with deep lines and a faint frowning V was sketched between her eyes. She wore a long brown knit dress over boots, her sleeves pushed up to her elbows.

"Are you Ms. Cavallero?"

She smiled. "Yes."

"I'm Kinsey," I said with a smile to match hers. "I was

wondering if I might take a peek at the 1967 yearbook. I'm
trying to track down an old friend."

"Of course. We keep the yearbooks in the other room. You
want to follow me?"

"Great," I said. I couldn't believe another closely held conviction was taking a hit. Now it turned out the faculty and staff
were as nice as the kids. What was Sutton's problem?

She moved to a door on our left and ushered me into the
room. "This was Albert Climping's study," she said. She
gave me a moment to appreciate the room and its furnishings. The study was smaller than the library and beautifully
proportioned, with a spiral staircase taking up one corner. I
counted twenty built-in file drawers, each labeled with old-
fashioned cursive on white cards slipped into brass frames.
I could see wide, shallow drawers that I imagined held maps
or documents intended to be stored flat. A massive desk took
up the center of the room, resting on an Oriental carpet in
muted browns and blues. A big stone fireplace with an impres-
sive carved mantel was centered in the wall across from the
door. On the far wall there was a second carved wooden door,
probably leading to the hall beyond. The remaining wall was
paneled in mahogany. The oil portraits that hung in the open
spaces between bookshelves were darkened with age and suggested successive generations of severe Christian gentlemen
and their long-suffering mates.

"Wow," I said, in all sincerity. From my perspective, the
prime item of interest was the spiffy-looking copy machine I'd
spotted just inside the door.

"The yearbooks are on the bottom shelf," she said. "I'll be
in the other room if you need anything else."

"Thanks."

She moved into the larger room and closed the door.

And just like that, I was given access to the information
I thought would require a mandate from the California State
Senate. I dropped my shoulder bag near the copy machine
and crossed to the shelves where the yearbooks were lined
up. The 1967 edition was there and I toted it with me, riffling
through pages while I activated the On button and waited for
the machine to warm up. The first twenty-five-plus pages were
devoted to the graduating seniors, half-page color head shots

with a column beside each photograph, indicating countless awards, honors, offices, interests. The juniors occupied the next fifteen pages, smaller photographs in blocks of four.

I flipped over to the last few pages, where I found the lower school, which included kindergarten through fourth grade. There were three sections for each grade, fifteen students per section. The little girls wore soft red-and-gray plaid jumpers over white shirts. The boys wore dark pants and white shirts with red sweater vests. By the time these kids reached the upper school, the uniforms would be gone, but the wholesome look would remain.

I turned the pages until I found the kindergartners. I checked the names listed in small print under each photograph. Michael Sutton was in the third grouping, front row, second from the right. His eyes were big and brown and worried even then. Most of his classmates towered over him. His teacher's name was Louise Sudbury. I looked for the two other Michaels, Boorman and Trautwein. Michael Boorman was a towhead, a goofy grin showing a blank where his two front teeth had been. Michael Trautwein was heavyset with a round face and a crown of dark curly hair. All the boys wore shoes that were comically large compared to their bony little six-year-old legs.

The copy machine wasn't old but it was slow. Nonetheless, my visit to the library and my return to the parking area, photocopies in hand, were accomplished in a snappy fifteen minutes. I couldn't believe my good fortune. Things seldom went this swimmingly for me, which should have been a clue.

# 5

The home address Sutton had given me was 2145 Hermosa Street, on the west side of town. His was a neighborhood of condominiums and single-family residences, many of which were rentals. The houses tended to be small and plain, with stucco exteriors and shallow-pitched asphalt roofs. Frame bungalows were tucked between two-story apartment complexes devoid of architectural interest. Mature trees towered over the tenth-of-an-acre lots on which they'd been planted, suggesting a lack of vision on the part of those first owners, who'd apparently failed to recognize that after forty-five years of California rain and sun, a red gum sapling or a two-foot spruce would dominate the front yard and dwarf the modest house it was meant to ornament.

I slowed, scanning the progression of house numbers on a stretch of pinched-looking, one-story board-and-batten cottages. The exterior of 2145 Hermosa was painted a gaudy yellow, the window frames and trim outlined in royal blue. The effect was not as cheerful as one might hope. The strong hues only emphasized the cheap construction and the sad state of disrepair. Above the small covered porch, a square window suggested habitable attic space, which would be unbearably hot and stuffy in the summer months and cold and damp at any other time of year. To the right of the wooden porch steps, a mass of pink snowball bushes obscured one of the two front windows. To the left, the thorny paddles of a prickly pear cactus had fanned out in a configuration that rendered the narrow side yard impassable.

I found a parking place, locked my car, and walked back to the house. Ordinarily, locking my car was more cautionary than critical, but not in this area. Hermosa came to a dead end at the 101, which was visible through a bare patch of wire fence that was otherwise blocked by weeds. Freeway traffic kicked up a buffeting wind, accompanied by an eddy of exhaust fumes. Trash had been sucked up against the fence where the rush of passing cars created a vacuum. How did a kid raised in Horton Ravine end up in a neighborhood as crummy as this? When Climping Academy boasted about entire graduating classes going on to college, there wasn't any mention of what came afterward. I'd always imagined a high-toned education guaranteed an equivalent high-toned lifestyle, but I lived better than this guy and what was that about?

I went up the porch steps and knocked on the screen, turning to continue my visual survey while I waited. The two houses directly across the street from Sutton's had been torn down and someone had taken advantage of the empty double lot to offer off-street parking for ten bucks a week. This was enterprising as parking at the curb was free. Every house I saw had iron grillwork secured across the windows to deter the burglars, who probably had the good sense to burgle the pricier houses in town.

When I heard the front door open, I turned. Sutton stood behind the screen, wearing the same shirt and tie I'd seen him in the day before. His dark brown eyes conveyed the usual unspeakable gloom. He said, "Oh, hi. I didn't expect to see you so soon."

"Sorry to stop by unannounced, but there's something I want you to take a look at."

"I was just on my way out. I have a doctor's appointment."

"This won't take long. A minute tops."

By way of a reply, he held open the screen door. I crossed the threshold and stepped into his front room. The light was muted, filtered through the pink hydrangea blooms that crowded against the window glass. The air smelled of bacon, scorched coffee, spilled beer, cigarettes, and dog hair. A golden retriever lumbered to its feet to greet me, long tail banging against an overstuffed chair. The room was too small to accommodate an animal that size. Dogs need a yard to wander in and a shady spot where they can curl up and snooze. A retriever might also appreciate the opportunity to actually retrieve something, like a ball or a stick. I've never even owned a dog and I knew that much.

There was a rail-thin girl stretched out on the sofa in shorts and a tank top, bra visible through the fabric. Her bare legs were thrown over the arm of the couch, treating me to a view of the blackened soles of her feet. She was pretty in a pouty sort of way. Her dark hair was long and her eyes were lined and smudged with kohl. She wore flashy dangle earrings that sparkled when she moved her head. A full ashtray rested within reach, but happily for me, she wasn't smoking just then. There were three beer cans on the coffee table, two of them empty and lying on their sides. Languidly she extended her hand, picked up the third can, and took a long swallow before she put it back again. I could see a series of overlapping circles on the tabletop where she'd placed the can. If I counted rings, I could re-create the timeline of her alcohol consumption.

Expressionless, she snapped her fingers and the dog crossed the room and settled on the floor close by. I looked at Sutton, anticipating an introduction, but none was forthcoming. I'm reluctant to discuss a client's business in front of someone else, especially in a circumstance like this when I had no clear sense of their relationship. I wasn't sure what he'd told her or how much I was at liberty to reveal.

Sutton said, "So what's up?"

I glanced at the girl. "Would you prefer to talk on the porch?"

"This is fine. She's cool."

I opened the flap on my shoulder bag and removed the pages I'd photocopied, handing them to him. "Take a look at these and see if you spot the kid whose house you visited."

He stared at the photographs, holding them close to his face. I watched his attention shift from face to face. He pointed and said, "That kid."

I peered over his shoulder. "Which one?"

"Him. I remember now." He indicated a kindergartner in the middle of the top row. A thatch of dark hair, receding chin, ears that protruded like the handles of a jug.

"Are you sure?"

"Of course. His name's Billie Kirkendall. I hadn't thought of him in years. His dad embezzled all this money, but it didn't come to light until the family left town. Overnight, they were gone. It was like this big disgrace. Does this help?"

"Absolutely. The address won't be hard to find unless Kirkendall was his bio-dad and the couple got divorced. If his mother remarried, we'd have no way of knowing who his stepfather was."

"Boorman would know. He was always good at stuff like that. He's the one who organizes our reunions. Not that I go," he added in haste. He checked his watch. "I have to run." He held up the picture. "Can I keep this?"

"I'll make a copy for my files and get it back to you."

Sutton returned the photograph and picked up his car keys. The girl on the couch watched us, but Sutton didn't say a word to her. I trailed out the door after him and we trotted down the steps together.

I said, "Give me a call when you're free and we'll pay a visit to the Kirkendall property. Maybe you'll find the spot you were talking about."

"I'll be home in an hour and a half. I can call your office then."

"Good," I said. "Mind if I ask about the girl in there?"

"That's Madaline. She was a heroin addict, but now she's clean. She needed a place to crash."

"And the dog?"

"She belongs to Madaline. Her name's Goldie Hawn."

We parted company with the usual insignificant pleasantries. Sutton turned to the left, angling up the driveway to the point where his car was parked, while I turned in the opposite direction. Once in the Mustang, I fired up the engine and waited until Sutton passed in his car before I pulled out. He drove a banged-up turquoise MG that dated probably from his high school days.

As long as I was downtown, I covered the seven blocks to

Chapel, where I hung a left and drove eight blocks up, then crossed State Street and took a right onto Anaconda. Half a block later, I turned into the entrance of the parking facility adjacent to the public library. I waited by the machine until the time-stamped parking voucher slid into my hand and then cruised up three levels until I found a slot. The elevator was too slow to bother with so I crossed to the stairwell and walked down. I emerged from the parking structure, crossed the entrance lane, and went into the library.

The reference department was directly ahead. The wall-to-wall carpet was a dusty rose with a muted pattern of teal green dots. The chairs were upholstered in the same teal green. Light flooded in through six tall arched windows on the far wall. Most of the tables were empty except for a lone man playing himself in a game of chess. In the fiction department to my left, an assistant librarian shelved novels from a cart piled high with books. At the nearest empty table, I set my shoulder bag on one of six empty chairs.

On the wall to my immediate right, the floor-to-ceiling shelves were lined with telephone directories for numerous California cities and towns. The shelves below were filled with additional phone books from assorted cities across the country. I circled the periphery in search of the Polk directory, the Haines, and the six decades' worth of Santa Teresa city directories that I knew were housed nearby.

The Polk and the Haines are both crisscross directories that offer a means of discovering and cross-referencing the name, address, and occupation of any individual or business in a given area. Where the target is a business, you can also determine the number of people employed and any relevant sales figures. If, as in my case, all you have is a name, you can usually find the person's home address. If all you have is an address, you can pick up the name of the occupant. By shifting to the city directory, you can check the list of residents against a second alphabetical listing of street addresses. The house numbers are sequential, providing the name and phone number of the resident at any particular address. While the information is redundant, each category supplies tidbits that can be pieced together to form a quick sketch.

I pulled both the Polk and the Haines for 1966 and then

selected three city directories—1965, 1966, and 1967—which
I carried to the table. I moved my shoulder bag to the floor
and pulled up the chair. From the depths of my bag, I removed
a notebook and a ballpoint pen. There was only one family
named Kirkendall: Keith (CPA) and Margie (grphic dsgnr) at
625 Ramona Road. I made a note of the address and added the
names and the house numbers of the neighbors on each side.
In Horton Ravine, the properties range from three- to ten-acre
parcels, with some larger ones as well. There are no sidewalks
and the houses are set back from the road. I couldn't picture
visits back and forth between neighbors or idle gossip across
a side-yard fence. I'd never seen anyone seated on the porches
visible from the road. My guess was that people were more
likely to get acquainted by way of church, the country club, or
the numerous civic organizations around town.

While I was doing a paper search, I looked for Michael
Sutton's former address on Via Ynez. I copied the house number in my notebook and then switched over to the Polk, where
I picked up the old phone number. In 1967, when Mary Claire
Fitzhugh was kidnapped, her family lived on Via Dulcinea.
Again, in the interest of being thorough, I found the names
of the neighbors on each side. After a twenty-one-year gap,
much of the information I'd gleaned would be out of date,
but having the names on hand might save me a return trip. I
checked the most recent telephone book and made a note of
the one listing that was still good.

I replaced the various directories and went downstairs to
the periodicals department. At the back desk, I asked the librarian for microfilm copies of the *Santa Teresa Dispatch*,
covering the stretch of dates that encompassed the Mary Claire
Fitzhugh kidnapping. I wanted to review the news coverage of
the crime before I did anything else. Sutton had sketched in
certain significant points, but his prime focus was the time
frame and mine was the bigger picture, including details he
might have missed.

The librarian returned with two boxed rolls of microfilm,
dated July 1–31, 1967, and August 1–31, 1967. I took a seat
at a nearby table, flipped on the microfilm reader, threaded
the reel under the glass plate, and caught the end piece on the
roller. I pressed the button and watched news pages whiz by at

a rate that made me dizzy. I paused now and then to check the date line at the top of the page and when I neared the 19th of July, I slowed and began to look in earnest.

The kidnapping garnered front-page headlines for the first time on Sunday, July 23, and occupied center stage for the following ten days, though the account in each edition was much the same. It was clear the FBI had kept a tight rein on the information released to the public, which forced the reporters into endless repetitions of the same few facts. The basics were much as Sutton had related, though I picked up several details he hadn't mentioned. Mary Claire vanished on Wednesday morning, July 19, though the crime wasn't reported until four days later. In that interval, which included the whole of Friday and much of Saturday, the police and the FBI had stepped in and put a lock on the case, ensuring that no whisper of the crime reached the public. Events leading up to the abduction were spelled out, but there was little information from that point on.

I started taking notes, in part to distract myself from the specifics of what went down. Even in the flat who, what, where, when, and how of journalism, the story made something in my chest squeeze down. What made the sensation worse was the black-and-white photograph of Mary Claire that appeared with every article. Her gaze was so direct I felt I was looking into her soul. Her smile was sunny, her eyes shaded by pale bangs. The rest of her hair was held back on each side with a plastic barrette. The dress she wore had ruffles down the front, tiny pearl buttons, and puffed sleeves over arms plump enough to kiss. The photographer had given her a stuffed bunny to hold so the occasion might have been Easter of that year.

I remembered reading about her disappearance at the time, but I hadn't understood the enormity of the crime. What had she ever done to warrant the evil that must have been inflicted on her? I knew without having met the Fitzhughs that they'd doted on her, laughed at her unexpected comments, hugged her when injury or disappointment made her burst into tears. I shifted my focus, blotting out the sight of her face. Then I looked again. This was as much of her as I'd ever know, and there was no way to shield myself from the knowledge that she was gone. Her parents would never have peace of mind, even if her ultimate whereabouts were discovered. In some ways, I wasn't sure what difference it would make. She was lost to them, the length and breadth of her life consigned to a few short years, beginning, middle, and end.

I forced myself to scrutinize the account of what happened that day. It all sounded so ordinary. The events leading up to her vanishing carried no hint of the horror to come. Mary Claire had been playing on the swing set in the Fitzhughs' backyard while her mother sat on the back porch reading a book. The only sound on that summer day was the stutter of a leaf blower on the property next door. A landscape company had dropped off a one-man crew. She hadn't actually seen him arrive, but she could hear him working his way up the drive, clearing the pavement of grass clippings from the lawn he'd mowed. The phone rang. Mrs. Fitzhugh set her book aside and went into the kitchen, where she picked up the handset mounted on the wall near the door to the dining room. The location of the phone prevented her from maintaining visual contact with the child, but the entire yard was fenced and there was no reason to think she was at risk.

The caller introduced himself, claiming he was a sales representative, conducting a brief survey. Mrs. Fitzhugh agreed to answer a few questions. Later she had no recollection of the caller's name or the name of his company. He hadn't identified the product he was promoting, but his questions were focused on the number of television sets in the house, the number of hours they were turned on, and the family's program preferences. In all, no more than four minutes elapsed between the time she took the call and the moment the salesman thanked her and disengaged.

When she returned to the porch, she noticed Mary Claire was no longer on the swing. She scanned the yard—sandbox, playhouse, shallow plastic wading pool—but Mary Claire wasn't visible anywhere. Puzzled, but not alarmed, Mrs. Fitzhugh called her name, but received no response. She went back into the house, thinking Mary Claire might have slipped in unseen while her attention was focused on the interview questions. When it became clear Mary Claire wasn't in the house, her mother returned to the yard and circled the perimeter, checking the shrubbery near the back fence. She peered into the playhouse, which was empty, and then continued around the house. She went through the gate, still calling Mary Claire's name, more alarmed as every minute passed. Frantic, she ran next door and knocked at the neighbor's house, but no one was home.

Mrs. Fitzhugh returned to the house, intending to call her husband and then phone the police. As she climbed the back steps, she spotted the note that had apparently been left on the side table and consequently fluttered to the floor. The message was block-printed and brief. The kidnapper said her daughter was safe in his keeping and would be returned unharmed in exchange for twenty-five thousand dollars in cash. If the Fitzhughs made any attempt whatever to contact the police or the FBI, the kidnappers would know and Mary Claire would forfeit her life.

All of this became public knowledge four days after the child had been taken. In the interim, the FBI questioned Mary Claire's parents, who were white-faced and stunned. After the news broke, neighbors, friends, and acquaintances were interviewed, many of them more than once. The case attracted its share of national attention because it involved the only child of a prominent Santa Teresa couple. After the first splash, however, the coverage became repetitive, which suggested that the FBI had cut off the stream of information to the media. No FBI agent was referred to by name, nor was there any mention of investigators at the local level. The Santa Teresa Police Department's community relations officer issued a statement from time to time, reassuring the public that the investigation was ongoing and that every effort was being made to identify the suspects and recover the child.

As with any major crime, certain critical details were withheld from the public, leaving investigators a means of weeding out the off-kilter citizen, driven by a need to confess. There was no further reference to suspects or persons of interest, though detectives must have combed the area, talking to pedophiles, registered sex offenders, and anyone else whose criminal history seemed relevant. The FBI received tips, sightings of the child in places all across the country. There were also countless calls reporting suspicious behavior on the part of strangers, who'd done no harm at all and whose actions were innocent. Mary Claire Fitzhugh had been swept into the Inky Void and there was no coming back.

Since that time, the papers had run a version of the same article year after year in hopes that something would break. Other kidnap victims were mentioned, anticipating the possibility that someone might recognize a detail and put it together with other facts previously unknown. If Mary Claire was lost, her plight might provoke a confession in another case. For the child herself, the prospects were bleak and had been once the first twenty-four hours had passed without word. At least I understood now why Michael Sutton had been so anxious to unravel the significance of what he'd seen. For my part, the thought of the child's fate was enough to make me ill.

# 6

# DEBORAH UNRUH

## July 1963

For the next three months, the mother-to-be ate so poorly, she gained fewer than fifteen pounds. Her diet consisted largely of beans and rice—a perfect protein, she proclaimed, completely disregarding her unborn baby's need for proper nutrition. She didn't believe in prenatal vitamins, claiming that women since the beginning of time had managed to conceive and bear children without the interference of the pharmaceutical companies. Patrick found her attitudes infuriating, but there was no arguing the point. She interpreted any opposition or rebuttal as an assault on her autonomy. He finally threw his hands up and took to leaving the room the minute she walked in.

Most of the time, she kept a sullen distance, but there were moments when she made a minor effort to get along, thus fostering Deborah's hopes that a bond could be forged, however limited it might be. Her optimism was always short-lived. Shelly's mood would darken. The unstable elements in her personality would combine, setting off the inevitable explosion. Once she blew up, Greg stepped into the role of mediator, traveling back and forth between the bus and the house. He made excuses, soothing and mollifying first Shelly and then his parents. Deborah almost preferred Shelly's hysteria to Greg's pathetic attempts to broker a peace.

Patrick and Deborah took to eating dinner with friends on Friday nights at the Horton Ravine Country Club. According to the gossip, many couples in their social set were experiencing the same dismay, as their offspring, now young adults, got caught up in "alternative lifestyles," which meant dope, secondhand clothes, long, unkempt hair, and a neglect of personal hygiene. The nights out were their only relief from the tensions at home and their only opportunity to blow off steam.

They'd known Kip and Annabelle Sutton since they'd joined the country club, shortly after moving to Santa Teresa from Boulder, Colorado. The Unruhs were in their forties, while Kip and Annabelle were ten years younger, with school-age children who took up a major portion of their time and energy. For the Suttons, the Friday-night get-together was a welcome respite from parental responsibilities.

Kip was an architect who specialized in commercial properties—office buildings, banks, department stores. Annabelle was a stay-at-home mom, just as Deborah had been in her day. The Suttons' four children were two, six, eight, and ten, the oldest a girl named Diana. During the first round of martinis, the subject of Greg and Shelly came up, as it did most Friday nights.

Patrick said, "Take a lesson from us. These kids are malcontents and they're spoiling for a fight. Our accomplishments are worthless as far as they're concerned. You two have the same trouble coming up only I'm betting it gets worse."

Annabelle said, "Don't say that. I have my hands full coping with the terrible twos. Michael was a doll until his second birthday and now here we are, turning to drink." She plucked an olive from her martini, popped it in her mouth, and then drained her glass.

Kip said, "I don't see this business with Greg and Shelly as anything new. Kids have always been rebellious at that age, haven't they?"

Patrick shook his head. "Not like this."

"Shelly's a beatnik," Deborah said. "She told me she lived for months in a crash pad in North Beach, where all the 'cool cats' hung out."

"A beatnik? That's passé, isn't it?"

"Not to hear her tell it. She claims she screwed Allen

Ginsberg and Lawrence Ferlinghetti in the same six-day period."

Annabelle looked askance. "She actually told you?"

"Oh, sure. Proud as Punch. I could see she was hoping I'd recoil in horror so she could accuse me of being uptight and out of it. I just sat there and blinked and then asked if she'd ever had the clap."

Annabelle cracked up. "What'd she say?"

"She said that wasn't the point. She was experiencing life to the fullest, which was more than I could say."

Patrick said, "I hadn't heard that bit. Where was Shawn all this time while she was getting it on?"

"They were all there together—kids, moms, strangers, potheads, and heroin addicts. They played guitars and bongo drums and made money writing poems they sold to tourists on the streets."

Patrick finished his drink and signaled the waitress for another. Kip raised his hand as well, like two guys bidding on the same lot at an art auction.

Patrick shook his head in exasperation. "What's wrong with these kids? You give them the best of everything and they end up spitting in your face. This girl knows it all. You should hear her mouth off. She doesn't have a brain in her head and she's got the gall to criticize the *president of the United States*, like she has a clue. She can't even run her own life. They're vegetarians, for god's sake. Do you know how much time and energy that takes?"

Annabelle said, "More than I'd be willing to expend. I guess you have to give her credit. I couldn't manage it."

"Oh, please. You think Shelly cooks? No, ma'am. She refuses to subordinate herself. Deborah's the one saddled with all the meals. You ask me, it's just one more form of narcissism, making everybody jump to their tune while they sit there thinking they're above it all."

Annabelle said, "That's ridiculous. Why don't you make them fix their own meals?"

"My point exactly. Ask her," he said, hooking a thumb in Deborah's direction.

"You know what she eats, Patrick. If it were up to her, every meal would be soy cakes, sprouts, and brown rice.

Shawn would starve to death if I didn't give him peanut butter sandwiches behind her back. You should see him wolf down his food. He's like a little animal."

The waitress set down two fresh drinks along with a basket of Parker House rolls and a plate of individual butter pats. Kip turned to Annabelle. "Sorry, I should have asked. You want another martini or you want to switch to wine?"

"I better lay off. I'm embarking on a new exercise program—a half-mile ocean swim three mornings a week."

"Starting on a Saturday? You're not serious!"

"I am. I leave the kids with a sitter. It's the only time I have for myself."

"Must be freezing."

"You get used to it."

Deborah said, "I'll make the sacrifice and drink her wine as long as you're ordering. It's the least I can do."

Kip asked the waitress for a bottle of Merlot, pointing to his selection on the wine list before he surrendered it.

Deborah raised her hand. "Here's one I almost forgot. Yesterday, I found Shelly sobbing her heart out. It was the first emotion I'd seen that wasn't anger, petulance, or disdain. I thought maybe she missed her mother, but when I asked, she said she was still in mourning because Sylvia Plath had killed herself."

Annabelle said, "Who?"

"A poet," Patrick said. "She was mentally ill."

Annabelle shrugged and chose a roll from the basket. She pulled off one segment and buttered it. She took a bite and tucked the nugget of bread into one side of her cheek, a move that slightly muffled her speech. "We know a couple who claim to be vegetarians. Talk about tedious. We had 'em over for dinner once and I served macaroni and cheese. After that I was stumped. They invited us back for a sumptuous bowl of vegetarian chili. The worst. Inedible. Not even close. What got me was they were wearing leather shoes. I voted to drop them and Kip was opposed until I told him he'd have to cook for them if they ever came back."

That set Patrick off again. "Here's the kicker as far as I'm concerned. Shelly doesn't *like* vegetables. The only vegetable she'll eat is beans. She doesn't like fruit either. She says bananas are disgusting and apples make her teeth hurt. She's got a list of food no-no's that includes just about everything known to man. Except quinoa, whatever the hell that is."

Kip was shaking his head. "Why do you put up with her?"

Deborah said, "She's carrying our grandchild. How can we turn our backs on her without rejecting an innocent child? Would you do that?"

"I guess not," he said. "Well, I might, but Annabelle would have my hide."

There was a pause while they studied their menus and decided what to have. Salads, rare New York strips, and baked potatoes with sour cream, green onion, and grated cheese.

Once the waitress took their order, Patrick returned to the subject. "It wouldn't be so bad if she weren't so opinionated and superior. She looks down her nose at us. We're materialistic and shallow. Everything we do is 'bourgeois.' She talks about the proletariat. God save the Queen."

Annabelle made a face. "And Greg goes along with it?"

"She's got him under her thumb. He sits there with his mouth hanging open, acting like she's reciting from the gospels of Matthew, Mark, Luke, and John," Patrick said. "And you know what else? She smells. She doesn't brush her teeth. She doesn't believe in shaving under her arms, or anywhere else. She's got leg hair that looks like beaver pelts. I don't see how he can stand being in the bus with her. Every time she leaves the room, we have to spray."

Kip and Annabelle were both laughing by then. She said, "Oh, Patrick. You're terrible."

"I kid you not. Ask Deborah if you don't believe me."

Kip lifted an eyebrow, his tone skeptical. "I hate to say this, kids, but I think your mistake was giving Greg too much. How else did he come up with this attitude of entitlement?"

Patrick held a hand up. "You're right. You're right. Deborah and I have talked about that."

He paused, looking up, as the waitress arrived at the table with the wine. She turned the bottle so Kip could read the label, and once he approved, she proceeded to open it. Kip sampled it, nodded, and said, "Very nice."

Annabelle covered her glass and once the other three were filled, Patrick picked up where he'd left off. "We both worked our way through college. Deborah's family didn't have the money and mine thought I wouldn't appreciate the value of an education unless I'd earned it myself. Frankly, the whole thing was a grind. I carried a full load, plus working twenty hours a week. We wanted Greg to focus on his classes so we told him we'd pick up the tab as long as he kept his grades up. So much for that. Two years of college and now he's a dropout and a bum."

Annabelle said, "What are they living on? I hope you're not giving them money along with everything else."

"Not so far, though I wouldn't put it past Greg to expect financial support."

Deborah said, "Which they get in any event. They don't pay rent and we're providing food and all utilities. They don't drive the bus because they can't afford the gas."

"Dollars to doughnuts, he's selling grass," Kip said.

Patrick looked at him. "You think? Well, that's worrisome."

Deborah said, "They're certainly smoking it. I can smell it halfway across the yard."

Annabelle made a face. "They smoke dope in front of the little boy?"

"Why not? They do everything else in front of him," Deborah said. "Shelly wants him in the delivery room with her so he can experience the miracle of childbirth."

"That'll be a cheery scene."

"What if they're busted selling pot?" Kip asked, harking back to his point.

Deborah smacked at Kip's hand. "Would you stop that?"

"No, I'm serious," he said. "Suppose the cops get wind of it? I'm just pointing out the kind of trouble you'd be in. For one thing, Child Protective Services would step in and yank that little kid right out of there."

"He's not Greg's. Shelly made that clear," Patrick said.

Deborah said, "None of this is his fault. He can be a pill, but it still breaks my heart watching the neglect. She has no concept of parenting."

"Isn't he in school?" Annabelle asked.

"She doesn't believe in the public school system. She feels that's just one more form of government propaganda so she's teaching him herself."

Patrick said, "Jesus. We can't keep talking about this. It's ruining my appetite."

Annabelle held up her water glass. "Let's look at the bright side. I propose a toast to the baby."

"Hear, hear," Patrick said. The four clinked their glasses together.

"May all your surprises be little ones," Kip added.

But the surprise was Shelly's. The baby was born two weeks before her due date. Neither Greg nor Shelly told his parents she'd gone into labor. When her water broke, he took her to the emergency room at Santa Teresa Hospital and settled Shawn in the waiting room with a pad of paper and a box of crayons. Initially, there was some confusion because Shelly didn't have an attending physician, medical records, or health insurance. The nurse asked Greg a series of questions, including his occupation, employer, and work address. Once she found out he was unemployed, she pressed him on the issue of who would be responsible for the hospital charges. Shelly was incensed and kicked up such a fuss that the nurse threatened to call security.

The two were left alone in the patient bay with the curtain pulled around it for privacy. Greg didn't see that they had any choice but to call his parents and ask for help. Shelly pitched the same fit she always pitched. Greg tuned her out. The hospital notified the obstetrician on call and he was there within the hour. There was a murmured conference at the nurses' station before the doctor came into the cubicle. He introduced himself as Dr. Frantz. Greg was asked to wait in the hall while he did a pelvic exam.

Greg went back to the waiting room to check on Shawn, who was watching television, an activity ordinarily forbidden. Greg returned to the admissions desk and asked to use the phone. He called his parents and told them what was going on. Patrick asked to speak to the admissions clerk and he apparently convinced her that all charges would be covered, saying he and his wife were on their way down. Greg returned to the curtained cubicle where he could hear Shelly shrieking at the doctor, telling him where he could stick his fucking finger in his fucking rubber glove. A nurse at the far end of the hall turned and gave him a look. Greg closed his eyes. He wished, just once, she'd act like a normal human being. Everything was a fight. Everything was a major uproar. He was exhausted by the strain of trying to soothe and contain her fury.

The doctor pulled the curtain aside and asked Greg to come in. Shelly's feet were out of the stirrups by then and she was sitting on the gurney with the sheet pulled around her and tucked under her arms, so furious she refused to look at either one of them. The nurse busied herself, studiously avoiding Greg as well. Dr. Frantz told them the presentation was breech, buttocks first, legs folded in front. He suggested a C-section, but Shelly was vehement about a vaginal birth. It was her right. Nobody could tell her what to do. The doctor was carefully neutral, his face blank. He acceded to her wishes "for the moment," as he put it. Shelly said, "Ha ha ha!" to his back. Greg thought the guy would turn around and punch her, but he continued down the hall, his heels clicking smartly on the polished tile floor.

She was admitted. After the nurse attached her hospital band she put Shelly in a wheelchair to take her upstairs to the labor and delivery unit. Greg accompanied them as far as the elevator and waited until the door closed before he returned to the waiting room. The quiet was a blessing. Deborah and Patrick arrived. By then, Shawn was curled up asleep on a plastic chair in one corner. Patrick took him back to the house while Deborah went up the elevator with Greg and sat with Shelly for the next four hours. Twice the doctor managed to turn the baby, but the baby flipped right back. Deborah had to give Shelly credit for the fact that she endured hard labor without uttering a peep. Of course, she was putting both herself and the baby at risk.

After thirteen hours, when little or no progress had been made, Dr. Frantz laid down the law. Deborah was allowed to remain in the room while he explained the impasse. If the fetus was born bottom first, there was a possibility the body would fit through the mother's pelvis, but the baby's head would most likely get stuck at the level of the chin. With this condition, known as a trapped head, the possibility of injury was high. Once the baby's body emerged, the umbilical cord would cease to pulsate, which would cut off the oxygen supply. With the baby's head still inside, the infant wouldn't breathe on its own. Without surgical intervention, there was a better than even chance the baby would die.

It seemed clear to Deborah there was only one choice. She wanted to shake Shelly until her head rattled, the answer was so obvious. Even Greg was in favor, urging Shelly to consent. By then, she was too worn down to protest. They prepped her for surgery and rolled her into the delivery room. Patricia Lorraine Unruh was born on July 14, 1963: six pounds, four ounces; twenty inches long; and bald as an egg. Greg and Shelly called her Rain.

Deborah went home and had a stiff drink.

Shelly and the baby were in the hospital three days. Greg spent most of that time at her side while Deborah was left to cope with Shawn. At first, whatever Deborah suggested, he would voice the doctrine according to his mother, reciting her tenets as an article of faith. It was nearly comical hearing Shelly's sentiments coming from a six-year-old. Deborah moved ahead without argument and soon Shawn was sharing lunch with her. The two of them had adventures—the botanical garden, the beach, the Museum of Natural History. The boy was not only bright but interested and quick to learn. Deborah revised her view of him and began to enjoy his company, especially once he went back to wearing clothes. He had a sense of whimsy she hadn't seen before.

Shelly came home, still in pain, incapacitated in the aftermath of the cesarean. Deborah offered her the use of the guest room while she recovered. Shelly was fragile and her defenses were down. She moved into the house without putting up a fight while Greg and Shawn remained in the yellow school bus. She withdrew, staying under the covers with the curtains in the room pulled shut. She seemed to be suffering postpartum depression, but Deborah realized it was something else altogether. She was humiliated, not angry so much as silenced now that Nature had betrayed her and she had nothing to boast about. How could she espouse her many closely held convictions when she'd failed something as elementary as the natural delivery she'd anticipated with such confidence? She'd had the wind knocked out of her sails. In the absence of dogma, she was strangely deflated. Deborah looked on from the side-lines, wanting to reach out but not daring to do so. Any gesture on her part would signal a compassion that Shelly was ill equipped to receive.

Contributing to the edgy cease-fire was the fact that Rain showed very little interest in nursing. Shelly had breast-fed Shawn until he was three, so she was an old hand at the process. Rain wouldn't cooperate. She'd whip her head back and forth, mouth barely brushing the nipple. If she finally managed to latch on, she became agitated, arching her back and screaming, red-faced, her fists flailing. After a few days, Shelly had no patience for the feedings. At the first sign of trouble, she'd thrust the baby back at Deborah and turn her face to the wall. Rain went from being fussy to crying non-stop. Deborah knew she wasn't getting enough to eat, but she wasn't sure what to do.

Greg appeared at one point. "Is everything okay?"

"We're fine. We have a few wrinkles to iron out, but it's nothing to worry about."

"Anything I can do?"

"Keep Shawn occupied, if you would."

"Sure, no problem," he said. "Any suggestions about how?"

Deborah had to bite her tongue. She already had her hands full and couldn't stop to educate Greg about amusing a child. "Let me give you a few bucks and you can take him to the zoo."

Greg frowned. "Did Shelly say it was okay?"

"She's asleep. I'm sure she won't object. You might also try the kiddy pool at the beach. He likes to wallow in the water playing hippopotamus. There are lots of other children. He'll have fun."

She put in a call to Dr. Erbe, a pediatrician she'd met at a cocktail party welcoming new members to the country club. She apologized for the imposition, not wanting to take advantage of their acquaintanceship to ask for free medical advice. She explained the problem as succinctly as she could. Dr. Erbe suggested waiting for a couple of more feedings before supplementing with formula. Maybe the baby would get the hang of it and all would be well. By then, Rain's crying was relentless, pitched at a level that would drive any ordinary mortal insane.

With Shelly in such a vulnerable psychological state, Deborah was afraid she'd take out her frustrations on the baby. She finally made up four ounces of formula and fed Rain herself. Rain settled in to eat, taking the entire four ounces before falling asleep. She put the baby in her crib, which they moved into the sewing room down the hall so Shelly could rest undisturbed if the baby fretted in her sleep. Deborah could remember how attuned she'd been to Greg as a newborn, when any slight sound from the crib would have her on her feet and standing over him.

She peered into the guest room where she saw that Shelly was awake. "You can try the breast again when she wakes up. Dr. Erbe says some babies take a little longer catching on."

"Who gives a shit?" Shelly said, and turned over on her side.

Deborah waited for a moment and when it was clear Shelly wasn't going to volunteer another word, she went downstairs and cleaned up the breakfast dishes. Twenty minutes later, the baby started crying again. Deborah heard Shelly's bare feet hit the floor and thump down the hall. Deborah dropped the flatware she was putting in the dishwasher and headed up the stairs, taking them two at a time.

Shelly was leaning over the crib. "Goddamn it, shut the fuck up!"

She was just reaching for the baby when Deborah blocked her arm. "I'll take care of her. You rest. Everything will be fine."

"What do you know, you fuckin' Pollyanna."

Deborah knew better than to respond. Shelly had reverted to her old ways and any reassurances would be met with hostility.

Shelly stared at her darkly and finally turned on her heel. "Have at it, *Deborah*. You think you're so smart, you do it."

She went back into the guest room and shut the door.

Deborah picked up the baby and took her downstairs. She settled in the rocker, put a diaper across her shoulder, and laid the baby up against her, patting her gently until she erupted in a satisfying burp. Rain was quiet then. Deborah continued to pat her, humming, until the baby drifted off to sleep. She debated about returning her to her crib and thought better of it.

Still holding her, Deborah crossed to the wall-mounted phone in the kitchen and lifted the handset. She called Annabelle and gave her a brief account of what was going on. "I need a cradle so I can keep the baby downstairs with me during the day. Do you still have Michael's on hand?"

"Sure. I set aside all the baby paraphernalia for the next garage sale. I've been letting it sit until I was sure I wasn't going to opt for one more. Let me haul it out and dust it off. I'll be there in a jiffy."

"Don't ring the bell. Come around to the kitchen door and I'll let you in."

Fifteen minutes later Annabelle pulled into the driveway with Michael in his infant seat next to her, David, Ryan, and Diana in the backseat. She got the kids out of the car, opened the back of the station wagon, and grabbed the cradle by one end. She herded everyone up the drive and around to the back. Deborah was waiting and opened the door before she had a chance to knock. She put a finger to her lips. "Thank you so much," she whispered.

"Not a problem. Anything else I can do to help?"

"This is fine. I'll call later. You're an angel."

Annabelle blew her a kiss and ushered her brood of kidlets back to the car. There was a delay while she got everyone settled.

Deborah heard the car start and caught a glimpse of Annabelle pulling out of the drive. She jiggled the sleeping baby on one arm, using her free hand to carry the cradle into the living room. The thick drapes and wall-to-wall carpeting would muffle Rain's cries if she woke. Maybe with rest Shelly would feel better able to handle the child. Annabelle had not only dusted the cradle, she'd tucked a crib sheet over the mattress and added a pile of flannel baby blankets at one end. Deborah lowered Rain into the cradle, shook out one of the blankets, and covered her. These were blankets Annabelle made by hand as gifts for the newborns among her friends. She also donated blankets to the nursery at St. Terry's, along with knitted booties and caps, so every new mom, even those without money to spare, would have something warm for her infant to wear home.

Deborah returned to her dishes, troubled by the conflict she could see looming on the horizon. She had never understood child abuse. She'd read occasional accounts of babies being shaken to death, babies being beaten and smothered by parents who lacked the patience or maturity to deal with their screaming infants. She'd even read of one young father who took his baby by the feet and swung her against the wall. Now she could see how such atrocities occurred, tempers simmering to a boil. She had no intention of leaving Shelly alone with the child, but she'd have a battle on her hands. Shelly hated interference, hated any action or comment on anyone's part that suggested she was falling short. She also hated being mothered and hated being perceived as needy, which didn't leave many options.

Midafternoon, Deborah knocked on the guest room door and then opened it a crack. "Would you like some lunch? I can make you a sandwich."

Shelly's refusal was scarcely audible.

Deborah had nothing else to offer. She fixed a sandwich for herself and sat down in the living room and read a book while she ate. She fed Rain two more bottles of formula at three-hour stretches. Rain was actually settling down; her periods of sleep and hunger falling into a routine.

Greg and Shawn came in at dinnertime, filled with talk of the zoo. Deborah had made a vegetarian lasagna and served it with a bowl of canned peaches and cottage cheese, not a dish she'd ordinarily serve. To her surprise, Shawn gobbled up everything on his plate and asked for more. With Shelly gone, the atmosphere at the table was actually pleasant. Now that Shawn wasn't subjected to his mother's running comments on the righteous way of doing things, he ate without being threatened or cajoled.

After dinner, Deborah cleaned up the kitchen while Greg and Shawn remained at the table playing Candy Land. The two of them left at 8:30 so Greg could put Shawn to bed.

Deborah said, "Why don't you fill the tub for Shawn before he goes down for the night? I left a container of bubble bath and a stack of fresh towels in the pool house."

Shawn gave a whoop and was out the door before Greg could get up. He skipped down the steps and galloped across the grass. Deborah gave Greg a kiss on the cheek before he left. Moments later, she saw the lights in the pool house come on. She looked up at the ceiling. Still nothing from Shelly, who was probably too proud to ask for anything, having been so stiff-necked and belligerent to this point. Deborah left the lasagna in the oven. She laid out a plate, a napkin, silverware, and a brief note. If Shelly came down of her own accord, she could fill a plate and take it back upstairs.

In the meantime, Deborah moved Rain to the sofa and placed pillows on one side to secure her while she took the cradle upstairs to the master bedroom. She came back for the baby, a fresh bottle, and a stack of diapers, and retreated to the bedroom, going about her business as quietly as she could. Later she realized how unnecessary the courtesy had been.

In the morning the door to the guest room stood open. The bed was unmade and there was no sign of the few belongings Shelly had brought into the house with her. Puzzled, Deborah carried Rain downstairs and peered out the kitchen window. The big yellow school bus was gone.

# 7

**Thursday afternoon, April 7, 1988**

I'd swung by Sutton's place to pick him up on the way over to Ramona Road. Gone was the dress shirt and tie. He'd changed into jeans, a red sweatshirt, and scuffed running shoes. I counted fifteen houses on my first pass down the street, circling the block to get a feel for the neighborhood. Ramona Road was one block long, looping back on itself like a lasso. The lots were hilly, largely given over to trees and scrub. The natural contours of the land left little room to build. Graders and excavators had gone to work, carving out the flats on which construction had gone up. The houses dated back to the '50s, all of them the work of one architect, whose modern style still looked fresh thirty years later. I parked the Mustang on a grassy patch across the road from 625. Sutton leaned forward in the passenger seat and looked searchingly through the windshield.

A swath of green lawn sloped upward toward the house, the long paved driveway forming a half-circle as it curved down and touched the road again. The Kirkendalls' former residence was a one-story structure in the shape of an inverted L, with the short arm extended toward the street. The exterior of the house was red brick and darkly stained redwood with bold horizontal lines and generous expanses of glass. The flat

concrete roof formed a wide overhang that shaded the verandah along the front. There were no flourishes, no embellish-
ments, and no unnecessary touches.

"This can't be right," Sutton said.

"Yes, it is. In 1967, there was only one Kirkendall in town
and this is where they lived."

"But where's the second floor? Billie Kirkendall was sick.
He stayed upstairs and I stayed down."

"Oh, shit. I'd forgotten that. Wait here and I'll see if the
owner's home. Maybe we can get permission to explore."

I got out of the car and dog-trotted across the road. The
driveway didn't appear steep, but I was winded by the time
I reached the top. The place had an air of emptiness, a house
enveloped in quiet. The windows were bare and there was no
sign of a doormat or any of the homely touches that indicate
someone in residence. A band of damp paving along the front
suggested that the sprinklers were still active, probably gov-
erned by the same automatic program that regulated indoor
temperatures and turned lights off and on. I went up a low step
to the entrance, where a panoramic wall of glass afforded me
an unobstructed view of the interior.

The architect had kept the non-load-bearing walls to a
minimum and the blond hardwood floors seemed to stretch
in all directions. Light poured in from everywhere. A stone
fireplace was offset on the far wall and I could see a length of
kitchen counter that had been stripped of small appliances. To
the right was the empty dining room, with a low-hanging light
fixture centered in the ceiling. I walked to my right along the
verandah, where I could see a large bedroom with white wall-
to-wall carpeting and mirrored sliding doors, one partially
open to reveal cavernous closet space.

I returned to the front door and noticed for the first time
an alarm company decal saying ARMED RESPONSE pasted to
one corner of the glass. The warning was probably more form
than content. It seemed unlikely that anyone would pay for
security services when the house stood empty. I was assuming the property was on the market, but there was no realtor's
lockbox and no stack of brochures detailing the floor plan, the
square footage, or the number of rooms. For Sale signs were
prohibited by the home owners' association. For all I knew,

every house in Horton Ravine was up for grabs. I rang the bell with no expectation of a response.

I left the porch, intending to circle the premises. Sutton must have been clued in to the fact that the house was vacant because he emerged from the Mustang and crossed the road as I had. I waited while he climbed the drive and then the two of us traced a path around the house to the rear. Below, on a wide concrete apron, there was a swimming pool and cabana surrounded on two sides by a plain concrete wall with an outdoor fireplace and built-in barbecue pit. Sutton turned and looked at the rear elevation. From this vantage point, the two-story construction was evident. The house had been tucked in against the steep hill and a series of windows looked out on the view. Beyond the patio, the property sloped down again sharply and thick railroad ties had been cut into the hillside to form a crude staircase. The neighbors' rooftops floated like rafts on a lake of dark green treetops.

"Look familiar?"

"I guess. I thought the house was much bigger."

"A lot of things look bigger when you're six."

"There wasn't a swimming pool. I'd have remembered it."

"I've done the research and this is where you were. The pool and barbecue could have been added later," I said. "Let's take a walk down the hill. If you wandered, that would have been your only choice."

The brush had been cleared within a twenty-foot radius along the slope, probably by order of the fire department. Sutton followed me reluctantly as I crossed the grass and made my descent. There was no handrail and the steps themselves were deep, with ten-inch risers that forced us to descend the stairs like toddlers, putting both feet on every step before moving to the next. This portion of the lot was useless to all intents and purposes. A series of terraces had been carved out of the hill. The first level was planted with dwarf fruit trees. The second offered shelter in a weathered wood pagoda lined with benches and bleached by the elements to a soft silver gray. The third was given over to rose beds that, at this point, were sadly neglected.

After that, the land fell away gradually. The bottom of the hill butted into a grove of trees that stretched out on either side, in varying degrees of density. I counted three large oaks and six mature black acacias. Clusters of pittosporum and eucalyptus were intermingled with saplings. I wouldn't have called this "the woods," but to Sutton, at the age of six, it might have looked like one. Where the undergrowth was thin, I could see sections of a paved road that must have been Via Juliana, one of the primary arteries through Horton Ravine. If I'd been searching for a secluded location to serve as a grave site, I wouldn't have picked this. From above, the hillside was open to view. Given the staggered pattern of trees below, the area would have been visible from the road as well.

Sutton stood there, his hands in his pants pockets, his gaze moving across the landscape as he struggled to get his bearings. I could see his confusion now that he was faced with a scene that had seemed so vivid in his mind. He moved to his right, traipsing through knee-high weeds before he came to a standstill. A fence blocked his path, the chicken wire sagging under a swarm of morning glory vines. The sign affixed to the fence post read:

DO NOT TRESPASS
Private Property  Keep Out
No Access to Bridle Trail
THIS MEANS YOU!!

He walked up the hill for a distance, peering at the trees in range of him. He stopped again and shook his head. "This is all wrong. I don't see the tree I used as a hideout and I don't see the oak I hid behind when I was spying on the guys."

"Maybe the oak was cut down."

"But the fence is wrong, too. Where did that come from? I didn't climb a fence. I'm sure of it. This is all screwed up."

"Sutton, it's been years. Take your time."

He shook his head in frustration.

"Would you quit being so negative?" I said.

"I'm not negative."

"You are, too. You should listen to yourself."

He turned and scanned the woods again, no happier than he'd been. The guy was getting on my nerves. I watched while he walked down the hill toward the trees. I followed the sagging fence line as he had, but where he went down the hill, I climbed up. A profusion of wildflowers had sprung up among the grasses. Grasshoppers skittered ahead of me as I walked. I turned and looked back as Sutton disappeared into the trees.

Below and to my right, I caught a glimpse of the rear of a house: patio doors, a deck, an outdoor table and chairs. Since I wasn't well acquainted with the neighborhood, I couldn't judge the relationships between properties. The irregular course the fence had taken suggested it had been erected in conformity with a meandering lot line, separating the parcel that fronted Ramona Road from the one that faced the secondary road below. Dimly I remembered the fork where a smaller tributary split off from Via Juliana. From where I stood, only the one house was visible, but there were doubtless others on that same street.

Sutton whistled, a shrill, piercing note forced from between taut lips and teeth. For years I'd worked to master the technique, but usually managed little more than an asthmatic wheeze and the risk of hyperventilation. I set off, trudging down the hill in his general direction. He emerged to the left of me and waved. I picked my way across the uneven ground, trying to avoid the numerous holes housing god knows what assortment of rodents.

I followed Sutton into a clearing shaded by a canopy of trees. Here the temperature was ten degrees cooler than the sun-drenched hill. The far side of the glade was open to Via Juliana. A riding trail angled across the open space, its muddy surface punctuated by hoofprints. The trail was clearly well used, dotted with fresh horse manure as well as desiccated mounds of previous equine BMs. In the center of the clearing there was a stone horse trough, three feet by six. The water was fed through a pipe linked to a circulating pump that kept the depths aerated and algae-free. The stone was darkened with age and the shimmering pool looked cold and black.

Sutton said, "I'd forgotten about this. The Horton Ravine Riding Club is just across the road. I played in the trough that day, floating leaves like boats. It was afterward I climbed the hill and came across the tree I used as my hideout."

"Nanny, nanny, boo boo. Told you so," I said.

"I'm not paying you to make fun of me."

"Then you shouldn't be such a pill."

"Sorry."

"Forget it. Let's focus on the job at hand. When you saw the guys, in what direction were they walking?"

"Actually, they were coming up the hill from here. They must have parked along Via Juliana and passed through this clearing. The tree where I was hiding was partway up the slope so I was looking down on them. They crossed my field of vision from left to right and moved off in that direction."

"So if the fence was there, they'd have had to climb over it, which means you'd have done the same thing."

"But I didn't . . ."

"Would you stop that? I'm not saying you did. I'm saying we should knock on some doors and see if someone knows what year the fence went in."

We climbed up the hill again, moving up the steps from terrace to terrace, until we reached the wide, flat patio with its pool, cabana, and built-in barbecue pit. We went around the side of the house and then crossed the front lawn to the house next door. I rang the bell.

Sutton stood behind me and to my right. To anyone inside, with an eye to the peephole, we'd look like Jehovah's Witnesses, only not as well dressed.

Sutton shifted uneasily. "What are you going to say?"

"Haven't made that part up yet."

The young woman who opened the door had a six-month-old baby clamped on her right hip. He had a pacifier in his mouth that wiggled as he sucked. His face was flushed and his hair had been flattened in a series of damp ringlets. I was guessing he'd recently awakened from his nap and, judging from his aura of fecal perfume, was in desperate need of a diaper change. He was at that clinging-monkey stage, where his hold on his mother was pure instinct. I could see clutch marks in the fabric of her blouse where his grip had made star shapes across the front. His resemblance to her was eerie—same noses, same chins, two sets of identical blue eyes looking back at me. His dark lashes were longer and thicker than hers, but life is basically unfair and what's the point of protest?

I said, "Hi. Sorry to disturb you, but is the house next door for sale? We heard it was on the market, but there's no realtor's sign and we didn't know who to contact."

She peered in that direction and made a face. "I don't know what to tell you. The couple got divorced and for a while the ex-husband was living there with his girlfriend, a ditz half his age. They moved out a month ago and we heard he's looking for tenants on a long-term lease. I can give you his number if you're interested."

With skepticism, I said, "Gee. I don't know about renting. I hadn't thought about that. How much does he want?"

"He's talking seven thousand dollars a month, which I think is way too much. It's a nice house and all, but who wants to spend that kind of dough?"

"That *is* pushing it," I said. "Do you happen to know how much property he has?"

"Five acres, give or take."

"That's a good-sized lot. When we walked up the hill just now, we saw a fence with a Do Not Trespass sign, but we couldn't tell if it was part of this parcel or the one next door."

She lifted a thumb, jerking it backward to indicate something behind her. "The guy down there could tell you. I know there was a lot-line adjustment years ago, but I'm not sure what changed. The utility company has an easement that extends along the hill and riders keep mistaking it for part of the bridle trail. The owner got fed up with all the horses crossing his land so that's where the fence came from."

"He's the one in that house I can see below yours?"

"Right. On Alita Lane. His name's Felix Holderman. He's retired and he's nice enough, but he's sometimes gruff. I don't know the house number, but it's the only Spanish-style on the block."

"Thanks. We may just pop down there and have a chat with him."

"If you catch him at home, tell him Judy said hi."

"I'll do that. Appreciate your time."

"I should thank you. This is the first adult conversation I've had since Monday when my husband left on a business trip."

"When does he get back?"

"Tomorrow, I hope. The baby's teething and I haven't

slept for days." She wrinkled her nose, looking down at him. "Pew-ee! Is that him or you?"

I could hear a phone ring somewhere in the house.

"Ooops. Sorry," she said, and eased the door shut.

Sutton and I headed down her drive to the car.

"I can't believe she didn't ask why you were quizzing her about the fence. If you're not buying or renting, then what's it to you?"

"I didn't say I wouldn't rent. I said, 'I hadn't thought about that.'"

"But you didn't get the guy's number when she offered it."

"Sutton, the trick in a situation like this is to behave as though your questions are completely reasonable. Most people aren't going to stop to ponder the inconsistencies."

"It still seems pushy."

"Of course."

We picked up my car and drove the short half-mile from Ramona Road to Alita Lane. It wasn't hard to spot the Spanish-style house, which was long and low, a cream-colored stucco with a small courtyard in front and a three-car garage on one end.

As I got out of the Mustang, Sutton said, "You mind if I wait here? I feel like a dunce standing behind you not saying a word while you chat people up."

"Suit yourself. I'll be right back."

I crossed the street and passed through the wrought-iron gate into the inner courtyard. The front door was inset with three panels of stained glass that depicted a rose, a donkey, and a saguaro cactus with a sombrero perched on top. I rang the bell.

The balding man who opened the door had a leathery face and a pate splotched with sun damage where hair had once been. He was roughly my height, five-six, with a barrel chest and a tangle of white hair sprouting from the V of his Hawaiian shirt. His shorts revealed bowed legs the color of caramel corn.

"Mr. Holderman?"

"Yes, ma'am."

"My name's Kinsey Millhone," I said. "I was just looking at a house for sale on Ramona Road and the woman next door thought you could answer questions about the property. Her name's Judy, by the way, and she said to tell you hi."

"Judy's a nice gal. Tell her hi back from me. You're talking about Bob Tinker's place. Well built, but it's overpriced. House is worth three-point-five tops and he's asking six, which is ridiculous."

"Judy says he moved out and he hopes to rent or lease."

"Man's a fool. Anything he has, he thinks is worth double the actual value. You said questions."

"I was wondering about the lot line. I have a friend waiting in the car who played on that hill as a child. There was an old oak he loved, but when we walked the property just now, he said the big tree he remembers is gone and the wire fence is new."

"I wouldn't say new. I put that fence in fifteen years ago, for all the good it does. Riders go over or around it. I might as well set up a toll booth and make 'em pay. You talk about trees. We lost a dozen or more in a storm some years back. Two eucalyptus and a big live oak went down. The oak was a beauty, too, a big guy, probably a hundred and fifty years old. It might well be the one he's talking about. The utility company should have kept the deadwood trimmed. Tree was on the easement and had nothing to do with me or I'd have pruned it myself. Winds came up and the damn thing split in half, taking out trees on both sides. Woke me up out of a sound sleep."

"Must have been a mess," I said.

"Big time. The utility company sent a fellow with a chain saw to clear the downed trees. He wasn't paid to work that hard so he took his sweet time—ten minutes' worth of sweat and then a cigarette break. Went on for days. I know because I watched. Pay minimum wage, you get minimum work. Nobody seems to get that. Took him three weeks."

I half turned, indicating Sutton in my car. "Would you mind if the two of us went up and looked around? It would mean a lot to him."

"Fine with me. Half the fallen trees were actually on the property next door. House has been sold twice. The current owners are off at work, but I don't think they'd mind if you wander a bit. You see anybody on horseback, you hightail it right back and let me know. I'm tired of the horseshit and horseflies."

"Amen to that."

# 8

Sutton and I walked between the two houses—Felix Holderman's on our left and his neighbor's to the right—with Alita Lane behind us. At one time the backyards might have been open to one another, creating a wide mantle of rolling lawns. With the introduction of swimming pools, fences had been erected to protect kids from mishaps and property owners from pricey lawsuits. Between the greensward on this side and the barren hill above there was a dense band of trees—pines and spruces, with a few sycamores and acacia thrown into the mix. Again, I wouldn't have called this "the woods," though it was more sheltered than the Kirkendalls' property, where we'd started our search. The full-skirted evergreens did shield the area from view. I couldn't see the wire fence with its burden of morning glories, but it had to be somewhere above us. Where we were, there was no reason to post a No Trespassing sign, because the natural undergrowth formed a barrier sufficient to block equestrian traffic. Riders following the marked trail wouldn't wander this far afield.

Once we entered the trees, the ground was matted with decomposing plant material that sent up puffs of peat scent as we passed. There was no path to follow so we were forced to create our own. We split up and tramped through the brush, snapping twigs and fallen branches underfoot. I heard Sutton's startled exclamation. "Found it!"

I waded through the scrub and waist-high weeds, holding my arms up like a swimmer moving toward the shallow end of a pool. When I reached him I saw the stump of the fallen oak, which was easily six feet across and hewn to eight inches or so aboveground. The tree trunk was hollowed by rot. The oak must have been dying from the inside out over a period of time, which meant the split wasn't due entirely to the weight of the branches as Mr. Holderman had thought.

"This is it?" I asked.

"I think so. I'm almost sure."

"Where were the guys when you caught up with them?"

Sutton pivoted and scanned his surroundings. "Down there."

His focus shifted from tree to tree, and his gaze finally came to rest at a point some fifteen feet away. He moved in that direction and I lagged a short distance behind, watching as he reached a small clearing and stopped to study it. The circular patch of ground was bordered by tall evergreens and mature live oak. The tree roots had sucked all the nutrients from the hard-packed soil, leaving bare dirt. He moved a few feet to his right. "This is where they were digging. The bundle on the ground was under that tree." He shook his head. "The place still smells the same. When you're a kid, everything is so intense. It's like you're filtering reality through your nose. Wonder why that is?"

"Survival. Catch the scent of a bear once and you carry the sense memory for life."

Sutton closed his eyes and took in a deep breath.

"Are you okay?" I asked.

"I'm fine. It just seems weird."


I took Sutton with me to the office, where I unlocked the door and flipped on a few lights. He slouched in the chair he'd occupied the day before, stretching his legs out in front of him. I settled in my swivel chair, picked up the handset, and punched in Cheney's number at the police department. As soon as he picked up I identified myself.

"How's it going?" he asked.

I laid out the sequence of events, starting with my trip to Climping Academy and ending with Sutton's identification of the area where he'd seen the two guys digging. When I was finished, there was a silence while he digested the information.

He said, "I have to talk to the detective sergeant. I'll call you back."

I wasn't sure how long we'd have to wait, but it was clear I needed to stay put so Cheney could get back to me, if need be. "You want coffee? I can make a pot," I said.

"No thanks. I'm wired as it is. You have a bathroom I could use?"

"Take a left in the hall. It's the only door on your right."

"Thanks."

It was 3:15 and I couldn't remember if I'd eaten lunch, which probably meant I hadn't. I opened my desk drawers in turn, but there wasn't so much as a Tic Tac in the way of nourishment. I picked up my shoulder bag and went into search-and-seizure mode, peering into every crack and crevice. I like a big bag with a lot of nooks and crannies—outside compartments for magazines and books; inside pockets, some with zippers, some without; and a pouch on one end for car keys. I found two red-and-white-striped peppermints in clear cellophane. They'd been in my bag so long, the mints had softened and were now welded to the wrapping. I could have popped one in my mouth as it was and made it last for days.

I heard a toilet flush, and moments later Sutton reappeared.

"Want a mint?" I asked.

"No, thanks." He resumed his seat and watched me peel the cellophane off the mint. He stirred restlessly. "So what happens next?"

I laid the mint on my tongue. It was heavenly to feel the sugar surge through my mouth. I tucked it in against my inner cheek so I could talk without spitting. I said, "No idea. I guess it depends on how seriously they're taking this."

We sat there in silence. I picked up a letter opener and tapped the point against the edge of my desk, practicing to be a drummer in case the private eye biz dried up. Sutton spent his time looking around the office at the bad paint job and the so-called wall-to-wall carpeting that had seen better days. I could tell he wasn't impressed. I make enough money to support myself, but I'm not big on "day-core." Then again, neither was he. Given what I'd seen of his place, he was hardly one to offer decorating tips.

I don't keep magazines in my office. I'm not a doctor or a dentist so what's the point? Someone comes to see me and I'm here, we sit down and talk. If I'm not here, the door's locked and they have to wait. Sutton didn't seem any better equipped than I was for chitchat. I'd known the guy one day, and now that we'd gotten the potty question and the mint behind us, conversationally speaking, we had nothing to say to each other. I'm deficient when it comes to small talk, which is probably why I have so few friends.

I sat in my swivel chair, willing the phone to ring, and when it did I jumped.

It was Cheney. "Roosevelt says we can take a couple of crime-scene techs and a K-9 unit out to the site. We're rounding people up now and should be ready to roll within the hour."

"Great. That's great."

I gave him the address and we spent a few minutes chatting about the logistics. Alita Lane was too narrow to accommodate vehicles and miscellaneous police personnel, so we agreed to meet at the roadside parking strip near the polo field on Via Juliana. That settled, I dropped Sutton off at his house so he could pick up his car.

On the way back to Horton Ravine, I stopped at McDonald's and scarfed down a Quarter Pounder and fries. I wasn't sure how long the excavation would take and I wanted to make sure I had a wholesome meal under my belt. The soft drink I ordered was a small one. No point in taxing my bladder when relief wouldn't be in range.

I arrived before Cheney did and used the time to change into an old pair of running shoes I kept in the trunk of my car.

I hauled out my navy windbreaker and shrugged into that as well. The light was still good, but the sun was sinking, taking the pleasant daytime temperatures with it.

Sutton arrived in his MG and parked beside my Mustang. He had the top down and Madaline, the ex-addict, was in the car with him, which annoyed me no end. This wasn't date night and it wasn't a public spectacle. We were dealing with life and death and I didn't want her hanging around like she was part of the scene. Goldie Hawn, Madaline's golden retriever, sat on her lap, with her chin resting on the lowered window. I'd swear the dog knew who I was and sent me a loopy doggie smile by way of recognition. Madaline's circulation must have taken a beating with eighty pounds of dog planted on her thighs. As I watched, she lifted a beer can to her lips and treated herself to a sip. So much for open-container laws.

Cheney finally showed up. The K-9 handler and cadaver dog were in a separate black-and-white that pulled in beside his car. Two minutes later one of the two evidence techs arrived, followed by the mobile crime lab with the second tech riding in the back. It looked like a circus arriving in town, men and equipment being set up for all the folderol to come. We had to wait for the photographer, but that gave Cheney the opportunity to approach the house on the property where they intended to dig. He was gone for ten minutes, talking to the couple whose hillside they wanted to invade.

The rest of us had emerged from our respective vehicles and we stood on the parking strip like extras on a movie set. We had nothing to do, but most people there were being paid for doing it. Sutton walked Cheney and the techs out to the burial site. Madaline and I were relegated to the sidelines while the professionals went to work. Two officers returned to the car to pick up traffic cones and the yellow plastic tape that would define the area. I wouldn't be allowed within a fifty-yard radius, so I occupied my time chatting with the canine officer I knew from times past. Gerald Pettigrew had been a beat cop in my neighborhood some six years before. In those days, he'd been hefty, a black guy in his thirties with beefy shoulders and a gut on him that would be a liability in a foot chase. By the same token, if he managed to overtake you, you'd wish you'd run a lot faster because the guy could hand out punishment. He'd lost weight since I'd seen him last, a side effect of his working with the golden Lab he introduced as Belle.

Madaline took the occasion to let Goldie Hawn hop out of the car. The two dogs went through the usual heinie-smelling nice-meeting-you routine. Anyone who knows me will testify I'm not a fan of dogs, but I hadn't felt at all hostile to these two. I took this as a sure sign I was getting old. Far from becoming set in my ways, my defenses were breaking down. At this rate, in another few years, the whole world would come rushing in and smother me with kindness.

I let Belle sniff my hand, which is something I'd seen other people do in the company of cats and dogs. I hoped the gesture would stave off a sudden snarling attack that would remove half my arm. I looked up at Gerald. "I pictured a bloodhound or a German shepherd."

"A lot of breeds are good for search-and-rescue, which is what they're usually trained for first. They learn to locate lost hikers or kids who wander off on a camping trip. You need a dog with a powerful retrieval instinct, a keen sense of smell, and a strong work drive. Even then, some are better than others. The last dog I worked with was a shepherd. He was good but high-strung, and he had a tendency to mope. Great nose, but it was clear the work upset him. I finally retired him because I couldn't bear the accusatory look in his eyes."

"What happened to him?"

"He's now the family watchdog, which suits him better than sniffing for dead bodies in the underbrush. I heard about Belle through a friend of a friend, who'd been breeding Labs for years. She was just a little fur ball when I got her, but smart as they come. Labs are easy to train and they're physically strong. They're also good-natured, which is great for PR purposes. I can take her into schools and nursing homes and everybody falls in love with her."

By then, Belle was lying on the grass at his feet, her gaze flicking across his face as he spoke. He smiled at her. "Look at that. She knows I'm bragging about her."

"Does she work on a leash or off?"

"That depends on the terrain. Here I'll take her off the leash and let her go about her business. If she finds something, she'll come get me and take me back with her."

Cheney reappeared and headed in our direction. Gerald signaled to Belle and the two walked out to meet him. A portable generator had been hauled out on the site, along with the big lamps that would make it possible to continue working when the daylight waned. I knew without even being present what the scene would look like. The digging would be done by hand. Two officers would run the loose dirt through a two-man sieve, hoping to capture any physical evidence left behind. The chances seemed slim to me, but these guys knew what they were doing and who was I to say? The entire process would be photographed and sketched, with relevant landmarks noted and measurements taken to ensure that a thorough record of the scene was kept.

The rest of us were left to amuse ourselves as best we could. A number of cars slowed and then moved on. As is usual, bystanders had begun to assemble. I assumed some were neighbors and others driving past the scene on the way home from work who had spotted the police cars and pulled in to see what was going on. There was nothing to do and not much to say after the first scanty explanations were passed along to new arrivals. People lingered, unwilling to leave before the final moments had played out. It was like being in a waiting room while someone else is giving birth. There was no drama in our immediate vicinity, but we all knew something important was going on. Such gatherings are often written off as morbid curiosity, looky-loos hoping for a glimpse of the injured or the dead. I prefer to attribute the behavior to a sense of community, people drawn together in the face of inconceivable tragedy.

Sutton had returned to the parking area and I could see him talking to a man nearby, filling him in. It was a story he'd tell repeatedly if Mary Claire's body came to light. Madaline, still wearing her short shorts, had pulled on a pair of leggings and a loose-necked sweatshirt that hung off one shoulder, exposing the same tank top I'd seen earlier. She sat in Sutton's MG smoking cigarettes with the passenger-side door open. I'd spent half a day in Sutton's company and I already felt a motherly urge to warn him about skanks and tramps like her.

"What's going on?"

I looked to my right and found a woman standing next to me, early thirties by my guess. She had shiny shoulder-length brown hair, blunt cut and very straight. Her glasses were frameless and the lenses accented the brown eyes behind them.

I said, "The police may have a line on an unsolved case."

"Really. What's the deal?"

"Remember when Mary Claire Fitzhugh disappeared? Someone came forward with information about two guys digging what might turn out to be her grave."

We exchanged idle remarks with our attention turned toward Alita Lane. I glanced at her outfit—brown blazer, tweed skirt, black tights, loafers—wondering how she managed to look so sensible and stylish at the same time.

"Where'd the tip come from?" she asked.

"Someone read an article about the kidnapping. He thinks he might have stumbled on the burial when he was a kid."

"Wow. That would be a break after all this time," she remarked. "So what's your connection?"

"I'm a PI in town. I know Cheney Phillips, the lead investigator."

"Cool. I've known Cheney for years."

"What about you? How'd you end up here?" I asked.

"I work for the *Dispatch*. One of the guys picked up chatter about it on the scanner and sent me to see what was happening."

"Not much at this point," I said. I'm not crazy about reporters and I didn't want her probing for my client's identity. I didn't even want her to know I *had* a client because she'd try angling for an interview.

"How'd you hear about it?" she asked. Her tone was casual and the line was delivered as a throwaway as though she had little or no interest in my response. This was crafty reporter small talk designed to elicit information.

"Long story," I said.

"Mind if I get your name?"

"You can keep my name out of it. This is not about me."

"No problem. If you don't want to be quoted, we can keep this off the record."

"What's to quote? I don't know anything."

"Fair enough. I'm Diana Alvarez, by the way." She held out her hand.

Without pausing to consider, I shook hands with her and said, "Kinsey Millhone." The second the words came out of my mouth I knew I'd been had. So much for keeping my name out of it. I was irritated at her for maneuvering me and irritated at myself for being so easily sucked in.

"Nice meeting you," she said, and then she wandered away.

While I watched, she removed a spiral-bound notebook from her blazer pocket and started scribbling on a page. She struck up a conversation with someone else, and I knew she'd weasel her way through the onlookers until she pieced the story together. No telling what kind of spin she'd put on it. I looked for Sutton, thinking to warn him, but he was nowhere to be seen.

I was happy I'd grabbed dinner, because it took until 8:00 P.M. for the techs to finish their work. Everything seemed to shut down at once. Cheney appeared at the mouth of Alita Lane and walked toward us on Via Juliana. One uniformed officer followed, toting cones and the yellow tape that he'd wound into a loose skein. Gerald Pettigrew and Belle followed, giving no indication whether the dig had served up anything of note.

Diana Alvarez separated herself from the guy she was pumping and made a beeline for Cheney, in full reporter mode. Cheney acknowledged her but his eyes were on me. I did a second quick visual search of the bystanders, looking for Sutton, thinking he should be first in line for the news, whatever it might be. Still no sign of him. His turquoise MG was parked on the berm with Madaline in the front seat, her feet propped on the dashboard. Goldie Hawn wandered from person to person, wagging her tail and receiving affectionate pats and praise from strangers, as was her due.

I couldn't read Cheney's expression. He looked serious but there was a suggestion of humor in his eyes. Diana Alvarez was close on his heels, eager for any news he intended to pass along.

When he reached me, he said, "Hold out your hand. I have a present for you."

I held out my hand and he dropped an object in my palm. I registered a mud-caked plastic disk attached to a length of dirty blue leather. "What's this?"

"What's it look like? A dog tag. That's what the two guys were burying—the family pet. Woof woof . . ."

He smiled and moved on.

# 9

## WALKER McNALLY
### Late Thursday afternoon, April 7, 1988

Walker McNally drove his black Mercedes through the entrance to Horton Ravine as he did every day on his way home from work. Occasionally he elected to use the back entrance, but he didn't much care for the associations. It was Thursday afternoon. Carolyn and the kids had left that morning for San Francisco, where they'd spend a long weekend with her mother, returning Monday afternoon. Fletcher, age four, and Linnie, age two, were still in preschool, so whisking them off for five days with Nana wasn't an issue. Though he'd miss them, he looked forward to the empty house, keenly aware that he was on his own and could do as he pleased.

He and Carolyn had moved back to California ten years earlier, when he'd been hired as VP of New Client Relations at Montebello Bank and Trust. He'd begun his financial career in the trust department at Chase Manhattan Bank in New York City and later joined Wells Fargo as a wealth-planning specialist. The job opening in Santa Teresa had been a blessing, since Walker had grown up in town, graduating from UCST in 1971.

He was a good-looking man, personable, charming, and articulate. A good part of his day he was on the phone, setting up meetings and lunch dates, arranging drinks and dinner with prospective clients whose business he was working to gain. He served on the boards of two nonprofit organizations and he was also involved in a number of planned-giving and development committees. He'd brought a goodly number of clients to the bank during his tenure, and he was rewarded accordingly.

Carolyn was the one who first raised the issue of what she referred to as his "drinking problem." She'd apparently been monitoring his intake, counting the number of beer, wine, and liquor bottles that went into the trash. He wasn't sure how long this had been going on, but she'd finally put her foot down. He was of Scots descent, fair-haired, blue-eyed, with a complexion that was ruddy by nature. Alcohol had added a tinge of pink to his cheeks and a faint puffiness to his face. He knew he'd packed on a few pounds the last couple of years. At thirty-eight, he was on the high side of the suggested boundaries for his height and weight. He'd quit smoking, and that had added the obligatory fifteen pounds. While he intended to work out, there wasn't much opportunity during the week. To his way of thinking, Carolyn's concerns were misplaced. Even when he'd belted down a few, he wasn't boisterous. His speech wasn't slurred. He was never goofy, or maudlin, or sloppy, or mean-spirited. Drunk, he looked and behaved exactly as he did when he was sober—at least according to his perceptions. Nonetheless, he'd promised her he'd rein himself in.

She'd urged him to join AA, but he'd balked at that. He didn't need outside help to get his drinking under control. He had absolutely no intention of standing up at a public meeting, with god knows who present, confessing his sins, and looking for approbation. He'd always been a man who held his liquor well, and his heft actually allowed him to metabolize alcohol more efficiently than many guys his age. He had to admit that after a couple of hours at the club, if he were stopped by the CHP, he could probably pass a field sobriety test, but he'd blow a blood-alcohol level that would put him in jail.

Happily for him he'd managed to restrict his drinking the past eight months. He'd have a beer or two after working in the yard, or he'd sip the occasional glass of Champagne, celebrating an occasion such as a birthday or an anniversary. He made sure Carolyn knew and approved of these exceptions because it underscored his stance of moderation. She'd never

believe it if he claimed he'd quit altogether. She knew him
better than that.

Now at business lunches and dinners he bypassed hard
liquor in favor of white wine, which scarcely registered on
his internal alcohol meter. Going dry was really no big deal.
He made do with iced tea, or soda water with lime. He slept
better and he had more energy, but he noticed he was often
bored. Friends and cohorts, who'd seemed so amusing when
he drank, began to get on his nerves. He wasn't as smooth or
relaxed as he'd been in the past and he was aware that certain
of his friends now shied away from him. And why would they
not? He thought teetotalers were a tiresome bunch and he was
sorry he'd been thrust into their ranks. It was also true that the
temptation to drink was with him every minute of every day,
like a low-grade headache he didn't know how to shake.

With Carolyn gone, he tooled along Via Juliana, actively
fantasizing about the highball he'd make for himself when he
got home. He planned to sit on the back patio, which Carolyn
had recently refurbished with faux wicker furniture, upholstered in a fabric impervious to the elements. Rain and sun
could beat down on the cushions without ill effect. The view
from the back terrace was still amazing to him, stretching
across the hills and treetops all the way to the ocean. The air
would be still, smelling of sage and bay laurel. He'd take his
time, savoring a predinner cocktail. Then he'd have a pizza
delivered and eat in front of the television set, maybe catch
a golf match or a guy flick of the sort Carolyn would find
tedious. He might allow himself a wee nightcap, but he'd wait
and see what his mood was when the time came. He didn't feel
the same compulsion to drink as he had in the past. This was
purely for the pleasure of it.

On his way home from the office, he'd stopped at the liquor
depot and picked up a pint of Maker's Mark, a quart of vodka,
and a six-pack of Bass Ale, which he intended to parcel out
to himself over the four nights his family would be gone. All
he had to do then was dispose of the empties before Carolyn
got home. Would she ever know? He thought not. He'd keep
his drinking simple—whiskey with a water back, vodka over
ice—and remove any telltale evidence first thing Monday
morning. No mixers in the liquor cabinet, no bottle caps in

the trash, no cut limes in the fridge, and no conspicuous rings on the glass-topped table, where he'd be sitting while the sun went down.

Ahead of him at the curve, cars had slowed and he wondered if there'd been an accident. Maybe someone had hit a deer. He hoped to god it wasn't a kid on a bike. Fletcher had just mastered his two-wheeler. Linnie was still riding a tricycle, and then only in the park. He wasn't sure he'd ever permit them to take their bikes on a public road. There wasn't much vehicular traffic through Horton Ravine, but at the end of the workday, when people headed for home, they often drove faster than the posted limit.

As he got closer, he spotted two cop cars and a mobile evidence van parked on the berm, which suggested an event of a more serious sort. He slowed. There was a smattering of people standing by the road, looking idle and indecisive. The crowd was modest, and it was clear they didn't quite know what to do with themselves. On impulse, he pulled onto the gravel strip where a number of other cars were parked. He killed the engine and got out. He still had no clue what was going on. An attractive redhead, in slacks and a sweater, stood leaning against the fence. She turned to look at him and gave him a little finger wave. Avis Jent. He recognized her from the country club, though she'd dropped from sight after her divorce.

She held her hand out. "Hello, Walker. Fancy meeting you here."

He smiled and took her hand, leaning forward to give her a perfunctory buss on the cheek. "Avis. It's been ages. What have you been up to?"

"I just got back from my second stint in rehab. What a drag."

"Ouch."

"Big ouch," she replied. "How are Carolyn and the kids?"

"Good, thanks," he said. "What's this about? Was there an accident?"

"The police got a tip about a body buried in the woods."

His smile faded. "You're not serious."

"I'm afraid so. Someone said it was a kid, but that's as much as I've heard. The cops are very tight-lipped." She removed a cigarette from a packet in her purse. "I don't suppose you have a match."

He patted his pockets. "No, sorry."

She waved him off. "Just as well. I smoke too much as it is. Can you imagine? Horton Ravine and cops are digging up a corpse."

"Unbelievable. No talk at all about what happened?"

"Nope. They brought in a cadaver-sniffing dog and once they pinpointed the spot, they went to work. They started digging a couple of hours ago and none of them looked happy," Avis said. "So what brings you out? Do you live around here?"

"A mile down in that direction. I was driving by when I saw the cars and I was curious. What about you?"

"Alita Lane. They blocked off the street so now I'm stuck. Shit, and it's the cocktail hour."

"Did this just happen today?"

Avis shook her head. "This was something old. They sent out an intrepid girl reporter so I suppose we'll read about it in tomorrow's paper."

Walker's attention was drawn to a surge of activity—two or three uniformed officers led by a guy who must have been the homicide detective assigned to the scene. Walker nodded toward the group. "It looks like something's going on."

"At long last," she replied.

He watched the detective make a brief remark to a woman in jeans. Walker saw him place an item in her hand, though he couldn't see what it was. A second woman zeroed in on the exchange, clearly peppering the detective with questions as he continued walking to his car.

Someone tapped Walker on the arm. "Sir?"

He turned to find a middle-aged man standing beside him, his expression anxious.

"Sorry to interrupt, but I wouldn't advise parking there. They've been asking people to move on to keep the area clear. They said they'd be writing tickets if motorists didn't cooperate."

"Thanks, but it looks like they're done. I'd hate to leave without knowing if they found anything."

The man glanced over at the commotion. "Oh. I guess you're right."

Walker could see word trickling through the crowd, those closest to the front turning to pass along what they'd heard.

Avis said, "Hang on." She moved forward and made her way through the bystanders. She tapped a woman on the shoulder and quizzed her for news. The two chatted briefly. Avis nodded, gesturing her thanks, and then returned to Walker's side. "Well, that's a relief," she said. "Turned out to be a false alarm. The only thing they managed to dig up was a dog."

"A dog?"

"Yeah, you know, dog, like a household pet. All this ruckus for nothing, but at least I can go home and belt back a few to catch up with myself."

Walker reached in his pants pocket for his car keys and realized he'd left them in the ignition. "I guess I better take off as well. Nice seeing you."

Avis said, "You, too. Behave yourself."

He returned to his car and noticed she was watching him with interest as he slid under the wheel. He smiled again and started his car, taking care as he backed out into the road.

Driving home he kept a close rein on his thoughts. He pulled the Mercedes into the garage and waited while the garage door rumbled down and closed with a thunk. He retrieved the liquor bag from the trunk and clutched it against him as he opened the door that led into the kitchen. When he set down the bag, the bottles of Maker's Mark and vodka made a satisfying clunk of glass on the granite countertop.

Carolyn had left a note he didn't bother to read. She'd be reminding him of things that needed to be done or couldn't be overlooked in her absence. "Leave the alarm system off Friday morning so Ella can come in and clean. She should be done by noon. Just make sure she hasn't left any outside doors unlocked. Garbage goes out for pick-up . . ." It was always like that, his wife directing events from afar.

He walked through the house, taking in the ordinary sights and smells. Carolyn had made an attempt to pick up after the kids in the minutes before they left, but it was still a house where unruly children lived—Fletcher's cowboy boots on the stairs waiting to be taken up; Linnie's jacket thrown over the newel post; shoes, doll clothes, coloring books on the floor. Carolyn had left her knitting in a heap on the side table near the couch, the same ugly afghan she'd worked on for years. He circled through the living room where she'd drawn the drapes, leaving the room in a golden gloom. He passed through the dining room with the round mahogany table and Chippendale chairs she'd inherited from an aunt.

He opened the china cabinet and removed an old-fashioned glass that was part of a set of Swarovski crystal he'd given Carolyn for their tenth anniversary. He went into the family room and crossed to the wet bar, where he opened the ice maker. He used the white plastic scoop to rattle ice into his glass. These were all sounds he loved, a prelude to the relief, the cessation of anxiety he knew was coming up. This was foreplay. He was setting the scene to maximize his pleasure. If he'd been into pornography, he couldn't have exercised greater care or self-control, teasing himself with his preparations, building his anticipation.

Glass in hand, he returned to the kitchen, opened the Maker's Mark, and poured himself a drink. By then a delayed reaction had set in. The mobile evidence van, police on the hill. His right hand started to shake so hard, the bottle banged against the rim of the glass. Carefully, he put both the bottle and the glass on the counter and leaned stiff-armed against the sink, hanging his head. Fear welled up like bile, and for a moment he thought he'd be sick. He took a deep breath, making a conscious effort to throw off his anxiety.

He reached for the wall phone and punched in Jon's number.

Jon picked up on his end. "Yes."

"It's me."

A brief, wary silence, and then Jon said, "Well, Walker. This is unexpected. What can I do for you?"

"You heard what's going on?"

"What would that be?"

Walker could tell Jon was sorting through papers on his desk, reminding him that whatever Walker had to say, it was of less interest than the task right in front of him. "They're digging up the hill off Alita Lane. Cops, cadaver dog, evidence van, the works."

The paper rustling stopped. "Really. When was this?"

"I saw them just now, on my way home from work. I pulled over and chatted with a gal I knew. She said they thought a child was buried on the hill. They dug up the dog."

"I'm surprised it hasn't come up before. One way or another, something was bound to surface. There was always that risk."

"Yes, but why now? Where's this shit coming from?"

"I have no idea. I'm sure we'll find out in due course. Are you all right?"

"So far. It's like waiting for the other shoe to drop."

"Don't be paranoid. Nothing's going to happen."

"So you've said, but here it is anyway."

"Cool it, man. Would you do that? Be cool. This won't blow back on us. I guarantee."

"Why after all these years?"

"No clue. The cops don't consult with me."

"But what could have happened?"

"Walker, it doesn't matter. It's a dead end so drop it. Where's Carolyn?"

"Up north. At her mother's. She took the kids."

"Until when?"

"Monday."

"Good. Gives you time to simmer down and get your head on straight."

"Take a chill pill," Walker said, echoing Jon's unspoken admonition from their teen years.

"Exactly."

"I'm sorry, but I had to call."

"Good you did. Let me know if you hear anything else."

Jon hung up without waiting for a response.

Walker replaced the handset in the mount on the wall. He lifted the glass and swallowed the whiskey in one smooth motion and then said, "Whooo!" Something loosened in his chest, the old familiar sensation he'd been longing for. He shook his head. He'd be fine. Everything was good.

He left his glass on the counter and went out to the mailbox. He brought in the mail and tossed it on the hall table. He made sure the front door was locked and then he returned to the kitchen and refilled his glass, two fingers of Maker's Mark, the rest water. Easy does it, he thought. He shucked his jacket and placed it on the back of a kitchen chair. He opened the French doors and went out onto the patio. He settled in an upholstered chair and set his drink next to him, as he'd imagined it. He removed his tie and unbuttoned his shirt collar, feeling he could breathe for the first time all day. He loved his life. He was a lucky guy and he knew that.

  · Restless, he got up and carried his drink with him as he crossed the grass. He strolled the perimeter of the yard, looking out over the wood-rail fence. In the distance, he could see the fairway for the fifth hole at the country club he and Carolyn had joined shortly after moving to town. The membership fees were steep—eighty thousand bucks up front and five hundred a month in dues thereafter. They also got assessed for any capital improvements. Not that he objected. He'd taken a secret pride in their acceptance, given the fact that his own parents had been turned down when they applied years before. Walker was coming up in the world.

    He turned to look back at the house, which was all charm, Cape Cod style, with white clapboard siding and a steeply pitched roof. The large central chimney was linked to fireplaces in two rooms, upstairs and down. Carolyn had insisted on an extensive remodel before the kids came along.

    There was more time for construction than either of them anticipated. Carolyn had no problem getting pregnant, but she miscarried four times and lost another baby at sixteen weeks. Faced with the prohibitive expense of additional infertility treatments after five failed intrauterine inseminations, they'd elected to adopt. Carolyn took charge of the process and powered everything through—background check, fingerprinting, a lengthy application with attendant paperwork, letters of recommendation, followed by home visits that included separate and joint interviews. It took three months to be approved and they expected to wait for a year before a baby came through. Fletcher, the wonder boy, dropped in their laps six weeks later when his intended adoptive mother learned she was pregnant with twins.

When Fletcher was two, Carolyn went back into high gear. The process was simpler that time since many of the same approvals were in place. Linnie came to them by way of a local adoption attorney who'd been chatting with Carolyn at a Christmas party. The bio-mom, unmarried and eight and a half months pregnant, had come into his office the week before. The baby's father refused to marry her, she'd lost her job, and her parents had kicked her out of the house. Would the McNallys be interested? There was no discussion at all. The birth mom moved into the McNally's guest room for the final weeks before the birth. Carolyn and Walker were both present in the delivery room when Linnie was born.

When his second drink was gone, he went back to the kitchen and fixed himself a short one. His tension had dimmed and the knot of anxiety in his gut was all but gone. He noticed that eight months of good behavior had boosted the effects of the booze. He loved the sensation. He couldn't help himself. Alcohol gave him access to his feelings. He experienced an extraordinary appreciation of his wife, his children, and the life he lived. Ordinarily, he held his emotions in check. He lived in a state of detachment, a stance he'd developed years before as a matter of self-preservation. He was present in his head but his sentimental side was seldom given free rein. It was in quiet moments like these that he let down his guard.

Walker still teared up on occasion watching his two little ones who resembled Carolyn closely enough to be mistaken for her "real" kids instead of the miraculous blessings they were. Where his love for his wife was constant, his devotion to his children overrode everything. Through them he'd been made vulnerable. His heart had opened to them in wholly unexpected ways. He'd been surprised by the depth and tenderness of his feelings because his soft side was in evidence nowhere else. The loss of either child would be a blow he could never recover from. His only prayer, on the rare occasions when he prayed, was that Fletcher and Linnie would be protected from evil and violence, spared illness and injury, disease and death. No one knew better than he did how fragile life was.

At 7:00 he called in an order for a large pizza with onions, jalapeños, and anchovies, a combination that would have made Carolyn shudder. The guy on the phone said it would be thirty minutes, which was fine with him. He changed into sweats and slippers and then went into the den where he unfolded a TV tray and set it with a paper napkin, a dinner plate, and silverware. When the pizza arrived, he'd make himself a proper drink that he'd nurse while he ate. He pictured an early evening, maybe reading in bed before he turned out the light. All he had to do was hang tight and act like everything was fine.

# 10

## Friday, April 8, 1988

I skipped my run the next morning and went into the office early. I knew a three-mile jog would wipe out the lingering sense of melancholy I felt, but sometimes when you're down in the dark, you lose the will to come up. The mood would pass as the day wore on. In some ways, I was sorry I'd seen the black-and-white photograph of Mary Claire. In that brief glimpse, I'd seen the mischief in her face and the light in her eyes. Before that moment, she'd been little more than a concept, Mary Claire Fitzhugh who'd vanished from the face of the earth. Now her life had touched mine and her fate had left a mark as delicate and distinct as a fingerprint.

I made a note in Michael Sutton's file and stuck it in the drawer, then went back to the rough draft of the report I'd begun writing two days before. I revised and polished and typed it into final form. I began work on the second report, knowing I'd have to take two or three runs at it. This part of the business always felt like high school to me, as if I had a term paper due and my final grade depended on it. I suffered so much performance anxiety at Santa Teresa High, it just about shut me down. Once Ben Byrd and Morley Shine had trained me and I was out on my own, I understood that the whole point of a client report was clarity, laying out the sequence of events in an orderly fashion with sufficient detail that a stranger reading the file years later could follow the course of an investigation. That, I could do. I'd even learned to enjoy the process, though it didn't come easily.

I paid my bills and made the bank run, depositing a collection of miscellaneous checks that had accumulated during the week, plus the five hundred dollars Sutton had paid me, which I'd removed from my office safe. While I was out, I picked up a sandwich and chips at the deli near the bank. The sandwich was a wicked one that I allowed myself once a year: a thick layer of liverwurst, with mayonnaise and thinly sliced dill pickle on freshly baked sourdough. While I would never dream of slapping a big glistening liver between two slices of bread, liverwurst was close to heaven, the poor man's pâté. I know organ meats play hell with my cholesterol levels, but I doubted the occasional indulgence would prove fatal. I was in the habit of eating so fast, maybe nothing would adhere. Halfway through the sandwich, I heard the outer office door open and close. I slid the sandwich, waxed paper and all, into my pencil drawer and wiped my mouth in haste.

When I looked up, Diana Alvarez was standing at my door. She wore a snug black turtleneck and a short preppy-looking pleated skirt over black tights. Her low-heeled patent-leather shoes had little brass buckles across the tops that were ever so pert. Her hair was pulled back in a ponytail, a style that magnified her dark brown eyes behind rimless glasses.

She said, "Mind if I sit down?"

"Be my guest."

As she settled in the chair, she straightened her skirt under her to avoid wrinkling the fabric. Over one shoulder she had a small bag on a thin leather strap. I'm constitutionally incapable of toting anything that small. Hers probably contained her driver's license, a tube of lipstick, her mad money, one credit card, and her little spiral-bound notebook with a pen stuck through the wire loops. I was hoping she had a tissue tucked in there somewhere for nasal emergencies.

"What's on your mind?" I anticipated a few follow-up questions about the dig the day before. Maybe she'd apologize for being pushy and deceptive, traits I found attractive in myself but unappealing in her.

"We need to talk about Michael Sutton," she said.

I went through an automatic sorting process, wondering:

1. How and what she knew about Michael Sutton;

2. Whether she was fishing to confirm my professional relationship with him; and

3. Whether I was still bound by ethical constraints now that our one-day business dealings had come to an end. What, if anything, was I at liberty to disclose?

"Where did that name come from?"

"Cheney Phillips told me he talked to Michael at the station and then referred him to you. I spotted Michael at the dig yesterday, and since you were at the scene as well, I'm assuming he hired you. Is that correct?" Even without her spiral notebook at hand, she was confirming the facts.

"Why not ask him?"

"I don't want to talk to him."

"Too bad. I don't intend to conduct a conversation behind his back so there you have it."

"We don't have to behave like antagonists. I'm here to save you a few headaches . . ."

I opened my mouth to interrupt and she held up one hand.

"Just listen to me," she said. "I didn't realize what was going on until I saw his MG parked by the side of the road. I'd been sent to cover the story, so I waited like everyone else to see what they'd find. I assumed the police were operating on an anonymous tip and then it dawned on me Michael was involved."

"That still doesn't tell me why you're here."

She cocked her head and the light glinting off her glasses was like a quick camera flash. "I'm his sister, Dee."

Ah. Dee, the difficult one. I looked at her closely, seeing for the first time Sutton's solemn brown eyes staring back at me. "Alvarez is your married name."

"I'm divorced. Pete's my ex."

"Peter Alvarez, the radio talk-show host?"

"The very one," she said. "I take it Michael mentioned me."

"Briefly. He told me you were estranged."

"Did he tell you why?"

"No, and I didn't ask."

"Shall I fill you in?"

"To what end?"

"I think you should know what you're dealing with."

"Thanks, but no thanks. A conversation about him is inappropriate."

"Hear me out. Please."

I debated with myself. Technically, I was no longer in his employ and nothing she said would have any bearing on the job he'd hired me to do. I couldn't imagine where she was headed and I confess my curiosity got the better of me. "Keep it short," I said, as though a brief airing of the dirty laundry would be less objectionable.

"I'll have to backtrack first."

"No doubt," I said. Long-winded storytelling must have been a family trait. Michael had done the same thing, making sure the facts were arranged in date order. I could see her composing sentences in her head.

"Michael's been depressed all his life. As a child, he was always anxious, subject to all manner of imaginary illnesses. He did poorly at Climp and barely managed to graduate. He couldn't find a job and since he had no income, he asked Mom and Dad if he could go on living at home. My parents agreed on one condition: he had to get help. If he'd find a therapist, they'd pay for it."

I was getting restless. Unless Michael Sutton was a spree killer, I didn't care about his psychiatric history.

She must have caught my impatience because she said, "Bear with me."

"It would help if you'd get to the point."

"Are you going to listen to me or not?"

She fixed me with a stony stare and I could barely keep from rolling my eyes. I gestured for her to continue, but I felt like an attorney questioning the relevance of her testimony.

"The family doctor referred him to a licensed marriage and family counselor, a psychologist named Marty Osborne. Does her name ring a bell?"

"Nope." I could tell she was teasing out the narrative for dramatic effect and it annoyed me no end.

"Michael seemed to like her and we were all relieved. After he'd been seeing her for a couple of months she suggested his depression was symptomatic of early childhood sexual abuse."

"Sexual abuse?"

"She said it was just an educated guess, but she felt they should explore the possibility. He didn't believe a word of it, but she assured him it was natural to block trauma of that magnitude. We didn't know any of this at the time. It all came out later."

"Shit."

"Shit is right." Diana shook her head. "Marty continued to work with him and, little by little, the ugly 'truth' came out. She was using hypnosis and guided imagery to help him recover his 'repressed' memories, sometimes with the aid of sodium amytal."

"Truth serum."

"That's correct. Next thing we knew, she'd diagnosed him with multiple personality disorder. As luck would have it— now here's a happy coincidence—she ran an MPD support group, which Michael joined. More cash changed hands, his to hers. Meanwhile, my parents were blissfully unaware of what was happening. My brothers and I were out of the house by then so we saw much less of him than they did. After three months, Michael started seeing her twice a week and talking to her on the phone three and four times a day. He didn't eat. He scarcely slept. We could see that, psychologically, he was disintegrating, coming apart at the seams, but we thought his getting worse was part of the process of getting better. Little did we know. She persuaded him it would be 'healing' if he confronted the past, which he did with a vengeance. He accused my father of molesting him from the time he was eight months old. He had these shadowy memories that he knew were real. Soon, his hazy mental movie came into focus and he 'remembered' my mother was also in on the abuse. Next thing you know, my younger brother Ryan was added to the list. We're talking nasty stuff—claims of satanic ritual, bestiality, animal sacrifice, you name it."

"Sounds preposterous."

"Of course. What made it worse was my parents had no way to defend themselves. Any attempt they made to refute his claims only served to reinforce his conviction that they were guilty as charged. Marty told him abusers always deny what they've done. He moved out of the house, cutting off all contact, which was actually a relief. Then she talked him into collaborating on a book and that's what blew the lid off.

"When Mom and Dad got wind of it, they hired an attorney and sued the crap out of her for slander and defamation. The night before they were set to go to trial, they reached a settlement. I don't know the terms because they signed a confidentiality agreement. Whatever it was, my parents were never able to collect a cent. Marty filed for bankruptcy and that's the last anybody ever heard from her. For all we know, she's still in private practice only somewhere else."

"I don't get it. Why would she do such a thing?"

"Because she could. She saw it as part of her job. In her eyes, she did no wrong. When they took her pretrial deposition, do you know what she said? That even if his story *wasn't* true, she was there to validate his feelings. If he was convinced he was abused as a child, then she would support him in his beliefs. In other words, if you think you were abused, you *were,* and that's all it takes."

"Without proof?"

"She didn't need proof. She said if that was 'his truth,' he could depend on her to keep the faith."

"Did the family doctor who referred him know what she was up to?"

"In his deposition he admitted he'd never met her. She'd been recommended by another doctor whose opinion he respected. In a way, it was beside the point. You don't need a doctor's referral to see a therapist. Just look in the yellow pages and pick anyone you like. Some of them even have little boxes advertising their specialties. Self-esteem issues, crisis counseling, anger management, stress, panic attacks. The list goes on and on. Who among us hasn't experienced the occasional rage or anxiety?"

"How do you know which therapists are legitimate?"

"I have no idea. I've never been in therapy. I'm sure most of them are honest and capable. Some might even be skilled, but sexual abuse is like a siren call. There's a ton of money to be made."

"That's a bit cynical, isn't it?"

"Not as cynical as you might think. Suppose you go into therapy because your relationships aren't working out the way you'd hoped. Turns out that's a symptom of early childhood abuse. Write me a check and come back next week. You don't remember what was done? That's called being 'in denial.' You've repressed the memory because it was all so traumatic and you don't want to believe something so horrible would happen at the hands of those you love. Pay me for this session and let's meet again next week so we can get to the root of it. In effect, my parents paid Marty Osborne six thousand dollars to drive a stake into their hearts."

"They must have been distraught."

"They were devastated, and I don't think they ever really got over it. I can barely deal with it myself and I wasn't one of the accused. After the case was settled, my parents swore they'd put it behind them. They shut the door on the whole ugly episode. They were desperate to believe Michael loved them and everything was okay. Here's how 'okay' it was. A couple of years afterward, my mother died in a drowning accident, and my father dropped dead six months later of an aneurysm. He never got around to changing his will, so after what Michael put us through, he inherited an equal share of their estate."

"That's a tough pill to swallow."

"What choice did I have? I've made my peace with it. The money was theirs and they could do with it as they pleased. Maybe that was always my father's intent, to look after him."

I could see where she was going. "So you think Michael's memory of the two guys digging is just more of the same."

"Basically," she said. "How did he come up with this story in the first place? Doesn't that sound suspect to you?"

"I'll admit I was skeptical at first," I said. "He says he read a reference to Mary Claire in the paper and it triggered his memory of the whole event."

"That was years ago. What makes him so sure?"

"He said he saw them on his sixth birthday, July 21, and that's how he made the association. Your mother left him at Billie Kirkendall's while she ran errands. He was wandering around the property when he saw them."

"It sounds bogus to me."

"It wasn't his imagination. There *was* something buried there."

"Oh, please," she said. "Michael's a drama queen. He can't seem to help himself. Sometimes I think he's delusional or spaced out on drugs. He's incapable of telling the truth. It's not in his nature. He can't tell the difference between what's really true and what he imagines."

That caught my attention. In my brief relationship with him, I could cite my experience in support of her claim. He was evasive, omitting critical information from his account of himself. When I called him on it, he'd corrected himself and filled in the blanks. If I hadn't, I would have ended up with an erroneous impression. I felt protective nonetheless. I didn't want to sit and say nothing while his sister trashed him. "I don't think he fabricated the story. He was six. Maybe he didn't understand what he'd witnessed, but that doesn't mean he lied."

"That's exactly my point. He takes a simple moment and he embellishes, invents, and exaggerates. Next thing you know, there's an elaborate conspiracy afoot. He sees two men digging a hole and suddenly it's about Mary Claire's murder and her being buried in that grave."

"You're implying that he did this deliberately, which I find hard to believe."

"I'm not telling you this stuff just to hear myself talk. This is how his mind works. You can't believe a word he says."

"This comes a little late from my perspective."

"Don't kid yourself. You haven't seen the last of him. It's never over with him. Have you met any of his friends?"

The shift in subject caught me off guard. "One. A girl named Madaline. He told me she was addicted to heroin . . ."

"And now she's clean, but not sober," Diana interjected, derisively. "Did he mention she's a lush? Twenty-two years old and she's on probation for public drunkenness. Of course, he's the one who ferries her to AA meetings. He collects losers like her, anyone in worse shape than he is, if you can imagine such a thing. Sutton's wounded birds. He gets into rescue mode so he can feel good about himself. There's usually two or three of them hanging around at any given time. They move in. They borrow money. They take his car without permission and wind up in fender-benders that he ends up paying for out of pocket. Some land in jail, while loudly protesting their innocence. He bails them out and brings them home again because they have nowhere else to go. That's when they steal his credit cards and go on a spending jag."

"Poor judgment."

"Very poor. I can't tell you the money he's gone through. What scares me is thinking about what'll happen when he's emptied all his bank accounts. He's never really worked. He's held jobs, but none for long. The money he inherited is the only thing keeping him afloat. Once that's gone, he'll end up on my doorstep, begging for help. What's my choice then? I take him in or he ends up living on the street."

"You're not obligated."

"That's what my brothers tell me."

"Why do it then?"

"I guess I feel guilty because he's such a mess and the rest of us are okay . . ."

As she went on, I could hear my own story echoed in hers. My grievances, my determination to hang on to everything that seemed unfeeling or unfair. Her complaints were legitimate, but so what? The recital of her woes only made matters worse, keeping the pain alive when it should have been laid to rest.

Diana must have realized I'd clocked out. "Why are you looking at me that way?"

"I have family issues of my own and they sound just like yours. Different scenario, but the angst is the same. Personally, I'm getting tired of hearing myself whine. And if I'm tired, what about the people around me who have to put up with my shit?"

"It's not the same."

"Sure it is. What's the point in going over and over it? I'll bet you've told the same story a hundred times. Why don't you give it a rest?"

"If I give it up, Michael wins. Bad behavior triumphs over good yet again. Well, I'm sick of it. After the havoc he's wreaked, why should I let him off the hook?"

I could feel myself getting irritated. I understood where she was coming from, but the events she'd described were years in the past. Waltzing into my office to unload it all on me was out of line. She'd turned venom into a lifestyle and it wasn't attractive. On first meeting, I'd been put off by her aggressiveness. Now I was put off by her attempt to rope me into Sutton bashing.

"What hook, Diana? He's not on the hook except in your mind. He's living his own life and if he's screwing up right and left, what's it to you?"

Her smile was tight. "You say that now, but you're not done with him. Trust me. You gave him credence which has been in short supply of late. He'll come back. Some new crisis will emerge, some disturbing turn of events . . ."

"That's my lookout, don't you think?"

"You really don't believe me, do you?"

"I've heard every word. I understand why you're pissed off at him, but I take offense at the wholesale condemnation. Give the kid a break. You came here to warn me. You've done that and I thank you. I'm on red alert."

That shut her down. She withdrew as though I'd slapped her.

She snatched up her shoulder bag and took out a business card. "Here's my number if you should ever need to get in touch. I'm sorry to have taken up so much of your time."

As she reached the door, she paused. "You want to hear the best part?"

I was going to fire off a smart remark, but I held my tongue.

"Six days after Daddy died, Michael saw the light. He became a retractor. He disavowed his claims about the sexual abuse. He said he realized Marty Osborne had planted all those memories. Oops. Big mistake. He took it all back. So that's who you're dealing with. Have a nice day."

She left the office, banging the door shut behind her.

# 11

I had dinner that night at Rosie's, the tavern located half a block from my apartment. It's the perfect setting for the neighborhood drinking crowd and serves as a ready substitute for my nonexistent social life. In the summer months the softball rowdies dominate the bar, celebrating victories so minor they scarcely warrant column space in the local sports pages. From time to time they put together touch-football teams, the losers paying off the winners with a pony keg. Prior to the Super Bowl, there are endless noisy debates, arguments, and wagers, which are finally settled by pitching in ten bucks each and drawing names from an oversized beer stein Rosie keeps behind the bar.

Rosie is Hungarian by birth and though she's been in Santa Teresa most of her life, she refuses to give up her accent or her tortured sentence structure. She and Henry's brother William were married Thanksgiving Day three and a half years ago. It's an unlikely match, but one that's turned out to be good for both of them.

I took a seat in my favorite booth at the rear of the bar. Before I could get my windbreaker off, Rosie appeared and set an empty wineglass on the table. She'd apparently just dyed her hair, which was a deeply saturated shade of red I'd never actually seen on a human head. She held up a wine jug with a screw top and a label pasted on the front, MONGREL WHITE, 1988. She upended the jug and poured the wine, which actually made a *glug-glug-glug* sound as it tumbled into my glass.

"I know you supposed to sip first and say if you like, but this is all I got. Take or leave him."

"I'll take."

"You need eating better. Is too thin so what I'm giving you is bean soup with pork knuckle. I'd say Hungarian name, but you forget so what's to bother. Henry's bring me fresh-baked rolls. I give you plenty with a side of Hungarian cheese spread you gonna love."

"Fine. I can't wait."

There was no point in arguing with her because she always gets her way. I find bossy women restful as they take all the decision making out of your hands. Conniving women are the ones who really set my teeth on edge, though Rosie probably does a bit of that as well.

She went to the kitchen, order pad in hand, and returned moments later with the promised repast on a tray. She balanced the tray on the table edge and set the big bowl of soup in front of me, followed by a basket of napkin-wrapped rolls and a ramekin of cheese spread. I placed a hand on the napkin and felt the warm rolls underneath.

I ate with a series of oinky little sounds consistent with a voracious appetite and a thorough appreciation of what was going down my gullet. At 7:00 I decided to head home, my intention being to change into my sweats and lounge around on my sofa reading the paperback mystery I was halfway through. I shrugged into my windbreaker and adjusted the collar. With the sun down, it would be chilly walking even half a block. I zipped up and hoisted my bag across my shoulder. When I tucked a hand in one pocket, my fingers curled around the tag Cheney'd dropped in my palm the day before. I pulled it out and studied it, which I hadn't had a chance to do. The plastic disk was encrusted with dirt. I crossed the room to the bar where William was working, dapper as usual in his dark gray wool serge suit pants, white dress shirt, and tie. He'd shed his suit coat and placed it on a coat hanger suspended on a wall hook nearby. His only other concessions to his job were the two cones of paper towel he'd secured over his shirt sleeves with rubber bands to keep his cuffs clean.

I put my check on the bar along with a ten-dollar bill. My meal was $7.65, including the bad wine. "Keep the change," I said.

William swooped up both. "Thanks. You want anything else? Rosie made an apple strudel that will knock your socks off."

"I better not, but I'd love a glass of soda water."

"Certainly. Would you care for ice?"

"Nope."

"A slice of lemon or lime?"

"Just plain."

I watched as he filled a Tom Collins glass with soda from an eight-button dispenser gun. "You have an extra bar towel I could borrow? A dirty one will do."

He reached under the bar and removed a damp towel he must have stowed earlier. William's a stickler for sanitation. He sees the world as one big petri dish fermenting god knows what microbes and death-dealing bacteria.

I perched on a bar stool where the light was good and cleaned the grunge off the tag. On one side there was a phone number; on the other, the dog's name, which was Ulf. I lifted the limp leather collar to my nose, noting that it still carried the faint scent of rot. I put the tag back in my jacket pocket, returned the bar towel, and gave William a quick wave.

Outside, the night air felt chilly and the street was deserted. It was only a little after seven, but the neighbors were home and buttoned up for the night. After twenty-one years, it probably wasn't possible to determine whether Ulf had died of old age or if he'd been put down because of illness or injury. The "pirates" probably had a good laugh at Sutton's expense, spinning the yarn about a treasure map. I was guessing Sutton would have been just as enthralled by a doggie funeral with a bit of pomp and ceremony thrown in.

I wasn't sure what had generated my musings except a lingering defensiveness about Sutton's ending up with egg on his face. How his sister must have loved that, seeing him make a public fool of himself. Ah, well. Once I reached my apartment and closed the door behind me, I secured the locks, turned on a couple of lamps, and adjusted the louvered shutters. Then I changed into my comfies, grabbed a quilt, and settled on the couch to read. Happily, I had a weekend coming up and I intended to goof off for the whole of it, which is exactly what I did.

Monday morning was a wash—busy, but otherwise forgettable. The afternoon was taken up with a due-diligence request for an Arizona mortgage company interested in hiring a high-level executive. According to his résumé, he'd lived and worked in Santa Teresa from June of 1969 until February of 1977. There was nothing to suggest he was hiding information, but the Human Resources director had been in touch, asking me to do a sweep of public records. If irregularities came to light, they'd send one of their investigators to do a follow-up. I was looking at half a day's work at best, but it wouldn't be strenuous. A paycheck is a paycheck, and I was happy to oblige.

At 10:00, I walked over to the courthouse, and spent the next two hours trolling the index of civil and criminal suits, property liens, tax assessments, judgments, bankruptcy filings, marriage licenses, and divorce decrees. There was no evidence of wrongdoing and no suggestion the fellow had ever crossed swords with the law. The problem was that there was no evidence of the guy at all.

I'd been given an address on the upper east side. On his application, the guy claimed he'd bought the house in 1970 and lived there until he sold it in 1977, but the owner of record was someone else entirely. Since the public library was just across the street, I left the courthouse and jaywalked, approaching the entrance with a suitable sense of anticipation. I love shit like this, catching liars in the act. His fabrications had been so specific and detailed, he must have felt safe, assuming no one would ever bother to check.

I returned to the reference department, where I'd spent such a satisfactory hour the week before. I shed my windbreaker and hung it across the back of a chair while I pulled the Santa Teresa city directories for the years in question. Again, a fingertip search turned up no trace of the guy. I cross-checked the address in the Haines and Polk and came up with nothing. Well, wasn't that a kick in the pants?

I was on my way out of the building when I remembered the dog tag. I took it out again and studied it, tempted by the phone number on one side. It wouldn't take five minutes to look it up in the Haines. Maybe I'd never know the whole story, but I might glean the odd bit of information. The issue wasn't pressing. My curiosity was idle and wouldn't have warranted a separate trip to the library. However, I was already on the premises and the effort required would be minimal.

I returned to the reference department, which I was beginning to regard as my adjunct office. I took out both the 1966 and 1967 Polk and Haines directories and sat down at what I was beginning to think of as my personal table. I put the tag down beside me and leafed through the Haines until I found the same three-digit prefix. I worked my way down the sequence of numbers until I found a match. In both directories, the number was assigned to a P. F. Sanchez. By flipping back and forth between the Haines and the Polk, I found an address for him, though it wasn't a street name I recognized. His occupation was contractor; no indication of a wife.

I returned the directories to the shelf and then crossed to the section where the telephone directories were lined up. I pulled the current Santa Teresa phone book and looked in the S's, running down the listings until I came to "Sanchez, P. F." His telephone number was the same, as was his address on Zarina Avenue. Where the heck was that?

I walked back to my office, sat down at my desk, and hauled out my *Thomas Guide to Santa Teresa and Perdido Counties*. Zarina Avenue was actually in Perdido County, one of half a dozen streets that formed a grid in the tiny coastal town of Puerto, a name that had morphed into the longer Puerto Polvoriento, which was then shortened to P. Pol and from there to Peephole. I sat and pondered the geography. I'd hoped to feel better informed, which in some ways I was. What puzzled me now was why a man who lived in Peephole would bury his dead dog in Horton Ravine, a good fifteen miles north. There must have been some quirky set of circumstances to explain the digging of the dog's grave at such a remove.

I put my feet up on the desk, leaned back in my swivel

chair, and put a call through to Cheney Phillips at the PD. After two rings he picked up and when I identified myself, I could hear the smile in his voice. "Hey, kid. I hope you didn't take offense at my teasing you about the doggie exhumation."

"You know me better than that. I'm just thankful Mary Claire Fitzhugh wasn't buried in that hole," I said. "I'm sorry about the waste of manpower. I owe you one."

"If I had a dollar for every lead that didn't pan out, I'd be rich. Anyway, I'm the one who referred the kid to you in the first place so it's not like you cooked this up on your own."

"I do feel for him. How embarrassing."

"He'll survive," Cheney said.

"So what's the story on Diana Sutton?"

There was a pause. "Refresh my memory."

"Sorry. I should have said Diana Alvarez."

"The reporter? What about her?"

"Did you know she was Michael Sutton's sister?"

"You're not serious. I knew she was persistent, but I wrote it off to her job. How do you know her?"

"I don't, or at least I didn't until Friday morning. She came into my office, took a seat, and unloaded with both barrels."

I filled him in on Sutton's sorry tale of woe, at the end of which he said, "Even if I'd known his sordid history, I'd have reacted the same way. I thought his story had a ring of truth."

"Me, too. Apparently, she's made it her mission to screw him over any chance she can. The dog gave her the ammunition to go after him again."

"Hold on a second." He put a hand over the mouthpiece and then came back. "I gotta scoot. Anything else?"

"One quick question. Can you tell me the dog's breed? I know the body must have been in bad shape, but could you tell anything about him from what was left?"

"Well, he was big . . . I'd say seventy to eighty pounds once upon a time. Most of his coat was intact. The hair was long and coarse, a mix of black and gray, with maybe some shades of brown thrown in. It looked like the tag was an afterthought, tossed in on top of him."

"A German shepherd?"

"Something like that. Why?"

"I was just curious."

"Oh, lord. Not again. Stay out of trouble if you can," he said, and hung up.

I took a moment to place a call to Phoenix, Arizona, filling in the HR director on her phantom executive. She gave me a fax number and asked for an account of my coverage. I typed up my notes and then walked one block over to a notary's office and used her fax machine. I had two pages to send and the process took five minutes, which I thought was nothing short of miraculous. One day I'd break down and buy a machine of my own, but to date I didn't need one often enough to justify the expense.

I retrieved my Mustang, gassed up at the entrance to the 101, and headed down the coast to Peephole (population 400). The area, like so much of California, was part of a Spanish land grant, deeded to Amador Santiago Delgado in 1831. His mother was distantly related to Maria Christina of Bourbon–Two Sicilies, the fourth wife of King Ferdinand VII, and the only one of his wives to bear him living offspring. There was no clear explanation for Maria Christina's generosity, but Amador inherited title to the land when his mother died. He and his young bride, Dulcinea Medina Vargas, traveled from Barcelona to Perdido, California, took possession of the tract, and established a large working ranch devoted to the raising of purebred Spanish horses. Within a year Dulcinea died giving birth to their only child, a daughter, Pilar Santiago Medina. Bereft, Amador sold off his horses and turned to the deeply satisfying solace of drink. On his death in 1860, Pilar inherited his massive landholdings, which had largely reverted to the elements. At the time she was thirty years old and not a beautiful woman, but she was clever and her wealth more than compensated for the hefty frame and plain countenance Nature had bestowed on her.

When the Homestead Act was passed in 1862, land-hungry settlers poured into California from all over the country, eager to claim the 160 acres (65 hectares) per person promised by the government. Harry Flannagan was one of these. He was a blue-eyed Irishman, with bright red hair, muscular arms, and a strong back and shoulders geared for hard labor. In Ireland, Harry Flannagan had been a poor man and the opportunity to own land was heady stuff to him. He took his time, traveling up and down the California coast for months before he chose his spot and filed a claim with the nearest land office in Los Angeles. As was required, he attested that he was twenty-one years of age and swore he'd never borne arms against the United States or given comfort to its enemies. He further declared his intention of improving the plot with crops and a dwelling, with the understanding that if he was still on the land in five years, the property would be his free and clear.

The rugged acreage he'd chosen was beautiful, but there was little or no fresh water on it and farming was precarious. Despite its proximity to the Pacific Ocean, the land was arid and the irony wasn't lòst on him: nothing but water as far as the eye could see and none of it was usable. No one bothered to tell him that for the past twenty-five years the idyllic-looking harbor had been known as Puerto Polvoriento, "Port Dusty." Regardless of its obvious shortcomings, he was convinced he could turn the land to his advantage and he set about it with a will.

The only small impediment to his ambition was the fact that the sixty-five hectares he'd laid claim to infringed in its entirety on the land that belonged to Pilar Santiago-Vargas. Not surprisingly, this came to her attention, which prompted her to mount her horse and ride out to challenge the audacious interloper. It was never clear how the encounter played out or what wiles the plucky farmer employed in defense of his hopes, but the upshot was that Harry Flannagan took Pilar Santiago-Vargas as his lawful wedded wife within the month. He was not, after all, a man to quibble about a few excess pounds. With regard to her homeliness, he was also motivated to make allowances. Some eight and a half months later she bore him a son—the first of seven boys who arrived at two-year intervals, a band of fiery-haired Hispanics. By agreement, Pilar and Harry took turns naming their boychicks, who were, respectively, Joaquin, Ronan, Bendicto, Andrew, Miguel, Liam, and Placido.

Harry and Pilar were married for fifty-six years, until he was struck down in the influenza epidemic of 1918. Pilar lived on another fifteen years and died in 1933 at the age of 101. Harry's crowning achievement was the founding of the Flannagan Water Company, which provided water to the citizens of Peephole for twenty-five cents a gallon, making him rich beyond imagining. Thereafter, he spearheaded construction of the Puerto Dam, which was completed in 1901 and provided a distribution system that delivered running water to the town.

Oddly enough, in the years I'd lived in Santa Teresa, I'd rarely been to Peephole, and I was looking forward to seeing it again.

# 12

## WALKER McNALLY

### Monday, April 11, 1988

"Mr. McNally?"

He became aware that someone was addressing him. He opened his eyes. He didn't recognize the woman who was bending close. She had a hand on his arm, which she was shaking insistently. Her expression showed impatience or concern and since he didn't know her, he wasn't sure which. The overhead light was bright and the ceiling tiles looked institutional, designed to dampen sound, though he couldn't remember the name for them.

"Mr. McNally, can you hear me?"

He wanted to reply but there was a heaviness that filled his body, and the effort was too great. He had no idea what was going on and no memory of events that might explain his lying on his back, immobilized, with this woman leaning over him.

Something hurt. Had he had surgery? The pain wasn't acute. More like a dull ache that radiated through his body with a thick layer of white on top, as cold and heavy as a blanket of snow.

The woman stepped aside and two copies of Carolyn's face came into his visual frame, one slightly offset, like a watery duplicate. Nausea stirred as the surface ripples widened and dissipated near the edges of his view.

She said, "Walker."

He focused and the two images locked into one, like a magic trick.

"Do you know where you are?"

Again, he wanted to respond but he couldn't move his lips. He was so tired he could scarcely pay attention.

"Do you remember what happened?"

Her look was expectant. Clearly, she wanted an answer, but he had none to give.

"You were in an accident," she said.

Accident. That made sense. He took in the words, searching for corresponding images of what had occurred. Nothing came to him. Had he fallen? Had he been struck in the head by a bullet or a stone? Here, he was on his back. Before here was blank.

"Do you remember going off the road?"

Nope. He wanted to shake his head so she'd know he heard her, but he couldn't manage it. Road. Car. The concept was simple and he got it. He knew there'd been an accident, but he couldn't imagine his relationship to it. He was alive. He supposed he'd been hurt and he wondered how badly. His brain must still function even if his body was temporarily . . . or perhaps permanently . . . out of commission. Carolyn knew and he was willing to take her word for it, but the idea was odd.

"Do you know what day this is?"

Clueless. He couldn't even remember the last day he remembered.

She said, "Monday. The kids and I got back from San Francisco late this afternoon and your car was gone. I unloaded the suitcases and I was letting the kids watch a few minutes of TV when a police car pulled into the drive. There was a wreck on the pass. Your car was totaled. It's a wonder you're not dead."

He closed his eyes. He had no recollection whatsoever. He had no idea why he'd been on the 154 and no memory of a collision. From his perspective, there was only a yawning black hole, a blank wall that separated this current moment from the recent past. Dimly, he remembered leaving the bank on Thursday, but the door had slammed shut on anything after that.

A doctor appeared, a neurologist named Blake Barrigan, whom he recognized from the country club. Barrigan was interested in Walker's cognitive functions and ran him through a series of tests. Walker knew his own name. He knew Ronald Reagan was president of the United States, even if he hadn't voted for the man. He could count backward from one hundred by eights, a task he wasn't sure he could manage ordinarily. Barrigan was middle-aged and solemn, and while Walker could see his mouth move and knew he was conveying reassurances about his condition, he was too tired to care.

The next time he opened his eyes he was in a private room and people were talking in the hall. He consulted his body; his right elbow ached and his chest felt compressed where they'd apparently taped his ribs. He touched the right side of his head and felt a painful knot. He probably had minor injuries he wasn't aware of yet. He could smell cooked meat and the scent of green beans with a metallic edge, reminiscent of the canned variety of his youth. The clatter outside the door suggested a meal cart with food trays.

A nurse's aide came in and asked if he was hungry. Without waiting for a response, she lowered the rail on one side, cranked up his bed, and placed a tray on his rolling bed table, which she pushed within range. There was a carton of orange juice and a small container of cherry Jell-O sealed with an elasticized plastic cover like a little shower cap. "What's today? Sunday?"

"Monday," she said. "You were admitted from the ER an hour ago, so you missed dinner. Do you remember coming in?"

"Is my wife here?"

"She just left. A neighbor was watching the children and she had to put them to bed. She'll be back in the morning. Are you in pain?"

He shook his head in the negative, stirring the headache he hadn't been aware of. "I don't understand what happened."

"Dr. Barrigan can explain everything when he gets here. He has a patient on the surgical floor and he said he'd look in on you again before he left for the day. Can I get you anything else?"

"I'm fine."

Once his supper tray had been removed, he opened the bed table drawer and found a pocket mirror. He checked his reflection. He had two black eyes, a purple knot on his forehead, and a smoky discoloration on the right side of his face. He must have hit the windshield or steering wheel on impact. He put the mirror away, realizing he was lucky he didn't have cuts or broken facial bones.

At 9:00 a nurse appeared with a tray of meds. She verified his name by checking his hospital bracelet and then handed him a small pleated paper cup with two pills in it. When he was a kid his mother had given him cups the same size filled with M&M's.

"To help you sleep," she said when she saw the look on his face. "Do you need a urinal?"

The minute she said it, he realized his bladder was full and the pressure close to painful.

"Please."

She set down her tray and removed a lidded plastic urinal from the cabinet beside his bed. The device had a handle and a slanted spout and looked like something his kids could invent a hundred uses for at the beach. "I'll leave this with you. You can ring when you're done."

"Thanks."

She pulled the curtain along its track, shielding him from the curious eyes of those passing in the hall. He waited until she was gone and then rolled to his left and angled his penis into the opening of the urinal. Despite his best intentions, nothing would come. He tried to relax. He put his mind on something else, but the only thing he could think about was his need for relief. He would have laughed if the need to pee hadn't been so imperative. He'd suffered something similar when he and Carolyn were undergoing infertility treatments and he was asked to ejaculate into a cup so his sperm could be examined under a microscope and then washed before each of the five fruitless intrauterine inseminations they'd undergone.

He took a deep breath, hoping his bladder would relent. A pointless enterprise. He gave up for the moment and when the pressure was unbearable, he rang the nurses' station. Fifteen minutes passed before the aide appeared. She palpated his abdomen and then went to consult a nurse, who returned to the room accompanied by a student nurse. She had a catheterization packet with her, and she opened it and took out the Foley, a pair of latex gloves, and a packet of lubricant. She viewed the situation as a teaching opportunity. She grasped his penis and explained how to pass the Foley into the bladder by way of his urethra.

"I hope you don't mind," she said to him, as an aside.

"That's fine," Walker said. If she didn't get on with it, his bladder would burst. He only half listened, distancing himself from what was going on.

"The size of a Foley is indicated in French units," she was saying to the student nurse. "The most common sizes are 10 F to 28 F; 1 F is equivalent to 0.33 millimeters or .013 inches, 1/77th of an inch in diameter . . ."

After she instructed the student nurse in the proper technique, she encouraged her to try her hand at it. The girl was apologetic. Her fingers were ice cold and trembling. After two failed attempts, the nurse took over and inserted the catheter with remarkable efficiency. The relief was a miracle. The whole encounter was humiliating, but he was already converting it to an amusing anecdote he'd tell at the next cocktail party.

He finally managed to fall asleep, though he was awakened four times in the night—twice for a check of his vital signs, once when the pain in his ribs became insistent and he had to ask for medication, and once because an aide came into his room by mistake, thinking he was someone else. At some point during the night he realized Blake Barrigan, the shit, had never stopped by.

At 8:30 the next morning Carolyn arrived. The timing was such that he figured she'd just dropped Fletcher and Linnie off at preschool. At least he was alert now and fully awake, though he still drew a blank when it came to the accident. He knew they had top-notch insurance coverage, so he wasn't worried about the expense. It was the hassle of paperwork and the inconvenience of being without transportation until he picked up a rental car. The headache was creeping up again, starting at the base of his skull.

Carolyn took off her coat and placed it over the arm of the upholstered chair. It took him ten seconds to register the fact she wasn't looking at him and another ten to realize how angry she was. Carolyn was ordinarily easygoing, but once in a while something set her off and then there was hell to pay. This mood he knew: cold, withdrawn, her face pale with rage.

"Is something wrong?" He didn't much feel like the verbal beating he knew would follow. He had no idea what she was so pissed off about, but if he didn't ask now, she'd freeze him out until he did.

"I take it Blake Barrigan didn't stop by last night to bring you up to speed," she said.

Fleetingly, he thought Blake's being remiss might explain her attitude. Carolyn took these matters seriously. She had high standards for herself and she expected others to anticipate her requirements and behave accordingly. If Blake said he'd stop by, then by god, he'd better do it.

Walker said, "Not that I'm aware. The nurse said he had a patient on the surgical floor—"

"You killed a girl."

"Excuse me?"

"You heard what I said."

In a flash, he felt his body disconnect from his soul, like a caboose uncoupled and left behind on the track as the rest of the train moved on. He found himself floating in one corner of the room, looking down on himself. He could see the expression of bewilderment on his face. He could see the crooked part in Carolyn's hair, her features foreshortened from his perspective. For a moment, he wondered if he'd died. Actually, he hoped he had because what she'd told him was too horrendous to absorb. His mouth was so dry he couldn't muster speech.

Carolyn talked on, her tone indifferent, as though she were speaking of matters unrelated to him. "She was nineteen years old. She was on spring break, her sophomore year at UCST. She'd driven to San Francisco to spend the weekend with friends. She told her mother she wanted to avoid the late-afternoon traffic, so she left the city Monday morning at nine. At four-twenty she came over the hill on the 154, just three miles from home. She was halfway down the pass when you crossed the center line and struck her Karmann Ghia head-on. She never had a chance." Carolyn closed her mouth, her lips forming a tight line while she got control of herself.

He shook his head. "Carolyn, I swear to god, I don't remember any of this."

"Oh, really," she said, all cynicism. "You don't remember going into the sports bar at State and La Cuesta Monday afternoon?"

"I didn't even know there *was* one."

"Bullshit. The Whizz Inn? We've passed it a hundred times and you always make a joke about the name. You were drunk when you got there Monday afternoon, loud and obnoxious. You insisted on service, but the bartender refused and when he asked you to leave, you were belligerent. He ended up calling the police the minute you were out the door. A motorist saw you getting on the 101, weaving all over the place, but by the time he got to a gas station and called it in, you'd taken the 154 off-ramp and you were heading up the pass."

"That's not right. That can't be."

"There were three other witnesses—two joggers and a guy in a pickup truck you barely missed. He ended up going off the road. He's lucky he didn't end up dead as well."

"I'm drawing a blank."

"That's called an alcoholic blackout in case you haven't figured it out. Forget what went on and you absolve yourself of blame. What better way to sidestep guilt than to blot it out of your mind?"

"You think I did this on purpose? You know me better than that. When have I ever—"

Carolyn rode right over him. "You know what's odd? We saw her—the girl you killed. The kids and I must have left San Francisco the same time she did. I didn't realize who she was until I came across her picture in this morning's paper. We'd stopped at that Applebee's near Floral Beach. The kids were cranky and hungry and needed a break. She was sitting in the first booth eating a burger and fries as we walked in. We sat in the booth next to hers and the kids were being silly, peeping at her over the top of the banquette. You know how they do. She started making faces at them, which delighted them no end. She finished her meal before ours arrived and she waved from the door as she went out. She was so fresh and so pretty. I remember hoping Linnie would be as sweet to little kids when she was the same age . . ."

Carolyn's face crumpled and she put a hand over her mouth, sobbing like a child, rocking back and forth. She held herself at the waist, as though she had a stomachache.

He wanted to reach out, but he was aware that any gesture he made would seem woefully inadequate. Had someone really died because of him? Carolyn's anguish was contagious and he felt tears spill from his own eyes, his weeping as automatic as yawning in the presence of someone who's just yawned. At the same time, in the most detached and clinical part of his brain, he was hoping she'd catch sight of his tears and feel sorry for him. She was capable of mood swings and emotional shifts, being outraged one minute and forgiving the next. He needed her on his side; not an enemy, but his ally.

"Baby, I'm sorry. I had no idea," he whispered. His voice cracked and he could feel the tension in his chest as he choked back a sound. "I can't believe it. I'm sick about it."

Her face snapped up, her tone incredulous. "You're sick about it? *You're sick?* You were drunk on your ass. How could you do that? How COULD you?"

"Carolyn, please. You have every right to be furious, but I didn't mean to do it. You have to believe me." He knew he was sounding too rational. This wasn't a time to try persuading her. She was too upset. But how could he survive if she turned on him? All their friends loved Carolyn. They'd take their cue from her. Everyone said she was an angel; considerate, warm, loyal, kind. Her compassion was boundless—unless or until she felt betrayed. Then she was merciless. She'd often accused him of being cold, but at the core of her being, she was the one with a stony heart, not him.

He said, "I'm not asking for sympathy. This is something I'll have to live with the rest of my life." Inwardly, he winced because the tone was off. He sounded petulant when he meant to sound remorseful.

She took a tissue from her handbag and wiped her eyes, pausing then to blow her nose. She made a sound that was an audible sigh and he wondered if the worst of the storm had passed. She was shaking her head with a small sad smile. "Do you want to know what I came home to? You've probably forgotten this along with everything else. I found an empty vodka bottle and six empty beer cans tossed in the trash. There was whiskey all over the patio where you'd knocked over the Maker's Mark. You must have fallen against the table because it was tipped up on its side and there was broken glass everywhere. It's a wonder you didn't cut your own throat."

She paused and pressed the tissue against her mouth. She shook her head again, saying, "I don't know you, Walker. I have no idea who you are or what you're about. I'm serious."

"What do you want me to say? I'm sorry. I'll never have another drink again as long as I live. I give you my word."

"Oh, for god's sake. Spare me. Look at you. You've been drunk for days and now an innocent girl is dead."

He knew better than to go on defending himself. He'd just have to ride it out, let her get it all out of her system, and then maybe she'd relent. He held his hand out, palm up, in a mute plea for contact.

She leaned forward. "I'm filing for divorce."

"Carolyn, don't say that. I'll quit. I promise you."

"I don't give a shit about your promises. You said you could quit anytime you wanted, but you meant as long as I kept an eye on you. The minute my back was turned, you were at it again and look at the result. I'm not your keeper. That's not my job. You're in charge of yourself and you blew it."

"I know. I understand. I have no defense. I'm begging you not to do this. We're a family, Carolyn. I love you. I love my kids. I'll do anything to make this right."

"There's no way to make it right. That poor girl died because of you."

"Don't keep saying that. I get it and you have no idea how horrible I feel. I deserve the worst. I deserve anything you want to throw at me—hatred, blame, recriminations, you name it—only please not right now. I need you. I can't get through this without you."

Her smile was mocking and she rolled her eyes. "You are such a horse's ass."

"Maybe so, but I'm an honorable man. I'll take full responsibility. You can't condemn me for one lapse in judgment—"

"*One* lapse? Perhaps along with everything else, you're forgetting your previous DUI."

"That was years ago. The whole thing was dumb and you know it. The cop pulled me over because the tag on my license plate was expired. The guy was a moron. You said so yourself."

"Not so much of a moron he didn't smell whiskey on your breath and haul you off to jail. I was the one who bailed you out. Because of you, the social worker nearly tossed out our application to adopt—"

"Fine. All right. I did that, Your Honor. I'm guilty as charged. I've apologized a hundred times, but you keep bringing it up. The point is, nothing came of it. No harm, no foul . . ."

She got up and reached for her coat. "Tell the judge 'No harm, no foul' at your arraignment. That ought to be good for a laugh."

The rest of the day went by in a blur. He feigned more pain than he felt, just to get more medication. God bless Percocet, his new best friend. He picked at his supper tray, then flipped from channel to channel on the TV set, too restless to focus. He ran through the confrontation with Carolyn a hundred times. What he hadn't dared confess, for fear of her heaping even more venom on him, was that he actually felt nothing one way or the other. How could he regret consequences when the before and the after and the in-between were gone?

At 9:00 P.M. he woke with a start, unaware that he'd fallen asleep. He heard footsteps in the hall and turned to the door expecting to catch sight of Blake Barrigan. He'd never had much use for the guy, but their wives were friends and he was sorely in need of a friend himself just now. Barrigan, like most doctors, was capable of keeping judgment at bay, appearing sympathetic whether he felt that way or not.

When Herschel Rhodes appeared in the doorway, Walker thought he was hallucinating. Herschel Rhodes? Why was he stepping into his hospital room? Walker had known him at Santa Teresa High School, where the two had occasional classes together. Herschel was a homely teen, awkward and overweight, with bad skin and no social skills. To compensate for his failings he was earnest and studious, the poor schmuck. Teachers fawned over him because he paid attention in class and actually participated. That's how out of it he was. The boy was hell on raising his hand and the answers he gave were usually right. He turned in his class assignments on time, even going so far as to *type* his term papers, including the copious footnotes. What a little kiss-ass. Herschel was one of those kids shunned and ignored by the popular kids. No one was ever outright rude to him and if he was aware of the smirks and eye rolling that went on behind his back, he gave no indication of it.

He was now in his late thirties, still round-faced, with his dark hair slicked back in a style Walker hadn't seen since the early 1960s. He'd been a merit scholar and graduated from Santa Teresa High third in his class. Walker had heard he'd graduated from Princeton and had then gone on to Harvard Law. He'd passed the bar the first time around. His specialty was criminal defense. Walker had seen his full-page ad in the yellow pages—murder, domestic violence, DUI, and drug offenses. It seemed like a sleazy way to make a living, but he must have done well at it because Walker'd seen his house in Montebello and the guy lived well. He'd become better-looking with age, and the traits that were deficits in his teens now stood him in good stead. He was reputed to be a ruthless competitor at anything he undertook—golf, tennis, bridge. "Cutthroat" was the word they used. He played hard, he played to win, and no one got in his way.

Herschel seemed startled at the sight of him. "Jesus, you look like shit."

Walker said, "Herschel Rhodes, of all people. I didn't expect to see you."

"Hello, Walker. Carolyn asked me to stop by."

"As an attorney or a friend?"

Herschel's expression was bland. "We're hardly friends."

"Nicely put. If you must know, I'm in the doghouse with her, piece of shit that I am. I can't believe she's taking pity on me."

Herschel smiled slightly. "She figured it was in her best interests. You go down, she goes down with you. None of us wants to see that."

"Oh, god no," Walker said. "Have a seat."

"This is fine. I can't stay long. I hope you know the kind of trouble you're in."

"Why don't you spell it out for me? I'm not sure if anyone's mentioned it, but the past four or five days are completely blank as far as I'm concerned."

"Not surprising. You came into the ER with a blood alcohol of 0.24—three times the legal limit."

"Says who?"

"They drew blood."

"I had a concussion. I was out."

Herschel shrugged.

"They drew blood when I was out? What horseshit. Can they *do* that?"

"Sure, under the implied consent law. When you apply for and receive a driver's license, you consent to a chemical test on request. Even if you'd been conscious, you wouldn't have had much choice. If you'd refused, or tried to, you'd have been charged with a refusal and they'd have taken the blood anyway pursuant to *Schmerber Versus California*—a U.S. Supreme Court case about the need to preserve evidence that's dissipating."

"Shit. I love it. *Schmerber Versus California*. Is that all? Give me the rest of it. You're bound to have more."

"You'll be charged with Penal Code 191.5—gross vehicular manslaughter while intoxicated. That carries four, six, or ten years, unless you have a prior, in which case it's fifteen years to life."

"Fuck."

"When did you get a DUI?"

"Two years ago. Look it up. The date escapes me."

"You'll also be charged with VC-20001, subsection C— felony hit-and-run after a fatal DUI accident—"

"What are you talking about? What hit-and-run?"

"Yours. You left the scene. The cops found you half a mile away, trudging down the pass all by your lonesome. One shoe off and one shoe on. Remember the nursery rhyme? *'Diddle diddle dumplin', my son John, went to bed with his trousers on; one shoe off and the other shoe on . . .'* "

Walker said, "Quit already. I know the one you mean." He would have denied it, but he suffered a quick flash of himself stepping on a rock. He'd cussed and hopped on one foot, laughing at the pain.

Herschel continued in the same mild tone, his gaze fixed

on Walker's. Walker wondered if it was malevolence he was seeing in his eyes, Herschel Rhodes's long-awaited and oh-so-delicious revenge for past slights.

"You'll also be charged with VC-23153 A and B—DUI causing injury. If you've been convicted of a DUI within the past ten years, you could be charged with second-degree murder under the *Watson* case—"

"Shit on you, Herschel. I just got done telling you I have a fucking prior so why don't you stick VC-23153 up your ass?"

"Have you talked to anyone else about this?"

"Just you and my wife. Believe me, that's more than enough."

Herschel leaned closer. "Because I have one piece of advice for you, pal: Keep your mouth shut. Don't discuss this with anyone. If the subject comes up, you button your lip. You're a deaf-mute. You no speaka da language. Are you hearing me?"

"Yes."

"Good. The doctor's talking about releasing you tomorrow morning—"

"So soon?"

"They need the bed. I'll see if I can talk the cops into waiting until you're home to take you into custody. Otherwise, they'll arrest you right here, handcuff you to the rail, and post a cop outside the door. Whichever way it goes, remember these two words. *Shut. Up.*"

Walker shook his head, saying "Shit" under his breath.

"In the meantime, you'd be smart to put yourself in rehab, at least make a show of cleaning up your act."

"I can't go into *rehab*. I have a family to support."

"AA, then. Three meetings a week minimum, daily if it comes down to it. I want you to look like a guy renouncing his sins and repenting his evil ways."

"Are you going to get me out of this mess?"

"Probably not, but I'm the best hope you have," Herschel said. "If it's any comfort, you won't go to trial for another three to six months. Speaking of which, I need a check."

"How much?"

"Twenty grand for starters. Once we get to court, we're

talking twenty-five hundred dollars a day, plus the cost of expert witnesses."

Walker kept his expression neutral, not wanting to give Herschel the satisfaction of seeing his dismay. "I'll have to move money over from savings. I don't keep cash like that in my checking account. Can it wait until I get out?"

"Have Carolyn take care of it. Nice seeing you."

# 13

## Monday, April 11, 1988

Peephole, California, is essentially two blocks long and ten blocks wide, a stone's throw from the Pacific Ocean. A Southern Pacific Railroad track runs parallel to the 101, separating the town from the beach. A tunnel runs under both the train tracks and the highway, making it possible to reach the water if you're willing to walk hunched over through a damp and moldy-smelling fifty yards of culvert. At the northernmost end of town there's a banana farm. The only other businesses are a service station selling no-name gas and a fresh-produce stand that's closed for most of the year.

I activated my left-turn signal and slowed, eyes pinned on the rearview mirror to make sure no one was plowing into me. At the first break in oncoming traffic, I turned off the highway and crossed the tracks, which put me at the midpoint, half the town to the right of me and half to the left. The ebb and flow of the surf and the surging and receding waves of cars on the highway created a hush of white noise. There was something lazy in the air. My driving tour was brief because there wasn't much to see. The streets were narrow and there were no sidewalks. There were roughly 125 homes in a hodgepodge of architectural styles. Many of the original summer cottages still stood, probably tricked out by now with proper insulation, forced-air furnaces, air-conditioning units, and triple-glazed windows. These were people with storage problems. The yards I passed were littered with everything from boat hulls to broken birdbaths to old suitcases. Discarded furniture had been tossed off the porch steps, perhaps awaiting a sweep by the alley fairies.

I turned onto Zarina Avenue, checked the house number, and found myself peering at a one-story shingle-and-adobe house with a crudely constructed chimney piercing the roof on one end. A flaking white-painted picket fence staggered around the property, enclosing a length of gravel driveway bordered by patches of overgrown grass. A chicken-wire fence surrounded the vestiges of a garden planted in winter vegetables. A shaggy-coated yellow mongrel roused himself from a nap and sauntered in my direction, wagging his tail. The mop of hair hanging over his face made it look like he was watching me from behind a bush. This was the third dog I'd encountered in the past week, and I could feel my resistance fading. The dogs I'd met were a good-natured crew, and as long as none of them barked, snarled, snapped, bit, jumped on me, humped my leg, or slobbered o'ermuch, I was happy to make their acquaintance. This one followed me to the front door and watched expectantly as I knocked on the frame of the screen. He studied the door as I did, glancing at me now and then to show he was attentive to the plan and supportive of my aims.

The man who opened the door had to have been descended from one of the blue-eyed Irish-Hispanic clan who'd prospered in Peephole since the mid-1800s. His hair was the color of new bricks, clipped short and threaded with gray. He was tall and thin, broad-shouldered, with ropy muscles and a weathered nut-brown complexion that suggested hours in the sun. His jeans were well worn and rode low on his hips, and his blue denim shirt had a rip in one sleeve. I placed him at the north end of sixty.

"Yes?"

I said, "Sorry to bother you, but I'm looking for P. F. Sanchez."

"That's me. Who are you?"

"Kinsey Millhone," I said. My impulse was to shake his

hand, but that would have necessitated his opening the screen and I could tell he was already wondering if I was selling soap products door-to-door, while I was wondering if he was married. The Polk and the Haines hadn't mentioned a spouse, and he wasn't wearing a wedding ring. The cornflower blue of his eyes was the same shade as Henry's.

"Mind if I ask what the P. F. stands for?"

"Placido Flannagan. People call me Flannagan, or sometimes Flan," he said. "I have an uncle and two cousins named Placido, so I use my middle name."

"So you're Harry Flannagan's, what, great-grandson?"

"Let me guess. You're an amateur genealogist. That's usually the story I get when a stranger asks about Harry."

"Actually, I'm a private detective."

He scratched his chin. "That's a new one. What brings you to my door?"

"I found your telephone number on an ID tag, buried with a dog. I was curious about the circumstances. In case you're wondering, you're listed in Peephole in two crisscross directories, which is how I came up with your address."

"A dog."

"A dead one."

His mouth pulled down with skepticism. "Woofer's the only pooch I own and you're looking at him. He may be old, but as nearly as I can tell, he's not dead yet. You sure about this?"

"Pretty sure," I said. "The dog's name was Ulf."

He stood stock still for a moment and then squinted at me. "*What* did you say your name was?"

"Kinsey."

He opened the door. "You better come in."

I entered the house, stepping directly into the main room with Woofer at my heels. The dog padded the perimeter with his nose down, following the scent of an unseen creature, very possibly himself. The place was old. The thick walls were stucco and the ceiling was exposed timber, dark with age. The fireplace itself was a half-round of stucco tucked into one corner. The mantel was a curve of raw wood with a pair of antlers mounted above it. The furniture was Victorian, four chairs and two sofas lined up against the walls as though the center had been cleared for dancing. Three dingy rag rugs had been tossed on the floor and Woofer chose the biggest for the next phase of his nap. The room smelled like damp ash, the lingering scent of last winter's fires.

Flannagan indicated that I should sit and I settled in a chair with an ancient black horsehair seat. Given my trivial mental processes, I was momentarily distracted by the notion of horsehair, wondering if the chair was literally upholstered in an equine hide. Couldn't be done in this day and age, but our forebears weren't troubled by the sorts of sentiments we harbor today, believing animals were intended for Man's use. Even in death, nothing went to waste.

Flannagan sat down to my right on a rose-colored velvet settee with an ornate dark mahogany trim. The nap had worn thin in places, but the tufting was still crisp and all the buttons were in place. He rested his elbows on his knees, his gnarly fingers loosely laced together. "What's your interest in Ulf? He's been gone the better part of twenty years."

"I know. If my information's correct, he was buried in Horton Ravine in July of 1967."

Flannagan was shaking his head. "That's not possible. You're mistaken."

"According to the best guess, he was a German shepherd." I reached into my jacket pocket and removed the blue leather collar with the tag attached. I handed it to him. He studied the disk, front and back, and then ran his thumb across the dog's name.

"Shit."

"I take it you know the dog."

"He belonged to my son. Liam died in a motorcycle accident in 1964. Eighteen years old. He laid his Harley down in a patch of gravel on the 101 and skidded into the path of an oncoming car."

I watched him without a word, letting him tell it his way.

He tilted his head this way and that to loosen tension, which created muffled pops. His blue eyes met mine. "Ulf wasn't a shepherd. He was a wolfdog. You know anything about the breed?"

"Wolfdogs? No clue."

"Ulf was what they call a high-content hybrid, meaning

genetically he was more *Canis lupus* than *Canis lupus famil-
iaris*. A hybrid is usually the result of a female wolf mated to
a male domestic dog. I'm generalizing here, but as a rule, they
don't make good pets. They're too high-spirited and demand-
ing. Smart as all get-out, but they're difficult to housebreak.
Chain 'em up in the yard and they go berserk."

"How long did your son have the dog?"

"Not much more than a year. Liam was in his biker phase
and probably sold dope, though I never pressed him on the
subject. He would have lied if I had so what's the point? He
bought the dog from a guy who had a litter of six in the back
of his pickup truck. I guess if you deal drugs, owning a wolfdog lends you a certain dangerous air. They're aggressive and
predatory and they have those eerie gold eyes that look straight
into your soul. Hold on. I'll show you something."

He got up and crossed the room to a carved oak break-
front he was using as a catchall—keys, junk mail, tools, paper-
backs, a silver tea set with the creamer missing. He picked up
a framed color photograph, looking at it for a moment before
he crossed the room again and handed it to me. "That's the
two of them."

I angled the photo to eliminate the glare. Liam must have
inherited his mother's coloring. Unlike his father, he was dark-
haired and dark-eyed. He did have his father's physique in a
lighter body style. He wore a black leather jacket, jeans, and
black boots. He was hunkered beside the young dog, which
stood facing the camera with a wary air of intelligence. He
looked like a German shepherd except that his torso was slim-
mer and his legs were longer. His coat was medium length and
appeared rough, a grizzled black with layers of gray near his
head. The mask of white across his face attested to the strong
genetic presence of wolf.

"He's beautiful. The name, Ulf, as in 'wolf'?"

Flannagan smiled. "Liam came up with that. He was just
a little fluff ball when he got him. Six weeks old. Even as a
pup, he was a handful. I never once heard him bark, but when
he howled, even as a baby, it would raise the hair on the back
of your neck. Dog like that is always testing—the more wolf,
the more testing. Liam was alpha male, which meant when he
died, no one else could really handle the dog."

"So he reverted to you?"

"That's about the size of it. Wolves are pack animals. They have a clear social structure. There's only room for one leader, and it better be you. You want alpha status with a dog like that; you have to teach him he's subordinate. You don't play tug-of-war with him. He doesn't sleep on your bed. You go through the door first and he eats when you say so and not a minute before. With Liam gone and me stepping in after the fact, there was no way the dog would accept me as dominant. I tried to treat him as Liam had, but he wasn't impressed. He put up with me. Beyond that, he obeyed if he felt like it, and the rest was my problem."

"Must have been a strange relationship."

"I'm not sure he ever felt much for me, but I admired him and I was grateful for his tolerance. My biggest problem was finding a vet willing to treat him. A lot of vets won't do it. There's no approved rabies vaccine for the breed so if the dog bites someone, the county will insist on putting him down, no ifs, ands, or buts. In some states it's illegal to own a wolfdog. I'm not sure what the California law was back then, but I remember Liam saying when you take a wolfdog to a new vet, to be on the safe side, you claim he's a husky or half malamute.

"That turned out to be a nonissue with Ulf. He developed what I thought was hip dysplasia, meaning the joint was unstable and started causing him pain. By the time he was four years old, the suffering was so acute he could barely get around. I'm not that good a liar so I made a lot of calls before I finally found a vet who'd see him. He suggested I drop him at the office so he could sedate the dog and take X-rays. Sedation's a risky business with wolfdogs, but he said he understood and he'd be cautious about the dosage. Anyway, I drove him up to Santa Teresa.

"While Ulf was still under, the doc called and told me it wasn't hip dysplasia at all. We were looking at osteosarcoma, a malignant tumor in the bone. In a young dog like Ulf, the tumor is usually fast-spreading and survival time is short. Amputation was a possibility, but I couldn't see it with a dog like him. The vet offered to show me X-rays if I needed to be convinced, but I believed him. He recommended euthanization and I agreed."

He lowered his head and then pinched the bridge of his nose and let the air out of his lungs. "Shit. I know I did the right thing. Own an animal and you're responsible for his comfort and safety. You do what you have to do, even if it breaks your heart. But I should have been with him. Losing that dog was like losing Liam all over again. I couldn't handle it. I should have driven back up there, even if he was already sedated and wasn't aware of what was going on. Instead, I told the vet to get on with it. I told him to just take care of it and when I hung up the phone, I stood here and wept. It was cowardly. He was a noble animal. I should have held him while he died. I owed him that and Liam, too."

I was busy thinking about six other things, breathing through my mouth in hopes I could keep my shit together. Meanwhile, Woofer, the yellow mongrel, had roused himself and crossed to Flannagan's side. He stood there with his chin on Flannagan's thigh, looking up at him through the mop of hair that hung over his eyes. Flannagan smiled and rubbed behind his ears.

I cleared my throat. "I've never owned a dog."

"Yeah, well, I swore I'd never own another one and here I am. This fellow's fifteen years old and so far, so good. Maybe I'll get lucky and go before he does. At any rate, that's the story of Ulf. You caught me off guard. I never thought I'd hear another word about the dog."

"I appreciate the information."

"What about you? You haven't explained how you ended up with his tag."

I gave him an abbreviated version of my meeting with Michael Sutton, his encounter with the two guys digging the hole, and his suspicions about Mary Claire Fitzhugh. Flannagan remembered the child's disappearance. None of the other names I mentioned meant anything to him. He hadn't known the Kirkendalls, the Suttons, or anyone on Alita Lane.

With a shrug I said, "Maybe there's no connection. Maybe Ulf being buried there was pure coincidence. It just seems odd. I don't know anything about the protocol when a dog is put down. The vet might have buried him."

"I don't know why he would. He only saw the dog once so it's not like there was an emotional connection between the two. I know *I* didn't bury him so how he ended up in Horton Ravine is anybody's guess. What else do you want to know?"

"I guess that's about it. Do you remember the vet's name?"

"Not offhand. I can sort through my canceled checks. It might take me a while, but I'll be happy to try."

"That was a long time ago. I can't believe you'd have records going back that far."

"Give me a number where I can reach you and I'll see what I can find."

"I'd appreciate it."

He watched while I jotted down my home number on the back of a business card and when I handed it to him, he said, "You might want to be careful referring to this town as Peephole. People around here can be stiff-necked. We call it Puerto."

"Thanks for the warning. I'll watch myself."


When I got back to my office there was a message on my answering machine. "Hey, Kinsey. Tasha here. I was hoping to catch you before you left for the day. We wanted to make sure you received the invitation to the dedication. Could you give me a call and let me know if you can make it? That's Saturday, May 28, in case the invitation hasn't arrived. We'd really love to see you. Hope all goes well."

She recited her number twice like I was standing by with a pencil writing everything down. As part of my brand-new attitude of open-mindedness, I did, in fact, make a note. Having done so, I tore the sheet from my scratch pad, crumpled it, and threw it in the trash. I wasn't even tempted to take it out again, in part because I knew this was Monday and the garbage wouldn't be picked up for another two days. Plenty of time for ambivalence.

I checked my watch. It was 5:15, time for me to pack it in for the day. I'd just locked the front door and I was heading down the walk when the turquoise MG came around the corner with Sutton at the wheel. He had the top down and his dark hair was ruffled. I waited while he parked, wondering why he was back. Even at that short distance, he looked closer to eighteen years old than twenty-six. I've noticed that once in a while, someone gets caught at a stage in life from which they never advance. Ten years from now, I suspected he'd look much the same, despite the close-up contradiction of crow's-feet and sagging jawline.

He got out of the car and approached with his head down, his hands in his pockets. When he spotted me, he stopped. "Oh! Are you leaving for the day?"

"That was my intention. What's up?"

"Can you spare me a few minutes?"

"Sure."

He stood there, apparently thinking I'd turn around and unlock the door. He said, "I'd prefer to talk in private."

I debated the point. When a client comes in, I offer a cup of coffee as a matter of course, usually hoping they won't take me up on it. Often, the coffee ritual is more of a commitment than I really care to make. Set up the machine, wait until the coffee's done, inquire about preferences (black, milk, sugar, no sugar), check the relevant supplies. I keep packets of sweetener on hand, but the milk is inevitably over the hill, and then what? We talk about the downside of powdered whitener and who gives a shit? I'd rather whiz past the chitchat and get to the point. Same with Sutton's coming into the office and taking a seat. If I let him in, how the heck was I going to get him out? "Is this urgent?"

"Pretty much. I mean, I think so."

"Can't we talk just as easily out here?"

"I guess."

We stared at each other for a moment.

"I'm ready anytime," I said.

"I was trying to think how to say this. Remember when we were standing around by the road while the officers were digging?"

"Thursday of last week. I remember it well."

"A bunch of people parked their cars and got out, curious about what was happening."

I said, "Right." Mentally, I leaped past the foreplay, guessing at his intent. I anticipated his mentioning his sister, Dee, as in Diana Alvarez, trying to offset any damage she might have done by regaling me with his tall tales of sexual abuse. I nearly

brought her name up myself in hopes of heading him off. I was
so close to interrupting, I nearly missed what he said.

"I caught sight of a guy I thought I knew and later I realized he reminded me of one of the pirates. I only saw him for a
second and I really didn't make the connection until yesterday.
You know how it is when you see someone out of context?
This guy looked familiar, but I couldn't think why. Then it
came to me."

"One of the two pirates," I said.

"Exactly."

I allowed myself time to absorb what he'd said, trying to
block the impact of his sister's revelations. In that split second, I understood how completely my perception of Sutton
had been tainted by what she'd told me. Even as I resisted the
pull, my response to him was skewed by the notion of his tentative hold on the truth. She'd sworn he'd come around again
and, sure enough, he had, offering me a new twist, the next
installment in a drama that would otherwise be dead.

"You're overthinking this," I said. "The guys were burying
a dog."

"I know, but I went over the incident and I wondered if they
might have switched the dog's body for Mary Claire's after I
interrupted them."

"Switched bodies? And then what? I don't understand
where you're going with this."

"Well, if I'm right and the guy saw me at the same time
I saw him, wouldn't he realize I was onto them? Why else
would the cops suddenly be digging up the hill? He'd know
the police were getting close and who else could have tipped
'em off but me?"

I closed my eyes briefly, forcing down the irritation that
was surging up my spine. "Sutton, honestly, you'll have to forgive my reaction, but I think you're beating this to death. You
were six. That was twenty-one years ago and there's no evidence whatever that the scene you stumbled on had anything
to do with Mary Claire. It's pure conjecture on your part. Why
can't you admit your mistake and let it go at that?"

The color came up in his cheeks. "You think I'm wasting
your time."

I don't like being transparent so naturally I denied what

he'd said. "I didn't say you were wasting my time. I under-stand your concern, but I think it's misplaced. You can't be this paranoid."

He stared at the ground and then looked up again. "I wanted you to have the information in case something happens to me. I didn't know who else to tell."

"Nothing's going to happen to you."

"But in case it did. That's all I'm trying to say. I've seen the guy somewhere, but it wasn't recently."

"Fair enough," I said. "I don't believe you're in any danger, but what do I know? If it makes you feel better, go ahead and tell me the rest. What did he look like?"

"He was kind of light-haired and not too tall and he was wearing a suit."

"Can you be more specific? There were six or seven guys out there who fit that description."

"Not that many. I'd say three, not counting the officers."

"But it still doesn't help. The information's too sketchy and it does me no good," I said. "I mean, I thought it was pure genius on my part that I found the burial spot based on the flimsy information you gave me the first time out, but I have my limitations . . ."

I stopped. Sutton was watching me with a look of such mute pleading that I relented. "But enough about me," I said. "What about his car? Did you see what he was driving?"

He shook his head. "I wasn't paying attention. I only no-ticed him when he'd already parked and he was standing by the road. Next thing I knew, he was gone again."

I stared at him.

"Sorry," he said, sheepishly. "I see what you mean. I haven't given you much to go on."

"Would you recognize him if you saw him again?"

"I think so. I'm pretty sure I would." He hesitated. "If I do, what should I do? Should I, like, follow him or maybe get the number off his license plate?"

"The plate number, sure, but I don't want you tagging around after the guy. He'll think you're a stalker. In any event, the chances of your spotting him again seem remote."

"True. Anyway, I feel better now that I've told you."

"Good. Is there anything else?"

He looked up, fixing me with those solemn brown doggie eyes. "I know my sister was there. I saw her talking to you."

"She's a reporter. That's what she does. She managed to buttonhole anyone who'd give her the time of day. So what?"

I could see him arranging his words with care.

Blinking, he said, "A long time ago, I caused big trouble in my family. Diana likes to tell people what I did because she's still furious with me. She acts like she's being a good citizen, warning people about the kind of person I am, but it's really her way of sticking a knife in my gut."

"Sutton, it's no big deal. You told me you were estranged so it's not like you were hiding anything."

"In a way, I was. I should have filled in the rest."

"You don't owe me an explanation."

"I was just thinking that after talking to her, you probably don't believe a word I say and I don't blame you. But you were polite and you listened just now and I appreciate it. If there's ever a way I can return the kindness, will you let me know?"

"Of course. Don't worry about it."

"Thanks."

He hesitated and then stuck his hands back in his pockets and started walking to his car.

When he turned with a half-wave, I felt a fleeting moment of dread. "Take care of yourself, okay?"

He waved again and then got into his car. How could I have known then that within days, he'd be laid out on a coroner's slab with a bullet hole between the eyes?

# 14

My encounter with Sutton left me with a load of guilt. If he'd been good at reading minds, he wouldn't have thanked me for being polite, because in truth, he'd annoyed the shit out of me. I couldn't decide if it was attention he wanted or emotional support, but I was unprepared to give either. Even with his collection of wounded birds, he seemed lonely and at loose ends. I didn't like feeling sorry for him because it clouded my judgment. Here I was bending over backward, trying to compensate for feeling one-up while he was one-down. Somehow he had me hooked in when I should have been moving on.

On the drive home, I operated by rote, rerunning the conversation so I could test the elements. Light-haired and not too tall? Spare me. I hadn't paid attention to the smattering of looky-loos who'd parked on the berm and it was way too late now for a mental review. A dog was a dog and even if Sutton was right about the guy, what difference did it make? I could understand his plaintive desire to persuade. He had no credibility. I tried to imagine myself in a position where any observation I made was automatically deemed false. Talk about feeling helpless and small. While I was no more inclined to believe him, I decided to set the subject aside without prejudice.

Once in my neighborhood, I scanned for a parking place and found a spot close to the corner of Albanil and Bay. I shut the engine down, locked my car, and walked the half-block to my apartment. I caught sight of a woman ahead of me standing by my gate. She was in her mid-seventies and probably physically imposing in her prime. I pegged her at six feet. Given the customary shrinkage of age, she must have been six-three or six-four in her youth. Her face was gaunt, though her bearing suggested she was accustomed to carrying substantial weight. She wore slacks that rode low on her hips and a crisply ironed white shirt with a lavender cardigan over it. I suspected her clunky running shoes were more for comfort than for speed. Her hair was iron gray, braided, and wrapped around her head in a thin chain. She had a leather purse over one arm and she held a scrap of paper with a note jotted on it, which made me wonder if she was lost.

"Can I do something for you?"

She didn't look at the paper, but I could see it tremble slightly. "Are you Miss Millhone?"

"Yes."

"I'm hoping you can help me."

"I can certainly try."

"I'm afraid there's been a misunderstanding. Something was sent to you by mistake and I need to have it back."

"Really. And what's that?"

"A photograph album. I'd appreciate your returning it as soon as possible. Today, actually, if it's not inconvenient."

I kept my face a blank, but I knew exactly what she was talking about. My Aunt Susanna had given me the album shortly after we met, just about this same time the year before. The package had arrived when I was out of town, so Henry had passed it on to Stacey Oliphant, who'd brought it down to the desert town of Quorum, where we were working a case. The album was old, half filled with Kinsey family photographs, and I'd been touched by the gesture. There was never any suggestion that the album was on loan, though now that I thought about it, I could see that it wasn't mine to keep.

I said, "I'm sorry, but I didn't catch your name."

"Bettina Thurgood. I drove down from Lompoc, hoping to divert any further trouble."

"Who's causing trouble?"

She hesitated. "Your cousin, Tasha."

"What's she have to do with it?"

"She's been planning an event. She said she sent you an invitation."

"Sure. I received it last week."

"She needs the old family photographs for a big display she's making, but when she asked Cornelia for the album, it was nowhere to be found. Tasha got very snippy and now Cornelia blames me."

"When you say Cornelia, I assume you're talking about Grand."

"Your grandmother, yes. Tasha thinks Cornelia's just being stubborn, refusing to hand over the album because she's so possessive about the family history. The two got into quite a tangle."

"Why didn't Aunt Susanna speak up? She's the one who sent me the album. If she wants it back, all she has to do is ask."

"Oh no, dear. Susanna didn't send the album. I did."

"*You* did?"

She nodded. "Last April."

"Why would you do that? You don't know me from Adam."

"Cornelia told me to. I argued until I was blue in the face, but she ordered me to send it to you and that's what I did. Of course, now she's forgotten the entire incident. She turned the house upside down in search of the album and when she couldn't lay hands on it, she accused me of sneaking it to Tasha behind her back. That's when I decided I'd had enough."

I squinted at the woman, trying to figure out what she was talking about. I understood what she'd said, but I'd never met Grand and I had no idea why she'd send me the family album. "Are you sure about this?"

"Oh my, yes. You don't have to take my word for it. I have the proof right here."

She opened her purse and pulled out a green postcard that I recognized as a return-receipt request. She passed it to me and I glanced at the notations that indicated the date and time the parcel was sent and provided a line for the person who'd signed for it. I recognized Henry's writing. He often signs on my behalf if I'm gone, as long as delivery isn't restricted. There was also a note that the package had been mailed from Lompoc, all of which coincided with what I knew. Why would the woman lie? How would she know about me or the album if she hadn't mailed it in the first place?

"Why would Grand order you to send it to me?"

"I have no idea. None of us dare question anything she does. Now that she's forgotten, there's no point in quizzing her."

Well, that was a comforting thought. Sending the album was the only gesture my grandmother had ever made toward me. Now not only was she taking it back, but she'd erased the incident from her mind. Here I'd been feeling all warm and gooey about Aunt Susanna and that illusion was gone now as well. Not that Bettina was at fault. She was looking at me plaintively.

"What's wrong?" I asked.

"Is there any way I might take advantage of your facilities?"

"You need a bathroom."

"I do."

"Why don't you come in?"

"I'd appreciate it."

"I can make you a cup of tea while you're here," I said.

"Really, dear. That would be lovely."

Bettina followed me through the gate and around to the rear where I unlocked my front door and ushered her in. My studio's perpetually tidy, so I wasn't worried about disgracing myself with dirty dishes in the sink. I worried I was out of tea bags and my milk would be old enough to smell like spit-up. I suggested she use the downstairs bathroom to "freshen up," which is old-people talk for pissing like a racehorse after a long drive.

Once the door closed behind her, I scampered into the kitchen to check on my supply of tea bags. As I opened the cupboard door, a little white moth flew out, which was either an evil omen or evidence of bugs. I opened the tea canister and discovered I had three tea bags left. A quick look in the refrigerator revealed that I was out of milk altogether, but I did have a lemon, the juice of which I'd intended to mix with baking soda to clean the inside of a plastic storage container that was dark with tomato stains. This was a tip from my Aunt Gin, who was famous for household remedies with little or no application to problems in the real world.

I filled the kettle and set it on the stove, turned on the burner under it, and sliced the lemon. I got out cups and saucers, placing a tea bag and a paper napkin neatly beside each cup. When Bettina emerged we sat down and had tea together before returning to the subject at hand. By then I was reconciled to handing over the album, which was sitting on my desk. I had no real claim to it and from what she'd said, my returning it was as good as saving her life. That issue out of the way, I thought I might as well pump her for information.

I said, "What happens when you put the album back? Won't Grand smell a rat?"

"I have that all worked out. I can tuck it under the bed or in the little trunk she keeps in the closet. I might even leave it someplace obvious and let everyone assume it was right there under her nose. There's a short story about that."

"'The Purloined Letter.' Edgar Allan Poe," I said.

"That's right."

"I'm still stumped about why she sent it in the first place."

Bettina made a gesture, waving the question aside. "She got a bug in her ear. When she comes up with one of her notions, you'd better do as you're told. She hates to be thwarted and she refuses to explain. Once she issues an order, you'd better hop to it if you know what's good for you. Not meaning to give offense, but she's a hellion."

"So I've heard. Why do you put up with her?"

She waved *that* question down as well. "I've kowtowed to her so long, I wouldn't have the nerve to stand up to her now. For one thing, I live on the property and I'd never hear the end of it."

"You're her assistant?"

Bettina laughed. "Oh no. You couldn't pay me to do a job like that. I help her out of gratitude."

"For what?"

"Cornelia may be difficult, but she can be kindhearted and generous. She did me a great service many years ago."

"Which was what?"

"I was abandoned as a child. I grew up in an orphanage. She and your grandfather took me in and raised me as their own. She fostered other children, too, but I was the first."

"Good news for you. I'm an orphan myself and she didn't take me in."

Bettina's smile faded and she looked at me with concern. "I hope you'll forgive my saying so, dear, but you seem bitter."

"No, no. I'm bitter by nature. I always sound like this."

"Well, I hope I haven't offended you."

"Not at all. Why don't you tell me the story? I'd be fascinated."

"There's not much to it. From the ages of five to ten I lived in an institution, the Children's Haven of Saint Jerome Emiliana. He was the patron saint of orphaned and abandoned little ones. My parents both died in the influenza epidemic of 1918. Any orphanage creates a loose association of pseudo-brothers and -sisters, so I suppose I had a family of sorts. We were fed and we had shelter, but there was little love or affection and no real bond with others. As harsh as this sounds, the nuns were cold. They entered the convent, leaving their families behind, for who knows what reasons. The devout ones didn't always make it. They became novitiates out of a passion for the church, but the life wasn't as they imagined it. They were often miserable: homesick and frightened. Passion doesn't carry you far, because it's transitory. The nuns who stayed, those who felt truly at home there, had little to give. Distance suited them.

"When your grandparents plucked me out of that environment they changed the course of my life. I don't know what would have become of me if I'd remained in the institution until I was of age."

"You'd have been marked for life like me," I said.

"What are you talking about, 'marked for life'? You were raised by your mother's sister, Virginia. Wasn't that the case?"

"A mixed blessing if there ever was one."

"A blessing that counts nonetheless," she said. She paused to glance at her watch. "I better skedaddle before Cornelia realizes I'm gone. Shall I tell Tasha we can expect you on the twenty-eighth?"

"I'm still thinking about it."

When we'd finished our tea I placed the album in a brown paper bag and walked Bettina to her car, where she gave my cheek a pat, saying, "Thank you for this. I was worried I'd fail and there'd be hell to pay."

"Happy to be of help."

She put a hand to her cheek. "I didn't think to ask, but you may have photographs of your own you'd like to see included in the display."

"Actually, I don't. My aunt left a box of photos, but none of them are of family members. It's possible she had some in her possession and destroyed them before she died. I wasn't even aware I had family until four years ago."

"Oh, you poor thing. Well, if you'd like some of these, we could have duplicates made. I'm sure Cornelia wouldn't object to the expense."

"Don't worry about it. I've lived this long without keepsakes. I'm sure I'll manage to muddle through."

"Well, if you're sure."

"I'm sure."

We voiced polite farewells and I watched her return to her car. Off she went, down the street, around the corner, and then she was gone. I turned and walked back to the studio with a mounting sense of dismay. What I was sure of, in retrospect, was my ass had been frosted and handed to me on a plate. Grand took in *orphans*? I was pissed off again.


I cleared the kitchen counter, tossing spoons, cups, and saucers into the sink. I ran hot water, squirted in a stream of liquid detergent, and watched the bubbles pile up. I turned the water off, washed the dishes, and put them in the rack. When I opened the kitchen cupboard, another little moth fluttered out.

"Shit!"

I began removing items from the shelves, inspecting them gingerly. The flap on a half-empty box of cornmeal bore a tiny slip of something in a web, like a wee insect hammock. I looked in and saw grubs crawling in the cornmeal like kids playing in the sand.

I got out a brown grocery bag and dropped in the box of cornmeal, followed by a bag of flour I didn't even bother to check. I couldn't remember now why I'd bought flour and cornmeal in the first place, but the two had been in my possession long enough to spawn vermin. In the interest of sanitation, I tossed out crackers, two stray packets of cereal, a package of dried pasta, and a round cardboard oatmeal container the lid of which I didn't dare lift. Impatient with the process, I put the bag on the counter and emptied the cupboard entirely. At the end of my rampage, there was nothing left, which meant I could scrub the shelves. Good. How perfect. I would start life afresh.

When the phone rang I left the kitchenette and crossed to the desk. I took a deep breath before I picked up the handset, lest I snap at the poor sucker on the other end of the line. "Hello?"

"Kinsey?"

"Yes."

"P. F. Sanchez down in Puerto. I came up with the vet's name and thought I'd pass it on to you."

"You did? Well, how cool! I didn't expect to hear from you." I pulled a scratch pad closer and opened the top drawer, looking for a pencil or a pen.

"I thought it might surprise you. I was pretty sure I knew where the file was, but I had to reorganize everything else while I was looking. That's the downside of hoarding. Things are always getting out of hand. You have a pen and paper?"

"I do. Fire away," I said.

"Guy's name was Walter McNally. He had on office on Dave Levine. McNally Pet Hospital. I've got the address and the phone number that were in service at the time."

He rattled them off and I made a note of the information.

"Did you say 'Walter' or 'Walker'?"

"Walter, with a *t*."

"Weird. I think I went to high school with his son," I said. "What about the date when Ulf was put down?"

"July 13, 1967."

"Thanks. You're a doll."

"You're welcome. Glad to be of help. If you learn anything of interest, will you call me back and let me know?"

"I'll do that."

After I hung up, I hauled out the telephone book and turned to the yellow pages, looking under the listing for veterinarians. There was no entry for Walter McNally or McNally Pet Hospital. I flipped to the white pages, but the only McNallys listed were Walker and Carolyn in Horton Ravine. I made a note of their address and phone number. I picked up the handset and paused.

While I knew Walker to speak to, our relationship was otherwise nonexistent. During my senior year Walker McNally and I had been in the same American history class. At the time, I was in my rebellious phase (which lasted all through high school), so I'd been more interested in cutting classes than attending. As a result, I hadn't done well. Then again, I didn't do that well when I wasn't truant, so no harm accrued as a result of my bad behavior. The only history class I remembered was the day we discussed the differences between the English and the American social structures. The teacher wanted us to appreciate the reasons the colonists had established this brave new land of ours and why they'd eventually broken away from the tyranny of the Crown. By his account, the Brits were rigidly class-conscious, while in America we were not. You can imagine my surprise. There followed a lively exchange of opinions, most of them voiced by the kids from Horton Ravine, whose families were well-off and therefore deeply committed to the notion that life was equitable. Of course, everyone in America was afforded equal opportunities! It was just that the Horton Ravine kids got more of them than the rest of us.

I remembered Walker as elegant, with a certain preppy nonchalance that I admired and feared from afar. He was a good-looking guy, aloof and self-aware. He and his entire social set took privilege for granted, and why would they not? Trips to Europe, Ivy League schools? Ho-hum for them. What piqued my interest was his wild side. He was into excess—fast cars and fast girls. The fast girls had money—nothing cheap about *them*—but they were reckless. I remembered two in particular—Cassie Weiss and Rebecca Ragsdale, with their perfect skin, perfect teeth, and trim athletic bodies. Both were friendly in the way of girls who know they're better than you.

Walker had dated Rebecca and then he'd broken up with her when Cassie made a play for him.

In those days the hot spot for making out was a hilltop pocket park dubbed Passion Peak. On Friday and Saturday nights the parking lot midway up the hill would be packed with cars, windows fogged over and much thrashing about in the front and rear seats. Those seeking greater comfort and privacy would climb to the top, where the city had installed picnic tables and benches and an oversized gazebo that served as a bandstand for summer concerts. The park had been closed to the public for the past two years because a group of teenagers had taken to building bonfires up there, one of which had set the autumn-dry grass ablaze and burned the gazebo to a charred shell.

By the end of the school year Cassie was pregnant and attended graduation in a robe that suggested she was hiding a basketball she'd stolen from the gym. Rebecca died that October in a fall from the third floor of a fraternity house back east. According to the gossip, the accident occurred while she and a Delta Upsilon pledge were having sex on the balcony, but surely he hadn't propped her up on the rail. It was more likely she took a tumble while barfing over the side.

As for Walker, he smoked heavily, drank heavily, and bought dope from the very low-wallers I considered my pals. Later I'd heard he was dealing dope himself, though I never saw proof of it. I never even considered selling dope because I knew if I were caught, the penalties would be far more stringent than the shit that would rain down on his head if he was busted for doing the same thing. This didn't strike me as unfair. It was just the way of the world.

So what was I going to do here, call the guy and reintroduce myself? What was the worst thing that could happen if I rang him up all these years later? I decided not to plague myself with the possibilities. Maybe the playing field was level now or, perhaps, at the very least, I wasn't standing in the same deep hole. I picked up the phone and dialed.

A woman answered and I said, "May I speak to Walker?"

"He's not here. You can contact him at Montebello Bank and Trust later in the week." Her tone was abrupt.

"Thanks. I'll try that. Is this Carolyn?" Little Miss Perky here.

"Yes."

"Could I leave a message in case I miss him at work?"

"Fine."

"Great. My name's Kinsey Millhone. Walker and I were in the same graduating class at Santa Teresa High. I'm hoping to contact his father. He's a veterinarian, isn't he?"

"He was back then, yes, but he retired."

"I gathered as much when I didn't see him listed in the yellow pages. Is he still here in town?"

A silence and then she said, "What's this about?"

"Look, I know this sounds odd, but I'd like to talk to him about a dog he put down."

"Is Walter in trouble of some kind?"

"Not at all. I have a couple of questions for him."

"Are you a telephone solicitor? Is that what this is? Because he's not interested and neither are we."

I laughed. "I'm not selling anything. I'm a private investigator—"

The line went dead.

My fault entirely. Usually I know better than to try to elicit information by phone. It's too easy for the other party to duck, evade, and deflect. In a face-to-face conversation, social conventions come into play. People tend to smile and make eye contact, defusing any hint of aggression. I'm five foot six and at a hundred and eighteen pounds, I don't appear dangerous to the average citizen. I smile a lot and talk nicely, conducting my business in a nonthreatening manner that usually nets me at least a *portion* of what I want.

All I'd garnered from my exchange with Carolyn was that her father-in-law was retired, which I'd suspected in the first place. She'd ignored my question about whether he was still in town, which led me to believe he was. If he were somewhere else—in another city or out of state—the easy way out would have been to say so. If he lived in Santa Teresa, I'd have a daunting job on my hands. Santa Teresa is chockablock with pricey retirement homes, nursing homes, and assisted-living facilities. If I tried a canvass on foot or by phone, I'd be at it for who knows how long, with no guarantee of success.

Once more, I weighed my need to know against the effort it would take. As usual, my fundamental nosiness won hands down. I knew that without much encouragement, I'd get into the spirit of the hunt and set aside all else until I prevailed. This is probably a form of mental illness, but over the years, it's served me well. First chance I had, I'd make a run to Montebello Bank and Trust. Maybe I could sweet-talk Walker into giving me the information out of affection for the good old days.

# 15

## JON CORSO

### November 1962–September 1966

When Jon was thirteen his mother died. She'd been asthmatic as a child and in later life suffered from countless pulmonary ills. Jon was aware that his mother often felt poorly. She was subject to coughs, colds, and various other upper-respiratory infections—pneumonia, bronchitis, pleurisy. She didn't complain and she always seemed to bounce back, which he took as proof that she wasn't seriously impaired.

In November she came down with the flu and her symptoms seemed to worsen as the days passed. By Friday morning, when she hadn't improved, Jon asked if he should call someone, but she said she'd be fine. His dad was out of town. Jon couldn't remember where he was and Lionel hadn't left a contact number. Jon's dad was an English professor, on sabbatical from the University of California, Santa Teresa. He'd recently published a biography of an important Irish poet whose name Jon had forgotten. Lionel was off giving a series of lectures on the subject, which is why Jon and his mother were on their own.

Jon offered to stay home from school, but she didn't want him to miss classes, so at 7:30 he rode his bike the two miles to Climping Academy. He was a husky kid, short for his age, and fifty pounds overweight. That fact, and the braces on his teeth, didn't contribute much in the way of good looks. He'd overheard his father make a remark about his turning into a swan—"Please, God," was the way he'd put it. Jon missed the first part of the sentence, but it didn't take much to figure out his dad thought he was an ugly duckling. It was the first time Jon had been jolted into the awareness that others had opinions about him, some of which were unkind. His mother had promised him a growth spurt when he reached puberty, but so far there was no sign of it. His dad bought him the bicycle to encourage outdoor activities. Jon far preferred having his mother drive him to school, which she did when she was well.

At 3:30 that day, he bicycled home and found the house exactly as he'd left it. He was surprised she wasn't up and waiting for him. Usually, even when his mother was sick, she managed to be showered and dressed by midafternoon when school let out. He'd find her sitting in the kitchen, smoking a cigarette, making at least a pretense of being normal. Sometimes she even baked him a cake from a mix. Now the rooms felt cold and dark, even though interior lights were on and he could hear the low wind of the forced-air furnace at work.

He knocked on the bedroom door and then opened it. "Mom?"

Her coughing by then was loose and wet and thick. She motioned him into the room while she patted herself on the chest and put a tissue to her mouth, depositing a wad of something.

Jon stood in the doorway watching her. "Shouldn't you call the doctor?"

She waved the suggestion aside, wracked by another bout of coughing that left her sweating and limp. "I've got some pills left from last time. See if you can find them in the medicine cabinet. And bring me a glass of water, if you would."

He did as she asked. There were four bottles of prescription medication. He brought all of them to her bedside and let her choose what she thought was best. She took two pills with water and then lay back against the pillows, which she'd stacked almost upright to help her breathe.

He said, "Did you eat lunch?"

"Not yet. I'll get something in a bit."

"I can fix you a grilled cheese sandwich the way you showed me."

He wanted to help. He wanted to be of service because once she was back on her feet, the world would right itself. He felt a responsibility since he was the only kid at home. His brother, Grant, five years his senior, had just gone off to Vanderbilt and wouldn't be back until Christmas break.

Her smile was wan. "Grilled cheese would be nice, Jon. You're so sweet to me."

He went into the kitchen and put the sandwich together, making sure both sides of the bread were well buttered so they'd brown evenly. When he knocked on her door again, plate in hand, she said she thought she'd nap for a while before she ate. He set the plate on the bed table within reach, went into the den, and turned on the TV set.

When he looked in on her an hour later, she didn't look right at all. He crossed to her bedside and put a hand on her forehead the way she did when she thought he was running a fever. Her skin was hot to the touch and her breathing was rapid and shallow. She was shivering uncontrollably, and when she opened her eyes, he said, "Are you okay?"

"I'm cold, that's all. Bring me that quilt in the linen closet, please."

"Sure."

He found some blankets and piled them on, worried he wasn't doing enough. "I think I should call an ambulance or something. Okay?" he asked.

When his mother didn't answer, Jon called the paramedics, who arrived fifteen minutes later. He let them in, relieved to have someone else taking charge of her. One of the two men asked questions, while the other one took her temperature, checked her blood pressure, and listened to her chest. After a brief consultation and a phone call, they loaded her onto a gurney and put her in the rear of the ambulance. From the look that passed between them, Jon knew she was sicker than he'd thought.

When the paramedic told him he could follow them to St. Terry's, he wanted to laugh. "I'm a kid. I can't drive. My dad's not even home. He's out of town."

After more murmured conversation, he was allowed to ride

in the front of the ambulance, which he gathered was against the ambulance company's policy.

In the emergency room, he sat in the reception area while the doctor examined his mom. The nurse told him he should call someone, but that only confused him. He didn't know how to reach his brother in Nashville and who else was there? It wasn't like he had his teacher's home telephone number. The school would be closed by then anyway, so that was no help. There weren't any other close relatives that he knew of. His parents didn't go to church, so there wasn't even a minister to call.

The nurse went back down the hall and pretty soon the hospital social worker showed up and talked to him. She wasn't much help, asking him the same series of questions he couldn't answer. She finally contacted a neighbor, a couple his parents barely knew. Jon spent that night and the next night with them. He left notes on the front and back doors so his father would know where he was.

His mother survived for a day and a half and then she was gone. The last time he saw her—the night his father finally showed up—she had IV lines in both ankles. There was a blood-pressure cuff on one arm, and a clamp on his finger to measure his pulse, a catheter, an arterial line in one wrist, and tubing taped over her face. He knew the exact moment the rise and fall of her chest ceased, but he watched her anyway, thinking he could still see movement. Finally, his father told him it was time to go.

Lionel drove them home and spent the next two hours on the phone, notifying friends and relatives, the insurance company, and Jon wasn't sure who else. While his father was occupied, Jon went into his mother's room. Lionel's side of the bed was untouched and still neatly made, while on his mother's side the sheets were rumpled, with pillows still stacked against the headboard. There were the same wadded tissues on the floor.

The plate with the grilled cheese sandwich was on the table. It was cold and the bread had dried out, but he sat on the edge of the bed and ate it anyway while his body warmth brought up his mother's scent from the sheets. Because of his braces, he couldn't bite down on a sandwich without getting bread sludge stuck in the wires, so he broke off bites one at a time and chewed them, thinking of her.

At ten that night, his father found him, sitting there in the dark. Lionel turned the light on and sat down beside him, putting an arm around Jon's shoulder.

"You weren't at fault, Jon. I don't want you to think anyone blames you for not getting help to her soon enough . . ."

Jon made no move. He felt the cold descend, moving from his chest to the soles of his feet. His cheeks flamed and he looked up at his father blankly. Until that moment, it hadn't occurred to him that any action on his part might have saved her life. He was only thirteen. His mother had reassured him, saying she was fine, and he'd taken her at her word. In the absence of adult counsel, he'd waited for a cue. In a flash, he saw how pathetic his ministrations had been, how immature and ineffectual he was in making the grilled cheese sandwich, as though that might heal her or prolong her life.

It wasn't until years later that it dawned on Jon his father had made the statement to assuage his own guilt about his failure to leave a contact number. In truth—and Jon wouldn't learn this until later still—Lionel had been in a hotel room, frolicking with a grad student he'd met while he was giving a talk at Boston College.

His brother came home for the funeral, but then he was gone again. The remainder of the school year was strange. Jon and his dad fashioned a life for themselves, like two old bachelors. His dad paid the bills and kept their world, more or less, on track. The house was a mess. For meals, they ate out, brought home fast food, or ordered in from any restaurant that would deliver. Lionel went back to teaching freshman English and two sections of literary history, spending long hours at UCST. Jon pretty much did as he pleased. Nobody seemed to recognize that he was grieving. He knew something black had settled over him like a veil. He spent a lot of his free time in his room. As a fat boy, he had no friends to speak of, so he was comfortable in isolation. His grades were mixed—good in English and art, bad in everything else. A cleaning lady came in twice a week, but that was about as much contact as Jon had with other people. His teachers gave him sympathetic

looks, but his demeanor was so dark they didn't have the nerve
to console him.

In the spring, without any discussion at all, Jon found out
his father had signed him up for two monthlong sessions of
summer camp, back to back. Lionel had committed to a series of speaking engagements that would have him zigzagging
across the country nonstop during June and July. The day after
school was out, Jon was shipped off to Michigan. This was
a so-called sports program, meaning an intense boot camp
for fat boys, during which they were weighed daily, lectured
about nutrition, berated for their eating habits, and forced into
long sessions of exercise, during which the occasional boy
collapsed. Oddly enough, Jon enjoyed himself. His loneliness, his guilt, the silence of the house, even the yawning loss
of his mother, all of that was set aside for two months, and
he needed the relief. The boys were encouraged to choose a
sport—basketball, football, soccer, hockey, lacrosse, or track.

Jon took up long-distance running. He liked sports where
individual achievement was the goal. He liked competing with
himself. There was nothing in his nature that lent itself to team
spirit. He wasn't cooperative by nature, not a rah-rah kind of
guy. He didn't want to wear a uniform that rendered him in-
distinguishable from fifty other boys on the field. He preferred
being on his own. He liked pushing himself. He liked the
sweat and the harsh laboring of his lungs, the pain in his legs
as he covered ground.

By the time he came home from camp, the promised
growth spurt had materialized. Jon's weight had dropped by
twenty-two pounds and he'd added three inches to his five-
foot-six-inch height. During ninth and tenth grades his braces
came off and he shot up another four inches. He also dropped
an additional ten pounds. Running kept him lean and filled
him with energy. He took up golf and in his spare time caddied
at the club. He and his father operated on separate but parallel
tracks, and Jon was fine with that.

In August of 1964, prior to Jon's freshman year at Climp,
Lionel appeared at the door to the den where Jon was slouched
on the sofa watching television. He had his feet propped on
the ottoman and he held a glass of Diet Pepsi balanced on

his chest. His father had been going out a lot, but Jon hadn't thought much about it.

Lionel stuck his head in the door and said, "Hey, son. How're you doing?"

"Fine."

"Could you turn that down, please?"

Jon got up and crossed to the TV set. He muted the sound and returned to his seat, his attention still fixed on the screen though he pretended he was listening to his dad.

Lionel said, "There's someone I want you to meet. This is Mona Stark."

Jon glanced over as his father stepped aside and there she was. She was taller than his father and as vibrantly colored as an illustration in his biology text. Black hair, blue eyes, her lips a slash of dark red. Her body was divided into two segments—breasts at the top, flaring hips below, bisected by a narrow waist. In that moment, he took her measure without conscious intent; she was a wasp, a predator. In his mind he could see the lines of print: *Some stinging wasps live in societies that are more complex than those of social bees and ants. Stinging wasps rely on a nest from which they conduct many of their activities, especially the rearing of their young.*

Jon said, "Nice to meet you."

"Nice meeting *you*," she said. And then to Lionel in a teasing tone of voice, "You bad boy. I can see I have my work cut out for me. I can't believe you haven't taught him to stand up when a lady enters the room."

Sheepishly, Jon set his soft drink aside and rose to his feet, mumbling, "Sorry. My fault, not his."

He shot a look at Lionel. What was going on? Jon knew his father had been dating, but as far as he knew, Lionel wasn't serious about anyone. He'd been carrying on a series of short-term romances with students in his department, skirting any suggestion of impropriety by waiting until the particular coed in question was no longer enrolled in his class.

Later that night, after Lionel dropped Mona back at her place, he returned to the den and settled in a nearby chair for the inevitable heart-to-heart. It was clear his father felt uncomfortable. For two years, he and Jon had functioned as pals, not the father-son duo that was now up for grabs. Lionel launched into a discourse about how lonely he'd been and how much he missed Jon's mother. Jon blocked out much of what Lionel said because the words didn't sound like his. Mona had doubtless primed him, making sure he touched on all the relevant points. Jon imagined Mona sitting there instead, explaining that no one would ever replace his mom, but that a man needed companionship. Jon would benefit, too, said she, talking through his father's lips. Mona knew how hard life must have been for him and now they had an opportunity to share their home. Mona was divorced and had three lovely daughters, whom Lionel had met. Mona was looking forward to merging the two families, and he hoped Jon would make the transition as smooth as possible.

Lionel and Mona were married in June of 1965. Now that they were a family of six, they needed a larger place. Fortunately, as part of her divorce settlement, Mona had been awarded a house in Beverly Hills, which she sold for big bucks, rolling the money into the new house in Horton Ravine so she wouldn't have to pay capital gains. At the same time, Lionel sold the modest three-bedroom house where Jon had been raised. That money was set aside for additions and improvements on the new place, which was situated on a bluff overlooking the Pacific Ocean. Jon moved into a newly remodeled two rooms and a bath built above the garage while Lionel, Mona, and the three girls occupied the main house. Mona told him how lucky he was to have independent living quarters that would allow him to come and go as he pleased. Not that he was permitted to do any such thing. His "pad," as she referred to it, was a not-so-subtle reminder that he'd been separated from the rest. His wants, needs, and desires were peripheral to hers.

From that point on, everything revolved around Mona. She had her tennis lessons, her golf, and her charities, activities his father didn't share with her because he was either teaching or secluded in his home office, writing. Jon was the outsider, looking in on a life that had once been his. He was miserable, but he knew better than to complain. At the same time, he wondered why he was expected to go on as though nothing had changed. His life had taken on an entirely different cast.

The following January, when he turned seventeen, he lobbied for his driver's license and a car of his own. Mona objected, but for once Lionel argued on Jon's behalf. After much ado and numerous debates, she finally gave in, perhaps because she realized having a car and driver at her disposal would work to her advantage. Lionel bought Jon a used Chevrolet convertible. By then, Mona's three perfect daughters were enrolled at the same private school Jon had attended since kindergarten. He caught sight of them in the corridors six and seven times a day. Of course, he drove them to school and picked them up afterward. He also kept an eye on them if Lionel and Mona went out for the evening. If he had other plans, if he resisted in any way, Mona would rebuff him with silence, cut him out of her field of vision as though he were invisible. This she was clever enough to do without Lionel's being aware. If Jon had brought it to his father's attention, he'd have been written off as paranoid or oversensitive. Lionel would have repeated it all to Mona and she would have doubled the penalties.

Lionel would have had to be a fool not to pick up on the chill in the air, but since neither Mona nor Jon would discuss the situation, his father was no doubt delighted to ignore the problem. One Saturday afternoon Mona took the girls shopping, and Lionel walked out to the garage and knocked at Jon's door. Jon hollered out, "It's open!" and Lionel dutifully trudged up the stairs. He took a moment to survey the place, which was as cold and bare as a cell.

He said, "Well, it looks like you've settled in. Very nice. Is everything okay?"

"Sure," Jon said. He knew his two rooms were without character or comfort, but he didn't want to offer his father the means to maneuver.

"Is it warm enough out here?"

"Pretty much. I don't have any hot water to speak of. I get five minutes' worth of lukewarm dribble before it runs out."

"Well, that's no good. I'm glad you brought it up. I'll have Mona take care of it."

Jon suspected he'd just given his father an opening to the Mona discussion that loomed. It was up to his father to proceed without any help from him.

"Mind if I sit down?"

Jon moved a pile of dirty clothes from a wooden desk chair

so his father could take a seat. Lionel began a long, rambling discourse about the new blended family. He acknowledged that things were sometimes tense between Mona and Jon, but she was doing her best, and Lionel said it was only fair that Jon meet her halfway.

Jon stared at him, bemused by the enormity of Lionel's self-delusion. Of course, his father was her defender. She and Lionel were allies. Jon had no recourse. There was no court of appeals. In effect, his father was announcing that Jon was totally at her mercy. Her whims, her sharp tongue, her uncanny ability to seize the upper hand: for all of this, she had Lionel's blessing. Jon couldn't believe his father didn't see what was going on.

"Well, Dad," he said carefully, "not to be obtuse about it, but from my perspective, she's a clusterfuck."

Lionel reacted as though slapped. "Well, son, you're certainly entitled to your opinion, but I trust you'll keep it to yourself. I'd appreciate it if you'd try to get along with her, for my sake if nothing else."

"For *your* sake? How do you figure that?"

Lionel shook his head, his tone patient. "I know the adjustment isn't easy. She'll never replace your mother. She's not asking for that and neither am I. You have to trust me on this; she's a caring person, amazing really, once you get to know her better. In the meantime, I expect you to treat her with the respect she deserves."

It was the word "amazing" that somehow stuck in Jon's craw. Mona was the enemy, but he could see how futile it was to battle her head-on. After that, Jon referred to her as the Amazing Mona, though never in his father's company and never to her face. The newlyweds' first Christmas together, the Amazing Mona had inveigled Lionel to play Santa for a Climping Academy fund-raiser, and every year thereafter, he donned his white wig, white beard, and white mustache, and then climbed into a red velvet fat suit, trimmed in white fur. Even his boots were fake. In Jon's mind, the photograph that exactly captured their relationship was the one in a silver frame Mona displayed on the baby grand piano in the newly decorated living room. In it she was decked out in a low-cut Yves Saint Laurent evening gown, perched seductively on Santa's lap. While she glowed for the camera, Lionel's identity was obliterated. She did manage to raise over a hundred thousand dollars for the school, and for this she was widely praised.

Jon unburdened himself bitterly to his brother by phone. "She is such a total bitch. She's a tyrant. I'm telling you. She's a fucking narcissist."

Grant said, "Oh, come on. You'll be out of the house in a year or two, so what's it to you?"

"She thinks she can run my life and Dad lets her get away with it. Talk about being pussy-whipped."

"So what? That's his business, not yours."

"Shit, that's easy for you to say. I'd like to see you try living under the same roof with her."

Bored with the topic, Grant said, "Just tough it out. Once you finish high school you can come live with me."

"I'm not moving away from all my friends!"

"That's the best I can offer. Stiff upper lip, old chum."

Jon discovered a new way to occupy his time. He began breaking into various Horton Ravine homes he knew were unoccupied. While he caddied at the club, he picked up all manner of information about members' travel plans. Guys chatted among themselves about upcoming cruises and European tours, jaunts to San Francisco, Chicago, and New York. It was a form of bragging, though it was couched in queries about exchange rates, good deals on charter flights, and luxury hotels. Lionel and Mona socialized with most of them, so all Jon had to do was look up their addresses in Mona's Rolodex. He'd wait until the family was gone and find his way in. If there was talk of an alarm system or a house sitter, he knew to avoid the place. People were careless about locking up. Jon found windows unlatched, basement doors unsecured. Failing that, he scouted out the house keys hidden under flowerpots and fake garden rocks.

Once inside, he cruised the premises, poking through closets and dresser drawers. Home offices were a rich source of information. He was curious about women's underwear, about the fragrances they used, their personal hygiene. He didn't steal anything. That wasn't the point. Breaking and entering gave him temporary relief from anxiety. The heightened fear level washed away the stress he carried and his equilibrium was restored.

Midway through his junior year, he started cutting classes at Climp, first occasionally, then more often. Not surprisingly, his grades tumbled. He was secretly amused at all the murmuring that went on behind his back. There were conferences at school and conferences at home. Notes went back and forth. Phone calls were exchanged. Lionel didn't want to be the bad guy, so Mona was the one who finally lowered the boom.

She was stern and reproving, and Jon made every effort to keep a straight face while she read him the riot act. "Your father and I have discussed this at length. You have great potential, Jon, but you're not putting forth your best effort. Since you're doing so poorly, we think it's a waste of our money to pay private-school tuition. If you're unwilling to apply yourself at Climp, we think you should transfer to Santa Teresa High."

Jon knew what she was up to. She thought the threat of public school would give her leverage. He shrugged. "That's cool. Santa Teresa High School. Let's do it."

Mona frowned, unable to believe he wasn't going to protest her ruling and promise to improve. "I'm sure you'll want to graduate with your classmates at Climp, so we'd be willing to discuss it after the first semester at Santa Teresa High, assuming you do better. If you show us you can bring your grades up, we'll see that you're transferred back. The decision is yours."

"I already decided. I'll take the public high school."

The fall of 1966, at the end of Jon's first day at Santa Teresa High, he was standing at his locker when a kid at the locker next to his looked over and smiled. "You're new. I saw you this morning. We're in the same homeroom."

"Right. I remember. I'm Jon Corso."

The kid extended his hand. "Walker McNally."

The two shook hands and then Walker said, "Where you from?"

"I was at Climp last year. I flunked out."

Walker laughed. "Good job. I like it. Welcome to Santa Teresa High." He opened his locker and dumped his books,

then took out a windbreaker and shrugged himself into it.
"Speaking of high, this seems like an occasion worth celebrating. You have a car?"

"In the parking lot."

Walker reached into his jacket pocket and removed a joint.
"Shall we adjourn, good sir?"

The first time Jon smoked dope was the first time he'd
laughed in years. The laughter was hard-edged and uncon-
trollable. Later he couldn't even remember what he found so
funny, but in the moment it had felt like happiness, however
empty and artificially induced.

# 16

**Wednesday, April 13, 1988**

Wednesday morning I came up against a stumbling block. As usual, I'd rolled out of bed, pulled on my sweats and running shoes, brushed my teeth, and headed out the door. I used the walk from my studio to Cabana Boulevard to warm up, setting a brisk pace to prime my pumping heart and soften the long muscles that kept my legs moving. By the time I reached the wharf at the foot of State Street, I'd break into a trot, picking up the tempo as I proceeded. Sometimes I jogged on the bike path and sometimes on the sidewalk, depending on the number of runners, walkers, and bicyclists out on any given morning.

Ahead of me a group of seniors had taken up a big chunk of the bike path, walking four people across and eight to ten people deep, in two separate clusters. I opted for the sidewalk to avoid the stragglers. On my left I passed a row of coin-operated newspaper stands and I gave them a cursory glance. A name popped out at me and I paused to read the headlines, most of which were dated the day before. The latest edition of the *L.A. Times,* the *Perdido County Record,* and the *San Francisco Chronicle* would replace the old issues as soon as the delivery truck made its morning rounds. What caught my attention was an article in the *Santa Teresa Dispatch,* on the left-hand side of the front page, just above the fold. The heading read:

UCST COED KILLED IN DRUNK DRIVER MISHAP

In the next line down, I saw Walker McNally's name.

I tried to peer past the frame, but the balance of the story was blocked from my view. I don't carry money when I run so I was forced to circumvent the tiny issue of the lock. I gave the window flap a quick couple of jerks and up it popped. I removed a copy of the *Dispatch* and let the window snap back into the locked position. I turned to the first section and read the article while I walked. When I reached the bus stop, I sank onto a bench and read the whole of it again.

On Monday afternoon, a UCST sophomore named Julie Riordan had been killed in a two-car collision on Highway 154 while returning home from San Francisco. Walker McNally had been at the wheel of the other car. According to witnesses, he'd lost control of his Mercedes, crossed into oncoming traffic, and slammed into her head-on. He'd then crawled out of the wreckage and taken off on foot. By the time the cops caught up with him, he'd collapsed on the side of the road. He'd been admitted to St. Terry's with a blood-alcohol level well over the legal limit. His injuries were non-life-threatening and his condition was listed as stable. Julie Riordan, age nineteen, was pronounced dead at the scene.

No wonder Carolyn McNally had hung up on me. Walker was probably still in the hospital when I'd called his house. She must have assumed I'd been hired to investigate the accident. When and if Walker returned to work—assuming he hadn't been thrown in the pokey in the interim—he wasn't going to be any friendlier than his wife had been. His colleagues at the bank would be on lockdown as well, warned about disseminating information of even the most benign sort. All I wanted was his father's current address and a few minutes of his time. If Dr. McNally had forgotten the dog, I'd be facing another dead end, but it made me crazy to think he might be in town and me with no access.

I flirted with the idea of contacting Diana Alvarez. She could probably bully or bullshit her way through to any source she pleased, but I didn't want to tip her to my interest in the wolfdog buried on that hill. Flannagan Sanchez had given me as much information as he had, so another chat with him would net me nothing. I abandoned the run and went home.

I tossed the newspaper on the counter and flipped on the TV. I tuned into one of the local stations, hoping the story would be covered in an upcoming news segment. All I caught was an endless stream of commercials. I tried two more channels with the same result. I left the TV on and went upstairs to shower. Once I was dressed, I put the coffee on and then ate a piece of toast while I read the article again. No two ways about it, Walker McNally was in deep shit. So now what?

On my way in to the office I stopped off at the market. I needed to replace the bug-infested foodstuffs I'd discarded on Monday. I wasn't likely to cook or bake, but my barren shelves looked pitiful. I stocked up on flour, cornmeal, cereal, and crackers, both graham and saltines, if you really want to know. I also bought baking soda and a container of baking powder. I'd noticed, as I tossed the old one in the trash, that the "best if used by" date on the bottom of the tin was March 1985. On a roll by then, I bought dried bow-tie pasta and long-grain rice, along with cans of tomato sauce, tomato paste, and diced tomatoes with onion and basil. I was shopping only to give my beleaguered brain a rest. I needed a new game plan and I wouldn't come up with one if I tried to tackle the problem directly.

I moved to the next aisle, piling tissue boxes, rolls of paper towels, and toilet paper in my cart. I had my hand on a container of liquid detergent when a possible solution occurred to me. I finished my shopping, paid for my groceries, and stowed everything in the trunk of my car. Then I slid under the wheel and took my notebook out of my shoulder bag, leafing through the pages until I found the address Sanchez had given me for the McNally Pet Hospital on Dave Levine Street. At the back of my mind, I'd been playing a little game of "suppose" and "what if " in my quest to find Walker's dad. I'd thought, What if, on his retirement, Dr. McNally had sold his practice to another veterinarian? The new vet might well know his current whereabouts.

I fired up my Mustang and pulled out of the lot. I hung a right on Chapel and drove the length of it until I reached the dead end at Miracle, where I turned left for half a block. This put me at Dave Levine Street, six blocks from the point at which it split from State. The address I wanted had to be somewhere to my left. I turned and continued at a greatly reduced speed until I reached Solitario Street. On the far side of the intersection, in a seven-tenant strip mall, I spotted Mid-City Cat Clinic with an address that matched the one Sanchez had given me. I snagged the only parking place available and sat for a moment, hoping the gods would be merciful. A wooden cutout of a Puss in Boots pointed at the clinic door, where the names of two veterinarians were stenciled on the pane— Stephanie Forbes, DVM, and Vespa Chin, DVM.

I got out, locked the car, and went in. The waiting room was small and neat, with a counter on the right that separated the receptionist's desk from the clientele. Behind her was a bank of charts, sporting a rainbow of tabs. A wall-mounted chart illustrated the difference between a fit cat and a fat cat. A nearby bulletin board was plastered with snapshots of cats that I imagined had been treated by the venerable Drs. Forbes and Chin. Through a doorway I saw wire cages that held an assortment of felines, some perhaps boarders and some being treated for various kitty ills.

The receptionist at the desk looked up at me as I came in. She was in her sixties. Her salt-and-pepper hair was heavy on the salt, shoulder length, and blunt cut. Her bifocals had beveled edges, with thin wire stems. The tops of the lenses were tinted blue and the bottoms tinted pink. I wondered how the world looked from her perspective. "Can I help you?" she asked.

"I'm hoping you can give me some information."

"I'll try," she said. Her smock was patterned with cats, every conceivable color combination, with real cat hair matted here and there. She looked like someone who'd carry a cat around while the office was closed for lunch. Belatedly, I noticed a small gray cat lying on her desk, curled in sleep like a hairy paperweight.

"I'm looking for the vet who used to own this facility."

"Dr. McNally?"

"Exactly. Did you work for him, by chance?"

"No, but he cared for all my animals over the years. Two dogs and I can't even tell you how many cats."

"Do you have any idea how I can reach him?"

She hesitated. "Why do you ask?"

"Well, I've got an odd little problem and this is what it is." I recited my strange request without a hitch. I glossed over the surrounding circumstances, not wanting to raise a red flag with regard to Mary Claire Fitzhugh. I did explain Ulf, the buried dog, the tag, and the former owner, who knew nothing of the dog's interment in Horton Ravine. "I'm hoping Dr. McNally can fill in the blanks."

"It's very possible and I'm sure he'd enjoy a visit. He's at Valley Oaks. Number 17 Juniper Lane. Hang on a second and I'll look up his phone number." She opened the bottommost drawer on her right and took out a leather-bound address book that looked like it was meant for her personal use. "Do you want me to call and let him know you'll be stopping by?"

"I'm not sure what my schedule is for the rest of the week, so it's probably better not to call in advance. I don't want him sitting around, thinking he'll have company if I can't get there for a day or two."

"Understood," she said. She made a note of his phone number and address, and passed it across the desk.

"Thank you so much. I really appreciate this." I tucked the note in my bag.

Hesitantly, she said, "I don't suppose you're in the market for a cat. We have so many strays dropped at our door. Some are older and harder to place, but you have no idea how loving they are."

"I'll keep that in mind."


The Valley Oaks Senior Settlement had been established on an old estate in Montebello. I liked the word "settlement." It suggested an encampment on the far reaches of life, where aging pioneers could find shelter and companionship. At the entrance a painted map-board showed a layout of the units,

and I took a minute to locate Number 17 Juniper Lane. I drove
through the gate at a crawl, obeying the sign that warned about
the speed bumps that appeared every fifteen feet. The landscaping was beautifully maintained. Many of the old oaks had
been left in place. Splitting off from the main thoroughfare,
a series of winding roads disappeared in all directions, each
marked with a discreet sign, indicating the name of the road
and the unit numbers thereon. A few of the units I spotted had
ramps to accommodate wheelchair users. Through the trees
I could see an imposing structure, which I imagined was the
original mansion converted now to public rooms where residents could visit, dine, or entertain.

Number 17 Juniper Lane was a cottage Hansel and Gretel
would have liked, a snug stucco structure with a roof that
looked like thatch. The front door was dark green, the shutters painted to match. A cluster of flowerpots took up one
corner of the porch, all of them empty at the moment. On
the drive over, as I rehearsed my approach, I'd decided not
to mention my sketchy acquaintance with his son. I assumed
Dr. McNally was aware of Walker's legal problems and it
wasn't a topic that would be productive. Walker's accident
had nothing to do with my quest. I parked in a four-car inset
between cottages.

I knocked and after a moment the door was opened by a
man in his eighties. His hair was a thick gray, cropped short,
and his bifocals had metal frames. I didn't see any particular likeness to Walker, but then again, I hadn't seen Walker in
years, so the two might appear more similar than I knew. He
had on a navy blue sweatshirt with the sleeves pushed up and
shorts that were creased across the lap. He wore slippers instead of shoes and socks, and his shins looked like soup bones
sparsely dotted with hair.

"Dr. McNally?"

"Yes?"

"I'm sorry for the intrusion, but I'm hoping to pick up information about a dog you euthanized some years ago."

He looked at me, waiting to see if I'd say more. "With what
in mind? I don't understand your purpose."

"The dog was found buried on a property in Horton Ravine.
This came to light last week and it's been puzzling me. I used

the dog's tag to track down his owner in Puerto and he was as puzzled as I was. I realize it's a long shot, but I'm hoping you can tell me how he ended up in Horton Ravine."

"I see." He thought about it briefly and then seemed to make up his mind. "Why don't you come in? I've got a good head for animals, but I don't remember much else. How many years ago was this?"

"Twenty-one."

"Oh, my."

He stepped back and I crossed the threshold into a foyer tiled in slate. He closed the door behind me and then led the way down a short hall toward the rear. I caught glimpses of a bedroom to my right and a book-lined study to my left. At the back of the cottage there was a great room with a seating area on one side and a kitchenette on the other. A small dining room table and two chairs were arranged against an oversized mullioned window that looked out on a patch of lawn. Everything was tidy. There was no sign of Mrs. McNally. I don't know how women can complain about the lack of single guys in this world.

He sat in a plump upholstered chair and I took one end of the matching sofa. He put his hands on his knees and said, "Tell me more about what you need. I'm not entirely clear how to help."

"This is the deal," I said. "In the summer of 1967, a fellow brought his dog into your office. This was a wolfdog, named Ulf. I'm told you sedated him and took X-rays that showed an osteosarcoma. You recommended putting the dog down."

Walter was nodding. "I remember. Young dog, maybe four or five years old."

"Really? You remember him?"

"I couldn't have told you his name, but I know the animal you're referring to. He was the only wolfdog I ever had occasion to treat. You see more of the mix these days, but back then it was rare. As I recall, the fellow called a number of pet hospitals in the area and none of the other vets would agree to see him. Beautiful beast, absolutely magnificent. He had so much wolf in him, he looked like he'd just come loping out of the woods. He'd apparently been experiencing episodes of lameness that seemed to be getting worse.

"I thought about osteosarcoma the minute his owner mentioned the joint being so extremely tender. An X-ray confirmed my suspicions. A tumor of that sort doesn't cross the joint space and invade other bones. It's a gradual expansion in the joint where it's found, destroying the bone from the inside out and causing excruciating pain. On the views I took, it looked like the bone had been eaten away. The dog couldn't be saved. That's the long and short of it. I knew the fellow was upset, but I gave him my best advice and that was to spare the animal further suffering."

"The man's name was P. F. Sanchez. The dog belonged to his deceased son."

"I see. Well, that's a sad situation that could pile misery upon misery. It's hard enough having to put an animal down, regardless of the circumstances, but when the dog belongs to a child you've lost . . ." He let the sentence trail off.

"What would have happened to the dog after he was put down?"

"County animal control picked up the remains and disposed of them. We'd place the body in a canvas bag that we left in a storage shed out back. This was a wooden contraption that could be opened from either side. I don't know how things are handled these days. I believe with recent budget cuts, the county has discontinued the pickup service and it's up to the individual veterinarian to deliver the remains to the animal control facility. Whatever the procedure, the animals are incinerated. That much is the same. I would have assumed that was Ulf's fate until you told me otherwise."

"Did the county make daily sweeps?"

He shook his head. "We called when we had a pickup and they'd be there by the end of the business day."

"Did you ever have reason to bury the remains yourself?"

"No. I understand the desire to bury a pet in the backyard, but I wouldn't have taken it upon myself. The animal wasn't mine."

"Would you know if the county kept a record of pickups?"

"There wouldn't have been any reason to. We had a form the pet owner signed, giving permission for an animal to be euthanized. Sometimes the owner would ask us to return the ashes and sometimes animal control was asked to dispose of them. I can't imagine why that would be subject to dispute."

"No, no. There's no dispute," I said. "Sanchez told me he gave you authorization by phone."

"I don't remember his doing so, but that sounds right."

"What about your records?"

"Those are gone. When I retired, some charts were forwarded to other vets on request and the rest I put in storage. I held everything ten years and then boxed up the lot and called a shredding company. It probably wasn't necessary, but I didn't like the idea of personal information going into the trash."

"Can you think of any reason why Ulf wouldn't have been picked up and cremated? Some special circumstance?"

McNally shook his head again. "That was the protocol."

"Most people keep the ashes?"

"Some do and some don't. What makes you ask?"

"I was just curious. I don't own a pet so I have no idea how these things are done."

"People get attached. Sometimes a dog or cat means more to you than your own flesh and blood."

"I understand," I said. "Well, I've taken up enough of your time." I reached for my shoulder bag and found a business card before I got to my feet. "I'll leave you this in case something else occurs to you."

He rose at the same time, still talking as he walked me to the door. "I'm sorry I couldn't be more help."

"You gave me more than I expected. It's frustrating, but I guess I'll have to live with it."

"What hangs in the balance? That's what you ought to ask yourself."

"I don't know yet. Maybe nothing."

"Don't let it keep you awake nights. It's bad for your health."

"What about you? Do you sleep well?"

He smiled. "I do. I've been blessed. I had a wonderful family and work that I loved. I'm in excellent health and I have all my faculties about me, as far as I know," he added wryly. "I managed to set aside enough money to enjoy my dotage so it's a matter now of staying active. Some people aren't as fortunate."

"You're a lucky man."

"That I am."

Getting in my car again, I wondered how lucky he'd feel when he heard about the trouble his son Walker was in. If he'd been informed, he gave no indication of it.


On my way back to the office I made a second trip to Mid-City Cat Clinic, this time turning into the alleyway behind the place. The name of each business was stenciled on the back door so it was easy to spot the shed Dr. McNally'd mentioned. I parked and got out, inspecting it at close range. It was smaller than the housing used for garbage cans, mounted on the wall to the right of the door. The wood construction was straightforward, with a simple metal hook that fit into a small metal eye. There was no other locking mechanism visible and no evidence there'd ever been one. There wasn't even a hasp where a padlock or combination lock could have been inserted and secured. I pulled the wooden knob and the door opened with scarcely a sound. Except for dried leaves and spiderwebs, the interior was empty and didn't appear to be in use. At the back of the shed, the door that had opened into the clinic in Dr. McNally's day had been boarded over.

I studied the alley in both directions. Across the way I could see a series of private garages, with gated walkways leading into backyards, most of which were separated by fencing. This was a public thoroughfare, utilitarian in nature but accessible from either end. Anybody could have known about the pickups—pet hospital staff and clientele, animal control officers, neighbors, adjacent businesses, trash collectors, vagrants. Cleverly, I'd narrowed the field of corpse-napping suspects to a couple of hundred unknown individuals. The question still remained: why would someone steal a dead dog and transport it to Horton Ravine for burial?

Unless, as Sutton had suggested, the two men felt compelled to substitute Ulf's remains for whatever, or whomever, they were in the process of burying when the six-year-old Sutton stumbled onto the scene. I'd dismissed the notion when he'd mentioned it, but now I reconsidered. An adult male wolf-dog would have been far bigger than a four-year-old child, but since I didn't have a way to determine what had actually happened, maybe it was time to approach the question from another point of view: not the motive for the dog's removal and subsequent burial, but the choice of the spot. Why there and not somewhere else?

# 17

After lunch I drove to Horton Ravine, taking Via Juliana as far as the Y where Alita Lane branched off. I parked in front of Felix Holderman's house, locked the car, and ambled up his driveway. To my right, at the far end of the house, the overhead doors were open on his three-car garage. A late-model sedan sat in the first bay and the other two had been converted into a workshop. Felix had his back to me but he sensed my presence. He looked up and lifted a hand to signal that he'd be with me momentarily, and then returned to the task in front of him. He wore dark blue denim overalls, a long-sleeve shirt, gloves, and goggles. In an open cabinet to one side, sheets of colored glass were stored vertically.

As I approached I could see that he was creating a stained-glass panel. On the workbench he'd laid out a design, a stylized pattern of trees, leaves, and branches against a white background. He'd cut paper templates for each section of the design, and these he'd glued to various pieces of glass. As I watched he ran a wheel glass cutter along the edge of one template. He'd already cut a number of sections, and I waited while he completed the straight line he was tracing. When he finished he tapped the glass and it broke neatly.

He lifted his goggles and pushed them up on his head.

I said, "Hi, Mr. Holderman. Sorry to interrupt your work."

He peeled off his gloves and laid them on the work surface with a shake of his head. "Don't worry about it. I was ready for a break. I get lost in this stuff and it's good to come up for air now and then. You were the one who knocked on my door and asked to walk the hill. You should have told me what you were up to."

"Sorry for the omission, but I didn't think I'd succeed. I should have laid it out for you regardless."

"I've blanked on your name."

"Kinsey Millhone," I said. "Did the officers bring you up to speed?"

"After the fact. They seemed to think you were onto something."

"I did, too, but I've been wrong before and such is life." I peered at the section of stained glass he was working on. "You made the panels in your front door?"

"I did. This one's a bit more complex, but I'm having a good time."

"That's the lead?"

He nodded. "It's called came. These are U-shaped cross sections for the circumference and H-shaped for the middle of the design. Lead came is meant for two-dimensional panes. You want to do three dimensions, you use a copper foil technique."

"What will you do with the window when it's done?"

"Give it away. Just about everybody in my family's had a window foisted off on 'em at some point. My daughter's house looks like a church." He smiled, showing dimples I hadn't seen before. "What brings you back to the neighborhood?"

"I'm curious about the people who owned the property where the dog was buried. You mentioned the house changed hands twice. Did you know the previous owners?"

"Oh, sure. Patrick and Deborah Unruh. Nice folks. The dog wasn't theirs, if that's what you're wondering."

"I know. I've talked to the real owner and he has no idea how the dog ended up in someone else's backyard. There's probably a simple explanation."

"That whole section of the hill was overgrown back then. Maybe whoever buried the dog didn't realize it was private property."

"Could be," I said. "When did the Unruhs sell the house?"

"You got me there. It's been at least fifteen years. I'd say closer to twenty."

"Did they buy another house in the area?"

"No. They moved to a gated community in Los Angeles. He owned a manufacturing plant, making uniforms, sports gear, and outerwear. He worked down there through the week and drove up here weekends."

"You think he wanted a place closer to his business?"

"That'd be my guess. The move was abrupt, which I thought was odd. They were here one day, gone the next. I remember chatting with them at a barbecue a few days before and neither said a word about plans to relocate. Next thing I know there's a moving van in the drive and guys are loading up the household goods."

"Do you remember when this was?"

"Not a clue. One of the other neighbors might know. The gal next door, Avis Jent, kept in touch for a while. She could tell you more."

"What about you? No exchange of Christmas cards?"

"We weren't close friends, more like social acquaintances. Patrick was killed in a plane crash a couple of years ago. After that, I heard Deborah moved back here, but I've never had it confirmed. A town this size, you'd think you'd run into people all the time, but you don't."

"Do you think she remarried? I ask because I'm wondering if she's still using the name Unruh."

"Probably. From what I saw of them, they were one of those magic twosomes who mate for life. They even looked alike. Both tall and trim, fair-haired."

"Any children?"

"Just one, a boy named Greg. She and Patrick ended up raising his daughter, Rain, so that might count as two kids."

"What's the story on him?"

"Typical of the times. Early sixties, he went off to college as a clean-cut kid and came home looking like a bum. I believe it was the summer after his sophomore year, he and this little gal showed up in a yellow school bus. He'd been traveling across the country, thinking what a free spirit he was while he borrowed money from his folks. Turned out his girlfriend was pregnant and the two of them were broke. Deborah and Patrick offered them a place to stay. Nothing permanent, just until the baby came. The girl already had one kid, five or six years old. Greg parked the bus on one side of the cabana and that's where they hung out. I used to see the little boy running around the front yard without a stitch of clothes on. Deborah and Patrick were fit to be tied. To top it off, once the baby was born, Greg and what's-her-face took off with the boy and left the little girl behind. After two years of no contact and no financial support, the court terminated their parental rights and the Unruhs adopted her."

"Sounds like a soap opera."

"It was. They thought they'd seen the last of them, but here they came again some time later, in the same yellow school bus, only now it was covered with peace signs in psychedelic paint. It was the talk of the neighborhood. Greg had changed his name to Creed and she was Destiny. I forget what her name was before. Her son was ten or eleven by then. They called him Sky Dancer, Sky for short."

"Oh dear," I said. "And the daughter was Rain?"

"Patricia Lorraine. The shortened version came before it occurred to them to rename themselves."

"Why'd they come back?"

"Beats me. They left again abruptly some weeks later. By then, Deborah was worried the day would come when the bio-mom would try getting her daughter back so that might have been another reason she and Patrick packed up and left. 'Gone, no forwarding' as far as those hippies were concerned."

"Could the bio-mom have done that, reclaimed the child?"

"Hard to say. The courts can be capricious when it comes to the welfare of a child. Judges sometimes put too much stock in nature and not enough in nurture. Deborah and Patrick were terrific parents, but why take the risk?"

"Who left first, Greg or his parents?"

"He did, definitely. It was the second time he'd decamped with his common-law wife. Deborah had no intention of putting up with that again."

"What happened to him?"

"Last I heard, he and Destiny were heavy into free love and dope. Flower children. That's what they called themselves.

Remember that? Sticking daisies down the rifle barrels of the National Guardsmen, like that would make a difference."

I laughed. "That's right—1967 was the Summer of Love. What were they thinking?"

He smiled and shook his head. "That's how you know you're getting old—when you start looking back with kindness on things you knew for sure were ridiculous at the time."

"At least they believed in something. Kids I see these days don't seem to have passions of any kind."

"That's the other way you know you're getting old. When you say crap like that," he said with a laugh. "Anyway, I didn't mean to get sidetracked. Do you think the dog's burial is significant?"

"I don't know, but I'll tell you what's bugging me. That dog's body was stolen from the veterinarian who put him to sleep. Does that make sense to you?"

"Not much." He nodded at the house next door. "Before you give up, you might want to talk to Avis."

"I didn't say I was giving up. I think the pieces are there. I just don't understand how they fit."

I left his house, walking past my car on my way to her place next door. In truth, I was talked out for the day and I would have preferred to head home. I had a lot to absorb and I wanted to make notes while the information was fresh. At the same time, the woman lived no more than fifty yards away and I figured I might as well make contact while I was close. I hadn't known her name before Felix mentioned it, but I'd put her on my mental list, along with the neighbors in the houses across the street. It had been a while since I'd done an old-fashioned canvass, trotting from door to door, introducing myself. As a PI apprentice, under the tutelage of Ben Byrd and Morley Shine, this was how it was done. You followed a trail of crumbs through the forest and pecked them up one by one. Thus far, I was still lost, but my appetite hadn't been satisfied so on I went.

Mrs. Jent's one-story house was plain, a typical 1950s construction that would probably hop off its foundation at the next big earthquake. I hoped her insurance premiums were up to date. While the neighborhood was affluent, there was the occasional house like hers tucked among the more prestigious properties. Once disaster struck, someone would come along and offer her top dollar just to get their hands on the lot.

In the meantime, there wasn't much to be said for the exterior: rough stucco painted a melon color with a low-pitched roof covered with rocks the size of popcorn embedded in tar. By way of contrast, the lawn was a lush green and the landscaping was well designed, which lent the house more grace than would otherwise have been in evidence.

When I rang the front bell, I found myself staring at one of Felix's stained-glass panes in the door. The design must have been one of his early ones, a simply rendered cluster of grapes beside a wineglass, shaped like a U on a stick and half filled with red wine. This was a portent since the woman who answered the door carried a wineglass much like it, only cloudy with fingerprints. In her other hand she held a cigarette. Her eyes were brown and her hair was a dark carroty red, cut into short wispy strands that curled up around her head like flames. I placed her in her fifties, though she might have been younger and suffering the aging effects of booze and smokes. She was barefoot and wore a vibrant green silk kimono.

"Mrs. Jent?"

"I am."

"Felix suggested I talk to you . . ."

Her movements were liquid and she swayed in my direction. "Sure. I can do that. You have a name?"

"Kinsey Millhone."

"You caught me at the cocktail hour. Would you care to join me?" Without waiting for a reply, she turned and the kimono blossomed out around her like a matador's cape. Fortunately, she had her back to me by then so I wasn't subjected to anything unseemly. Was she wearing underpants? She padded down the hallway, talking over her shoulder while I followed in the wake of smoke and alcohol fumes.

Surreptitiously, I checked my watch. It was 2:30.

"Don't be a fussbudget," she said, apparently catching my move out of the corner of her eye.

"Sorry. Wine would be great."

"White or red?"

"White."

"Chardonnay or Sauvignon Blanc?"

"Chardonnay."

She held a finger up. "Bingo! That's correct."

The interior of the house was surprisingly modern. The living room walls were painted cobalt blue and the hall was done in rust. The floors were polished hardwood and the furniture design was stark and uninviting. The paintings were oversized and abstract, bright splashes of red, white, and yellow.

"I'm Avis, by the way. That 'Mrs. Jent' malarkey is for the birds. Archie Jent was my third. I was married to him the longest, but I'm not anymore. He was an engineer, if you know the type. He walked around looking like he was trying to shit a bowling ball. I went on the wagon for a while and realized I liked him better when I was drunk. I decided to keep his last name as long as he's paying my rent. Are you married?"

"Not now."

"How many times?"

"Twice."

"Oh, good. We can compare notes. I had a couple stinkers. How about you?"

"I wish I could say they were at fault, but I carried half the blame."

"Oh, please. Don't pretend you're fair-minded. It's unbecoming."

We'd arrived in the kitchen, which was stark white, anchored by dark green marble surfaces. The appliances were stainless steel. Copper pots hung from a rack. She opened the door to an under-counter, glass-fronted wine cooler, pulling out first the top rack and then the next one down. She removed a bottle and read the label, saying, "Talbott, Diamond T."

She held it out so I could see the label as well. "You know the wine?"

"I don't." I peered at the year, which was 1985, and wondered if that was a good one.

"Well, you're in for a treat. I go through a case of Diamond T every other week. In between assorted other cocktails. Shit." She'd knocked the live ember from her cigarette and it settled on the floor near her bare foot like a small red bug. "Would you get that for me? Paper towels are under the sink."

I stepped on the ember and then found the roll of paper

toweling. I tore off a sheet, wet it, and made quick work of the ash, which I tossed in the wastebasket.

While she struggled to uncork the wine, I said, "Mind if I look around?"

"Have at it."

I circled the kitchen, glancing into the three adjoining rooms—a glassed-in back porch that ran the width of the house, formal dining room, and den. By the time I finished my minitour, she'd taken out an enormous wineglass and poured me enough Chardonnay to float a small school of fish.

"We can sit on the porch unless you have a better idea."

"I'm with you," I said.

I tagged after her as she crossed the kitchen in a billow of silk. Windows, mounted above wainscoting, now enclosed what had probably once been a bare concrete patio. A sisal carpet covered much of the floor, and the windows could be protected with roll-up blinds if the sun hit at a blinding angle at odd times of the day. The furniture was white wicker, old-fashioned compared to the rest of the house. Looking out, I realized the house to the right of hers was where the Unruhs had lived. I couldn't see the spot where the techs had gone to work, but it felt odd to know I was in range of a site that had occupied so much of my imagination of late.

She settled on one of two love seats that faced each other across a wicker coffee table. She leaned forward and snagged an ashtray, pulling it closer so she could light another cigarette. The ashtray was metal and the spent paper match made a tinking sound when she tossed it in. She took a deep drag on her cigarette and blew out a stream of smoke, lifting her head slightly to avoid blowing it in my face. "Now then. Why did Felix send you over here? Natural charm aside, I'm sure you have a deeper purpose in mind."

"I'm interested in talking to Deborah Unruh. Felix thought you might put me in touch."

"Really. And what's your interest?"

"I'm a PI."

"Excuse me?"

"I'm a private investigator. My client was the one who motivated the cops to dig up the Unruhs' backyard."

"How did your 'client' talk them into it? That must have been a trick."

"He remembered something that happened when he was six years old and thought it was connected to a crime."

"And what crime was that?"

"I'd prefer not to say."

"I see. So you want information from me, but you won't pony up yourself."

"Good point. I'm talking about the Mary Claire Fitzhugh kidnapping."

"What's that have to do with Deborah? They dug up a damn dog. I don't see the relevance."

"The dog was buried in 1967 when she and Patrick were still living in the house."

"I'd say 'So what,' but I don't want to sound rude."

"It was right around the time Mary Claire Fitzhugh disappeared."

She studied me briefly. "You're not drinking your wine."

"It's a little early in the day for me."

"I usually start at noon, so this is late as far as I'm concerned. You really ought to loosen up. One little taste won't kill you."

I took a sip of wine, which I confess was head and shoulders above the crap I'm used to drinking. "Wow. That's really lovely."

"Told you so." She was silent for a moment, pressing a wrinkle out of the silk in her lap. "Funny you should mention Mary Claire."

"How so?"

She studied the end of her cigarette. "Don't think I'm telling tales out of school here, but Deborah had a similar experience. Her granddaughter, Rain, was abducted maybe ten days before Mary Claire was kidnapped. Happily, Rain was returned unharmed, but Deborah believed Rain was what she called the 'practice child.' Rehearsal in preparation for the real deal."

# 18

---

# JON CORSO

### Summer 1967

The Amazing Mona had arranged an eight-week trip to France and Italy, departing after the school year ended in June. She and the girls had been to Europe when she was married to her former husband, and now she wanted to relive the joys of foreign travel with Lionel in tow. Lionel saw the trip as an opportunity to do research for a book on the lesser-known American expatriates writing in Paris after World War I. In May of Jon's senior year at Santa Teresa High, his academic performance was still so poor that it was clear he wasn't going to graduate. As a consequence, he was excluded from the family vacation.

He was three credits short of what was required for his diploma and he'd managed to exasperate just about everyone, including his English teacher, Mr. Snow, who snagged him one afternoon after class. Mr. Snow was thirty-five years old, dedicated and energetic, new to Santa Teresa High School, where he taught English and creative writing. He'd had two novels published and he was working on his third. He perched on the edge of his desk, with his grade book open in front of him. He ran his finger down the column of Jon's classroom grades, many of which read "incomplete." He shook his head while Jon sat in the front row, posing as a kid busy contemplating his sins.

Mr. Snow said, "I don't know what to do with you, Jon. This class is an elective. This is all you needed to graduate and you blew it. You're a bright kid and you write well—when and if you get around to do it. You might even have some talent lurking in that thick skull of yours. If you'd done even half the assignments, you'd have passed with no problem. Why are you doing this?"

Jon shrugged. "The topics are boring. I can't relate."

"You can't *relate*. Are you kidding me?"

"What do you want me to say?"

"Where's this horseshit coming from? That's what I don't get. You did well at Climp, until your junior year. I know because I called the school and checked. Now your GPA is in the toilet. I don't think you've lost any IQ points, so what gives?"

Jon shrugged. He kept his eyes pinned on Mr. Snow's but his expression was blank.

Mr. Snow stared at him. "Are you having problems at home?"

"Not really."

"You want to talk about it?"

"There's nothing to talk about."

Mr. Snow closed his eyes for a beat and tried another tack. "You have plans for college?"

"City College maybe. I haven't decided yet."

"Well, you better pull your thumb out. If you don't get into *some* college, you risk being called up."

"I thought they were mostly taking older guys."

"You want to take that chance? The last two years, they've bumped up the draft to thirty-five thousand a month. That's a lot of young men."

"Yes, sir. I'm aware of that," he said, polite but unyielding.

Mr. Snow set the grade book aside. "Do you *like* to write? I'm asking because when you bother to do it, you're not half bad."

"Writing's okay. I like it pretty well. I mean, not all the time, but sometimes."

Mr. Snow studied him. "Here's what I'm willing to do. I'll set you up in an independent-studies program, just the two of us. You turn in the work and you'll pass. I guarantee it. Mr. Albertson might even let you go through the graduation ceremony. He can leave your diploma blank and we'll take care of it at the end of summer school, assuming you haven't dropped the ball."

"What would I have to do?"

"Well, *Jon,* this is a writing class. You'd have to write, as wacky as that might seem. If you're bored with my topics, you can tackle your own."

"Like what?"

"That's up to you. You can't have it both ways. You either do the pieces I assign or you come up with your own. At the end of each week, you turn in everything you've done, and I mean everything—false starts, cross-outs, bad paragraphs, ideas that bomb. The first time you fail to deliver, you're out. Do we have a deal?"

"I'll think about it," Jon said.

"I'm making a sales pitch. The offer's on the table for ten minutes." Mr. Snow glanced pointedly at his watch.

"Okay, fine. We have a deal." Jon was thinking it would be a breeze. He liked Mr. Snow. The guy was blunt and aggressive and Jon trusted him. "When would I have to start?"

Mr. Snow said, "The day school gets out. After that, you report to me here every Friday morning at nine."

Jon got to his feet and ambled to the door. As he was leaving the room, Mr. Snow said, "You're welcome."

Jon closed the door behind him, but he was smiling.

The Friday morning Lionel, Mona, and the girls left in the limousine for LAX, Jon managed to look somber and contrite. He'd been excluded from the family fun, but he was taking his punishment like a man. Mona knew he was faking, but that was his intention. Lionel gave him a big hug, like there was oh-so-much affection between them. His dad patted his shoulder. "You take care," he said. "You have everything you need?"

"Hot water would be nice."

Lionel frowned. "I thought we bought you a new water heater. I mentioned it to Mona after our last chat, but that was months ago."

"I guess she forgot." Jon's tone was neutral and the gaze he fixed on his father was without guile.

Lionel flashed an irritated look at her and then said, "Call
the plumber. Mona has the number in her Rolodex. Tell him
we need an eighty-gallon water heater and the charge comes
to me. The two of you can work out a time for the installation,
but make it soon."

"Thanks."

The minute the limo turned out of the driveway, Jon felt relief wash over him. It was like getting out of prison. He loved
having the big house to himself, though he spent most of his
time in his rooms above the garage. The big house was pure
Mona—her taste, her style, expensive and overdone. He went
through all her drawers but didn't learn much, except she used
K-Y jelly.

Lionel had left him sufficient money to cover meals and
gas for his motor scooter while the family was gone. In March,
Jon had totaled the used car his dad had given him, and Mona
was adamant about not replacing it. Fine with him. He went
back to tootling around on the Vespa his dad had bought for
him his freshman year. As the end of school approached, Jon
asked if he could use his father's old Olivetti typewriter for
summer school, but Mona said she needed it for one of the
girls. Jon had to suppress a smile. When it came to sheer pre-
dictability, the Amazing Mona was a champ.

He cruised garage sales that weekend until he came across
a Smith-Corona portable electric typewriter with a manual
carriage return. He paid fifteen bucks for that and then stopped
at the hardware store and bought four gallons of paint. For the
two years he'd been living in his aerie above the garage, he'd
been content to leave it in its original bare and shabby state.
Now he saw it differently. Three dormer windows looked out
on the ocean and the sharply slanting eaves made the rooms
feel garretlike, perfect for a writer in residence.

He painted the walls a dark charcoal gray, close to black,
in part to annoy Mona, but more nearly because it soothed
and quieted the chatter in his head. He went through the
main house, scavenging items from linen closets and storage
areas. For bedding, he'd been using a sleeping bag, flung on
top of the bare mattress, but now he made up his bed with a
set of Mona's expensive cotton sheets and two quilted cover-
lets his mother had made. From the attic he brought down a

secondhand chest of drawers and a hat rack, and he mounted a series of wooden pegs on the wall for hanging his clothes. He scrubbed his small bathroom until it was immaculate.

For the larger of the two rooms he'd found a deep, down-filled easy chair—another garage sale acquisition, this one for twenty-five dollars, with a reading lamp thrown in. He moved his desk under the middle window, placed his typewriter in the center, and laid in a supply of paper, carbons, typewriter ribbons, and Wite-Out. Once everything was arranged, he sat there for four days, drinking coffee and staring at the view. During his preparations, he was brimming with ideas. Now that he was ready to go to work, his mind was blank.

He wrote the occasional paragraph, but he spent most of the time thinking about Walker. He couldn't figure out why Walker was so successful with girls while he remained so out of it. Walker had had a string of girlfriends his senior year. Two of them Jon found attractive, but neither one would give him the time of day. It was always "Walker this, Walker that." Their only purpose in talking to Jon was to ask how Walker felt about them. Having heard Walker trash both in private, Jon wondered if they'd lost their tiny minds. Walker treated girls badly. He ignored or snubbed or insulted them. He'd date them, screw them, and break up with them. Given the tears and upsets and phone calls and public scenes, they were totally smitten, absolutely gaga about him. Jon detached himself, mystified by the unspoken rules underlying love, flirtation, passion, and sex.

Just to feel like he was doing something, he went into his father's study and pulled out a copy of Hemingway's *The Sun Also Rises*. He took it back to his desk and typed out the first two chapters. He liked the plain, choppy feel of the prose, but transcribing someone else's work didn't spark inspiration. While he liked the language, he wasn't connected to the content. The words belonged to Hemingway and the images were his. For Jon, the subject matter carried no emotional energy. If he could write about anything, what would it be? He couldn't think of a thing.

He had to laugh at himself. He hadn't written a word and he was already suffering writer's block. Just to shake himself loose, he closed up shop for the day and broke into a house

four doors down. The owner was a Hollywood producer who
spent the occasional weekend in Horton Ravine. Jon knew
their habits because the couple had come to a number of dinner parties Mona had given and they talked nonstop about
themselves. The guy had a son Jon's age that Jon had no use
for. Mona liked him, of course, because his manners were
good and he wore a coat and tie and said sir and ma'am. It was
therefore doubly amusing to discover the kid's stash of dope
and pornography. Farm animals? Come *on*.

In the master bedroom, at the back of a closet, Jon came
across a wooden box. There was no lock on it and when Jon
opened it, he found a handgun. It was a Mauser HSc .380 ACP.
He took it out of the box and hefted it in his hand. Pasted in the
lid of the box there was promotional material in German and
English that he read with interest. The pistol was a double-
action, all-steel small-frame automatic with checkered wal-
nut grips. Very cool. According to the pamphlet, the gun had
open, fixed recessed sights, a positive thumb safety, a maga-
zine safety, and an exposed hammer for additional safety. Jon
tucked the gun in his waistband and helped himself to a box
of ammunition. Maybe he'd write about a crook who carried
a gun just like it. He returned the empty wooden box to the
back of the shelf where he'd found it. Chances were the guy
wouldn't pull the box out to check. He'd assume the gun was
where he left it.

Back in his garage apartment, Jon took a few minutes to
decide where to hide the Mauser. He finally went into the bathroom and unscrewed the plumbing-access panel. He wrapped
the gun and ammunition in an old towel and pushed it into the
gap on the right, snug against the underbelly of the tub. He returned to his desk feeling fresh and renewed. Again, he raided
his father's study, this time taking out William Faulkner's
*Light in August*. Typing the first ten pages taught him something about the power of language in the hands of someone utterly in control. Faulkner was extravagant, while Hemingway
was spare. The stylistic differences seemed appropriate to the
tale each was trying to tell. While Hemingway stripped away,
Faulkner painted layer on layer, using long, lavish sentences.
Neither narrative voice was natural to Jon, but at least he was
beginning to understand range and tone.

Jon had a stack of *Playboy* magazines, dating back to the first of the year. The girls all had perfect bodies, but they seemed brainless to him. What difference did it make how big their tits were when the girls themselves were shallow, egotistical, and self-involved? Yeah, right. Like he'd really turn one down as unworthy of him. Since he didn't have a prayer of meeting any of them in real life, he might as well enjoy the illusion of them as lush, sensual, and available. Leafing back through the January issue, he got sidetracked by a Ray Bradbury short story called "The Lost City of Mars" and after that, the second part of a new Len Deighton spy novel called *An Expensive Place to Die*. Now he'd seen two more writers with entirely different literary effects.

His first few stabs at fiction were erratic, prose that fell flat and ideas that died in half a page. The problem, as he saw it, was that he had nothing to draw on. He'd done a lot of reading, but he didn't have firsthand experience at much of anything. The only job he'd had was the unpaid babysitting he'd done for the Amazing Mona. Weekends, he caddied at the club, but aside from the intelligence gleaned, it was mostly step-and-fetch-it stuff—cleaning club heads and humping golf bags up hill and down. He'd had no travel adventures, no athletic triumphs, no physical challenges to overcome. Well, the latter wasn't quite true. He'd been a fat boy and he remembered how shitty that was. He thought it best to avoid stories about prowlers lest he seem too well informed.

He wrote part of a short story based on a notion he had about a kid contaminated by radiation, who turned into a zombie and infected his entire family before his dad shot him dead. He ran out of steam in the middle of that one because he couldn't think where to go with it. He wrote a mawkish essay about loneliness that struck him as funny when he read it the next day—not quite what he was hoping to achieve. He wanted to write about a kid seduced by his tennis instructor, but that wasn't exactly an area of expertise. The tennis pro at the club had put her hand over his once, showing him how the face of the racket should feel on contact with the ball, but that was as close to having sex as he'd come, so to speak.

The best part of writing, at least the best part of *trying* to write, was that it allowed him to spend time alone, tuned to the static in his head. Once in a while a line came through, like an unexpected message from the outer limits of the universe. He recorded those isolated images and phrases, wondering if one day there might be more. At the end of the week he didn't have much to show for his time, but he gathered up what he'd done and stuck the sheaf of papers in a file folder that he handed to Mr. Snow, who said, "Have a seat."

Jon sat down in the front row, looking on self-consciously while Mr. Snow went through his pages.

"What's this about? You plagiarized Hemingway?"

"I typed a couple of chapters as warm-up. I tried Faulkner, too. You told me to bring everything so I did."

Mr. Snow rolled his eyes and read on.

Jon watched his face, but he had no idea how his work was being received. When Mr. Snow was done, he straightened the pages, lined up the edges, put them in the folder, and handed it back.

He didn't make a comment so Jon was finally forced to clear his throat and say, "So what do you think?"

"As a general rule, beginning, middle, and end are nice, but at least you kept at it. Go back and try something else."

"Like what? I mean, I'm really having trouble coming up with stuff."

"Fancy that."

Jon went back to work. He wrote at night, usually until three, when he fell into bed. In the morning he slept late. At lunchtime he showered and dressed and headed over to Walker's house at the top of Bergstrom Hill, half a mile from his house. If he kept to the winding streets, the travel time was five minutes by scooter, but Jon found another route, skirting the Ravine along its easternmost edge, putt-putting along the bridle paths that formed a warren of meandering trails. It required his crossing one two-lane road, but there was scarcely ever any traffic. Late afternoons he'd spend forty minutes lifting free weights in Mona's home gym and then do a long run of six or seven miles. After that he'd shower, put on his slippers and sweats, and sit down at his desk. For most meals he ate cold cereal or Top Ramen, which was all he could afford after the money he'd spent on furnishings.

Meanwhile, Walker was spending his summer vacation

selling dope. His parents were clueless and didn't seem to grasp the import of his frequent absences from the house or the unannounced visits from an assortment of friends whose names they were never told. In the fall Walker would start his freshman year at UCST. He had no interest in living at home, but he didn't have the money to pay for off-campus digs. Even if he went in with five other guys, he'd be coming up short, dope money notwithstanding. Jon was in the same boat. Once Mona and the family returned, she'd make his continued residency dependent on his paying rent. Lionel would explain this was for his own good, a means of building character, not just a variation on Mona's abuse. Jon could see he'd have to find a job and juggle work with classes at City College. Mr. Snow had a point about avoiding the draft.

# 19

## Wednesday afternoon, April 13, 1988

Deborah Unruh agreed to meet me on the beach in front of the Edgewater Hotel. The spot she suggested was across from the hotel entrance, at the bottom of the concrete stairs that led down from the frontage road. It was a point she'd be passing in the course of her regular weekday walk, a loop that extended from her Montebello condominium to the wharf downtown. Avis Jent had called her on my behalf and after the preliminary chitchat, she'd summed up my mission as succinctly as I might have done in her place. Deborah didn't seem to require much in the way of persuasion.

I arrived fifteen minutes early and parked on the narrow road that ran behind the hotel. I locked my shoulder bag in the trunk of my car and took a shortcut through the property. I crossed the frontage road and trotted down the stairs. A dense fog was rolling in, spreading a thick marine layer that blotted out the offshore islands, twenty-six miles away. The April air, mild to begin with, was changing its character. Erratic winds topped the waves, creating whitecaps in the chop. It was close to 3:00 by then, and I was already operating on sensory overload. I needed time to breathe and I hoped the bracing ocean air would clear my head. My usual morning jog didn't bring me down this far. My circuit began and ended at the wharf, with its complicated history of good intentions gone wrong.

Coastal Santa Teresa, despite its many assets, wasn't blessed with a natural harbor. Early trade by sea was inhibited because shipping companies, fearful of exposure to rough seas, were unwilling to risk their cargo when faced with the rocky shore. In 1872 a fifteen-hundred-foot wharf was finally constructed, allowing freighters and steamers to unload goods and passengers. Over the next fifty years, earthquakes, winter storms, and arsonists laid siege to the wharf, and while it was rebuilt time and time again, it failed to solve the problem of safe mooring for the swelling number of yachts and pleasure boats owned by its wealthy citizens and sometimes wealthier summer visitors.

In the early 1920s an informal engineering survey (which consisted of setting empty jugs and sacks of sawdust afloat at Horton Ravine beach and watching which way they drifted) indicated that locating an artificial harbor to the west of the town would be folly because prevailing currents would denude the beaches of sand and deposit it all directly into the proposed moorage basin, barring both ingress and egress. A $200,000 harbor bond issue was offered in support of this ill-conceived scheme, and voters approved the measure on May 4, 1927. Tons of rocks were barged from the islands and dumped just offshore, forming a thousand-foot breakwater. Thereafter, as predicted, 775 cubic yards of sand per day shifted to the inside aspect of the barrier, creating a sandbar of sufficient mass to choke the harbor entrance. It wasn't long before the taxpayers were forced to buy a $250,000 dredge and a $127,000 tender in a perpetual effort to keep the harbor open, at an annual expenditure of $100,000. The sum has grown exponentially since then, with no permanent remedy in sight. All of this by way of improvement.

I did a few preliminary stretches, keeping an eye on the beach. Ten minutes later I caught sight of Deborah Unruh, approaching from my left. Avis Jent's description hadn't prepared me for how attractive she was. She was barefoot and the wind had buffeted her silver hair into a choppy halo. She had to be in her late sixties, looking trim and fit in black velour pants with a matching jacket that she'd left unzipped, showing a red cotton T-shirt. Her eyes were brown and her face was youthful, despite numerous soft lines that came into focus as she reached me. "Kinsey?"

"Hi, Deborah." I reached out and the two of us shook hands. "Thanks for meeting me on such short notice."

"Not a problem. I'm just happy I wasn't asked to give up my afternoon walk. I usually go as far as the wharf and back if that's doable for you."

"Absolutely. What's that, four miles round trip?"

"Close enough."

I took a minute to pull off my running shoes and socks. The socks I stuffed in my jacket pockets. I tied my shoelaces together and hung my shoes around my neck, letting them dangle in back. I wasn't crazy about the persistent bump-bumping between my shoulder blades as we trudged through the soft sand, but it was better than walking fully shod.

She was already moving toward the surf at a pace I might have found daunting if I hadn't been faithful to my jogging routine. On the ocean, waves broke a dozen yards out, and once we reached the hard pack, the water rushed forward in an icy flurry, covering our feet with foam before sliding out again. The Pacific is cold and unforgiving. You can usually spot a few hardy souls swimming in its depths, but no one had braved it that day. Two sailboats tacked toward the islands and a speedboat, at full throttle, paralleled the shoreline, keeping a parasailor aloft, attached by a towrope scarcely visible against the pale blue sky. Hang gliding and parasailing are second and third down on my list of the one thousand things I never want to do in life. The first is have another tetanus shot.

Deborah said, "I understand this whole business originated with Michael Sutton. What's the nature of your relationship?"

"I wouldn't call it a relationship," I said. "I met him for the first time a week ago when he hired me for a day's work."

I sketched in the situation, starting with his appearance in my office and his story about the two pirates he'd seen in the woods. "They claimed they were digging for buried treasure, but he noticed a bundle on the ground nearby. A few weeks ago, he came across a reference to the Fitzhugh kidnapping and the penny dropped. Now he's convinced he saw Mary Claire's body wrapped for burial. The only snag is when the police excavated the site, they found a dead dog. According to the ID tag, his name was Ulf."

She seemed taken aback. "Well, that's bizarre. I can assure you he wasn't ours."

"I know. I drove to Puerto and talked to the man who owned him. He said he'd taken Ulf to Dr. McNally for hip dysplasia. X-rays revealed a nasty tumor instead and the vet recommended euthanasia. Someone removed the dog's remains from a shed at the rear of the clinic and transported the body to your property, where they buried him."

The look she turned on me was perplexed. "Pardon my skepticism, but it sounds like all of this is predicated on the notion that it was Mary Claire's body he saw. What makes you so sure? It seems like folly to operate on the idea when all you have is his word for it."

"Agreed. I'm not even sure we could say we had his word on it. Call it a hunch."

"Call it anything you like, it's still odd. If something went wrong in the course of the kidnapping and they had to dispose of her body, why would they bury her in *our* yard when Horton Ravine has acres of woods?"

"I've been asking myself the same question. If we're lucky we'll find answers. On the other hand, we may never know."

"There's a certain irony in here somewhere. I haven't heard Michael's name in years. His parents, Kip and Annabelle, were our best friends."

I looked over at her with interest. "Really. Michael's parents? When was this?"

"During that same period. We met at the country club when she was six months pregnant with him. They were the dearest people in the world. I lost Annabelle, Kip, and Patrick in a span of two years."

"Avis told me your husband died in a plane crash," I said. I was reluctant to bring up the subject of his death, but it seemed to me the conversation we were embarking on had better be rooted in reality. The fact that we were walking, with our attention directed outward, allowed a more intimate exchange than if we'd been chatting eye-to-eye over a cup of tea.

"Some days I think I'm reconciled, that I've dealt with the pain and it's over and done. Other days the grief is just as fresh as it was the first moment I heard."

"What were the circumstances?"

"Rain was just starting graduate school, working toward her master's degree in social work at the University of Wisconsin, Milwaukee. This was the fall of 1985. She and Patrick drove out in her car, with all her stuff in a four-by-eight cargo trailer. His plan was to get her settled and then fly on to Atlanta for a business meeting. I'd have gone with him, but it made more sense for me to tend the home fires and let the two of them have the time together. The Midwest Express flight to Atlanta went down after takeoff. The right engine failed and then a whole series of things went haywire. I was here in California without any intuition whatever. It's hard to realize your life can change so radically with no warning at all. When Rain phoned, she couldn't even speak. I thought it was a crank call and nearly hung up on her."

"I don't know how anyone gets through something like that."

"You do because you do. Because you have no choice. I had Rain to consider. I set my own pain aside and focused on helping her."

"Tell me the time frame. I heard about Michael's accusations against his parents."

"The lawsuit was settled in 1981. By then, Kip and Annabelle were crippled by the strain. Between the public outcry and the drain on their emotions, they were whipped. Let's not even talk about the thousands of dollars in legal fees it cost them. Annabelle died in the summer of 1983, and Kip six months later."

"They must have been a mess after what he put them through."

"You have no idea. The four of us talked about it for hours on end and there was just no way out. Suing his therapist was their only hope of putting a stop to it. Even when it was over, the bad feelings remained. Some people were convinced he was actually abused, even after Marty Osborne as good as admitted the whole of it was her doing. The general attitude seemed to be that if Kip and Annabelle were accused, there must be a grain of truth to it. Both drank. I'm not saying they were alcoholics, but they hit the bottle pretty hard at times. Patrick and I were in much the same boat. We called it 'social' drinking, but we were social every chance we got. When this came up, they couldn't suck down the martinis fast enough, and that set tongues to wagging on top of everything else. At the club, feelings ran so high, the four of us resigned. That's how bad it got. I still run into people who refuse to make eye contact. They know Patrick and I were loyal, which apparently put us on the same dung heap as the Suttons, like we were somehow guilty by association."

"Diana told me Michael recanted."

She shook her head in disgust. "That was the last straw. I wanted to kill the little shit. Patrick and I were incensed, absolutely livid. Not that it made a whit of difference. Kip and Annabelle were both gone by then and the damage was done."

"Diana says her mother drowned."

Deborah gestured toward the surf. "She was swimming a few hundred yards offshore when she got caught in the undertow. She must have used up all her strength trying to fight her way back. In the end, the ocean took her." She was quiet for a moment and all I could hear was the chunking of sand under our feet as we walked. "I wouldn't mind a touch of justice for Michael, some small sign he was getting back his own. I look at the lives he destroyed and it seems unfair that he gets to enjoy the same sun that shines down on the rest of us. That may sound monstrous, but I don't care."

"I can understand how you feel," I said. "It's not about vengeance. It's about balance, the sense that good and evil are in a state of equilibrium. At the same time, I have to admit I like the kid. I think he should be held accountable for the harm he did, but he's paid a price like everyone else."

"Not enough of one." She broke off, impatiently. "Let's change the subject. It doesn't do any good to dwell on it," she said, and then glanced over at me. "You wanted information about Rain's abduction. How much did Avis tell you?"

"Nothing. She said the story was yours, which is why she

set this up. I do know you had a son and you ended up raising his child."

"Rain is the good part. She's the love of my life. At the time we took custody, I was forty-four years old, way past the point of parenting a newborn, but there she was. The birth itself was hard and Shelly ended up having a C-section. She had absolutely no interest in mothering the child. Rain was a fussy baby and didn't nurse well. I suspect Shelly was suffering from postpartum depression. I wasn't entirely unsympathetic, but I was seriously concerned she'd harm the child. My worries were pointless, as it turned out. She and Greg and the boy vanished in a puff of smoke, leaving Rain behind."

"How old was she?"

"Five days. After the initial shock wore off, we realized how totally blessed we were. I still laugh when I think about all those PTA meetings. Which I ran, by the way. All the other moms were in their twenties. I'd been chairing committees for years and I couldn't help myself. They'd start floundering and I'd take over. That was another reason we were so close to Kip and Annabelle. They had four kids underfoot and suddenly we had one, too." She smiled. "Sorry to run on like this."

"Don't worry about it," I said. "How long was it before you saw Greg and Shelly again?"

"Four years. June of 1967. I thought they were gone for good. I should have known better."

"Why did they come back?"

"Well, it certainly wasn't for love of Rain or the two of us. Patrick's father had left forty thousand dollars in a trust fund for Greg. He wasn't entitled to the money until he turned thirty, but he wanted it right then. Patrick and I refused to knuckle under to his demands. He and Shelly were furious, and I was terrified they'd retaliate by taking Rain."

"Why was Greg so insistent on the money?"

"I couldn't see the urgency myself. They told us they wanted to buy a farm so they could establish a commune. Their claim was they'd paid a thousand dollars down and needed the balance by the end of the month. Patrick asked to see the contract, but Greg said there wasn't one; it was a gentlemen's agreement. Patrick thought it was hogwash, and so did I."

"Had they lived in a commune?"

"Not that I ever heard, though by then they were full-blown hippies. Greg was calling himself Creed and she was Destiny. Shawn was Sky Dancer. The plan was to be self-sufficient, farming the land. Others would join them—at least in their fevered imaginations. They'd share the chores and pool their money, which I guess would go into an account to pay expenses. They thought Patrick should advance the funds, but he wouldn't budge. Neither of us liked Shelly anyway. She was poor white trash, arrogant, foulmouthed. Shawn was born out of wedlock, just as Rain was."

"When was Rain abducted?"

"Tuesday, July 11. There'd been a series of blowups. Lots of screaming and yelling and hysterics. The uproar finally died down and we thought they'd backed off. Then suddenly, on the sixth, they disappeared. It was the same as the first time around—no note, no goodbyes, no here's where we'll be. Five days after they decamped Rain was 'kidnapped.' I put the word in quotes because we knew it was them."

"You're saying they snatched Rain to force the issue?"

"More like they were getting even, making us suffer because we hadn't done as they asked," she said. "It wasn't a sophisticated plan, but they were stoned all the time and that's how their minds worked. Anyway, they didn't demand the entire forty thousand. They asked for fifteen, which I guess was their way of being clever. I'm sorry for all the editorializing. I should probably stick to the facts."

"Actually, I find it helpful to know what was going on in your mind. How'd they pull it off?"

"That was largely dumb luck. Rain was out in the backyard, playing in her sandbox. I'd given her some cookie cutters and a rolling pin. She had her bucket and shovel and she'd pour water on the sand, flatten it, and then cut out cookie shapes. The phone rang; some fellow taking a survey. He asked ten or fifteen questions that I answered. I wasn't much interested, but it seemed harmless enough. By the time I looked out the back door to check on her, she was gone. Later she told me a man came with a yellow kitten and said she could play with it at his house. Don't ask me to go through that part of it blow-by-blow. It was horrendous when it happened and it's horrendous every time I think of it. Those first hours, I thought I'd die. I can't revisit the trauma. It gives me heart palpitations even now. Look at that. My hands have started to sweat."

"Understood," I said. "I'm assuming the man on the phone wasn't Greg or you'd have recognized his voice."

"I'm not so sure. He'd already left and he was gone for good as far as I knew. I didn't expect to hear from him so it wasn't his voice I was listening for."

"If it wasn't Greg on the phone, there must have been someone else involved. Another guy."

"So it would seem. Greg certainly could have picked her up and taken her without a fuss."

"When did you first realize she'd been kidnapped?"

"Another phone call came in."

"The same guy or someone else?"

"He sounded the same to me. I called Patrick in L.A. and he was home ninety minutes later, breaking every speed law. I was a basket case. I didn't care who'd taken her or what it cost as long as Rain came back to us alive."

"You called the police?"

"Later. Not at that point."

"Why?"

"Because the man on the phone said they'd kill her if we did."

" 'They'd kill her.' Plural?"

"It might have been a figure of speech. Maybe they wanted us to picture a gang of thugs. Who knows?"

"But you were convinced her life was at stake."

"Let's put it this way: we weren't in a position to argue the point. I wasn't going to take the chance and neither was Patrick. He was convinced Shelly and Greg were behind the scheme, but that didn't mean Rain was safe. We had no idea how far they'd take it. Patrick withdrew the money from four different banks. He managed to stall delivery while he made a quick trip to the plant to photocopy the bills. It was a time-consuming job and he had to do it while the office staff was gone for the night. While he was about it, he marked the back of each with a fluorescent marker he used when he exported inventory. The bills looked fine, but the kidnappers might have been suspicious."

"Were the marks visible?"

"Under a black light, sure. Every kid seemed to have one in those days. If my guess is right, they'd have worried about putting that many marked bills in circulation, which can't be as simple as it seems."

"Couldn't they have passed the bills in small lots? Maybe not locally, but somewhere else. Seems like Los Angeles would have been the natural choice."

"Yes, but what fun would fifteen thousand dollars be if it was spread out like that? Patrick notified the local banks about the marked bills when Mary Claire was kidnapped. None of the money ever surfaced as far as we know."

"Avis referred to Rain as the 'practice child.'"

"Of course. She was their rehearsal for Mary Claire. If you know anything about her disappearance, you'll recognize the . . . what do they call it . . . the MO. We didn't believe they'd harm Rain, but we were frantic they'd refuse to return her. She was ours. We'd formally adopted her, but if they absconded with her, we'd have no way of getting her back. They had no permanent address, no phone, no employment." She shrugged. "We did as we were told. We received another call, telling us where to drop the ransom."

"Which was where?"

"Near the back entrance to the Ravine. One of them kept me on the phone while Patrick drove over with the gym bag and tossed it out on the side of the road. Then he came home. The other kidnapper must have picked up the money and counted it, making sure the entire amount was there. They told us to wait an hour and then we'd find her in the park off Little Pony Road. She was asleep on a picnic table, covered with a blanket, so they weren't entirely heartless. I don't know what would have happened if they'd realized Patrick marked the bills before we had her back in our keeping."

"She'd been drugged?"

"Clearly. She wasn't completely out, but she was groggy. She was fine once the sedative wore off, whatever it was. She'd been properly looked after. Fed well, at any rate, and she was clean. We had her examined and there was no evidence of sexual abuse. Thank god for that."

"What did she tell you about what went on?"

"Nothing coherent, bits and pieces. She was four—not what you'd call a reliable witness. The only thing she was upset about was that she didn't get to keep the kitten. Aside from that, she wasn't traumatized. No nightmares and no psychological problems in the aftermath. We were thankful she came out of it unscathed. To Patrick's way of thinking, this was further support of his conviction that Greg and Shelly had a hand in it."

"If the two of them took her, wouldn't Rain have said so?"

Deborah shook her head. "One of the kidnappers wore fake glasses with a big plastic nose attached and the other dressed like Santa Claus. We'd taken her to see Santa on two previous occasions so she was used to seeing him. He made her promise to be a good girl and she was."

"Here's what I don't get. If they'd already picked up the fifteen thousand, why kidnap a second child?"

"I can tell you Patrick's theory. When Mary Claire was taken the ransom demand was twenty-five thousand dollars. Add twenty-five to the fifteen we paid for Rain's return and you're looking at forty thousand dollars, which is what Greg and Shelly wanted in the first place. That's hardly proof, but I can't believe the total was a coincidence."

"It does seem like an odd amount. Too bad they weren't satisfied with what they got the first time around," I said. I let a short silence fall while I thought about what she'd told me. "How soon after Rain's abduction was Mary Claire kidnapped?"

"A week or so. By then we had the house on the market and we were looking at places in gated communities down south. The minute we heard about Mary Claire, we went to the police and told the detectives everything we knew. The FBI had been called into it by then. We gave them Greg and Shelly's names and descriptions, plus a description of the school bus along with the license plate number. None of this ever made the papers. They did put out an APB, but there was never any sign of them."

"Have you heard from them since?"

"Not a peep," she said. "I saw Shawn when Patrick died.

He spotted the obituary in the paper and drove down for the funeral."

"Drove down from where?"

"Belicia," she said, mentioning a little town an hour and a half north of us. "He was calling himself Shawn again, using Dancer as his last name. He looked wonderful. Tall and handsome. He has a shop up there where he builds furniture. He showed me photographs and the pieces are beautiful. He also does custom cabinetwork."

"You think he'd talk to me?"

"I don't see why not. You're welcome to use my name, or I can call him if you like."

"When you saw him at the funeral, did you ask about Greg and Shelly?"

"Briefly. He told me both of them were gone. To tell you the truth, I didn't care that much. As far as I was concerned, Greg had been dead to me since the summer of 'sixty-seven. We parted from them on bad terms, and anything that happened to them afterward was irrelevant. Except for the business with Rain, of course."

It bothered me that much of what she'd told me ran counter to my intuitions. "I'm sorry to keep harping on Mary Claire, but I have trouble believing they'd resort to snatching her. That's hard-core for a pair who weren't seasoned criminals."

"Look. I know what you're getting at and I agree. I can't imagine Greg doing any of this even under Shelly's influence, but Patrick felt if they were desperate enough to take Rain, they wouldn't be all that scrupulous about trying again. We paid without hesitation. If the plan worked once, why not twice?"

"I wonder how they fixed on Mary Claire? Did you know the Fitzhughs?"

"To speak to. We didn't socialize with them, but we were all members of the Horton Ravine Country Club."

"But the Fitzhughs said they'd pay, didn't they? I mean, they agreed to the ransom the same way you did."

"They also notified the police, which they were told not to do. The kidnappers must have figured it out."

"But how?"

"I have no idea. Maybe they sensed their luck had turned. Somehow they understood if they picked up the money, they'd be caught, so they left it where it was."

I said, "If they decided to forfeit the ransom, why not just hit the road? Why kill the child?"

"I can't believe they meant to hurt her. Greg might have been stupid and greedy, but he'd never harm a child. Not even Shelly could have talked him into going that far. To be fair, I've questioned whether she was capable of anything so heinous. Patrick thought it was totally in character. As for the hole being dug on our property . . . whatever the intention . . . Greg and Shelly could have chosen the location, thinking it was safe. To my way of thinking, the similarities between Rain's abduction and Mary Claire's are too obvious to discount."

I said, "The one obvious difference is the introduction of a ransom note during the second kidnapping. As I understand it, when Rain was taken, the contact was strictly by phone."

Deborah slowed and I was surprised to see we'd almost reached the wharf by then. I'd been so focused on the conversation I hadn't been aware of the walk itself. By now the fog had fully enveloped us and the air was so saturated with mist that my sweatshirt was damp. I could see beads of moisture in Deborah's hair, a veil of diamonds.

I was quiet, running the information in a quick loop, and I found myself itchy with misgivings. "Something's off. You and the Suttons were good friends. If Greg was one of the two guys digging in the woods, Michael would have recognized him."

"That's true. On the other hand, Greg and Shelly had their druggie pals who kept them supplied with dope. They sat out in the bus and smoked so much weed, I could have gotten high myself. I realize now I should have turned them in to the police, but I was still hoping the problem would go away of its own accord."

"Did you meet their friends?"

"I never laid eyes on them. They'd park around the corner and approach on foot, which allowed them to bypass the house and go straight to the cabana where the bus was parked. One of them had a motor scooter. I remember that because every time he left, I could hear it puttering down the street."

"I wish I could make sense of it."

"You and me both," she said. "Oh, before I forget. Rain's driving up from L.A. for a few days. She took over the family business after Patrick died. I'm sure she'd be willing to tell you what she remembers. It isn't much, but you might pick up a useful tidbit."

"That's great. I'll call and set something up."

# 20

The four-mile beach walk with Deborah had warmed me, but once I cooled off and my body temperature dropped, I could feel the chill in my bones. I returned to my car and pulled on my socks and running shoes. My feet were still wet and so grubby with sand that the cotton sawed against my flesh like a wood rasp. While I was out and about I made a quick stop at the drugstore and stocked up on blank index cards.

At 5:00, I unlocked the studio door and let myself in. My first order of business was to strip off my damp clothes and hop in a hot shower, after which I put on my sweats and went down to the living room. For supper I made myself a peanut butter and pickle sandwich. Recently I'd been making an effort to upgrade my diet, which meant cutting down on the french fries and Quarter Pounders with Cheese that had been my mainstays. A peanut butter and pickle sandwich was never going to qualify as the pinnacle on the food pyramid, but it was the best I could do.

I set my plate and napkin on the table at one end of the sofa, then opened a bottle of Chardonnay and poured myself a glass. I returned to the living room, a round-trip of twenty feet. I found a ballpoint pen and curled up on the sofa with a quilt tucked around my legs. I opened the first packet of index cards and started taking notes.

I had a lot of ground to cover, consigning everything I'd learned to note cards, one item per card, which reduced the facts to their simplest form. It's our nature to condense and collate, bundling related elements for ease of storage in the back of our brains. Since we lack the capacity to capture every detail, we cull what we can, blocking the bits we don't like and admitting those that match our notions of what's going on. While efficient, the practice leaves us vulnerable to blind spots. Under stress, memory becomes even less reliable. Over time we sort and discard what seems irrelevant to make room for additional incoming data. In the end, it's a wonder we remember anything at all. What we manage to preserve is subject to misinterpretation. An event might appear to be generated by the one before it, when the order is actually coincidental. Two occurrences may be linked even when widely separated by time and place.

My strategy of committing facts to cards allowed me to arrange and rearrange them, looking for the overall shape of a case. I was convinced a pattern would emerge, but I reminded myself that just because I *wished* a story were true didn't mean that it was. As my Aunt Gin used to say, "It's like the Singer sewing machine repairman said to the housewife, Kinsey. 'Wishing won't make it sew.'" I confess I didn't get the point until I was in third grade and realized that "sew" and "so" sounded the same but served different functions. More pertinent in my experience was another saying of hers: "Wish in one hand and shit in the other and see which fills up first." Sometimes a dog tag is just a dog tag, and two guys digging a hole are gathering worms in preparation for a fishing trip.


I devoted most of Thursday to other business. Despite my fascination with Mary Claire Fitzhugh, I had other work-related responsibilities. I'd been asked to comb public records for hidden assets in a nasty divorce. In that case, a husband was suspected of playing fast and loose with certain real property he claimed he'd never owned. I was also in the process of tracking down a witness to a hit-and-run accident and that required a lot of knocking on doors, so I was out of the office for most of the day. I stopped by at 4:00 and spent the next forty-five minutes transcribing my field notes to rough-draft reports. I'd been so caught up in work I hadn't noticed the message light blinking on my answering machine.

I punched Play.

Tasha said, "Hi, Kinsey. I'm down in Santa Teresa to meet with a client and I was wondering if you'd be available later this afternoon. I have something I think will interest you. It's roughly noon now, so I'm hoping I'll hear from you. I'll be staying at the Beachcomber on Cabana until tomorrow morning." She recited the number, which I ignored.

I went back to typing notes, but I'd lost my train of thought. I pressed Play and listened to the message again, this time jotting down the number at her hotel. She must have known me better than I thought, because nothing is more irresistible than veiled references to a topic of interest. I couldn't imagine what she was up to, but I was willing to give her the benefit of the doubt.

I dialed the number and the switchboard put me through to her room. She was out, but a very pleasant automated woman told me that the party I was calling was not available at this time. She invited me to leave a message at the tone and that's exactly what I did, saying, "Hi, Tasha. Kinsey here. I just got your message and I was hoping to catch you. I'm on my way home, but if you like, we could meet for a drink. Why don't you join me at Rosie's on Albanil, where we met before. The desk clerk can give you directions if you've forgotten where it is. The place still looks like a dive, so don't be put off. Five-thirty works for me if it works for you. Hope to see you soon."

I left the office at 5:00 and was home again at 5:10, stripping off my clothes as I scrambled up the stairs. For someone indifferent to her kin, it's amazing how hard I work at looking good in their eyes. Since I tend to deal with only one aunt or cousin at a time, I don't want reports going back to the clan that my boots are scuffed or my hair is sticking out in all directions, as is usually the case. I showered and shampooed. I even shaved the requisite legs and armpits just in case I fell in a swoon and one or the other was exposed to view. How did I know how the evening would proceed?

I stood in front of my closet, wrapped in a towel, staring at my clothes for one full minute, which was a long time, given that in ten minutes more I was expected to present myself fully dressed. I nixed the all-purpose dress. Though comfortable, the garment is looking a bit shopworn, which is not to say I won't be wearing it for years. I considered my tweed blazer, but if I remembered correctly, I was wearing that very blazer the last time Tasha and I met. I didn't want her to think I had only the one blazer, though that was close to the truth. I pictured Diana Sutton Alvarez. As much as I disliked her, she did dress with class. What was it about her? Black tights, I thought, and quickly rooted through my sock drawer until I came up with a pair. I put on clean choners and then shimmied into the black tights and added a skirt. The fabric was wool and the color was dark so I figured I couldn't go wrong there. I found my tassel loafers and then struggled to find a top. I put on a white blouse and discovered a button missing. I tucked my shirttail into the waistband of my skirt and then pulled on a hunter green crewneck sweater. The "ensemble" (which means: a bunch of clothes all worn at once) didn't look half bad, but it needed another touch. I looked around the bedroom. Ah. I'd been using a hand-knit wool scarf along the bottom of the door to the upstairs bath, keeping out the drafts that crept through the crack where there should have been a threshold. I snatched up the scarf, shook off a few woofies, and slung it around my neck. I checked my reflection in the full-length mirror. I was, as they say, a sight for sore eyes.

I grabbed my jacket, my shoulder bag, and my keys, and headed out the door.

By 5:27 I was comfortably ensconced in my favorite booth at Rosie's, my gaze pinned on the door while I feigned indifference. Rosie took one look at me and knew something was up. I wasn't sure whether it was my hair, still slicked down and damp, or the blusher and mascara I'd taken such care to apply. I could feel myself squirm under her scrutiny.

As she handed me a menu her penciled-on eyebrows went up. "You heving a date?"

"I'm meeting my cousin Tasha," I said, primly.

"A cousin? Well, that's heppy news. Is this the one you can't stand?"

"Rosie, if you say anything of the sort to her, I'll sock you in the mouth."

"Ooo, I'm loving when you talk tough."

I glanced up in time to see Tasha enter. She paused in the doorway to survey the room. I waved and she waved in return. She took a moment to peel off her coat and hang it on one of the wall-mounted hooks near the entrance. She retained the long scarf she'd worn under her coat collar and rearranged it over her sweater and skirt. She wore high heels and I wore flats. Aside from that, the similarities in our outfits were unsettling, as they were in most other aspects of our personal appearances.

I stood when she reached the table and we did that fake kissing thing, looking like a pair of budgies about to peck each other to death.

Rosie appeared to be transfixed, the same reaction she'd had on prior occasions when she'd seen Tasha and me. Her gaze shifted from my face to Tasha's.

I turned to her. "Rosie, this is my cousin Tasha. I believe the two of you met before."

"A cousin. And here, I'm thinking you was an orphing."

"Not quite. My parents died, but my mother had four sisters so I still have aunts and cousins in Lompoc."

"And a grandmother," Tasha put in.

"You hev a grandma?" Rosie said, feigning surprise. "Why you don't hev her down for visiting?"

"That's what *I've* been asking her," Tasha said, not wanting to pass up the chance to get under my skin. I refused to react. If I offered resistance the two of them would gang up and turn on me like chow dogs.

Rosie turned to Tasha. "I'm bringing you good wine. Not like your cousin drinks."

"Great. I'd appreciate that. The cuisine's Hungarian?"

Rosie nearly purred when she heard the word "cuisine," which she took as a compliment. "You know Hungarian dish what is carp in sour cream? Is special tonight. You be my guest." She turned to me. "I'm giving you some as well in honor of your friend. You lucky to have someone so close. My own sister Klotilde is died."

"I'm sorry to hear that," Tasha said.

"No big loss. She wus crabby to the end. I'm getting wine now. You sit and I'm bringing right beck."

"Looks like you've made a conquest," I remarked, as Rosie moved away. I took a seat again on my side of the booth and Tasha slid in across the table from me.

"She's adorable," she said.

"That's one word for it."

"She speaks English well. How long has she been in this country?"

"Sixty years, give or take."

We confined ourselves to chitchat until Rosie returned with the wine in a dusty bottle with an actual cork. For me, she's quick with a screw-top jug and wine so close to vinegar you could use it to clean windows. The wine she poured for Tasha was like drinking elixir from an orchard—soft, subtle, with a fragrance of apples, pears, and honey.

We let Rosie order for us, which she'd have done anyway. It was better to give her permission to be bossy and thus retain a modicum of control. She was otherwise a food dominatrix. The carp with sour cream turned out to be lovely. Maybe I'd have dinner here with Tasha more often.

As is the case every time we meet, I couldn't help making a secret study of her. She looks not the way I look, but the way I think I look when I'm at my best. We have the same square teeth, the same nose, though mine has suffered a few indignities where hers has survived in its original state. My eyes are hazel where hers are dark brown, but the shape is the same. I could tell she plucked her eyebrows, and I envied her both the skill and the courage. Sometimes I try, usually closing my eyes while doing so in hopes it won't hurt. Inevitably, I pull out the wrong hair, which makes my brows look patchy and incomplete. Then I have to use eyebrow pencil to fill in the blanks, which gives me the fierce demeanor of a Kabuki.

When we'd finished our meal and Rosie had removed the plates, Tasha reached into her tote and pulled out a bulky manila envelope. I expected her to hand it across the table to me, but she held it against her chest.

"I've been sorting and cataloging Grandfather Kinsey's papers for the historical preservation group that raised the money to move the house. Grand asked me to take charge because his files are so voluminous and so disorganized. She's never had the patience to tackle them herself. She wants me to put together a chronological account of the house—when it was built, the architect, the plans, and that sort of thing. Grandfather Kinsey kept *everything*—and I mean *everything*—so with a bit of digging I've been able to come up with summaries of his meetings with the builder, various construction proposals, invoices and receipts documenting the project from beginning to end. In the midst of it, I came across some letters that by rights belong to Grand. I haven't told her I found them, because there's no way to predict what she'd do with them. Destroy them, most likely. I thought you should see them first."

"Well, you've got my attention."

"I hope so," she said.

I held out my hand and took the envelope. While she watched, I unfolded the clasp, opened the package, and peered in. There were three or four sheets of letterhead stationery and a series of letters bound together with two thick rubber bands, old ones apparently, because both snapped when I tried removing them. I did a finger walk through the envelopes, some of which were addressed to me and some to Virginia Kinsey, my Aunt Gin. The postmarks were assorted dates in the latter half of 1955—the same year my parents were killed—starting in June and extending through the next two calendar years. One had been opened but the rest were still sealed. Across the front of each envelope there was either an emphatic "RETURN TO SENDER!! ADDRESSEE UNKNOWN!" in Aunt Gin's unmistakable bold printing or equally forceful messages delivered by way of post office rubber stamps with a purple-ink finger pointing accusingly at the return address. You'd think a federal crime had been committed from the savagery expressed.

I knew what I was looking at. In one of my last conversations with Tasha, we'd argued this very point. Her mother, my Aunt Susanna, had said that the day my parents were killed, they were traveling to Lompoc in hopes of a reconciliation with my grandparents. She claimed that after they died, Grand tried for years to establish contact with me and had finally given up. I'd assumed it was all bullshit, Aunt Susanna's attempt to put a better spin on the tale of my abandonment. Having never spoken to my grandmother, the gist of my quarrel with her was that she'd been content to let me languish, bereft of family solace and support, for the twenty-nine years following my parents' deaths. Aunt Gin's parenting, while adequate, had been curiously deficient in matters of warmth and affection. Her remoteness might well have been something she learned at her mother's knee, but whatever the origin, I was affected. She'd taught me many valuable lessons about life, most of which still serve me, but of comfort, closeness, and nurturing, there was little. The letters were proof Grand had made an effort that Aunt Gin had rebuffed.

I found myself without a word to say. I might have mustered a weak protest, but what would have been the point? I'd been wrong in my assumption. Grand wasn't to be faulted for neglect. Aunt Gin had refused her letters, thus cutting off communication. I cleared my throat. "I appreciate this."

"Go ahead and open them if you want."

"I'd prefer to be alone if it's all the same to you. Unless the letters turn out to be too personal or too painful, I'll be happy to make copies and get them back to you."

"Take your time."

"Will you tell Grand you found them?"

"I don't know yet. If you return the letters, I won't have much choice. The minute Grand sees the seals are broken, she'll know the secret's out, whatever it may be."

"And if I don't return them?"

"Let's put it this way, she's never going to ask. She might not even realize they were sitting in the files. Actually, there's something else that may prove more important."

I stared, unable to imagine what could trump the ace she'd laid on the table the moment before.

She took the envelope from my hand and pulled out a thin sheaf of letterhead stationery. She offered me the pages, which I read through rapidly. They were invoices submitted to Grand by a private investigator named Hale Brandenberg, with an office address in Lompoc. The information was sketchy—no reports attached—but a cursory look at his charges suggested he'd been in her employ for more than a year. He'd billed her four thousand bucks and change, not a trivial amount given his rates, which were low by today's standards.

Tasha said, "Grandfather Kinsey was still living when this was done, so she either browbeat him into paying for it or she did this behind his back. In any case, the work was done."

"I don't see any reference to what he was hired to do."

"It's possible the invoices became separated from his reports or maybe the reports were destroyed. Grand hates to lose and she hates being thwarted, so nothing of this was leaked to the rest of us. I believed Mom when she said Grand tried to make contact, but I was startled to see the proof. I have trouble believing she'd go so far as to hire an investigator, but there it is. I'm guessing when all those letters came flying back, Hale Brandenberg was the next logical step."

I said, "Well."

I thought she was on the verge of taking my hand, but she made no move. Instead, she watched me with a sympathy I chose to ignore. She said, "Look. I know this is hard for you. Once you've read the letters, you might end up feeling the same alienation, but at least you'll know more than you do now. If you're like me, you'd rather deal with hard facts than speculation and fantasy."

"That's been my claim," I said, with a pained smile.

"I'll leave you to it then." She turned and opened the handbag sitting on the seat beside her, looking for her wallet.

"I'll take care of it," I said.

She hesitated. "Are you sure?"

"Of course. You brought me a gift."

"Let's hope that's what it is."

"If not, you owe me a dinner."

# 21

## DEBORAH UNRUH

### May 1967

Deborah picked up Rain at preschool and dropped her off at a friend's house for a playdate. She had a couple of hours to kill and thought she'd give the kitchen and bathrooms a good scrub. This was midweek and she wanted to get meals planned for the next few days so she wouldn't have to think about it once Patrick got home. He reserved the weekends for the family, the three of them going off on outings of one sort or another. Deborah liked to have all the work done, leaving the time free to play.

She talked to Patrick three and four times a day, consulting about his business dealings and her household decisions, trading perspectives and advice. Rain stories charmed him, and Deborah tried to pass along the adorable moments as they occurred. Only another smitten parent would understand what constituted "cute" where a child was concerned. Rain was pretty and precocious, sweet-tempered, sunny. She wasn't perfect only in their eyes. Everybody else agreed she was remarkable, especially after Deborah and Patrick browbeat them into it.

As she turned from Via Juliana onto Alita Lane, she caught sight of a vehicle parked in the drive. It was Greg's yellow school bus, the paint job embellished by crude red, blue, and

green peace symbols and antiwar slogans. She pulled the station wagon over to the side of the road and sat for a moment,
engine running, thinking, *Shit!*

She tilted her forehead against the steering wheel, wondering if there was still time to escape. As long as they hadn't
spotted her, she could turn the car around, fetch Rain from her
playdate, check into a motel, and then let Patrick know where
they were. She and Annabelle had talked about this at length,
the possibility that the three of them would make another appearance one day. She'd been a complete wuss where Shelly
was concerned. Looking back, she couldn't believe she'd
allowed herself to be so mistreated. How had Shelly managed to intimidate her? Shelly was a pipsqueak, a twerp. She
was half Deborah's age. Deborah knew a hell of a lot more
about how the world worked than Shelly had ever dreamed.
If Deborah didn't face the girl now, she was only postponing
the inevitable.

She took a deep breath. She had to do this or she wouldn't
be able to live with herself. She certainly wouldn't be able to
face Annabelle, who'd given her strict instructions. Deborah
put her foot on the accelerator and pulled away from the berm,
then continued the few hundred feet to the house, where she
eased into the garage. She entered the house through the door
that opened into the kitchen. Of course, they'd let themselves
in. Greg knew where the key was hidden, and even if she and
Patrick had been clever enough to move it, he'd have found
his way in.

The house had been spotless when she left, less than an
hour before, but Greg and Shelly had made themselves at
home, unloading backpacks, sleeping bags, and duffels by the
door to the dining room. This was territorial marking, like a
dog pissing in each corner of the yard. She wasn't sure why
they hadn't left their stuff in the bus . . . unless they anticipated
being houseguests. Oh lord, she thought.

She called, "Greg?"

"Yo!"

She crossed the kitchen and looked into the den where the
three of them were sprawled, almost unrecognizable. They
looked like ruffians, people who'd wandered in off the street.
Greg had a scraggly beard and mustache. Patrick had never

been able to grow convincing facial hair and usually ended up looking like someone on a Wanted poster. Greg had inherited the same sparse fuzz. He'd let his hair grow long, dark and frizzy and unkempt. She wondered if he knew how unattractive he looked. Or maybe that was the point.

Shelly was sitting on the floor, leaning against the couch with her bare feet out in front of her while she smoked a cigarette, using one of Deborah's Limoges saucers for an ashtray. She wore the familiar black turtleneck, torn black tights, and a long skirt. She'd kicked off her Birkenstocks and those lay in the middle of the room. Her earrings were big silver hoops. In the tangled mass of dark hair, she now sported a series of small braids with beads woven into the ends. She was no longer the petite, thin creature she'd been. She had an earthy air about her, the residual weight of two pregnancies having caught up with her.

Most alarming was the boy, Shawn, who was ten years old now, according to Deborah's calculations. His dark hair was shaggy, worn long enough to brush his shoulders. His cheeks were so gaunt he looked like a young Abraham Lincoln. He had Shelly's huge hazel eyes set in darkly smudged sockets, which gave his face the solemnity of a lemur's. He was tall for his age, and very thin. His flannel shirt was pale from wear or too many runs through the washing machine. The cuffs rode above his wrists. His hands were thin and his fingers were long and delicate. His pants hung on him.

He'd found a spot in one corner of the room and he had his nose buried in a copy of Frank Herbert's *Dune*. Deborah had read it two years before, when it first came out, and she was surprised that his skills were so proficient. Maybe Shelly's homeschooling hadn't been so bad after all. It was possible he was only hiding in the pages, pretending to read so he could observe what was going on without having to participate. He glanced at her once and then went back to his book. She wondered how much he remembered of her hostility toward him when he was a child of six. She'd eventually seen him in a kinder light, but her early disapproval had been savage and must have wounded him. She was ashamed that she'd blamed him for his behavior when Shelly was the one who should have been held accountable.

Greg crossed the room and gave her a bear hug. "Good to see you," he said. "We were on our way south and thought we'd stop by. I hope you don't mind." He was treating their arrival as a common occurrence, like they popped in every week.

When Deborah put her arms around him, tentatively returning his embrace, she could feel his rib cage through the fabric of his shirt. She held herself stiffly, unaccustomed to the display of affection. She didn't reciprocate his feelings, or what he pretended to feel.

He stepped back. "Whoa. What's this? Are you mad about something?"

"You took me by surprise. I would have appreciated a call," she said. She could have kicked herself for the stupidity of the comment. This was like coming face-to-face with home invaders, making nice in hopes they wouldn't slaughter you where you stood.

Shelly snorted. "Yeah, sorry about that. Like we have a phone on the bus." She hadn't said "a fucking phone," but the expletive was buried in her tone.

Deborah ignored her, addressing her attentions to Greg. "When did you get in?"

"Fifteen, twenty minutes ago. Long enough to use the bathroom and take a look at what you've done. New paper and paint. The place looks great."

"Thank you. I'm sorry I wasn't here when you arrived."

"We figured you were out running errands. Anyway, we needed time to cool it after being on the road."

"Can I fix you something to eat?"

Shelly said, "Don't bother. We already looked in the fridge. What a waste."

"I'm sure I have something. I went to the store yesterday and stocked up for the weekend. What were you thinking of?"

"Nothing that involves cruelty to animals," Shelly said.

Greg said, "We're vegans. No meat, no dairy, no eggs, no animal products of any kind."

"In that case, I guess you'll have to have your meals somewhere else. I don't know the first thing about vegan cooking."

Shelly sounded put-upon. "We don't have the money to eat out. We used all our cash to pay for the trip."

Greg said, "We left San Francisco this morning and drove straight through."

"Ah. Is that where you've been? We had no idea you were so close."

Shelly said, "Something else while we're on the subject." She pointed at Greg, then Shawn, and then herself. "He's Creed, he's Sky Dancer, and I'm Destiny."

Deborah lowered her gaze, keeping her expression neutral. She couldn't wait to tell Annabelle, who'd howl with laughter. "I see. Since when?"

"Since we realized our birth names were completely meaningless. We each chose a name that represents the future, like a higher calling. Our vision of ourselves."

" 'Destiny.' I'll make an effort to remember."

Greg said, "Don't worry if you forget. Everybody goofs at first."

"I can well imagine," Deborah said. "I'll see if I can round up some towels for you. I assume you'll be sleeping in the bus."

Greg said, "Sure, if that's what you want."

From the way he'd phrased his reply, she knew he was waiting for her to offer them the guest rooms, with assurances they were welcome for as long as they liked. Their insistence on living like vagabonds must have lost its appeal. Nothing like clean sheets and flush toilets, especially when someone else is doing all the work. Shelly was giving her the hard stare she'd used so often before. Deborah felt a certain stubbornness take hold. She didn't intend to let Shelly take advantage of her hospitality.

"We don't want to put you to any trouble," Greg added. "I mean, you might be using the guest rooms for something else these days."

"No, not really. You probably saw for yourselves if you had a look around."

"Yeah, that's right. It's just the way you said that about our sleeping in the bus—"

"Creed," Shelly said. "It's obvious she doesn't care to play hostess, which is her prerogative."

Greg looked at his mother. "Is that true? You don't even want us in the *house*?"

"It's entirely up to you," she said. She knew full well they wouldn't take her up on it. She and Shelly were in a power play. Shelly couldn't ask for anything. She only won if she could outmaneuver Deborah, who was supposed to extend herself of her own accord, graciously bestowing favors on her guests to save them the discomfort of making their wishes known.

Now it was Greg's turn to look pained. "Man, this is like a major bummer. We didn't mean to intrude. We thought you'd be pleased to see us. I guess not, huh?"

"Creed, dear," Deborah said carefully, nearly tripping on the name. "You and Destiny left four years ago without so much as a by-your-leave. We had no idea where you'd gone or what your intentions were. I don't think you should expect to be welcomed back with open arms. That's not how these things work."

"Sorry we didn't keep you informed about our busy lives," Shelly said.

Deborah turned on her in a flash. "I'm not going to put up with any shit from you so you can knock that off."

Shelly shut her mouth, but she made a comic face, eyes getting wide, mouth pulled down in mock surprise. Like, *Lah-di-dah, the nerve. Did you hear what she just said?*

Greg made a gesture, indicating that he'd take care of it.

At least he was starting to stand up to her, Deborah thought. Watching them, she felt like she'd developed X-ray vision. She could see all the little nuances in their communication, the ploys, the dodges, the way they tried using emotion to throw her off balance. This was like the children's game of hot potato, where the object was to leave the other guy holding the bag.

Greg said, "So where's Rain? Shawn's been looking forward to seeing her."

"I'm picking her up at three. How long did you plan to stay?"

"Couple of days. Depends. You know, we haven't decided yet."

Shelly cupped a hand to her mouth, like she was making an aside that no one else could hear. "Notice how she's ducking the subject of Rain," she said to Greg.

Deborah kept her voice in a singsong range, as though speaking to a child. "Well, Shelly—oh, *excuse* me. I meant Destiny. What is there to say? We didn't think you were interested in Rain. There was never a letter or a phone call and not a penny of support for her. The child is ours now."

"What, like you gave birth to her? News to me."

Deborah didn't think it was possible to loathe another human being more than she'd loathed Shelly in the past, but apparently, there were untapped reservoirs of hostility that Deborah could call upon at will. "We adopted her. We went through the court system. Your parental rights were terminated. That's what they do when parents abandon a baby at the age of five days."

Shelly said, "Fuck you, bitch. I'm not putting up with any shit from you either!" She got up, agitated, and snatched up her shawl. "Come on, Sky Dancer." And to Greg, "We'll be in the bus when you get done kissing butt. Jesus, what a mama's boy."

Greg made his excuses shortly afterward. There was no graceful way to exit the conversation. He went out to the bus, and Deborah went upstairs to the master bedroom and called Patrick, who said he'd drive up for the night, but he'd have to return to L.A. first thing the next morning. "Keep away from them if you can," he said. "I'll take care of it when I get home."

"That might not be necessary. Now that Shelly—oh, excuse me, Destiny—has worked herself into such a state of righteous indignation, they may take off of their own volition."

But such was not the case. Deborah picked up Rain from her playdate, half expecting the yellow school bus to be gone on her return. Instead it was parked where it had been, which seemed curious in itself. Flouncing off in a huff was a typical Shelly move, meant to alert you to her displeasure. Emotional one-upsmanship.

Shawn knocked on the back door soon after Deborah and Rain got home.

"Is Rain here?" he asked.

"Of course." Deborah let him into the kitchen. He stood by the door, not quite sure what to do with himself. It was almost as though he held a hat in his hands, turning the rim while he waited for what came next. Deborah said, "Did your dad send you?"

"Greg's not my dad."

"Sorry."

"He and my mom are asleep."

"I see. Well, why don't you have a seat? Rain went up to her room. I'll tell her you're here. She'll enjoy the company."

Shawn perched on the edge of a kitchen chair. His tennis shoes were ill-fitting and he wore no socks. Deborah wanted to weep at the sight of his ankles, which looked as frail as a fawn's.

She said, "I'm happy to see you, Shawn. I mean that."

She didn't wait for a reply. She went upstairs to Rain's room and told her she had company. "His name is Shawn. His mother calls him Sky Dancer and it would be polite if you did, too."

She took Rain by the hand and the two went downstairs. Shawn was actually Rain's half brother, but Deborah thought the concept would be confusing to a four-year-old.

Shawn got up from his chair when Rain entered the room. She stood there looking at him and he looked at her. There was an unmistakable resemblance between them. Both had Shelly's dark hair and big hazel eyes. Rain's hair fell into natural ringlets, and she was rosy with good health, where Shawn looked like a prisoner of war.

Shawn said, "You want to read stories?"

"I can't read."

"I couldn't either when I was your age. What about the alphabet song? You know that?"

She nodded.

"You feel like singing it?"

"Okay." Without any self-consciousness at all, Rain sang the alphabet song, bungling the order of the letters but otherwise presenting herself earnestly.

When she finished, Shawn said, "Wow. That was good. If you don't know how to read yet, I could read to you."

Deborah said, "Her books are in the chest under the window in the den. That's sweet of you, Shawn. She loves having someone read to her."

The two disappeared, and after a moment she could hear

Shawn reading aloud to her. She peered at them through the crack in the open door, keeping herself out of sight. Rain had climbed up on his lap, leaning her head back against his chest in the same way she did with Patrick. Later she found them stretched out on the floor, with Shawn looking on while Rain formed her letters with a fat red pencil. "B goes the other way," he was saying. "Here, let me show you."

"I can do it!"

"Okay. Let me see you, then."

When Patrick got home Deborah told him what had transpired since she'd spoken to him by phone. "Creed" and "Destiny" (whose names she always said as though surrounded by quotes) had spent the afternoon in the bus. Rain had talked Shawn into a game of Chutes and Ladders. His patience seemed infinite. Meanwhile, Deborah was at a loss. The dinner hour was coming up and Creed and Destiny had shown no signs of entering the house or moving on. She'd been tempted to make something for Shawn, but the idea of no meat, no dairy, and no eggs left precious little.

Patrick said, "What do you think they're up to?"

"I'm sure we'll find out. Maybe they've given up life on the road and they're ready to move in with us."

Rain came into the kitchen with Shawn close behind. "We're hungry."

"Well, we'll have to take care of that," Deborah said. "Shawn, this is Patrick. You remember him?"

Patrick reached over and shook Shawn's hand. "Hey, Shawn. It's been a while. Nice seeing you again. I understand you like to be called Sky Dancer."

"Sometimes."

"We'd be happy to have you join us for supper, but Deborah's stumped about what to fix for the two of you."

"Pasta with olive oil is good. Or tomato sauce," Shawn said. "And salad. I eat lots of vegetables and fruit."

"Well, I'm sure we can rustle up something. Thanks for the suggestions."

Deborah made enough supper for Creed and Destiny as well. She knew she was allowing hospitality to take precedence over hostility, but she couldn't help herself. People had to eat. This wasn't a third-world country where starvation was the rule. She sent Shawn out to tell his parents there was food on the table if they were interested. Creed and Destiny appeared, looking as though they'd showered in the interim. Nothing was said about the earlier friction. The six of them sat down to eat, keeping the conversation superficial, which was easier than she'd expected. Aside from dogma, the pair knew little about the world and seemed to care even less.

Deborah noticed Greg making a covert study of his daughter, and once she saw him offer her a tentative smile. Shelly was chilly throughout the meal. She had no interest in Rain and made a point of giving Greg a warning look when she caught him starting to clown around with her. After that he avoided any show of warmth. Fortunately, by then Rain was so enamored of Shawn that she paid no attention to either one.

It was after supper, when Rain had been put to bed and Shawn relegated to the bus, that Creed and Destiny got down to business. Given their agenda, it wasn't hard to understand why the two had been so patient to this point. Creed explained the project they had in mind. "We saved up a thousand dollars as a down payment on a farm. We'd been thinking about it for a long time before we heard about this place. The problem is, we need to have the rest of the money by the end of the month."

Patrick said, "A farm. Well, I guess that's one way to make a living. I didn't know you were interested in farming. You know much about it?"

"Not right now, but I can learn. That's the whole point, you know, working the land."

"And where is this place?"

"Up the coast. Close to Salinas," Greg said.

Deborah was sitting there wondering if there was a word of truth in anything he'd said.

"Actually, we're setting up a commune," Shelly said. "Anyone who joins us will share whatever money they have and we'll divvy up the chores. We'll share everything equally. Even child care."

Patrick nodded. "How many acres are you buying?"

"Maybe a hundred?" Greg said.

"Mind if I take a look at the contract?" Patrick appeared to be taking them seriously, but Deborah knew it was his way of pointing out how ill prepared and ill informed they were.

"We don't have a contract. This is like a gentlemen's agreement. We did it on a handshake. We know the guy and he's really supportive of our idea."

"Good. I like the sound of it. What do you intend to grow?"

"Mostly vegetables. We'll plant enough to live on and then put stuff by. We plan to do a lot of canning and we'll sell or trade the produce we can't use. We might put in wheat or corn or something like that if we want to turn a profit. I mean, we don't want to turn a profit per se, but we want to be self-sustaining. We've visited a couple of communes in Big Sur and they're keen. They even said they'd help."

"Well," Patrick said. "That's a hell of an idea. You have my blessing if that's what this is about. I wish I had advice to offer you, but farming's not my bailiwick."

Greg was grooming his facial hair. He'd taken to spinning strands of his scruffy beard between his fingers, making little upturns like the villain of the piece. "We were thinking about the money Granddad left me. Didn't you talk about that once?"

"Sure. Forty thousand dollars, but it's all in trust. The money won't be available until you turn thirty. I thought I'd made that clear."

Greg frowned, baffled by the very idea. "Why? That's five years from now."

Deborah got the impression they were getting to the heart of the matter. Greg had a point of view he was prepared to argue if he could work his way around to it.

Patiently, Patrick said, "Those were the terms of the will. If you'll remember he gave you ten thousand dollars when you were eighteen."

"And that was part of the forty?"

"No, no. He was curious what you'd do with it. If it's any comfort, he did the same thing with me and I went through mine about as fast as you did."

"What, that was like a test or something?"

"That's precisely what it was. Your grandfather was a

bit of a pissant. This was his method of teaching money management."

"That's not what he told me. He said the money was mine and I could do anything I wanted."

"He didn't want to influence your process. If you made a mistake or turned out to be a financial whiz, he wanted it to come from you. Do you remember what you did with it?"

"Some of it, sure. I went to Oregon to see my friend Rick, and ended up lending him a few hundred dollars because the transmission on his truck went out."

"He pay you back?"

"Not so far, but he said he would. And I mean, you know, I trust the guy. He's a good dude."

"You also bought a Harley, if I remember correctly."

"Well, yeah, a used one. And I paid off some credit cards."

"That was smart. I remember the credit card companies were really on your case by then."

"I don't know what *their* deal was. If they were going to be such butts about it, why offer me a card in the first place?"

Destiny said, "Creed, would you wise up? Your dad's a shit-ass. He has no intention of giving you forty thousand dollars. Don't you get that?"

"I'm not asking him to *give* it to me. This would be like an advance."

"Yeah, well he's not going to do that either. God, you are so dense sometimes. This is all bullshit. He's having a big laugh at your expense. He thinks you're an idiot when it comes to money. He won't give you a dime."

"That's not what he said. Anyway, this is between him and me, okay?"

Destiny got up, ignoring Patrick and Deborah. "You're pathetic. You know that?"

She banged the back door as she left.

Patrick said, "You found a charmer in that one."

"We could really use some help," Greg said, not looking at his father.

"I don't doubt it, but you'll have to come up with something better than this business about a farm, Greg. I'm willing to listen, but you know me well enough to know that's never going to fly. You don't even have a business plan."

"What? Like I'm supposed to petition my own dad for a break?"

Patrick said, "Do you have any idea how much farm equipment costs? You want to farm, you better know how much water you have available and what soil conditions are—"

"Would you quit with this shit? All I want is what's mine. Granddad left me forty grand and you know he did so what's the big deal? It's not coming out of your pocket."

"You'll get the money when you turn thirty, at which point you can piss it all away."

"You just can't let go, can you? It's all rules and regulations and shit-ass stuff that nobody cares about."

"Say anything you like, son. The money's in trust. There's nothing I can do."

Greg got up. "Skip it. I'm sorry I brought it up."


Thursday morning, Patrick left after breakfast, saying he'd be back late Friday afternoon. Greg stuck his head in the door after Patrick took off, saying, "Mind if we borrow the Buick? We're going to do a little driving tour so Destiny can see the town, and then we may bomb up the coast to Calida. Destiny's never been there, but I was telling her how cool it was."

Deborah jumped at the chance to have them gone, even for a short time. "That's fine. I just filled the tank with gas. The keys are on the hook by the back door," she said. "What about Sky Dancer?"

"He doesn't want to come so we're leaving him here."

"Would you object to his coming with Rain and me? She has her swimming lesson this morning."

"He doesn't need babysitting. He's fine on his own."

"I thought he might enjoy being out and about."

"Sure, whatever. I doubt he'll do it, but why not? If we're back late, don't worry about it. He doesn't like to be fussed over. He can take care of himself."

"What time does he go to bed?"

"He's a night owl. He gets hyper. It'll be one A.M. before he falls asleep."

"I see," she said, and then hesitated. "You know, it wouldn't hurt you to get to know your daughter. She's an adorable little girl. In many ways, she reminds me of you."

"Yeah, well, Shelly's kind of touchy on the subject."

Deborah bit back a remark. She was sick to death of his catering to the woman. "Fine. I just thought I'd mention it."

Deborah waited until she saw Greg and Shelly pull away and then she went out to the bus. The day was overcast and inside there was hardly enough light to see by. She knocked on the folding front door and Shawn opened it. He wore a T-shirt and a pair of ragged cutoffs. He'd been lying on his futon, his flat pillow rolled up to support his neck. On the floor around his bed there were piles of dirty clothes.

"Would you like to come inside where the light's better?"

"Did Mom say it was okay?"

"Greg did."

"You mean Creed."

"That's right. Creed. I keep forgetting. You might round up a jacket while you're at it."

Shawn picked his way toward the back of the bus, lifting up garments in search of his jacket. Deborah removed the dead pillow from its case and stuffed dirty clothes into it until it bulged. Shawn came back, pulling on a sweatshirt of Greg's that hung to his knees.

"I thought we'd give this a quick wash," Deborah said of the pillow-case full of dirty clothes. "I can show you how to use the washer and dryer."

"My mom showed me once at the laundromat."

"Ours might be different. It won't hurt to take a look."

Shawn pulled on his tennis shoes and followed her.

Deborah loaded his clothes and showed him how to operate the washer. As soon as the cycle was under way she said, "I'm taking Rain for her swimming lesson this morning at the Y. Would you like to come along? You and I can paddle around in the pool."

"I don't have a suit."

"I can stop at a store and pick one up. You probably need a new toothbrush, too. You know how to swim?"

"Not really."

"Well, we can practice."

While Rain had her lesson with six other little kids on the

far side of the pool, Deborah and Shawn sat with their legs dangling in the water. In his bathing suit he looked younger than ten, more like a seven-year-old, with his bony shoulders and his collarbones exposed. He was afraid of the water, though he pretended he really wasn't interested. When Rain joined them half an hour later, they persuaded him to get into the shallow end with them. Rain had a set of weighted rings that Deborah dropped into the water, one by one. Rain would upend herself like a duck, kicking to the bottom to retrieve them. Shawn didn't want to get his face wet, but Rain made the game look like fun and at the end of an hour, he would at least hold his nose and sink to the bottom briefly. He and Rain would look at each other underwater and blow the air out of their mouths before they shot to the surface.

After they'd showered and dressed again, Deborah ushered them into the station wagon. "On swim days, we have a late lunch at McDonald's and then we skip dinner unless we decide to have popcorn," she said.

"That's a hamburger stand."

"Yes, but they have other things as well. I can get you lettuce and tomato on a bun. It'll be fine."

Once at McDonald's, she told Rain and Shawn to secure a booth while she ordered their lunch. She came back to the table with their order number and sent the two off to get paper napkins, salt, mustard, and ketchup in small packets. When their number was called, Deborah went back to the counter and picked up their food, which was piled on a plastic tray. She brought a glass of ice water for Shawn and a large chocolate milkshake that she and Rain would share. She doled out a paper-wrapped sandwich for each and put a large container of fries in the middle of the table where everyone could reach them.

Shawn opened his sandwich. In addition to the lettuce and tomato there was a meat patty with cheese melted on top. He put his hands in his lap and looked at her.

"Do you see lettuce and tomato?"

"Yes."

"You want condiments? You're allowed to eat mustard and ketchup, aren't you?"

"Sure."

Rain was munching on her burger, dipping fries in a puddle of ketchup and eating them rapidly. Deborah bit into her cheeseburger, and a moment later Shawn picked up his and took a hesitant bite. Neither of them said a word, and she kept her attention focused elsewhere. The next time she looked, Shawn had devoured his lunch.

"That was quick. You want another one?"

He nodded.

She ordered him a second cheeseburger, and when that was ready she brought it to the table, passing him an extra straw so he could help with the milkshake, which she said she and Rain couldn't finish without help.

After they got back to the house, she moved Shawn's clothes into the dryer. Later the two of them folded his clean clothes and made a neat pile of them. Then he and Rain read stories and worked on her printing skills. For supper they had a huge bowl of popcorn, corn being a vegetable, as Deborah pointed out. She made sure they bypassed the television set, and played board games until Rain's bedtime at 8:00.

Deborah asked Shawn if he wanted to sleep on the couch. She had a knitting project she was working on and said she'd work in the next room.

The idea made him anxious. "I better not. Mom and Creed might come back and wonder where I am."

"We can leave them a note," she said. "That way they won't wake you up when they get in. With Patrick gone, I could use the company. I don't know about you, but I sometimes get scared on my own."

"Okay."

She let Shawn write two notes and he went off to brush his teeth while she taped one to the back window of the bus and slipped the second into the front bifold door. She settled him on the couch under a big puffy quilt and a spare pillow she told him he could keep. Then she sat in the den with her knitting, leaving the door open between the two rooms so the light would slant in.

At 9:00 he called, "Deborah?"

"I'm here."

"Do you think my mom will get mad about what I ate?"

"I don't see why she would. You had lettuce and tomato on

a bun with a glass of ice water on the side. We won't mention anything else, okay?"

"Okay."

And after a few minutes, "Deborah?"

"Yes?"

"You know what?"

"What, Shawn?"

"This has been the best day of my life."

"Mine, too, sweetheart," she said. Her eyes filled and the knitting blurred in her lap. She had to put a finger on her lips to maintain silence while she blinked back tears.

# 22

**Thursday night, April 14, 1988**

I let myself into my studio at 7:00, the manila envelope full of letters tucked under one arm. I tossed the package on the desk and then went and poured myself a glass of wine. I confess I was looking to alcohol to bolster my courage. This might have been the first step on the road to a drunken downfall, but I doubted it. Twice I picked up the envelope and turned it over in my hand. I was reminded of that old question that comes up occasionally at a cocktail party: if you knew that in your top dresser drawer there was a piece of paper on which was written the date and time of your death, would you peek?

I've never known the right answer. There probably isn't one, but the dilemma is whether you'd opt for total ignorance or for information that might affect the rest of your life (however short it might be). Since all of the letters had been returned, it was clear Aunt Gin had rejected Grand's peace offering—if, indeed, that's what it was. Maybe the messages were Grand's berating of Aunt Gin for failings real and imagined, impossible to know unless I sat down and read them. I hesitated for the following reasons:

1. It was bedtime and I didn't want to spend the next six hours stewing about the past. Once I climbed on my emotional carousel, especially in the dark of night, I'd circle for hours,

up and down, around and around, often at speeds that threatened to make me sick.

2. Once I knew the content of the letters, I'd be stuck. In my current state of innocence, anything was possible. I could cling to my long-held beliefs about Grand's indifference without the pesky contradiction of the truth. What if the letters were filled with hearts and flowers and gushing sentiment? Then what? At this point, I wasn't prepared to lay down my sword or my shield. My defensive stance felt like power. Surrender would be foolish until I understood the nature and strength of the enemy.

I went to bed and slept like a baby.

In the morning, I went through my normal routine—the run, the shower, clothes, a cup of coffee with a bowl of cereal. I picked up my shoulder bag and the packet of letters and drove to the office, where I made yet another pot of coffee and settled at my desk. This was an environment where I felt safe, the arena in which I experienced my competence. What better setting in which to risk personal peace?

Before launching myself into uncharted territory, I made one more quick evasive move. I called Deborah, asking if Rain would be willing to meet with me. She put Rain on the line and after a brief discussion, we agreed to get together Saturday morning at a coffee shop on Cabana Boulevard, in walking distance of my studio. The place was a favorite of hers and she'd been looking forward to having breakfast there while she was in town.

I made a note on my calendar. That done, I got down to business. I divided the letters into two piles. In the first I placed those addressed to Virginia Kinsey; in the second, those addressed to me. I began with Aunt Gin's. The earliest was postmarked June 2, 1955, three days after the accident in which my parents died. A quick examination suggested that this was the only letter she'd opened before sealing it up again and sending it back.

*Dearest Virginia,*
   *We write you with heavy spirits, our hearts burdened with sorrow as we know yours must be. The loss of Rita Cynthia is more than any of us should have to bear, but*

*I know we must push forward for little Kinsey's sake. We were heartened by news that the doctors had examined her and found her unharmed. I spoke to the pediatrician, Dr. Grill, and he suggests that given the trauma she's suffered, we'll want to have her reevaluated in a month or so, pending her response in the aftermath of the accident. Children mend so much more quickly than adults do under the same circumstances. Dr. Grill cautioned that her physical recovery and her psychological well-being might be at odds. While the child might give every appearance of having adjusted, an underlying depression could well manifest itself as she begins to realize the finality of her parents' passing. He urged us all to be alert to the possibility.*

*We were disappointed that we weren't allowed to see her during her overnight stay in the hospital here. Of course, she was under observation and I'm sure the doctors were busy seeing to her care. We would not have disturbed her for the world and I thought I'd made that clear. Our only desire was to peep into the room so that we could see with our own eyes that her condition was stable. We had hoped she might spend time with us, but we perfectly understand your desire to take her straight home to all that is known and familiar. At the same time, Burton and I are praying to visit the child as soon as possible so we can personally offer the comfort and support she so desperately needs. If there's anything we can do for you, in terms of emotional or financial relief, please let us know. We stand ready with our arms open to you both.*

*On another note, we would love to sit down together and discuss Kinsey's future. We believe it would be in the child's best interests to be settled here with us. Burton and I are putting together a proposal that should satisfactorily address both your needs and ours. We look forward to an account of Kinsey's progress.*

*Your loving mother, Grand*

I closed my eyes, marveling at the sentiments expressed. Did Cornelia Straith LaGrand know nothing about her two

oldest daughters? I couldn't be sure, but I suspected my
mother would have reacted badly if she'd received such a letter. Virginia, younger by a year, was doubtless incensed. The
Aunt Gin I'd known growing up, was volatile, opinionated,
and fearless in the face of authority. She'd have been livid
at Grand's barely disguised attempts to gain the upper hand.
The pointed omission of my father's name must have infuri-
ated Virginia further. Grand's reference to "a proposal" would
have been especially offensive, as though my future were
subject to a carefully constructed business plan that Aunt Gin
would warm to as soon as she understood its many virtues and
advantages.

I returned that letter to its envelope and took up the next in
date order, postmarked June 13, 1955.

*Dearest Virginia,*

*My letter of June 2, 1955, was inadvertently returned
to me. Perhaps the address I have is incorrect. If so,
I'm hoping the post office will forward the address correction. In the meantime, I'm sure you're doing everything possible to assist little Kinsey during her recovery
from recent tragic events. Given your own deep sorrow
for your sister's passing, you must be under a strain
as well. I'm hoping both you and Kinsey are bearing
up under your sorrow as best you can. Burton and I
are hard-pressed to know where to begin the process of
putting all our lives back together. It would do us such
good if you could see your way clear to having Kinsey
spend a few days with us.*

*I called your workplace and was told you were un-
available, so it's possible you've taken a brief leave of
absence. If there's any way we can help tide you over,
please accept the modest sum I'm enclosing by check.
We are willing to supply anything else you need in the
way of aid in this heartbreaking transitional period. We
want only what's best for you and the child.*

*We hope you've been giving serious thought to our
previous suggestion about Kinsey's living with us. We
have the stability essential to a child in her position,
unsettled by the sudden loss of those so dear to her . . .*

The check she'd enclosed was written for twenty-five dollars. There was no sign of the proposal she'd mentioned, so maybe Grand had reconsidered the wisdom of tendering the plan.

The next two letters were variations on a theme, offers of comfort, solace, and cash in just about that order, with the continuing suggestion that "little Kinsey" would benefit from their generosity and long experience with young children. I started skimming, picking up a paragraph here and there to see if the tone or content changed over time.

In a letter from Grand dated August 8, 1955, she began to pick away at Aunt Gin's lifestyle. The school year was rapidly approaching, and Grand probably wanted me settled with her in Lompoc so I could be properly enrolled. Since the envelopes were still sealed and being returned to Grand as soon as they arrived, she knew her good counsel was falling on deaf ears. This forced her to operate in the dark, without feedback of any kind, spurring new efforts on her part to break down Virginia's resistance, which was steely to say the least.

> Given your limited resources and your lack of experience with child rearing, we feel we have more to offer Kinsey. Perhaps by now you've come to understand the impossibility of raising a child alone. We feel our position has merit, and while the idea might not seem tenable to you at first, we beg you to keep an open mind. Whatever our differences, I'm sure we're united in our desire to do what's best for her. We feel we can provide her a loving family, good schooling, and the best prospects possible on her journey to adulthood. Of course, Burton and I would want you to remain a constant in Kinsey's life, and we assure you we'd make every effort to nurture and protect the bond you have with her.
>
> Granted, there were difficulties between us these past few years. I don't know that either of us could trace the short sad history of our disagreements. Suffice to say, in light of Rita Cynthia's passing, all such conflicts should be set aside so that we may act in concert. We're hoping to avoid giving Kinsey the impression we're engaged in a tug-of-war. She should not be put in the middle of this

*discussion—that could only leave her feeling torn and
confused. We'd appreciate the opportunity to present
her with options without prejudice or undue influence.
Since you've been in her life, her natural inclination
might be to cling to what's familiar, but working together we can demonstrate the many advantages that
await her.*

The irony wasn't lost on me. Here all these years I'd re-
sented Grand's apathy when, in fact, she'd been doing her ut-
most to pull me into her orbit. My wants, needs, and desires
were scarcely mentioned except to suggest that she could serve
me better than Aunt Gin. Two letters later, she was saying,

*You've always valued your career goals and your inde-
pendence, issues that would be strongly curtailed by the
rigors of parenting. Given your full-time employment,
Kinsey would, of necessity, be relegated to day care,
which we can't help but think would be disastrous in
light of her losses . . .*

I set the rest aside and turned to the small bundle of letters
addressed to me.

*Dearest One,*
  *How are you today? I bet you can't guess who sent
you this letter. I don't believe you know how to read yet,
so I'm hoping your Aunt Virginia will do me the incredible honor of making my thoughts known to you.*
  *I hope you haven't forgotten your Grandfather
Kinsey and me. We love you so very very much. You
may not remember, but the last time I saw you, you were
three years old and we took you to the circus. You had
a wonderful time watching the clowns and the trained
animals. I promised you another visit and now I'm hoping your Aunt Virginia will make this possible.*
  *You might wonder what you would do in this big
house of ours. We've set aside a special bedroom for
you with lots of toys and books. We can paint it any
color you like. Pink or blue or yellow. Which do you*

*prefer? We have an orchard with some trees that grow big red apples and some that grow oranges. In front of the house, there's a big oak with a tire swing, and there are grassy fields where you can run to your heart's content. And guess what else? We have two Shetland ponies and a nanny goat named Joan, who might have babies soon. A baby goat is called a kid. Have you ever seen one? Your cousins are begging you to come so you can all bake cookies in our big kitchen. If you tell us your favorite kind, you can have a dozen and one! I was going to keep this a secret, but I can't resist . . . we have a new puppy! His name is Skippy and he says "woof, woof," which means please come to see us.*

The rest of Grand's letters to me were the same saccharine and simple-hearted tomes, addressed to an imaginary child, as she knew nothing about me. I could hardly fault her for that. It had been years since her mothering had been called upon. She might have done a bang-up job raising five daughters when the role was hers. Here she was, working to insinuate herself into my life while Aunt Gin blocked her every move.

I had to admit Grand's question about child care was legitimate. I hadn't thought about the fact that Aunt Gin, working full-time, would have had to find someone to watch me during the day. I was certain she'd done no such thing. My memory of those early days is sketchy at best, but I would have shrunk in horror if I'd been left in the hands of anyone else. Aunt Gin was my anchor. The death of my parents was probably what triggered the overwhelming sense of timidity with which I lived all through my school days. If Aunt Gin had tried handing me off I'd have set up such an unrelenting howl she wouldn't have tried it again. I knew she hadn't asked for time away from her job, as Grand had suggested. From early June until September, she took me into work with her. Virginia Kinsey was high-energy, a tireless worker, with no patience at all for slackers. She'd been with California Fidelity Insurance since she was nineteen years old, probably without having taken a sick day or a vacation day, both of which she considered a form of self-indulgence.

When I started school that fall, she dropped me off in the

morning and then picked me up at twelve-thirty, when she'd usher me into the office with her. I had a little table and chair on one side of her desk, and I would amuse myself with picture books, coloring books, and other quiet pursuits. I wondered how California Fidelity Insurance felt about having a child underfoot. By the time I went to work for the company myself, investigating arson and wrongful-death claims, there was a child-care facility on the ground floor of the building, where parents could drop off their children on their way to work.

I felt the penny drop. Virginia Kinsey had done that. When she assumed the role of faux mother, it was the '50s and I was sure CFI had no provision for child care and no interest in initiating such a program. The idea of children on the work premises was years in the future, but she was a force to contend with. It would have been exactly like her to compel the company to bend to her wishes, allowing me to spend half-days with her. CFI would have jumped for joy at the chance to do as she required. Unless they capitulated, they'd have never heard the end of it. My guess was that once she established the precedent, other employees with youngsters leapt at the opportunity to have their little ones close at hand. The company must have balked at providing trained teachers or teachers' aides—there were none on the premises during my tenure—but they did provide child-care workers whose salaries the parents paid. Having their children under the same roof must have been well worth it.

I was smiling to myself when the phone rang.

"What's this crap I hear about you opening a can of worms in the Mary Claire Fitzhugh case? I can't believe you'd have the gall to meddle in police business . . ."

The guy was yelling so loud it took me a minute to figure out who it was. "Lieutenant Dolan?"

My relationship with Lieutenant Dolan had spanned a number of years. Health issues had forced him to retire, but he was still plugged into the department grapevine. Having knocked heads early on, we'd finally come to an understanding based on mutual admiration and respect. I should have been inured to his occasional sharp tone, but it always took me by surprise.

"Who the hell else?"

"What can of worms are you talking about?"

"You know damn well. You're off on some tangent, stirring up talk."

"That's a good thing, isn't it?"

"Not from Mrs. Fitzhugh's perspective. She's had enough wackos making claims about the child over the years."

"Could you just tell me what you've heard and who you heard it from?"

"Cheney Phillips. He says he talked to some kid who thinks he saw Mary Claire's body being buried. Phillips sends the guy to you and you get the cops all in a lather, thinking there's been a break. Turns out it's all bullshit and you're responsible."

"You want to hear my side of it?"

"No, I do not! How come I'm calling you when you're the one who should be calling me? You should have told me about this on day one."

"Why would I tell you?"

"Because it was my case," he snapped. And then, grudgingly, "At least until the FBI stepped in."

"How was I supposed to know?"

"Because everybody knew."

"I was in high school. We didn't meet until years later."

"Didn't Cheney mention my name when he sent the Sutton kid your way?"

"No. If I'd known you were involved, I'd have been on your doorstep, begging for information. I've been working out here on my lonesome and I could have used the help."

"You didn't know I was the lead detective?"

"Cheney never said a word. This is the first I've heard."

"Are you blind? It's right there in the files."

"The files are sealed. And even if they weren't, the police aren't going to invite me down for a cozy chat about the case."

"Well."

"Yeah, well," I said.

"Maybe I spoke in haste."

"You certainly did. You owe me an apology."

"Consider it done."

"I want to hear you say it."

I could hear him take a puff on his cigarette. "Okay, then. I'm sorry. Is that good enough?"

"Not quite, but I'll give you the opportunity to atone."

"How so?"

"Invite me over for a drink. You and Stacey and I can sit down and talk about old times while I pick your brain."

A pause while he took another puff. "What have you come up with so far?"

"I'm not telling you without an invitation."

Dead silence.

"Be here at three," he said, and hung up.

# 23

Friday afternoon, April 15, 1988

Con Dolan's house was on a narrow side street on the east side of town. It hadn't occurred to me that he might have information to share. Cheney Phillips hadn't mentioned him, and since Dolan was retired, I had no idea he had a hand in the case. I parked in front of a large brown clapboard bungalow with long horizontal lines, open porches, mullioned windows, and widely overhung eaves. Dolan came to the door, cigarette in hand, wearing bedroom slippers, baggy chinos, and a T-shirt under a flannel robe cinched at the waist like an overcoat. He motioned me into the house and I followed. I'd never had occasion to visit him at home, and I was making a secret study of the place.

"Sorry I went off on you," he murmured.

"Think nothing of it. I didn't," I said, netting a smile.

Dolan's housemate, Stacey Oliphant, sat in the living room with a small battery-operated fan that he directed at Dolan's burning cigarette. This place couldn't have been more different from Stacey's rented apartment, which I'd visited when he was being treated for cancer. He'd been told he was dying and he was in the process of vacating the premises. I'd found him disposing of the bulk of his possessions and packing up the rest for delivery to the Salvation Army. I walked in on him shredding family photographs, which made me shriek. It seemed sacrilegious to destroy the images of his kinfolk and I'd begged him to give the pictures to me. I didn't know most of my relatives anyway so his would serve. I adopted them as my own, the odd assortment of unknown faces from times gone by.

Once he'd rid himself of all the paraphernalia, his intention was to kill himself before the cancer put him in a position where he had no choice. Con Dolan was vigorously opposed to the plan, in part because his wife, Grace, had taken a similar route before the disease had a chance to mow her down. But Stacey had been given a reprieve, which took the subject off the agenda for the foreseeable future. In the meantime, he and Dolan ended up sharing a place, which suited them both, even with the occasional snit.

The year before, they'd invited me to work a cold case with them since both were limited by physical ills. At the time, I'd introduced Stacey to junk food, which he'd never eaten in his life. Thereafter, I tagged along with him as he went from McDonald's to Wendy's to Arby's to Jack in the Box. My crowning achievement was introducing him to the In-N-Out burger. His appetite increased, he regained some of the weight he'd lost during his cancer treatment, and his enthusiasm for life returned. Doctors were still scratching their heads.

Dolan took my blazer and hung it on a hat rack, which was already decked out with a number of Victorian bonnets. We went down two low steps into the living room. The floor plan was open, with differences in elevation defining the rooms. If there were doors at all, they came in glass-paned pairs so that each area could be expanded to include those adjacent. The entire interior was dark-stained wood, including the walls, woodwork, cornices, window frames, and low ceiling. The furnishings were quirky. In addition to track lighting, Tiffany lamps were set on marble columns. The chairs were thrift-shop finds. The paintings looked like originals, not necessarily masterpieces, but an interesting mix of abstracts, landscapes, and portraits, in styles that ranged from photorealism to impressionistic to Grandma Moses crude.

The glimpse I had of the kitchen showed a 1920s stove and a kitchen window filled with a display of Depression glass on clear glass shelves. The measuring cups, vases, candlesticks, bowls, and pitchers cast a soft green light onto the linoleum floor. Headless mannequins in vintage clothing stood here and there, like guests who'd arrived early for a party. Everything smelled like cigarette smoke. Stacey sat in the living room in what looked like a Stickley chair. He, too, was in his robe, and his ginger hair was covered by a bright green watch cap. He pointed at the fan. "I'm doing this in self-defense," he said. "Sit, sit. Where's your manners, Dolan? Get the girl a beer. We have some catching up to do."

I set my shoulder bag on the floor and sat down. "Water's fine. A beer will put me to sleep."

Dolan went into the kitchen and came back with a coffee cup of tap water that he set on the arm of my chair, which was wide enough to serve as a desk.

I glanced from one to the other. "Don't you two get dressed anymore?"

Stacey smiled. "Sure, sometimes. You know, if we're going out and like that. We don't get gussied up for company. We're too old."

"Quit that," I said, waving the idea aside. "I take it you're doing okay? You look good."

"I'm better than I have any reason to hope. I figure my days are numbered, but so far, so good. We've been taking a lot of trips. We drove all the way up the coast and fished every chance we got."

Dolan said, "We also drank a lot of beer and ate all the crap we could find. Stacey's health is getting better and mine's getting worse. Last time I had blood work done, my cholesterol was through the roof. I cut back on cigarettes and booze. That's the best I can do."

"So tell me about your house. I don't know what I pictured, but it wasn't this. It looks like a Frank Lloyd Wright."

"That's everybody's guess, but it was actually an architect passing himself off as Wright's brother, Fred. Last name was the same but there was otherwise no relationship. People took one look at his portfolio and jumped to the wrong conclusion. He made a point of denying the connection, but he did it with a wink and a nudge, claiming he'd had a falling out with a 'partner' of his, who'd lifted most of his ideas. After that, he'd mention Frank Lloyd Wright's name in a tone that implied phone calls were passing back and forth between the two, more Frank asking his advice than the other way around."

"Clever," I said.

"Well, he made it work for him. His ploy was to ask them to list their favorites among Wright's houses, and then he'd draw up plans that borrowed the same elements. Since his prices were low, prospective home owners felt they were getting the real deal at half the cost."

Stacey said, "Let's talk about the kidnap business before I take my siesta. I'm like a little kid these days. Half an hour more of this chitchat and I'll be comatose."

I went through what I'd been up to, again starting with Michael Sutton and including Dr. McNally and assorted others I'd talked to along the way.

When I finished, Dolan said, "You know, Deborah and Patrick took a lot of flak for not coming to us when Rain was kidnapped. By the time they gave us a description, Greg and Shelly and the school bus were long gone. The draft board was close on Greg's heels, so chances are he was heading out of the country. Sweden or Canada. Probably the latter. Canada had numerous support groups for draft evaders. Students United for Peace. The SDS. Immigration made it easy for people to come in from all over."

"Is Deborah aware of this? I talked to her a day ago and she never said a word."

"She and Patrick might have been embarrassed. In the minds of most conservatives, draft dodgers were scum."

"Did you interview Rain after she was returned?"

"Three times. The Unruhs insisted on being there, which was fine with us. We didn't want any suggestion that the child was being coached or intimidated. After the second interview, we weren't getting anything we hadn't heard before."

"Nothing useful at all?"

"Nothing that went anywhere. She talked about the yellow kitten, which is how they snagged her cooperation in the first place. She said she slept in a big cardboard box that they'd done up like a little house with windows cut into it. When she woke up, she played with the kitten or the paper and crayons that had been left for her."

"Deborah says one of the kidnappers was dressed as Santa Claus."

"Same thing Rain told us. She said there were two of them and one was fat and had a long white beard. The other one had glasses with paper eyes and a big nose attached."

"Which I assume was a novelty item."

"Exactly. We showed her a pair from a local costume shop and she recognized them right off. The shop had no record of a recent sale, but an item like that could have been ordered from the back of a comic book."

"Was she scared?"

He shook his head. "She said she liked Santa Claus. She'd sat on his lap before. When she asked where her mommy was, he said she'd be back in a bit and then he had Rain drink her lemonade and she went back to sleep. The naps were short and from what she says, she did a lot of bouncing around."

"In the box?"

Dolan nodded. "They'd made up a little bed for her. They told her it was a playhouse just for her."

"What about the blanket? Deborah says she was found in the park on a picnic table, covered with a blanket."

"No help. It was the kind wrapped in plastic on airplane seats. There are thousands of them out there. Pan Am, in case you're wondering which airline. That's as far as we got."

"And in all of this, no fingerprints?"

"The only print we ever picked up was on the back of a ransom note after Mary Claire was taken. We've run it half a dozen times and we've never found a match."

"What about suspects? You must have had your eye on someone," I said.

"Pedophiles and other registered sex offenders, drifters, hired help in the neighborhood, and anyone else who might have seen someone coming or going. We talked to the friends and acquaintances of both families. Mrs. Fitzhugh said there was a yard guy with a leaf blower next door, working his way up the drive. She assumed he was from a lawn company, but the couple who owned the house were off at work and when we talked to them, they said they didn't have a service of any kind. The husband handled all the yard work himself."

"Did you find the leaf blower?"

"No sign of it. A gas-powered mower had been removed from the garage and it was sitting in the drive, but the guy must have worn gloves, because there were no prints on it."

"How'd he get into the garage?"

"The doors into the house were locked, but not the garage doors. Most days they were left open. Too much trouble to get out of the car and close them."

"No barking dog on the premises?"

"Nope."

"Interesting that Mrs. Fitzhugh saw the guy."

"From a distance. She said he was in coveralls and since he had the leaf blower, she assumed he was the gardener."

"How'd the kidnappers get to Mary Claire?" I asked. "I thought the yard was enclosed."

"They cut through the wire fence behind her playhouse. They might have been hiding there, waiting until she was left by herself. We're not sure how they got her out of there. No one reported seeing anyone with a kid. Chances are, they used the bridle trails. There's a whole network of trails that winds through Horton Ravine. If they stuck to those, probability is no one would have seen them. Someone on horseback maybe, but we never had a report to that effect. We know Rain didn't make a fuss, so it's likely Mary Claire didn't either. Little girls tend to be compliant anyway, and Rain says they were nice to her."

"So Rain wasn't carried off kicking and screaming."

"No need. The one fellow offered to let her play with the kitten and off she went. Kids that age are trusting. It's likely they pulled the same thing with Mary Claire."

"What'd they feed her?"

"Nothing fancy. Peanut butter and jelly sandwiches."

"And as far as she knew, she hadn't encountered either one before?"

"Nope. They were either smarter than we thought or the luckiest sons of bitches on the planet."

"You're convinced there were only two?"

"Two would have been optimal; one on the phone to the mother while the other took the kid. If more guys had been involved, we might have had a better chance for a break. With three or four guys, somebody's bound to blab or start throwing money around."

For the next twenty minutes we kept the subject afloat, like a badminton cock being lobbed back and forth over a net. With the right mix of minds, tossing ideas around can be productive, not to mention endlessly entertaining.

"Deborah tells me Patrick photocopied the bills and marked them before he paid."

"She told us as well. We made photocopies of his copies and sent 'em out to all the banks and savings and loans. Businesses, too, for all the good it did."

"They could have circulated the money somewhere else."

"Or they might not have spent a dime. In effect, the ransom was radioactive. Not literally, of course."

"I got that," I said. "So far, I haven't talked to Mrs. Fitzhugh because I didn't want to intrude. You think I should contact her?"

"She'll probably get in touch with you. That's how this whole thing got started. She's been calling me once or twice a year for the last twenty-one years, asking for updates. I told her we had nothing new as far as I was aware, but I'd check with Cheney Phillips and get back to her. That's when I heard Michael Sutton had come in and Cheney'd sent him over to you."

Stacey said, "What about this Sutton kid? How solid is his claim? He sounds like a nutcase to me."

I had to shrug. "Well, it's really not such a stretch. He was playing on a property owned by a family named Kirkendall, just up the hill from the Unruhs. As Dolan says, there are horse trails running through that area. The spot where he saw them digging was not far from the horse trough off Via Juliana."

"You believe him?"

"What he says makes sense. He sees the two guys and they see him so they know they've been busted. They can't count on a little kid to keep his mouth shut so they swap out the little girl's body for the dog's. That way if he properly identifies the place, it looks like he's made a mistake."

"Why'd they choose that property?"

"I've been wondering the same thing," I said. "It might have been an attempt to point a finger at Shelly and Greg. The Unruhs were convinced the pair had a hand in it because the total they asked for—adding Rain's ransom to the demand made of the Fitzhughs—was forty thousand dollars, exactly what Greg's grandfather left for him in trust."

Dolan said, "That's a detail I find puzzling—and this has bugged me for years—a ransom demand for fifteen thousand dollars seems odd to me. Even a forty-thousand total seems screwy. Why not a hundred thousand? Better yet, half a million? Why risk the electric chair for chump change? I mean, who kidnaps a kid and asks for so little?"

"I'll tell you who," Stacey said. "Amateurs, that's who. Which is why they never tried it again. The second kidnap blew up in their faces and that was the end of it. Two career criminals cured of the urge. Speaking of which, I'm out of here. You come up with anything good, you can wake me later on."

"I have a question before you go," I said. "Have either of you ever run across a Lompoc PI named Hale Brandenberg?"

Stacey said, "Sure, I know Hale. He started out about the same time I did, only he was younger by a goodly number of years."

"You think he's still around?"

"Last I heard. You want to talk to him?"

"I'd love to. It's not about this case. It's something else."

"Let me make a few calls and see if I can find out where he ended up."

"Thanks. I'd appreciate it."


Saturday morning I slept in until 8:00, a luxury for me. My breakfast meeting with Rain was scheduled for 9:00, which gave me time to dawdle over the newspaper and my first cup of coffee. Once I'd showered and dressed, I walked two blocks over to Cabana and two blocks down. On the beach I could see where ropes of kelp had washed up on the sand. The tide was going out and the waves rushed forward and then receded, tugging the gray-green fronds into the depths again. The wind was up and I could see whitecaps ruffling the water beyond the surf. In the harbor the masts of sailboats swayed back and forth in a rhythm of their own. Countless gulls formed a gray funnel cloud and descended on the beach, two of them squabbling over an abandoned cellophane bag half filled with

Cheetos. The public swimming pool was still closed for the season and the children's play area was deserted.

At the entrance to the coffee shop I paused. There was only one young woman at a table alone. She raised a hand and waved, having identified me by the same process of elimination. I indicated to the hostess that I was joining a friend. I slid into the padded Naugahyde booth across from her and signaled to a waitress who was passing with a fresh carafe of coffee. She turned my mug right-side up and filled it.

Rain passed the stainless steel pitcher of milk and I added enough to turn the coffee beige. We introduced ourselves properly and then chatted about nothing in particular, which gave her a chance to study me while I made a study of her. She had the fresh look of youth. Her complexion was clear and her features were delicate. She had Betty Boop lips and hair like a cloud of platinum-blond frizz, bobbed level with her ears. Discreet pearl-and-diamond earrings caught the light. She wore jeans and a gossamer white shirt over a white lace camisole, a combination more elegant than I'd have imagined. Two booths over, a busboy wiped down the table with his eyes pinned on her, as though she might be a celebrity.

"Have you ordered yet?" I asked.

"I was waiting for you."

The waitress returned with her order pad in hand. I asked for a small tomato juice, rye toast, and a soft-boiled egg. Rain ordered the breakfast special. When the meal came I watched her work her way through orange juice, scrambled eggs, home fries, bacon, link sausages, and buttered biscuits with strawberry jam. Though she ate as rapidly as I did, I finished first, leaving her with two biscuits to go.

"How old are you?" I asked.

"I'll be twenty-five in July. Why?"

"Please tell me you don't eat like that and then go to the ladies' room and barf it all up again."

"And waste all this food? I wouldn't dream of it."

"No laxatives? Ipecac? Finger down your throat?"

She laughed. "I've got the metabolism of a bird."

"That's what the skinny actresses say to cover up their eating disorders."

"Not me. In my teens I had migraines and I barfed enough

for a lifetime. I admit I was pretty good at it, but eating's too much fun."

"Can I ask you about your father's business? Deborah says you took over after he died."

"I did. He was actually my grandfather, as I'm sure you know, but I called him Daddy because that's what he was to me. He owned a plant in downtown L.A., manufacturing sports uniforms. Later, he created a line of foul-weather gear—raincoats, rain hats, anoraks, rain jackets, slickers, umbrellas . . ."

I stared at her. "Are you talking about Rain Checks?"

"That's him."

"You're kidding. You're the 'Rain' in Rain Checks?"

"Yep."

"How did he come up with the idea when California has so little rainfall? What is it, fifteen days a year?"

"He was smart. Early in his career he worked for a company that made sports apparel. He was on the road a lot, mostly in the Northwest, Oregon and Washington States. He could see the niche. People had raincoats, umbrellas, and boots, but it was all a hodgepodge and none of it was stylish. He decided to tackle the high-end market, where Burberry and London Fog were the only competition. Now we sell through all the luxury department stores; Neiman Marcus, Bloomingdale's, Bergdorf Goodman. We have a huge worldwide presence as well. London, Rome, Prague, Tokyo, Singapore. 'When foul weather threatens your day, take a Rain Check.'"

"I love those ads," I said. "You know how to run a business?"

"I'm learning," she said. She popped the last bite of biscuit in her mouth and wiped her fingers on her napkin. "After Daddy died, I changed my major from social work to business and got my MBA. I have a team of experts holding my hand, and we've done well so far. Knock on wood."

"I am totally amazed."

"You're not the only one," she said. "Anyway, I know your primary interest is the kidnapping—abduction, or whatever."

"I'm curious about the experience."

"It was fine. Really. I was four. I didn't know what was going on so why would I react badly?"

"No unpleasant associations?"

"Not at all. The guys were nice. I got to play with this adorable yellow kitten. The only thing I was ever upset about was not getting to keep her when it was all over with."

"There were two guys?"

"Two that I saw. One was Santa and the other was just this goofball who wore glasses with cardboard eyes in the frames and a big plastic nose. He had a wig, too—bright red fake hair like Raggedy Andy. There might have been other guys, but I doubt it."

"Your mother says they made you a house out of a cardboard box."

"That was great. They put in a pile of blankets for a bed and they cut windows along one side so I could look out. That's where I slept, though I didn't do much of it. They kept coaxing me into drinking lemonade laced with something. I'd get sleepy for a while, but I didn't stay down long. Whatever it was, it had the opposite effect. Instead of tired, I'd get wired. The more they gave me, the more amped I got."

"But no aftereffects?"

"None."

"What about the box? Was it a carton an appliance might have come in?"

"I guess. Not big enough for a refrigerator or a stove. I was little, but even then the box didn't seem gigantic. I'd say more or less the size of this table. Longer, but about as wide."

"You didn't miss your mom?"

"Some, but they told me my mother wanted me to be a good girl, just for a little while, and then they'd take me home."

"And they stayed with you the whole time?"

"One or the other did. Usually not both. I think that's why they wanted me asleep—to make their job easier. One would keep an eye on me while the other one left, probably to call my folks."

"Did you have nightmares afterward?"

"Nope. Honestly, there was nothing traumatic about it. Weird as it sounds, I had a lot of fun." Her expression shifted when she caught sight of my face. "What?"

"I have trouble reconciling your experience with Mary Claire's disappearance. Clearly, these guys weren't thugs or hardened criminals. I can't believe they were kiddie-killers either, at least from what you've said. It sounds like they wanted money and not very much of it at that. Somehow they were spooked into abandoning the twenty-five thousand dollars, which was more than they got for you."

"You think something went wrong?"

"I can't imagine any other explanation for the fact that you were released while she vanished forever."

"I feel guilty about that and I have for years. If there's anything negative in the aftermath, it's knowing I escaped with my life. She wasn't as lucky and look at the price she paid."

# 24

## WALKER McNALLY

### Monday, April 18, 1988

Walker took a seat near the back of the small conference room at the city recreation center. There was a separate door on the side of the building, its purpose to promote privacy. The furnishings were plain—folding chairs set up in ordered rows, a lectern that had been removed from its stand and placed on the floor. Wooden tables had been herded into a corner where they'd be out of the way. There were maybe twenty people in attendance, most keeping a chair or two between themselves and others. This was the third AA meeting he'd sat in on. The air smelled like construction paper and library paste. As an after-school project, the kids had cut out a number of tree silhouettes that were pinned to the bulletin board. THIS IS MY FAMILY TREE was written across the bottom of each. The branches were covered with cutout leaf shapes in primary colors, each bearing a name printed in block letters. MATTHEW, JESSICA, CHRISTOPHER, ASHLEY, JOSHUA, HEATHER. Walker could see leaves with the names of siblings as well, one or two leaves for Mom and Dad, depending on their marital status. A generation of grandparents appeared above the immediate family, with great-grandparents closer to the tippy-top. He doubted grade-school kids could conceive of ancestors more remote in time.

His sponsor was a guy named Leonard whom he'd met through the Episcopal church he and Carolyn attended sporadically. He'd been aware Leonard didn't drink. They had few acquaintances in common, though they ran into each other at the occasional dinner party. Leonard's wife, Shannon, was a kick, bright and funny, and Carolyn had been interested in getting the four of them together. Walker had resisted the idea. Being in Leonard's company was like being in the presence of a born-again, and Walker preferred to keep him at arm's length. Once Herschel laid down the law about Walker's pulling himself together, he'd called Leonard and talked to him about getting help. Leonard had agreed to sponsor him and the two chatted frequently by phone. He was gradually warming to the man. He wanted his life back, and Leonard understood exactly where he was, even his ambivalence in the face of despair.

He had to admit alcoholism was democratic, encompassing every age, race, social status, and financial standing. So far he hadn't run into anyone he knew, but he was braced for the possibility. After his release from the hospital, he'd gone down to the police station with his attorney and surrendered himself to the authorities. The booking process had been matter-of-fact, for which he'd been inordinately grateful. He'd been more than cooperative, thinking to demonstrate that he was a cut above most of those who passed through their hands. It was a mark of how low he'd sunk that he deemed their opinions relevant. Later, at his arraignment, he'd pleaded not guilty and now he was waiting for a court date. When the cops caught up with him after the accident, he'd been forced to surrender his driver's license, so he'd had to hire a car and driver to ferry him around town.

Betty Sherrard, the bank vice president and portfolio manager, had offered a solution to the transportation problem. Her son, Brent, was living at home until school started in the fall. He was twenty and worked part-time stocking shelves at Von's supermarket. He needed the extra money and he was able to tailor his hours to accommodate Walker's needs. Walker paid him fifteen dollars an hour, plus mileage on his mother's spare car, a 1986 Toyota. It was all a pain in the ass, but he had no choice.

The woman standing up in front was speaking about the trajectory of her drinking woes, a spiral as relentless as a toilet being flushed, according to her report: First, the family intervention, which had shocked her into good behavior. She'd been one year sober and then her mother died and she'd begun to drink again the day of the funeral. Three months later, she swore off alcohol again, but there were countless falls from grace, each one more degrading than the one before. Her husband divorced her. She lost custody of her kids. She was a mean drunk and her friends had taken to avoiding her. One morning she woke up in her car, which was parked at a shopping mall a hundred miles from home. She had no idea how she'd gotten there. Her purse had been stolen and she'd had to hike to the nearest service station, where she bummed enough money to call and beg her ex-sister-in-law to pick her up. Waiting, she'd finally accepted the fact she couldn't do it on her own. Now she was fifty-one days clean and sober, which netted her a big round of applause.

Walker thought his circumstances were tame by comparison. True, Carolyn had forced him to leave the house, but he was confident she'd relent. He still saw his kids every chance he got and he still had a job, for god's sake. He'd messed up badly, but his problems didn't hold a patch on some he'd heard here. This was a bump in the road, a wake-up call. He'd stumbled off course and now he'd righted himself. All these stories about people losing everything and living on the streets? He sympathized, but his situation was entirely different. One guy had made it clean and sober for five years, two months, and five days. The best Walker could offer up was seven days, not even worth one hand clapping. He'd have felt like a fool if he'd stood up and shared that. Belatedly, he flashed on the fact that while he'd been busy patting himself on the back, he'd forgotten about the girl he'd killed.

Sitting there, he could feel his demons stir. It wasn't that he wanted a drink as such. It was the *option* to drink that he found hard to renounce. At some point in the future—five years or ten, he was unclear on the time frame—he wanted to believe he could enjoy a cocktail or a glass of wine. How many special occasions would come and go with him sipping soda water or a Diet Coke, detached and disengaged? Not drinking for the remainder of his life was too extreme a penalty. Surely, he'd regain the privilege once he learned to moderate his intake.

Carolyn would have told him he was kidding himself, but it wasn't true. He was grappling with his so-called drinking problem and he was doing his best. How much more did she expect? He wanted a drink. He admitted it, especially now with this other business coming to the fore. The subject was like a cracked tooth he kept feeling with his tongue to see if the fissure had progressed.

He checked his watch. Half an hour yet. All he could think about was how burdened he was. Over the years guilt had chafed at him, and now his only relief occurred during that magic moment when a drink went down and the warmth spread through his chest, untying the knots, loosening the noose around his neck. He was losing his capacity to tolerate the weight of anxiety that dogged him from day to day. How would he grow old with such a canker in his soul?

An eternity later, the meeting ended and the room emptied with a clatter of chairs being folded and stacked against the wall. He felt a touch on his arm that made him jump.

"Fancy meeting you here."

He turned. Avis Jent stood close by, in a spiky blaze of dark red hair, the scent of whiskey pouring off her skin. Shit, he thought, had she come to the meeting drunk? His right arm was still in a sling so he didn't make a move to shake hands.

Her eyes widened at the sight of his face. "Oh, I *love* that blend of purple and yellow. The black eyes make you look like a raccoon. You got yourself banged up good."

"I take it you heard about the accident."

"Me and everyone else. The whole of Horton Ravine is abuzz."

"Thanks. I'm feeling so much better for having talked to you."

Walker hadn't seen Avis since their chance encounter on Via Juliana, that nightmare of patrol cars, police personnel, and rumors of a dead child. He hadn't read a word in the paper about the incident, unless an article had appeared while he was in St. Terry's and out of commission.

Avis wasn't looking good. He'd once thought her attractive, but the fluorescent lighting didn't do her any favors. In her current state of inebriation, her eyes were out of focus and her loose-limbed swaying was such that he had to put a hand out to steady her.

She said, "Whoa."

"I hope you didn't drive over here in this condition."

"I came by cab. My license was permanently yanked. What a drag," she said. "And you?"

"I have a kid who squires me around town."

"Lucky you. How many meetings? Is this your first?"

"Third."

She smiled. "Clever move. Paying lip service so you'll look good when your case goes to trial. I've done the same thing myself."

Her tone was bantering but smug, and it annoyed the shit out of him. "How's Carolyn holding up?" she asked, eyes wide with sympathy.

"Great. She's been very supportive, a real brick."

Avis made a face. "Well, that surprises me. I don't think of her as understanding. She let you stay at the house?"

"Not at the moment. I'm at the Pelican in Montebello, two blocks from the bank, which simplifies life to some extent. I still see the kids."

She looked around the room, which was empty except for the two of them. "I don't suppose you could give me a ride home. I'm low on cash and the taxi over cost me twenty bucks. We could have a quick drink."

"Jesus, Avis. Would you give it a rest?"

She laughed. "It was a joke."

"Not a funny one."

"Oh, lighten up. This isn't the end of the world."

"Thanks for the encouragement. Nice seeing you. Have a good life."

"Good-bye to you, too. Change your mind, you know where I am. Second house on the right as you turn on Alita Lane."

He moved past her, crossing to the exit, aware that she followed him with her gaze as he stepped out of the room. Four middle-aged men were standing on the patio, smoking, oversized coffee cups in hand. This was the life that awaited him, endless cups of coffee and a cloud of cigarette smoke.

Avis, still plastered, represented the other end of the spectrum, which was no more attractive than the one in front of him. How had he ended up in this hell on earth?

Brent was parked across the street. Walker waved and he started the car, swinging around the block to pick him up. Walker got in the backseat. Sitting up front with Brent was a little too chummy for his taste. Fortunately, Brent was discreet and he knew his place. He and Walker exchanged only the most banal of remarks. Walker didn't want to be Brent's buddy and he was sure Brent wasn't interested in being his. This was a business arrangement and Brent seemed to understand that Walker didn't want to hear his observations or opinions. Brent conducted himself as though he were invisible, squiring Walker from one place to the next without comment.

Walker stared out the window as Brent navigated through the heart of town, following Capillo to the top of the hill. At the crest, he turned right on Palisade. The road curved down to Harley's Beach and up the hill again on the far side. The route took them through the back entrance to Horton Ravine, stone pillars marking the outer limits of the enclave. Earlier in the day Walker had called Carolyn, asking if she objected to his stopping by after his AA meeting to pick up a load of clothes. He passed off the reference to AA as an afterthought, but he knew it would register with her, perhaps winning him points.

When possible, he avoided the motel he'd moved into. He'd have preferred a place with more class—the Edgewater Hotel being his first choice—but he didn't want to give Carolyn the impression he was being extravagant. She was already pissed off about the money he paid Brent, but what was he supposed to do, take public transportation? He could just picture himself on a city bus. The Pelican Motel was perched on a rise overlooking the main road through what was known as "the lower Village" in Montebello. The building had a drab air about it, just the place for a penitent. All he needed was a hair shirt and a cat-o'-nine-tails and he'd be set.

Brent pulled up in front of his house and parked. Walker let himself out of the backseat, wondering what Brent's impression was. The place looked good. He'd never liked the word "quaint," but that's how it struck him now. This charming home was forbidden turf until he'd straightened up his act.

Carolyn was the keeper of the gate. He'd have to kiss serious butt for the rest of his life to get back into her good graces. The very idea made him tired, the pretense, the carefully guarded behavior, the facade of virtue when all he wanted was the life he'd had before. Plus, a drink, he thought.

Brent accompanied him to the door. Politely, Walker rang the bell, feeling like a door-to-door salesman with a trainee at his side and a traveling case full of wares.

When Carolyn opened the door she scarcely looked at him. She said, "Oh, it's you" like she was expecting someone else and had suffered a disappointment. He thought a pleasant greeting would have been nice, some semblance of goodwill for the children's sake. At the moment they were off at school and Carolyn was having none of it. Brent didn't warrant a greeting of any kind, so Walker should have been grateful she spoke to him at all.

She turned away and proceeded down the hall, talking to him over her shoulder. "I'll be in the kitchen. Let me know when you're done. I put the mail on the table. Remind me and I'll tell you about a call I should have mentioned before."

Walker wondered if she was worth the effort it would take to win her back. She'd lord it over him from this point on. She had all the power and he was the supplicant, begging to see the kids, begging for an audience with the Queen, begging for attention, which she'd decided was undeserved. In return for crumbs, she'd want all his paychecks deposited to her account. She'd dole out a few bucks to him from week to week—not enough for a binge, but a modest sum she'd say was his to do with as he pleased. Maybe he'd appeal to the pastor of their church, citing Christian forbearance as a means of bringing her to heel. Ha. Like that would do any good.

He went upstairs with Brent tagging behind. Walker's ribs still pained him and he wasn't allowed to lift anything, which was why Brent was forced to follow him around like a dog. Walker went into the walk-in closet and pushed through the hangers on his side of the hanging rods. With his left hand he pulled out sport coats, four suits, his raincoat, and his leather jacket, passing them to Brent, who laid them on the bed while Walker went through the dresser drawers removing underwear, socks, and T-shirts. He'd have to borrow a suitcase or go down to the kitchen and find a paper bag to carry all his stuff. He went out into the hall and looked in the storage area under the eaves. After a grubby search he came up with a duffel into which he jammed the pile of personal items.

Idly he wondered what would happen if he just walked away from the entire situation. He'd pack the car, cancel credit cards, empty all the bank accounts, and leave the state. By the time Carolyn realized what he'd done, he'd be out of her grasp. He pictured her at Saks, pricey merchandise piled up on the counter while the saleswoman rang the sale and returned her card, looking mystified. "I'm sorry, Mrs. McNally, but this was declined."

"Declined? There must be a mistake. My husband pays our bills in full the first of every month."

"Would you like to try another card?"

She'd pull out her Visa or MasterCard, her embarrassment mounting as one after the other was rejected.

Without him busting his ass to keep the coffers full, her life would grind to a halt. She didn't have a dime of her own. She was dependent on him for everything. The problem was, if he stuck it to her, he'd be sticking it to his kids. He didn't want Fletcher and Linnie to suffer, which meant he'd be tied to Carolyn for all eternity.

Brent made a couple of trips to the car, ferrying Walker's clothes. Meanwhile, Walker went into the kitchen, where Carolyn was unloading the dishwasher, a job she'd always insisted was half his to share. He stood and watched her, making no effort to pitch in, a gesture she noticed but refrained from remarking on. Looking at her without the filter of affection, he realized she wasn't pretty anymore and she was picking up weight. She was thick through the middle and her pants were riding up. Maybe his losing the marriage wasn't such a big deal after all. He had wealthy women clients who'd made it clear they were interested in him. He'd been bemused by their attentions, but he might be more receptive now that he was on his own. Where would Carolyn find a guy willing to take her on, a plump premenopausal woman with two kids underfoot?

He leaned against the counter. "You said something about the mail?"

"It's out on the hall table in a manila envelope. You must have walked right by."

"Fine. What about the phone message?"

"Oh, right. This was last week and I apologize. It completely slipped my mind. A woman called and asked for you. Someone you went to high school with. She said she was a private eye and she was looking for your dad."

"Dad?"

"That's what I said. She wanted to get in touch with him."

"What for?"

"I don't know. She told me, but it went in one ear and out the other. It didn't sound all that urgent."

"What did you tell her?"

"I didn't tell her anything. I hung up on her."

He thought about it, wondering what he'd missed. "What would a private investigator want with Dad?"

"Why are you asking me? I don't have a clue."

He stared at her, trying to make sense of what she'd said. "Did you get her name?"

"Millhone. I forget the first. Something odd."

"Kinsey?"

"You remember her? I thought she was feeding me a line of bullshit."

"Senior year we had a class together," he said, distracted. "*What* did she want again?"

"Walker, I just told you. I have no idea. Something about a dog. She didn't say anything more than that."

The floor shifted under his feet. For a moment he thought there'd been a temblor. He put out his left hand and grabbed the counter with Carolyn looking on like he was losing it.

He murmured an excuse and left the house, not even sure later how he got to the car. He felt like he'd been walking, looking in the other direction, and slammed into a door. The shock was making the blood drain out of his head, taking his blood pressure down along with it. His body was shot through with a clamminess that carried nausea in its wake. The outside air helped. He leaned against the car, feeling shaken to the core.

Brent slammed down the trunk. "Are you all right, Mr. McNally?"

"I'm fine. Let's get moving, if you don't mind."

"Sure thing."

Walker got in the backseat. Brent fired up the engine and was on the verge of pulling away when Carolyn called from the front door and then trotted down to the car. Walker lowered the rear window.

"You forgot the mail," she said. She leaned down to look at him. "Are you all right? The way you bolted out of there, I thought you'd seen a ghost."

Walker wanted to make a withering reply, but Brent was sitting in range and he didn't want to make a scene. He took the mail and dropped it on the seat beside him. "Fuck you," he said under his breath. He pushed the switch that rolled the window up so Carolyn was forced to yell through the glass.

"Fine. I'm sorry I asked."


Brent drove along Ocean Way toward the stone pillars at the rear of Horton Ravine.

Walker said, "On my way back to the Pelican, I'd like to see my father. He's at Valley Oaks. I'll direct you once we get there."

"No problem."

Walker glanced out the window and realized they were passing Jon Corso's house. Jon still lived in the sprawling two-story, gray-shingled monstrosity his father and stepmother had bought when Jon was sixteen. Walker hadn't met Jon until their senior year at Santa Teresa High, but he'd heard plenty about the Amazing Mona and her three perfect daughters. Jon had confessed to screwing all three before each went off to college. The sisters were married now and living in the East with an assortment of kids. Two years before, when Lionel died of a heart attack, Mona packed up and moved to New York so she'd be closer to her girls and all the grandkids. She'd inherited the house and the bulk of Lionel's estate. Jon's inheritance was ten thousand dollars and a life interest in the studio apartment above the garage. Since the business with Mary Claire, Jon insisted that Walker keep his distance, so they'd never discussed the issue. Nonetheless, Walker knew to a certainty that Jon was still chafing at the paltry sum he'd been left. He earned staggering sums from the sales of his books, so it wasn't about the money. It was the insult of it all, his father's final slap in the face; game, set, and match to Mona. She was perfectly content to have Jon living at the house. The arrangement bound him to her. Walker was willing to bet she was still sticking it to him any way she could. Eventually she'd put the place on the market, but for the time being, it was a nice vacation spot when she or the girls felt like a jaunt to the West Coast.

The drive continued in silence. Occasionally Brent flicked a look in the rearview mirror. Walker leaned his head back against the seat. He was aware of Brent's scrutiny but he made no remark. It wasn't up to him to explain his complicated family life. How had this happened? Everything was fine. Everything was good, and then, in one swift stroke, he realized he was going under. An unseen force, subtle and relentless, had taken him unawares and now he was being dragged toward open water with no way back.

He tried to reason with himself as a defense against fear. There was no reason to think Kinsey Millhone had talked to his dad. How would she do that? Carolyn said she hadn't given her any information, certainly no means by which she could have tracked him down. And even if she did and she asked about the dog, what would his father be expected to remember? The man was old. He'd been retired for years. In the course of his practice, he'd seen hundreds of animals. What kind of threat could she be?

Walker leaned forward as Brent turned into Valley Oaks. "It's this lane on the right. Number 17. You can pull into the parking pad and wait. It should be half an hour or so."

Brent shut down the engine and Walker got out. He hadn't seen his father since the accident, and while he dreaded the coming conversation, he had no other way of finding out if Kinsey Millhone had succeeded in reaching him. He could see his father peering at him from the window as he came up the walk. Walter opened the door, standing erect, his manner cautious. He seemed to be avoiding the sight of Walker's facial bruises, which Walker tended to forget about.

"I didn't expect to see you."

"Sorry about that, Dad. I should have called, but I was in

the neighborhood and thought I'd stop by. There's something I'd like to ask about."

"Come in, come in," Walter said, stepping back. "You have time for a cup of coffee?"

"I could probably manage that," he said. "Don't go to any trouble—"

"No trouble. Let's go back to the great room, where you can make yourself comfortable. How are Carolyn and the children?"

"Doing well, thanks. I just came from the house, as a matter of fact. And yourself?"

"Tolerable. That pain in my hip is largely gone and I've been increasing my walks. I'm up to two miles these days."

Walker perched on the couch and watched as his father set about putting together a pot of coffee, carefully filling a carafe of water, which he poured into the tank. He added six small scoops of ground coffee, double-checking everything before he pressed the button that set the coffeemaker in brewing mode.

His father returned to the sitting area. "Coffee will take a minute," he remarked.

Walker couldn't think of a response. He was casting about for some way to introduce the subject of the accident and all of its attendant horrors.

His father cleared his throat. "I don't suppose I need to tell you how distressed I am about this recent business of yours. Carolyn stopped by and told me. She made a special point of coming over because she didn't want me to hear about it from a third party."

"I appreciate her consideration. I would have told you myself, but I've been down for the count."

"Yes."

The word seemed like a non sequitur. Walker had hoped for some help getting through the awkwardness of the discussion. "I was horrified, as you might imagine."

"And rightly so. If your mother were alive, this would break her heart."

"Well, I guess we can both be grateful she was spared," Walker said. Wrong tone, he thought. He tried again. "I understand how upset you must be, but I've been knocked to my knees as well. How do you think I feel, knowing that poor girl is dead because of me?"

"Carolyn said you'd blanked on all of it."

"I had a concussion. I was knocked unconscious. The doctor says amnesia is pretty common under the circumstances."

"Carolyn believes you suffered an alcoholic blackout, which is a horse of another color."

"That's ridiculous. I didn't *black* out."

"Perhaps not. I thought she made a good case."

"Well, I'm glad the two of you had such a happy chat at my expense."

"She's entitled to her opinion."

"She's hardly the reigning expert—"

"Son, you'd be wise to cut the sarcasm. She's a wonderful woman and you're fortunate you have her standing by you."

"I don't know where you got the impression she was 'standing by' me. She's barely civil."

"I'm sure she'll come around in time. You have the children to think of. It would be a pity if this tragedy ruined their lives as well as hers."

The coffee was done and his father left the sitting area to attend to cups and saucers. He set up a tray with the sugar bowl, a cream pitcher, and two spoons.

While he was occupied, Walker debated how best to approach the matter of Kinsey Millhone. The name had no more than crossed his mind when he glanced down at the coffee table and saw her business card propped up against a potted plant. He picked it up, noting her office address and phone number. There was nothing about the kinds of cases she handled. Walker fingered the card.

His father returned with a tray, cups rattling against the saucers as he walked. He set the tray on the coffee table and passed a cup to Walker. "I forget what you take with your coffee. I have half-and-half."

"Black's fine," he said. "What's this?"

"What's what?"

"This is what I wanted to ask. Carolyn told me a private investigator called the house looking for you. According to my attorney, a conversation with this woman would be out of line."

"I've already met with her and you needn't be alarmed. Her reasons for seeing me had nothing to do with you. She stopped by a few days ago and asked about a dog I treated once upon a time."

"A dog?"

"She had questions about the protocol when a pet was put down. I told her what I could, and she left her card in case I had something to add. She was a very pleasant young woman. We chatted for a bit about this and that, and then she left. I doubt she was here thirty minutes, if that."

"Did she mention I went to high school with her?"

"I wasn't aware of it. She was here on an entirely separate matter."

"What did you tell her?"

His father stopped with the cup halfway to his lips. "I'm quite capable of having a conversation independent of your oversight."

"Sorry. I didn't mean to butt in. I don't want her to take advantage of our prior acquaintance."

"Your name didn't come up. She sought me out of her own accord, though it's no concern of yours. I suggest you get your own house in order and let me worry about mine."

He let the subject drop, stung by the rebuke. The conversation bumbled on until he felt enough time had passed to make his excuses and return to the car. His father declined to walk him to the door.

He was barely aware of the drive home. He rolled down the nearest window and let the air whip through the car's interior, cooling his face and buffeting his hair. He loosened his tie and unbuttoned the collar of his shirt. Brent shot him a look in the rearview mirror. Walker didn't feel he had to explain. He was hot. What business was that of Brent's? The same thoughts assailed him persistently. Kinsey knew about the dog. He couldn't figure out how she'd arrived at his father's door. By what circuitous logic had she linked his father and the dog's remains? Walker had seen her at the dig and within a week, she was six steps behind him and gaining.

By the time Brent dropped him off at the Pelican, the combination of caffeine and anxiety had triggered something close to a panic attack. Walker locked the door behind him and staggered to the bed. His heart was thudding at a rate that made him pant and sweat. It was like an overdose of speed, which he'd experienced twice in his lifelong association with drink and drugs. He sat on the edge of the bed, clutching his chest, afraid to stand up again for fear of passing out. He was dying. He would die. The terror would mount until it crushed him under its weight.

Seven days sober. He wondered if it was possible to make it even one more hour. There was a cocktail lounge two blocks away. He pictured the quick walk, the glittering rows of bottles behind the bar. The lighting would be muted and he doubted he'd see anyone he knew. One drink would calm him. One drink would tide him over to the next day. Mornings were easier anyway, though the day would stretch before him like eternity. All he had to do was get up, cross the room, walk the two blocks to the bar. His hands began to shake.

He picked up the phone and called Leonard.

# 25

## Monday, April 18, 1988

Monday afternoon I dialed Information and picked up a phone number for Dancer Custom Woodwork in Belicia. Deborah hadn't given me the business name, but when I checked the local yellow pages, most custom cabinetmakers seemed to use their own last names by way of a designation. I was prepared to try Dancer Woodworking, Dancer Cabinetry, and variations on that theme. Fortunately I hit it the first time out. I punched in the number and the line rang twice before a man picked up.

"Dancer Custom Woodwork."

"Is this Shawn Dancer?"

"It is. Who's this?"

"My name is Kinsey Millhone. I'm a private investigator in Santa Teresa. Deborah Unruh suggested I talk to you about Greg and Shelly. Would you be willing to meet with me?"

"I can save you a trip. Anything I know, I can tell you by phone. It doesn't amount to much."

"I'd be happier talking face-to-face if it's all the same to you. I won't ask for any more time than you're willing to spare."

"Up to you," he said.

He gave me his work address and said he'd be in the shop all of Tuesday and Wednesday. He had an installation on

Thursday so he'd be gone Thursday and Friday. I told him
Tuesday afternoon would be fine. Stacey had called that morning to tell me Grand's private investigator was still in business,
operating out of the same office he'd occupied at the time. My
plan was to stop first in Lompoc and talk to Hale Brandenberg,
then drive the additional fifty miles north to Belicia, covering
both sources in one day.

Tuesday morning I gassed up my car and hit the northbound 101. I had the manila envelope of letters on the passenger seat, along with the invoices Brandenberg had submitted.
I assumed there'd once been reports attached, but he might
have agreed to convey his findings verbally to avoid written
accounts. I've done the same thing myself when the issues are
sensitive and a paper trail seems unwise. As long as the client
is satisfied, I can work either way. I keep a set of notes for my
own files, as a hedge against an investigation coming back to
bite me in the butt, but the client doesn't need to know.

The drive was uneventful. The day was gorgeous, temperatures in the low seventies with a light breeze coming off the
ocean. I'd had the Mustang serviced the week before and the
car was driving like a dream. We'd had intermittent rain in
February and March, and the rolling hills on either side of the
road had turned a lush green. Thirty-five miles later, I took the
132 off-ramp and drove west toward Vandenberg Air Force
Base.

The town of Lompoc boasts a population of roughly thirty-
six thousand, with single-family homes ranging in price from
$225,000 to $250,000. There's a small airport, a U.S. peniten-
tiary, an attractive public library, pocket parks, good schools,
and three percent more single men than single women, if you
happen to be husband hunting. The surrounding area produces
half the flower seeds grown in the world, which means that in
May, thousands of acres of flowers are visible from the road.
This was early in the season, but in another couple of months
the fields would be sprouting the colors of a Persian carpet.

The business district was low-key, with wide streets and
few structures over two stories high. Hale Brandenberg was on
the second floor of a chunky office building. At ground level,
to the right, there was a real estate company, its front windows
papered with photographs of houses for sale; on the left, a title

company. A glass-paneled door between the two opened onto a wide carpeted staircase. The directory posted on the wall showed his suite number as 204.

I went up the stairs, marveling at the proportions of the place. The windows in the upper hallway were huge and the ceilings were easily twenty feet high. A race of giants could have moved in and had headroom to spare. The corridor was dead quiet. I counted eight offices, each entrance marked by a transom above the door, the old-world equivalent of air-conditioning. I was taking a chance he'd be out, but when I tapped on his door and then opened it to stick my head in, he was sitting on the floor in the middle of his one-room suite, rubbing saddle soap into one of two worn leather-upholstered chairs.

His office was sparsely furnished—leather-top desk, the two leather chairs, and a bank of filing cabinets. His windows, like those in the corridor, were big and bare, spotlessly clean, revealing an uninterrupted expanse of blue sky. I caught sight of a patch of green across the street, trees just leafing out.

"Housekeeping chores," he said, explaining his homely activity.

"So I see. Mind if I come in?"

He was a rangy-looking man somewhere in his sixties, with a thin face and a cleft in his chin. His fair hair, cropped short, was threaded with gray. He wore faded jeans and cowboy boots, a Western-cut shirt, and a string tie. He looked like he'd be happier outdoors, preferably on horseback. He'd finished conditioning one of the leather chairs and was working on the second. The sections he'd finished looked darker and more supple. "If you're looking for Ned, he's across the hall."

"I'm looking for you, if you're Hale Brandenberg."

"You selling something?"

"No."

"Serving papers?"

"I'm looking for information."

"Come on in and have a seat. You can use my desk chair since it's the only one available. You mind if I work while we talk?"

"Fine with me," I said. Taking advantage of his offer, I circled his desk and sat. His swivel chair was upholstered where mine was not, but I felt at home anyway because the squeaks were similar. As I watched, I was struck by a sense of familiarity. "I know you. Don't I know you?"

"I get that a lot. People tell me I look like the Marlboro Man."

I laughed. "You do."

He moved his rag across the tin of saddle soap, which he applied to the chair arm with a circular motion. "You have a name?"

"Oh, sorry. Kinsey Millhone. I'm a PI from Santa Teresa. Are you sure we haven't met? I could swear I've run into you. Maybe a professional meeting?"

"I don't do those. Do you socialize up here?"

"I hardly socialize anywhere."

"Nor do I. So what can I do for you?"

"Does my name ring a bell?"

He took his time answering. "Possibly, though the context escapes me. Refresh my memory."

"You worked for my grandmother once upon a time. Cornelia Kinsey."

He moved from the side of the chair to the back, the leather looking almost wet as he rubbed in the saddle soap. "What makes you think I worked for her?"

"I have the invoices."

"Mrs. Kinsey still alive?"

"Yes."

"I'm not at liberty to discuss her business without her consent."

"Admirable."

"You said you're a PI. You must find yourself in the same boat every now and then."

"As a matter of fact, it happened in the last two weeks."

"Then I don't have to spell out the ethical implications. She paid for the information. It belongs to her."

"Don't you think the statute of limitations has run out where I'm concerned?"

"Depends on what you want to know."

I opened the manila envelope and dumped the letters on his desk. "Know what these are?"

"Not from down here. You want to hold something up where I can see it?"

I picked up a handful of letters, which I fanned out and held in view. "Some of these were sent to my Aunt Gin and some to me. All of them were returned unopened. Well, except the first. It looks like Aunt Gin read that one before she put it back in the mail to Grand."

"You steal them?"

"No, but I would have, given half a chance. A cousin of mine came across them when she was going through my grandfather's files. I figured the letters are mine since they're addressed to me."

"You'd have to take that up with an attorney. I'm not well versed in the laws governing intellectual property," he said. "What happened to Virginia Kinsey?"

"She died fifteen years ago."

"Ah. Well, I'm sorry to hear."

"I was the sole beneficiary of her estate, which means her letters are mine as well."

"You won't catch me arguing the point."

"Did you know her?"

"I met her in the line of duty, so to speak."

"You want to hear my theory?"

"I can't prevent you from voicing an opinion."

"In the two or three years after my parents' death, my grandmother was hell-bent on gaining custody of me. It's all in the letters. I'm guessing you were hired to investigate my Aunt Gin in hopes of impugning her parenting ability."

Hale Brandenberg said nothing. His rag went around and around while he squinted in the manner of a man who's accustomed to working with a cigarette in one corner of his mouth. His was a type I'd run across before. The rugged outdoor sort. His humor was dry and understated, and his persona had a comforting appeal.

"No comment?" I asked.

"Don't think so. I understand your interest, but the same principle applies. You want the information, talk to your granny."

"She's in her nineties and losing it, from what I hear. I doubt she'd remember what you did for her."

"That doesn't mean I'm free to discuss it with you."

"Mr. Brandenberg, in less than a month, I'll be thirty-eight

years old. I'm not up for adoption so I don't see what difference it could *possibly* make if you confirmed what I've said."

He smiled faintly. "The name's Hale and you have a point.
At your age, I'm sure the court would take your wishes into
consideration before making a decision about placement."

"That's safely nonresponsive. What if I ask about process
instead of content?"

"You can try."

"What happened to the written reports? I've got invoices
but nothing else."

"There weren't any."

"How so?"

He smiled. "I'd have to cite confidentiality again."

"Were you supposed to grab me and run?"

"Oh, god no. I wouldn't have hired out if that was the
point."

I sorted through the invoices. "She paid you close to four
thousand dollars."

"I put in a lot of hours."

"Doing what?"

He was quiet and I could see him brooding.

I said, "Look. This is all ancient history. There's nothing
at stake. Whatever Grand's intentions, she couldn't have succeeded because here I sit."

He was quiet for a moment more. "Can I buy you a cup of
coffee?"

Surprised, I said, "Sure. I'd like that."

I pictured a coffee shop, but Hale had something else in
mind. We went into the lobby of an office building three doors
down. In one corner, there was a coffee cart, complete with
wee containers of half-and-half, sugar packets, stirring sticks,
and freshly baked cinnamon buns. He glanced at me. "Have
you had lunch?"

"It's ten A.M."

He smiled. "How about a sticky bun?"

"Sure, why not? I skipped breakfast this morning along
with my three-mile run."

He pointed to three big cinnamon buns that the woman behind the cart picked up with a sheet of waxed paper and placed
in a sack. He asked for two jumbo coffees to go, which she

poured, and then set in a collapsible cardboard tray. He picked
up a handful of half-and-half containers the size and shape of
bonbons, and then he added a pile of sugar packets.

After he paid, I followed him out the lobby door and from
there to the grassy park across the street. I got the impression
this was his morning ritual. The bench he chose was in dap-
pled shade. By the time he sat down, setting the cardboard tray
between us, a Disney-like assortment of birds and squirrels
had appeared in anticipation of the third pastry, apparently intended for them. Our conversation proceeded by fits and starts
while we sipped coffee and munched on sticky buns, tossing
nuggets to the little creatures gathered at his feet.

"You understand I could have my license yanked if this got
back to her."

"How would it get back to her? I won't breathe a word of
it. Scout's honor."

He sat and thought about it. "What the hell. I'm close to
retirement. I'll take you at your word."

"Please."

"You're right about the job. Mrs. Kinsey hired me to do a
background check on Virginia."

"She wanted proof Aunt Gin was unfit to act as my guardian, right?"

"Basically. Your grandmother had enough money to pay
for the best attorneys. Still does, for that matter. She also had
enough to pay for my services, which didn't come cheap . . .
as you so kindly pointed out. She thought she could influence
the social workers and the judge and she wasn't too far wrong.
Virginia Kinsey was an odd duck."

" 'Eccentric' is the word," I said. "So what went on?"

He smiled, conceding the point. "Your parents left no instructions about guardianship if something happened to them.
Your aunt had no experience with kids. You must have discovered that yourself if you had half a brain. She was one of
a kind. She could knock back whiskey with the best of them
and she cussed like a stevedore. I could have made a case for
your grandmother being the better equipped to care for a five-
year-old."

"Is that what you did?"

"No."

"What happened?"

"I'll get to that in a bit. Two things I should tell you first. I didn't like your grandmother then and I don't like her now. Maybe she reminds me too much of my own granny, who was stingy and bad-tempered, as hateful as they come. Mrs. Kinsey's the same, self-centered and autocratic, which won't fly with me. I've worked for her a time or two after that job, but it's been years now, which is why I asked if she was still alive."

"Fair enough."

"Here's the other thing. That was the only job I ever did strictly for the money. I was just getting into the business. I'd borrowed from the bank to set up my office, but clients weren't exactly breaking down my door. The loan officer . . . the cranky so-and-so . . . expected payment and I didn't have a dime. I put him off as long as I could, but I was running out of excuses. I don't know what the bank would've done if I'd defaulted. I figured the last thing they wanted was an empty office filled with my used furniture. I knew the location was good and I was convinced I'd have business enough to support myself—at least modestly—within a short period of time. I just didn't have the cash in hand.

"Mrs. Kinsey came along and told me what she had in mind. Even as desperate as I was, I didn't want to work for her so I named an exorbitant price. She agreed to pay it and I was stuck. I sat surveillance on Virginia off and on for weeks— first in 1955, then again in '56 and early '57. In truth, I never saw your aunt as a motherly type. She provided you with the basics, but I didn't witness much in the way of affection."

"I can testify to that."

He smiled. "You were a tiny little thing and you clung to her like a monkey. So much so that I wondered about your emotional stability. You'd taken a hit. The loss of your parents was a blow I wasn't sure you'd recover from. Virginia wasn't nurturing, but she was solid and she was constant. She was also a firecracker when it came to protecting you. In my opinion, that was enough."

"You decided all this sitting in a car parked down the street from us?"

"Not quite. I'd been out there less than a week when she spotted me. I thought I'd been discreet, but she was sharp. She must have known her mother was up to no good. One day she came out to the car, gestured I should roll the window down, and then invited me in. She said if I was going to spy on her I might as well do it up close and net myself a cup of coffee in the bargain. After that, she knew I was following her, but she made no concessions. She did exactly what she always did. What I thought of her and what I reported was of no concern."

"I'm missing something here," I said. "My grandmother was ancient even then. What made her think she had any chance of gaining custody?"

"It was the other way around. She thought she had the means to knock your Aunt Gin out of the running. If she managed to do that, who else was going to step in?"

"My mother was the oldest of five girls. Aunt Gin was next, and after her there was Sarah, Maura, and Susanna. I should think any one of them would have been preferable."

"They were financially dependent on the senior Kinseys. All the girls made respectable marriages, but their husbands didn't have the kind of money your grandparents did. As I heard the story, Sarah and Maura didn't approve of your mother anyway and neither one of them was willing to defy Mrs. Kinsey once they knew she wanted you."

"What kind of leverage did she have aside from that? I'm still not getting it."

"I've probably said enough."

"Come on."

"Don't you ever give up?"

"It doesn't hurt to ask. I figure you'll tell me as much or as little as you want."

He took a bite of sticky bun and chewed for a while, then took a sip of coffee. "Your grandmother believed Virginia was a lesbian."

I stared at him, astonished. "You're not serious."

"You asked about the leverage. That was it. In those days, the accusation was damaging, even if there wasn't any proof. That's why I wouldn't give her written reports. I didn't want Mrs. Kinsey to have anything to hold over Virginia's head."

"Aunt Gin was gay?"

"That's not what I said. I said I wouldn't put anything in writing one way or the other."

"How'd she come up with the notion in the first place?"

"I have no idea. When she came to my office, she told me what she wanted, which was to get 'the goods' on her daughter. That was the phrase she used. She said no judge would permit custody to go to someone of such a 'bent.' I told her I wouldn't tailor my findings to suit her purposes. She said she'd be happy to hire someone else who'd give her what she was paying for. I told her I didn't give a shit who she hired. If she didn't care about the truth, she wouldn't be doing business with me."

"She let you talk to her that way?"

"She took offense, but I think she liked it. Hardly anyone stood up to her in those days."

"They still don't. Go on with your story."

"She was irritated, but in the end she agreed. The thing about her, she was an egomaniac, but there was a line she was hesitant to cross. Virginia was still a Kinsey. If your grandmother was right, exposing Virginia would be an embarrassment to her as well as to the rest of the family."

"You're saying if she was right, she wouldn't have used the information?"

"Not publicly, no. I was worried she would do something underhanded. She was devious and I didn't want to give her the ammunition."

"So you told her Aunt Gin was straight?"

"She was."

I squinted at him. "Are you leveling with me?"

"Why wouldn't I? To me, the idea was ridiculous. There was never a shred of evidence Virginia Kinsey was anything other than a dyed-in-the-wool heterosexual. She preferred being single, but that's not aberrant behavior. A lot of folks are like that. I'm one."

"Me, too," I said. "I don't understand why Grand would even raise the question."

"It must have been the worst thing she could think of, so naturally, she wanted it to be true."

"As old-fashioned and proper as she seems, I can't believe she even knew about such things."

"Don't kid yourself. Even Victorian women had their 'special' friends. When two 'single' women settled in together, eyebrows went up. The arrangement was referred to as 'a Boston marriage.' "

"Did Aunt Gin know what Grand was up to?"

"I believe she did."

"I don't know what to do with this. For years, I've been feeling sorry for myself because I thought my grandmother didn't give a shit. Now it looks like she cared so much, she'd have blackmailed her own daughter to achieve her ends."

"That's about the size of it. On the bright side, she failed."

"Yeah, and on the dark side, look at what it cost. My poor Aunt Gin. I had no idea what she was going through. She made sure no whisper of it ever reached my ears. For years, I wasn't aware I had family beyond her. I only learned about my relatives when she was gone."

"A woman of contradictions. Forthright and secretive in the same breath."

I studied him, wondering if I was missing something. "I don't want you bending the truth. I'm truly fine with it either way."

"Why so suspicious? You must have 'trust issues,' as they're referred to in the common parlance."

I laughed. "Maybe. And what about you?"

"You'd have to be a fool to trust most people. I credit myself with more intelligence."

I glanced at my watch. "Oops. I have a meeting in Belicia, so I should hit the road. I appreciate your confidence. My lips are sealed." I made a zipping motion across my mouth.

Hale wadded up the paper sack and tossed it in the trash. "If you have other questions, don't hesitate to call."

It wasn't until I was on the road again that I realized he hadn't actually answered my question about whether he'd lie.

# 26

The business address Shawn Dancer had given me in Belicia turned out to be his home address as well. The town itself was small, spread out like a net between the highway and the beach. The main source of income was the tourist trade, visitors attracted by the setting and the work of local artisans, who made everything from cheeses to breads to boutique wines. I spotted seven art galleries on the main thoroughfare, where there were also shops selling jewelry, handmade furniture, textiles, and other one-of-a-kind crafts. Countless small hotels and bed-and-breakfast places lined the narrow streets, with high-end restaurants, cafés, and bistros sufficient to service the locals as well as the numerous travelers who'd come to explore the area. At this time of year, rates were reasonable and I saw a number of No Vacancy signs.

Shawn Dancer lived in a one-story gray-painted frame house, with a suggestion of Victoriana in its steep gables, fish-scale shingled roof, and gingerbread trim. I pulled up in front and parked. I knocked at the front door and waited the requisite few minutes, wondering if anyone was home. The door was opened by a young woman I judged to be scarcely out of her teens. She was just a slip of a thing, with large hazel eyes and a halo of black curls. She was barefoot, wearing cutoffs and a T-shirt that she'd knotted in the front. Her right arm was weighted with silver bracelets.

I said, "Hi. I hope I have the right house here. I'm looking for Shawn."

"He's in his shop around back."

Since she offered nothing else, I thanked her and then went down the porch steps, turned right, and followed the drive. The workshop was the main house in miniature, connected by a breezeway. The door was standing open and the scent of glue and raw wood perfumed the air. I could hear the high-pitched singing of a lathe. Shawn, in coveralls and goggles, was intent on his task, which allowed me a moment to study him without his being aware.

He was tall with a mop of dark curly hair. The seams of his white coveralls were etched in sawdust. Unacquainted as I was with the tools of his trade, I could still identify buffing and drilling machines, routers, planes, disk sanders, miter and band saws. He'd glued the edge joints of two wide flat panels together, then placed them in a big C-clamp. Rough lumber was stacked on end against one wall. Hundreds of drill bits, small tools, and wooden templates were arranged neatly on wall-mounted pegboard panels.

He turned, and when he saw me he shut down the lathe. "Hey."

"Are you Shawn?"

"Absolutely. You must be the investigator from S.T."

"Kinsey Millhone," I said. "Nice meeting you. I see I caught you hard at work."

"Always. I'm glad you figured out where I was."

"The girl who came to the door told me you were back here."

"You met Memory."

"I assume so, though she didn't introduce herself."

His expression was wry. "She sometimes comes up short in the manners department. Sorry about that. She doesn't mean to be rude."

"No need to apologize. You're the one I came to see."

"Hope I can help. How's Deborah doing these days?"

"Good. We did a beach walk last Wednesday, and she's in better shape than I am."

"Have a seat if you can find one," he said.

"This is fine."

He hoisted himself onto a bare patch of workbench while I leaned against the table, keeping us eye-to-eye. We chatted for a bit, working our way around to the subject at hand.

Finally, he said, "Why don't you tell me what's going on?"

"I'll try to be succinct about this," I said. I launched into my tale, distilling it down to the salient points. "An old kidnapping case has popped into view again for reasons too complicated to go into. A little girl named Mary Claire Fitzhugh disappeared in July of 1967 and hasn't been seen since."

"That's bad."

"Very bad, but at least there's hope we'll find out what happened to the child. As I understand it, you and your mom and dad were in Santa Teresa that same summer—"

"Greg wasn't my dad," he said. "Just want to be clear on that since Mom was."

"Sorry. I'm hazy on the details, which is why I'm here."

"Matters not. Go on."

"I know the three of you were staying with the Unruhs. Deborah tells me Greg was pressing them to hand over the money his grandfather had left him so he and Shelly could buy a farm . . ."

Shawn was already shaking his head. "I heard 'em cooking up the story, but it was fiction, every word of it. Nitwits. I don't know what they were thinking. Patrick wasn't going to underwrite their cockamamie plan, even if it had been legitimate. The money was in trust and there was no way they could've busted into it. Well, maybe with a legal hassle, but Greg wasn't in a position to stick around for that."

"What was he up to? Can you fill me in?"

"Sure. Greg dropped out of Berkeley in his sophomore year, which meant he lost his 2-S student deferment and was reclassified as 1-A, ready for immediate induction. His draft notice caught up with him and he promptly burned it. He and Mom were both paranoid about authority, her more than him. He decided to go to Canada. She wasn't keen on the idea, but he had friends in hiding up there and he figured he could take advantage of the connections. If he got his hands on his inheritance, they'd have enough to live on while they applied for citizenship."

"I can understand the kind of pressure he was under."

"Well, yeah, from his perspective. I'll tell you what was dumb. I didn't realize this until later, but in July of 'sixty-seven, Greg was twenty-five years old. Once he turned twenty-six, he'd be off the hook, so all he had to do was wait. I don't think they were taking married guys, so if he and Mom had been willing to go that far, he'd have been home free. Not that they'd have done anything so pedestrian. They were hippies and way too free-spirited for anything as mundane as a civil ceremony. Anyway, once it was obvious the Unruhs weren't going to cooperate, we hit the road, which was their solution to just about anything."

"Why such an abrupt departure?"

"They did everything on impulse, though there might have been something more going on. I heard a lot of heated whispers from the back of the bus. Greg was in a panic."

"Any idea when that was?"

"Not a clue. I was a kid. What did I know? I remember Mom lobbied hard for San Francisco. There was all this talk about the Summer of Love and she was pissed she'd be missing out. She said it wasn't like they'd have a posse on their tails. There were thousands of guys ducking the draft, so all they had to do was keep on the move and they'd be fine. Cut no ice with Greg. He was anxious to get out of Dodge, so to speak. As far as she was concerned, that was his problem, not hers. She knuckled under in the end, but not without a lot of knock-down, drag-out fights. You want my take on it, I got the impression somebody called the draft board and dimed him out."

"If they left empty-handed, what'd they do for money?"

"The usual—panhandled, sold dope, stole stuff. It's what they always did when they were down and out, which I might add was their permanent state. The trip took weeks because of all the stops we made, scoring cash for gas and food. To this day, I bet I could support myself standing at a four-way stop with a funky cardboard sign."

"They didn't turn around and head back to Santa Teresa for any reason?"

"No way. Greg was freaked out. They were happy to be gone."

"Patrick believed they'd come up with a scheme to get money. He was convinced they never really left town."

Shawn shook his head. "I'm the only one who ever came back and that was three years ago when I read about Patrick being killed. I wanted to pay my respects."

"Are you aware that Rain was kidnapped right about the time Greg and Shelly left?"

"Rain was?"

"Less than a week after they took off. The ransom demand was fifteen grand, which Patrick paid. She was returned in good shape and ten days later, the other little girl was snatched. The Unruhs thought Greg and Shelly had a hand in it."

"Not true. Once we left the States, that was it. Why would Patrick blame them?"

"Because it made sense. At least in his mind. The two were desperate for money. The Unruhs refused and the next thing they knew, Rain was abducted and they were forced to pay. The plan was lame, but Deborah says their brains were addled from all the dope they smoked."

"Well, that's a fact. I was stoned half the time myself."

"At ten?"

"That's what life was like in those days. Don't get me wrong. Mom had her principles. Until I turned sixteen, she wouldn't condone peyote, cocaine, or heroin. She also drew the line at LSD. Very strict, she was. She got into the heavy stuff herself, but not until later."

"You were homeschooled?"

"That was her claim, but it was BS. She quit school when she was fifteen and pregnant with me. That was ninth grade so she didn't know enough to teach me anything. I survived by looking after myself. If I'd been a pain in the ass, she'd have dumped me the way she did Rain."

"When did you last see your mom?"

"She died of AIDS in 'eighty-six. Ugly business. I could have done without that."

"What about Greg?"

"He died of an overdose when I was fourteen. That's when Mom and I came back to the States. Mom's first thought was

San Francisco. Man, she was really burning up the road. Of course, the Haight was dead by then, but she was ever hopeful. We lived in Berkeley for a while and then Santa Cruz. Eight months in Mexico and I can't remember where else. We didn't stay long in any one place. It was a crappy way to grow up."

"How'd you end up in Belicia?"

"It was one of our many stops along the way. I met a guy here who handcrafted furniture, and he said he'd mentor me if I was ever interested. By the time I was twenty, I'd had it with all the moving around so I settled here. He taught me everything I know."

"It looks like you're doing well."

"This is true," he said, with mock modesty.

"How long have you and Memory been together?"

He smiled. "She's not my girlfriend."

"I'm sorry. I just assumed."

"She's my sister."

"Really? I'm not sure Deborah knows about that."

"No reason she would. We left Santa Teresa in July. Memory was born in Canada the next April. Greg was pissed about the whole deal. He said the last thing they needed was another mouth to feed. He wanted Mom to put the baby up for adoption, but she was having none of it. They went after that subject hammer and tongs. He said since she'd dumped Rain, she could dump this one, too. Mom wouldn't budge. Personally, I don't believe the baby was his."

"Wow. Whose, then?"

"Who knows? Anyway, if we've covered the subject, I'll get back to work."

"Sure thing. I may call you later if something new comes up, but for now I appreciate your time. Do you mind if I tell Rain about Memory? I'm sure she knows about you, but I'm guessing she'd want to hear about her sister. Deborah, too."

"You can tell them anything you like. I'd love to see Rain if she ever has the inclination to come up. Or maybe Memory and I will drive down."

"If I talk to her, I'll tell her you said so."

"Give both of them my love."

Driving south again I had a lot on my mind. I was still mulling over the account Hale Brandenberg had given me about Grand. When it came to Greg and Shelly's departure, I confess I felt vindicated. They hadn't turned around at all, let alone snatched first Rain and then Mary Claire. I understood Deborah's reasoning, but the points she cited were circumstantial, a crude cause and effect that didn't hold up to scrutiny. This was the kicker from my perspective: if Greg and Shelly weren't guilty, then who was?

When I reached the office, I parked, snagged my shoulder bag, and got out of the car, locking it behind me. I noticed a car parked directly across from mine, a sleek white Corvette with a woman in the driver's seat and a guy in the passenger seat next to her. The sun reflecting off the windshield prevented a clear view of the driver so I shrugged to myself and continued up the walk. I unlocked the office door, and as I was letting myself in I heard two car doors slam in quick succession.

I glanced over my shoulder and saw Diana Alvarez moving in my direction. Her male companion was someone I'd never seen before. Oh, joy, I thought. She looked as buttoned-down as ever—loafers, black tights, and a black corduroy jumper worn over a white turtleneck. I could see that any outfit looked spiffier when paired with black tights, and I vowed to add more to my wardrobe. Since I was already the proud owner of two skirts, I'd be all set.

Diana carried a large leather tote, bulging from the weight of an oversized book. "I'm glad we caught you," she said. "We were just about to take off. This is my brother, Ryan."

Belatedly I saw the resemblance. The solemn dark eyes were clearly a family trait. "Nice to meet you," I said.

Ryan and I shook hands. He wore gray slacks and a charcoal sport coat over a pin-striped dress shirt. His red tie introduced the only note of color. Offhand, I pegged him as a salesman working in the retail clothing business, maybe Sears. I couldn't imagine why she was back again.

"Mind if we come in?" she asked.

"Might as well."

I stepped back and let them move into the office ahead of me. They settled in the guest chairs, Diana adjusting her skirt before she placed her tote on the floor. She tilted the case against the modesty panel on the front of my desk. There was something self-satisfied in her demeanor, a quality I'd seen before and one that made me testy.

I sat down in my swivel chair. "What can I do for you?"

Even before she spoke I could tell she'd rehearsed her remarks, eager to present herself as someone organized and in control. "I told Ryan about the conversation we had—"

I interrupted, hoping to throw her off balance. "We've actually talked twice—once at the dig and again the next day."

"I'm referring to our meeting here. Something nagged at me when you talked about Michael's seeing the two men in Horton Ravine. If you'll remember, I asked you then what made him so certain of the date and you told me it was because it happened on his sixth birthday."

"Okay."

"Even at the time it seemed off and I remember saying so."

"You know you really don't have to go through the whole thing again."

"I'm touching on the salient points," she said. "I hope you don't object."

"Far from it. I'm begging you to get on with it. I've got work to do."

She ignored that and went on. I half expected her to whip out her little spiral-bound notebook, but she'd committed her recital to memory. "You told me Mary Claire Fitzhugh was kidnapped on Wednesday, July 19, 1967. Michael claims he saw the two men two days later, on Friday, the twenty-first."

I waved a hand in the air, dismissing the details, which I didn't feel bore repeating. As far as I knew, none of this was in dispute.

She shot me a dark look and then went on. "According to his account, Mom dropped him off at the Kirkendalls'. Billie was sick so his mother let Michael wander on the property and that's when he came across the two men. I'm repeating this for Ryan's sake since he was the one who pointed out Michael's error."

"The error?"

"A whopper," Ryan said.

"And what might that be?"

Diana reached for her tote and removed what I could see

then was a scrapbook, the pages thick with newspaper clippings, programs, souvenirs, and party favors, some of which were sticking out. The assemblage was clearly the work of someone suffering from obsessive-compulsive disorder, who couldn't bear to throw anything away. She'd marked a particular page and she turned to it, reversing the album so I could see the contents without craning my neck.

Looking down, she said, "I started this when I was eight. To remind you of the family order, by the time Michael turned six, David was ten years old, Ryan was twelve, and I was fourteen."

"I'm aware of that," I said. I could see she was stringing it out and I could hardly keep from rolling my eyes.

"I can assure you, you're unaware of *this*," she said. "To celebrate his birthday that year, Mom and Dad took us all to Disneyland. You can see for yourself."

She pointed to a photograph that showed a costumed Mickey Mouse and Cinderella in the background. All four kids were seated at a table in an outdoor café, leaning toward the center so the photographer could get them all in one shot. Michael and his siblings wore paper hats, all of them grinning for the camera. The paper tablecloth, napkins, and cups were decorated with Happy Birthday greetings in several different fonts. The birthday cake was at Michael's place, with six candles burning away merrily.

I nearly said, So what? I was thinking, *Shit, a birthday doesn't have to be celebrated on the actual day. Parents can throw a party anytime they please.*

Diana sensed my response and moved her finger to the date along the bottom of the photograph. July 21, 1967. "You might note these as well if you're not convinced."

She turned the pages for me like a teacher reading a picture book upside down so I'd have it in perspective. She'd pasted in dated programs, ticket stubs, receipts, and additional snapshots that showed the kids on a variety of rides. Every item that bore a date supported her claim.

Ryan spoke up as though on cue. "There's something else."

"I can hardly wait."

"It's about the Kirkendalls."

He was hoping I'd prompt him, but I was tired of their routine. I said nothing, forcing him to flounder on without an assist. He cleared his throat and coughed once, saying, "Sorry. Keith Kirkendall was a CPA who embezzled $1.5 million from the firm he worked for. The discrepancies showed up during an independent audit and the authorities were closing in. He took his family and vanished overnight."

"So I've heard."

"Good. Then I'll get to the point. By July 17, when the news of Kirkendall's crime appeared in the local paper, the family was gone. On Friday, the twenty-first, the house was empty and not a stick of furniture remained. Even if Michael hadn't been at Disneyland, he couldn't have been there."

I was silent for a moment, calculating rapidly. "Maybe it was the week before. July fourteenth instead of the twenty-first." I was talking off the top of my head, desperate to salvage the story Michael had told me with such conviction.

Diana wagged an index finger. "No, no, no," she said, as though correcting an errant child. "Mary Claire was kidnapped on the nineteenth. If Michael had seen the men the week before—even if he was correct about what they were up to—the bundle couldn't have been her. She was still alive and well."

I closed my mouth and stared at them.

Diana Alvarez's eyes were bright with triumph. I could feel the color rising in my cheeks. Offhand . . . except for an incident in first grade . . . I couldn't think when I'd felt so humiliated. I'd believed Sutton. I'd persuaded others he was telling the truth. Now here I sat, feeling like an ass. I didn't care that my ego had taken a hit. I cared because we were back to square one where Mary Claire was concerned. The link, as tenuous as it might have been, was gone.

Diana reached into her tote again, this time pulling out a file folder that she then pushed across the desk. "I made copies of the photographs from Disneyland. I also made copies of the clippings about Keith Kirkendall so you can read them at your leisure. I knew you wouldn't be content to take our word for it."

I pushed the folder back across the desk. "I appreciate the offer, but you'll want those for your latest scrapbook."

She left the folder where it was. "I made duplicates. That's yours to keep. We've already dropped off a set for Lieutenant Phillips."

Ryan fixed his big brown eyes on me with a phony look of pity and regret. Briefly I considered leaping across the desk and biting him until he bled.

"Sorry you had to go through this," he said. "It's typical of Michael, but that doesn't make it any less infuriating."

"Have you told him?"

Diana said, "No. As you know, we're not on the best of terms. We thought the blow might be softer if it came from you."

"In other words, you want me to stick it to him instead of you."

Ryan said, "There's nothing personal at stake. We're setting the record straight. If you want us to put copies in the mail to him, we will."

"I'll take care of it."

He reached into the inner pocket of his sport coat and took out a checkbook and pen. "We're assuming he didn't have the money to pay for your services."

"Which is another reason we're here," Diana said. "I have no idea how much time and energy you've devoted to this wild-goose chase, but we're prepared to cover what he owes."

Ryan leaned forward to use the desk in writing the check.

"Michael's paid in full."

Diana's smile flickered. "Really? I find that hard to believe."

"Life is a barrel of surprises, Diana. Was there anything else?"

Ryan put the checkbook away and the two exchanged a look, apparently at a loss as to what should come next. They'd probably hoped to hear me rage about Michael and his tenuous hold on the truth, but I'd have cut my own throat before I gave them the satisfaction. Their departure was awkward, hard-pressed as they were to detach themselves with any ease or grace. I didn't offer to escort them to the door, but I did trail after them without the usual end-of-meeting pleasantries.

Once they were gone I locked the door and returned to my desk, where I sat and stewed for the better part of an hour.

# 27

## JON CORSO

### June 1967

A week after the family left for Europe, Jon arrived at Walker's house on his scooter just as Walker was coming down the drive in the secondhand 1963 Buick Skylark his father had given him the day he was accepted at UCST. The car wasn't new, but it was better than the crummy Chevrolet Lionel had bought for Jon. Walker leaned across the passenger seat and rolled down the window. "I gotta make a run. Leave the scooter in the carport and hop in."

Jon walked his scooter up the incline, parked it, and then hustled down the driveway to the street where Walker was waiting. He got in on the passenger side and slammed the door. "Where to?"

"Alita Lane. You won't believe this pair. They're living in a school bus. Creed and Destiny. He's an asshole but she's a trip. They went over to the high school, hoping to score some dope, and Chapman turned them on to me."

"Good deal."

When they reached Alita Lane, Walker parked around the corner and the two hoofed it back. Walker was careful to avoid parent types when delivering weed. He mentioned, in passing, that the house belonged to Creed's parents, Deborah and Patrick Unruh, whom Jon knew distantly from the country club. Mona was particularly enamored of Deborah Unruh and took every opportunity to fawn over her. Immediately Jon anticipated the moment when he could casually refer to the time he'd spent at Deborah's. Soon afterward, however, he decided the connection would never pass his lips. There were things Mona wasn't meant to know and most began to unfold on that day.

Jon followed Walker around the side of the house to the cabana in back, where the school bus was parked. A boy of ten or so was splashing naked in the pool, probably peeing in the water when it suited him. The school bus was ratty on the outside, but when Jon finally saw the interior he thought it was cool—decked out with mattresses, a camp stove, storage boxes. An Indian-print spread served as a privacy screen, dividing the vehicle into two parts. The couple crashed in the back while the kid sacked out on the futon in front.

The bus doors were open and the boyfriend was fussing around with something inside. The chick was cross-legged in the grass, knotting a length of hemp, using hitches and half-hitches to make a wall hanging, or something equally useless since the bus had no walls to speak of. She looked up as they approached. "Hey, Creed? We have company."

Creed emerged from the bus and Walker made the introductions. Nobody bothered to shake hands. Even years later, it was odd how vivid the moment seemed. Destiny was in her mid-twenties, six or seven years older than he. He'd never encountered anyone as hang-loose as she was. Her nails were bitten to the quick and her hair was a mass of curls. Her earrings were big silver hoops. She wore a scoop-necked peasant blouse, a long skirt, and Birkenstocks. She was chunky and smelled sooty from all the dope and cigarettes she smoked, but the scent reminded him of his mother. Destiny was a walking warning about the health hazards of poor nutrition and substance abuse. Within minutes, she mentioned she wasn't married to Creed.

Jon said, "Is that your kid in the pool?"

She laughed. "Mine, but not his. Sky Dancer's dad could have been any one of half a dozen guys."

Was she for real? Jon couldn't believe she'd said that.

After the preliminary chitchat, Creed handed Walker a

wad of wrinkled bills in exchange for a lid. Destiny set aside her macramé and invited them to "partake," as she referred to it, and then proceeded to roll the tightest joint he'd ever seen, about the size of a bobby pin. The four of them settled on the mattress at the back of the bus, smoking and making idle conversation. She had a husky laugh and she peppered the conversation with the sorts of expletives he associated with guys. After a time, he became aware that she was watching him. Creed, while dim, had to be aware of it, but seemed unconcerned.

Smoking dope made Jon paranoid and he was anxious about the kid who'd been left to play in the pool unsupervised. Now and then he'd find a pretext to hop out of the bus so he could check up on him. It wasn't his responsibility, but the kid's mother didn't seem to care. At one point, while he was paddling around the shallow end, she appeared at Jon's side, managing to stand closer than the situation required. The heat pouring off her skin left Jon mute. When she spoke, angling her face to his, it reminded him of those movie moments when the lovers are on the verge of kissing. Why was she coming on to him with Creed no more than fifteen feet away?

Jon shifted his focus to the kid, who was doing cannonballs off the side of the pool, plumes of water splashing up.

"Hey, Sky Dancer, shit-for-brains!" she snapped. "What's the matter with you? You want to hit your head and drown? Get over here before you crack your skull and die."

The kid grabbed the side of the pool and worked his way around to her. She leaned down and hauled him out by one arm, after which he sat hunched and shivering on the side.

Jon peered at her. "*What's* his name?"

"Sky Dancer. It's like his spiritual designation, the same way Destiny's mine. Why, you think it's weird?"

"It's not that. I just wasn't sure what you said."

She made a remark half under her breath and then turned to him, waiting for a response.

"Sorry, I didn't catch that."

"Yeah, you did," she said with a slow smile.

He stared at her for a moment and then made an excuse and returned to the bus. What kind of game was she playing?

From that day on, he and Walker hung out with Creed and

Destiny most afternoons. In her company, Jon was detached, seldom making eye contact. Surreptitiously he studied her, noting her gestures, absorbing her raucous laugh and her air of confidence. She didn't shave her legs or armpits, and she exuded an animal smell that stirred him in some curious way. She'd taken to ignoring him, but he knew she was as aware of him as he was of her. She was the antithesis of the *Playboy* centerfolds and he wove her into his daydreams.

On the occasions when Walker had other deliveries to make, Jon rode over on his scooter so he'd have his own transportation. Later he couldn't remember how the discussion about the money came up. Walker arrived fifteen or twenty minutes after he did that day. The three of them—Jon, Creed, and Destiny—were sitting around smoking dope, as usual, while Creed bitched and whined about his parents. Walker stretched out on the mattress, toking on the joint when it came around to him.

Jon sent Walker a look and then turned to Creed, saying, "Start over and tell him. Walker's big on finance."

Creed said, "Like I was telling Jon before you got here, my grandfather left me money in his will and my parents are refusing to let me have it. They claim I can't collect until I'm thirty. How fucked up is that?"

Destiny said, "His dad is such a butt. Creed's entitled to the money so what gives him a say in the matter one way or the other?"

"How much are we talking about?" Walker asked.

Jon said, "Forty grand."

Walker said, "Groovy. So what's the deal? Was it left in trust?"

"Technically, but that's bullshit. Dad could fork it over. He's got money up the wazoo."

"What do you need forty grand for, you planning a cruise?" Jon asked, his tone mild.

Creed and Destiny exchanged a look, and Creed said, "We're buying a farm. We put a thousand dollars down and we need the rest by the end of the month."

Jon laughed. "A *farm*? You're shittin' me."

Creed scowled. "What's wrong with that? We're planning

to work the land. Raise chickens and goats and sheep and like that."

Destiny said, "I'll learn to make soap and I can sell my macramé. We'll be completely self-sufficient. It'll be way cool."

"You're not buying a *farm*," Jon said. "What the hell are you talking about? How do you propose to 'work the land' when you don't know jackshit about anything?" He'd developed a very low opinion of Creed and loved egging him on. Sometimes Destiny sided with her boyfriend and sometimes she turned on him, mocking him as Jon did. Today she was standing by her man.

She said, "We're talking about a *commune,* dickwad. Don't be such a prick. Everyone will pitch in."

Jon could barely suppress a smile. "Oh, excuse me. A commune. Well, that explains it."

Destiny bristled. "God, Jon. Who the fuck asked you? Why are you always trying to bring us down? Keep your opinions to yourself."

"Hey, Des, come on. Why not tell 'em the truth?" Creed said.

"Because it's none of their business!"

"What isn't?" Walker asked.

"Nothing. Just drop it," she said.

Creed ignored her. "We're immigrating."

"Knock it off, Creed. You've said enough."

"Where to?" Jon asked.

"Canada."

Destiny pushed Creed sideways. "You know what your problem is? You don't know how to keep your big mouth shut."

"Baby, cool it. Would you just cool it? These are friends of ours, okay?" Creed turned to Jon. "I got my draft notice three weeks ago. We were having mail forwarded to a post office box in Oakland and there it was. I knew it was only a matter of time before they caught up with me. Short of shooting off my toe or claiming to be a bed wetter, my proverbial ass is grass. I'm cannon fodder. Big time."

Walker said, "So you're heading to Canada? Far out."

"I thought Sweden was the haven of choice," Jon remarked.

"Nah, Canada's easier. We take the old yellow school bus and head north. We don't even need passports."

"The forty's to cover us while we apply for citizenship," she added.

Jon's gaze shifted to her. "What if you get caught?"

Destiny flashed a look at him. "Man, you are bumming me *out*. What's all the negativity about? I'm getting bad vibes from you."

"I'm not putting you down. I'm just asking what you'll do if they catch up with you," he said.

"We don't need your counsel, shitbird. You're eighteen years old."

"You think Creed's mom and dad are going to buy your cock-and-bull story about a farm?"

"That's it, Jon. You're outta here. We don't have to put up with your shit," she said.

He smiled. "So okay, ignore me, but I'm telling you the truth. Creed's parents aren't stupid. You talk about starting a commune, they'll laugh in your face."

Creed said, "They already did when we first brought it up."

"You won't get a cent unless you come up with something better than that."

"Maybe we have. We've been giving it some thought."

"Creed!"

"What's wrong with running it by them?"

"Great. And have 'em rat us out? That'll be a big help."

Irritated, Walker said, "Get off it. We're not snitches."

"I'll just bet."

Jon watched her with interest. "Now you got me curious."

Creed took two quick hits from the joint and passed it to Jon. "Destiny came up with this. We could make it look like Rain's been abducted and someone's holding her for ransom. Dad would fall all over himself, forking up the dough."

"So how much ransom? Forty thousand? That'll fool 'em," Jon said.

Destiny said, "Shit, Jon, would you lighten up? We're still

working out the details, okay? We're tossing ideas around. We figure she's our kid so it's not like we're really doing any harm."

Jon drew on the joint, making the tip glow a bright red before he passed it on to her. "I thought his folks adopted her."

"Technically, sure, but she's still our kid," she said.

Creed said, "Yeah, Jon. You're missing the point. We scare 'em shitless, wait a couple days, and then hit 'em good like it's a one-time deal. Pay and you get the kid back. You don't pay, she's dead. They'll come through in a heartbeat, no questions asked."

Destiny brightened, warming to the subject. "It'll look like someone's snatched her, only she won't be in danger."

"Well, that sucks, right there," Jon said.

"Jesus . . ."

"Don't look at me like *that*. I'm playing devil's advocate. What if they call the cops or the FBI? I sure as shit would. You'll have the law swarming all over you."

"Not if we set it up right."

"Which would be what?" he asked.

"We're brainstorming. I'm not saying we've got all the answers," she said.

"You don't have *any* answers."

Walker cut in. "Where you going to keep her?"

Destiny considered the issue and then shrugged. "I don't know. Maybe a motel."

"Who's going to babysit the kid while the two of you walk around pretending to be innocent?"

"Maybe we'll be gone by then."

"Then how would you collect the dough?"

"We'd find a way," she said, irritated with his persistence.

Jon said, "Why don't you do the obvious? Tell them you have her stashed somewhere and you won't turn her over unless they make it worth your while. They don't pony up, they'll never see her again."

"I don't think my dad would go for it," Creed said. "So far he's turned us down cold."

"Don't ask for forty. Ask for fifteen. That's enough to get you out of the country."

"Yeah, but what if they balk?" she asked. "I mean, what if they tell us to take her and shove off. Then what?"

"Then I guess you get your daughter back," Jon said.


It was the weekend after that that their relationship changed. The last two weeks of June, Walker went to Hawaii on vacation with his folks. With Walker gone, Jon was at loose ends. The first couple of days he hung out at his place, watching TV. On day three he decided it was time to get out. He fired up his scooter and headed over to the Unruhs', arriving just in time to see the family pulling out of the drive. Looked like Patrick at the wheel, Deborah in the front seat, and Creed, Rain, and Sky Dancer in the back. He wasn't sure if Destiny was with them or not.

He parked the scooter and then peeked in the yellow school bus, which was empty. He could see her half-finished macramé lying in the grass. "Hey, Destiny? You here?" No response.

He shrugged and circled the house to the cabana, surprised at the pang of disappointment that shot through him.

"Is that you, Jon?"

He followed the sound of her voice and found her sitting on the edge of the pool, her gypsy skirt pulled up around her as she dangled her legs in the water. She wore a tank top, a white one, and he could see the freckles that covered her shoulders and chest. "Sun damage," she said when she caught his look.

"Where'd everybody go? I saw Creed and his folks in the car with the kids."

"It's Sky Dancer's birthday and he asked if he could go to the band concert in the pocket park on the hill. Deborah packed a picnic lunch. They'll be gone for hours."

"Why didn't you go?"

"Because I was hoping to see you. You want to see me?" She lifted her skirt, showing him that she was naked from the waist down. She opened her legs, exposing herself.

Irritably, Jon said, "What's the matter with you? Would you cut that out?"

She laughed. "Don't be a stick in the mud. It's just us."

He scanned the surroundings, realizing how sheltered the area was from the eyes of neighbors. The trellised fencing that stretched out on each side of the cabana was overgrown with wisteria that obstructed the view into the Unruhs' backyard.

"This is a very bad idea," he said.

"I think it's a very good idea."

He put his hands in his pockets, his gaze restlessly searching the perimeter of the property. The air was hot and he could hear birds. Two houses away, a lawn mower buzzed, and even at that remove he could smell the cut grass.

She ran her hands down along her belly and between her legs. "What would you give for a piece of this?"

"I'm not going to *pay* you."

"I'm not talking about money, shithead. I'm talking about what it's worth to you."

"What about Creed?"

"We have an open relationship."

"He knows you're doing this?"

"He probably has a pretty good idea. As long as we don't rub his nose in it, so to speak, then what's it to him? Creed doesn't own me and I don't own him."

"Anyone could walk in," he said. "What if the mailman comes by or the UPS guy, delivering a package?"

"If you're so worried about being seen, why don't we go into the cabana where we can talk and get to know each other a little bit. If you feel uncomfortable, all you have to do is say so. I'm not going to knock you down and jump your bones."

She held a hand up, wanting him to pull her to her feet.

Jon ignored her.

"You'd prefer to do it all out here?"

"No."

"Then help me up."

Jon grabbed her hand and pulled her to her feet. Primly she shook her skirt down. "All nice and neat," she said.

She moved toward the cabana. Jon followed her with a mounting sense of disbelief. This couldn't be happening. Passing through the door, she lifted her crossed arms and pulled the tank top over her head.

Inside, she'd made a pallet of blankets. Two joints at the ready with a roach clip, a pack of matches, and an ashtray. She unbuttoned her skirt and stepped out of it. Her figure was womanly—generous ass, small breasts with brown nipples as big and flat as fifty-cent pieces. The thatch of hair between her legs was dark and bushy. She knelt on the blanket, picked up a joint, and lit it. She took two or three quick draws and held the smoke in. She closed her eyes and toked once more before releasing the smoke in a thin stream. "You're wasting time, Jon. Don't just stand there with your clothes on. You can do better than that."

He hesitated, looking down at her as though measuring the drop from a ten-meter board. He stripped off his T-shirt and then stepped out of his pants. When he took off his jockey shorts, he saw the change come over her face.

"Oh my god, you're beautiful. Incredible. I'd forgotten what eighteen looks like." She crawled to the edge of the blanket and ran a hand along his bare flank and then looked up at him. He bent and kissed her upturned mouth.

# 28

### Wednesday afternoon, April 20, 1988

Wednesday afternoon I took Cabana Boulevard up the hill to Seashore Park, a city-owned stretch of palm trees and grass that skirts the bluff overlooking the Pacific. That morning I'd called Michael and asked him to meet me there. In my shoulder bag I had the file folder of clippings about Keith Kirkendall and copies of the photographs his sister had given me the day before. My body hummed with dread, but there was no avoiding the conversation. I couldn't bear to lay the revelation at his feet, but there was no escape.

The day was sunny and the air mild with scarcely any breeze at all. While I waited I walked the length of the chain-link fence that had been erected to prevent citizens from tumbling off the cliff. The drop to the ocean below was a good sixty feet. At high tide, the surf concealed the rocks. At low tide, the rocks were laid bare. Either way, a fall would be fatal. Looking down I could see the telltale muddy plume where a sandbar had formed, and the waves were breaking differently from how they did a hundred yards on each side. Most people think of the effluence as a riptide, but the proper term is "rip current." Tides are the function of the moon's gravitational pull. A rip current is a treacherous outflow that runs in a narrow line perpendicular to the beach, sometimes extending as far as twenty-five hundred feet. The term "undertow," used to describe the same phenomenon, is a misnomer as well. A rip current moves along the surface of the water, a function of the hidden shape of the shore itself. This one, like the rip current that swept Sutton's mother to her death, was an artifact of the same attempt by the city engineers to create a safe harbor where there was none before. As with so much in life, good intentions often generate unexpected results.

I heard Sutton's MG approaching long before I saw him pull into the small parking lot. He had the top down and his hair had been whipped into an untidy thatch that he smoothed as he stepped out of the car. He wore a sweatshirt and shorts, and the sight of his knobby knees nearly broke my heart. As before, I was struck by his youthfulness. When he was fifty instead of twenty-six, he'd look the same. I couldn't picture him portly or bald. I couldn't picture him with heavy jowls or a double chin. As he aged, his face would shrink away from his skull, but it would otherwise retain its boyish cast.

On the phone I hadn't specified the reason for the meeting. I felt badly about it now because he suspected nothing, which made him all the more vulnerable. Though I didn't understand the psychological dynamic, I sensed that after the destruction he'd brought down on his family, he'd moved from villainy to victimhood. By rights, the family should have been the ones to lay claim to all the suffering. Instead the burden was his.

There was a bench situated at the halfway point between us. As he approached from the narrow parking strip, I crossed the grass and sat down, placing the folder beside me, saying, "Hi, Michael. I appreciate your meeting me."

He sat down. "I was going into town anyway, so it was easy enough to swing by. How are you?"

"Not bad," I said. "How's Madaline?"

"Good. I'm on my way to pick her up, as a matter of fact."

"Good? I heard she was arrested for public drunkenness."

"She was, but the judge said he'd give her probation if she promised to straighten up her act."

"I see. And what does that consist of?"

"AA meetings twice a week. She doesn't have a car so I take her over and pick her up afterward."

"Has it occurred to you she's taking advantage of you?"

"This is just until she gets back on her feet. She's trying to find a job, but there's not a lot available here in her field."

"Which is what?"

"She's a model."

"And in the meantime, you provide meals, housing, transportation, bail money, and Goldie's dog food, right?"

"She'd do the same for me."

"I'm not convinced of that, but let's hope."

His smile faded. "You don't seem happy with me. What's wrong?"

"I don't even know where to start," I said. I blew out a big breath, marshaling my thoughts. Try as I might, I couldn't find a nice way of putting it. "Yesterday Ryan and Diana came to the office. She brought in a scrapbook that included memorabilia from your sixth-birthday party."

"Memorabilia?"

"Yeah. You know, snapshots, ticket stubs, stuff like that."

"Ticket stubs. What are you talking about?"

"July 21, you were all at Disneyland. Your mom and dad, Ryan, David, Diana, and you."

I watched the animation draining out of his face. "That can't be right."

"That was my first response."

"She's making things up, trying to get me in trouble."

I indicated the folder on the bench. "She made copies of the photographs. You can see for yourself."

"She's wrong. She has to be."

"I don't think so. She's a reporter. She may be irritating, but she knows how to write a story and she knows she better get her facts straight. Take a look."

"I don't need to look. I was at Billie's house. My mother dropped me off."

"The Kirkendalls were gone by then. Billie's dad stole a shitload of money. You said so yourself. He knew the police were closing in on him so he took his family and fled. The house was empty."

"You think I lied?"

"I think you made a mistake."

"I saw the pirates that day. The two of them were digging a hole. It could have happened before we left for Disneyland."

"The timing is off. Whatever you saw, it must have been the week before. And as Diana so aptly pointed out, if you saw the guys on July 14 instead of July 21, it couldn't have been Mary Claire's body wrapped for burial. She wasn't kidnapped until five days later."

He stared off at the sky, rocking his body on the bench. It was the self-comforting motion of a kid whose mother's an hour late picking him up from nursery school. He was almost beyond hope.

"Look, Michael. No one's faulting you," I said.

When dealing with someone else's emotional distress, it's best to gloss over the enormity of the disaster. It doesn't change reality, but it makes the moment easier . . . for the onlooker, at any rate.

"Are you kidding? She must have had a good laugh at my expense. Ryan, too. They were always in cahoots."

Shit. Now he'd turned it into a conspiracy. I kept my mouth shut. I'd already offered as much comfort as I could muster.

"What about Lieutenant Phillips? Does he know?"

I glanced away from him, which told him what he'd already guessed.

"She told him, *too*?"

"Michael, don't do this. Yes, she told him. She had to. He was in on the story from the first. She gave him the same file folder she gave me, and so what?"

He blinked and put his right hand to his face, pulling down until his hand covered his mouth. "I saw the pirates. They knew I'd caught them in the act."

"Okay, fine, but not when you thought you did. July 21, 1967, you and your family were a hundred miles away."

"They were burying a bundle . . ."

"I believe you saw *something,* but it wasn't Mary Claire."

He shook his head. "No. They took the body somewhere else and put a dog in the hole. It was right where I showed you."

"Let's quit with the arguing and deal with what's true instead of what you dreamed up."

He lifted a hand. "Never mind. You're right. I wasted your time and I misled the police. Now all parties concerned are fully aware of it. So much for me and anything I might say."

"Would you stop that shit? I can't sit here and sympathize when you're wallowing in self-pity. I understand your embarrassment, but take your licks and move on."

He got up abruptly and walked away.

Watching him, I could see how he wanted the scene to play out. My role was to hurry after him, offering reassurances. I was supposed to fling myself into the conflict to help him save face. I couldn't do it. The bottom had dropped out. The search for Mary Claire was over and he knew it as well as I did. She might be buried somewhere, but it had nothing to do with him. While I understood his humiliation, his behavior was calculated to generate a response. He was the vacuum. I was meant to be the air rushing in to fill the space. Stubbornly, I stayed where I was.

I heard the car door slam. The engine roared to life. I looked over and watched him back out in a wide arc before he threw the car in first and drove off with a chirp of his tires.

To no one in particular, I said, "Sorry about that. I wish I could help you, but I can't."

I picked up the folder and returned to my car. I slid under the wheel and sat for a moment, watching pigeons pecking in the grass. I was only five blocks from home and my instinct was to run for cover. What I was facing wasn't new. Past investigations had occasionally come apart in my hands and I hadn't felt the need to fall on my sword. I'm an optimist. I operate on the assumption that if a question is legitimate, there's an answer out there, which is no guarantee I'll be the one to find it. While the current failing wasn't mine, I couldn't shake the sense that I'd messed up somehow.

It was midafternoon and I probably could have talked myself into quitting for the day, but one can only do that so often before it becomes habitual and, therefore, unprofessional. Playing hooky wasn't the antidote to disappointment. Work was. I had a business to run and I needed to get back to it. Easier said than done.

When I reached the office I set up a pot of coffee and then I sat at my desk and did nothing. I'd chastised Sutton for feeling sorry for himself, but it wasn't such a bad idea. When you've been dealt a blow, self-pity, like rationalization, is just another way of coping with the pain.

A sound penetrated my consciousness and I realized someone was tapping on one of the panes in my outer office door. I glanced at my calendar. I wasn't expecting anyone and there was no note of an appointment. For a moment I had the bizarre sense of skipping back in time. I pictured myself getting up to look around the corner at the front door. Through the glass, I'd catch my first sight of Michael Sutton. It would be April 6 again and I'd be forced to relive the same series of events.

I left my desk and crossed to the inner-office door, where I peered into the reception area. There was a woman on my doorstep, pointing at the knob. For the second time in two weeks I'd locked up automatically after letting myself in. I turned the deadbolt and opened the door. "Sorry about that. Can I help you?"

"I wondered if I might talk to you."

"Sure. I'm Kinsey Millhone. Have we met?"

"Not really. I'm Joanne Fitzhugh. Mary Claire's mother. May I come in?"

"Of course."

I stepped aside as though admitting an apparition. She was probably in her mid-fifties, with one of those lovely mild faces assigned to dead saints on Catholic calendars. She was half a head shorter than I, with shoulder-length blond hair worn in the sort of flip I'd longed for in high school. She wore a dark skirt and a matching cropped jacket with a green silk blouse under it. For having thought about her so often, I was unprepared for an encounter. What was I going to say to her? I'd come up against a blank wall. How could I explain where I'd started and where I'd ended up?

"Would you like a cup of coffee?"

"I'm fine. Don't worry about it."

She sat down in one of the guest chairs and pulled the other one closer, giving the seat a quick pat as a way of encouraging me to sit near her instead of on the other side the desk. She was clearly in charge. When I settled in the chair, the two of us were almost knee to knee.

Her features were finely drawn: small blue eyes, light brows and lashes, a straight nose, and lips thinned by age. Usually,

I think of beautiful women in terms of the overblown—high cheekbones, big eyes, plump lips. Hers was a beauty of a different kind—soft, subdued. Her cologne smelled like fresh soap, and if she wore makeup at all, it was discreetly applied. I can't make small talk with someone whose only child has been kidnapped and killed, so I left it up to her.

"I spoke to Lieutenant Dolan this morning. He's been gracious about keeping in touch with me since he retired. He called, saying your name had come up with regard to Mary Claire's disappearance. He tells me a young man named Michael Sutton has come forward with information that looks promising."

"I don't know what to say. May I call you Joanne?"

"Of course."

"Michael was wrong about the date. This came to light yesterday and I'm still adjusting to the disappointment. He was a kid at the time, six years old, and the incident he remembered actually happened a week earlier, if at all."

"I don't understand. Lieutenant Dolan said he came across two men digging what appeared to be a grave two days after Mary Claire was kidnapped. You're saying his report was false?"

"He made a mistake. There was no malice intended. He read a newspaper article and Mary Claire's name triggered a vivid recollection. His story sounded reasonable. Detective Phillips thought it was worth pursuing and so did I.

"Yesterday, Michael's sister came in with evidence showing he wasn't anywhere near Santa Teresa on the date he claimed, so it looks like he conjured the memory out of whole cloth. Whatever he saw, it had nothing to do with Mary Claire. I wish we had more, but it's not there."

"Well." She stared down at her hands.

"I know all of this is hard on you, and I'm sorry."

"Not your fault. I should be used to it by now. I should have detached years ago, but I've never found a way to do it. Something like this comes up . . . a scrap of information surfaces and even against my better judgment, I feel a flutter of hope. I can't tell you how many people have come up with 'clues' in the last twenty years. They write, they call, they stop me on the street, all of them claiming to know Mary Claire's whereabouts. Any reference in the paper and the 'tips' come pouring out. Some ask for money and some just want to feel important, I suppose."

"Believe me, Michael wasn't doing this for gain. He was hesitant about going to the police and uneasy when they sent him over to me. As odd as his story was, it seemed to hold an element of truth. In the end, it just didn't hang together."

"I'm not blaming anyone. It's all just so endless."

"Look, I know this is none of my business, but can you tell me what happened afterward? I can't imagine what it must have done to your personal life."

"It's simple enough. My husband and I divorced. It might have been unfair to fault Barry for the way he handled the situation, but watching him those three days taught me things I hadn't fully understood. He took over. He called all the shots. I was relegated to the sidelines while he dealt with the police and the FBI. My opinions and my reactions meant nothing to him. For the first time, I saw the sort of man I was married to."

"What would you have done if it had been up to you?"

"Exactly what they asked. I'd have kept the matter quiet instead of bringing in the police. I'd have paid the ransom without a second thought. That's what the Unruhs did and their daughter survived. I'm sure the FBI would have deemed it the worst possible tactic, but what did they have at stake? Twenty-five thousand was nothing to us. I found out later Barry had twice that much in a secret account—money he used to establish his new life after we separated. For all I know, that was always his intention, saving up so he could leave. I reached a point where I didn't care one way or the other. I suppose if Mary Claire had been saved . . . if she'd come back to us alive . . . we might have smoothed things over and gone on as we had before."

"Is he still in town?"

"He moved to Maine. I think he wanted a location as unlike California as he could find. He remarried and started another family. So much for us."

"Do you have any idea why you were targeted?"

"Barry owns a wealth-management firm. It's a company he started years ago and he's always done well. He felt that's what put us in the line of fire. That and because Mary Claire was an only child."

"How long were you married?"

"Eight and a half years." She hesitated. "I'll admit when he left me, I took revenge, spiteful little thing that I am. According to our prenuptial agreement, if we divorced, he'd have paid me a pittance in alimony for the next ten years. He was older. He'd been married twice before. I knew the risk I was taking and I did what I could to protect myself, though it didn't amount to much. When our relationship collapsed, he was hoping for a quick divorce so he'd be off the hook. My attorney argued the prenup should be set aside because I'd signed under duress. By the time the divorce became final, he'd been forced to settle for six million, plus a million in legal fees. So here we are. He's stuck with me for life, for better or for worse, in sickness and in health."

"Do you work?"

"I don't have a job, if that's what you're referring to. I'm a part-time docent at the art museum, and I volunteer two mornings a week at Santa Teresa Hospital in the newborn nursery."

"Is there any chance your daughter had medical problems? Allergies, asthma, anything like that? I'm trying to understand what might have happened to her."

"She'd had the occasional seizure since infancy and the pediatrician had her on Dilantin. I take it you ask because you think something might have gone wrong."

"Exactly. I don't believe those guys were hardened criminals. Rain tells me she was treated well. She believes they mixed sleeping pills in her lemonade, but instead of going down for the count, she got hyper and slept less and less. Suppose they upped the dose, trying to induce sleep? If Mary Claire was already on an anticonvulsant, the combination of medications might have been fatal."

"I see what you're saying, and it makes sense. My poor little one," she said. She covered her eyes for a moment as though she might block out the very idea. I watched her work to compose herself and she finally sighed. "What now? Is this as far as it goes?"

"I don't know what to tell you. I'm fresh out of leads. On

the other hand, I can't quite let go. I don't like feeling I haven't done my job right."

She leaned forward and put her hands over mine. "Please don't give up. One of the reasons I came here was to tell you how much I appreciate your efforts. Even if you're facing a blank wall, don't concede. Please."

"I'll do my best. I can't promise you anything beyond that."

# 29

## WALKER McNALLY
### Wednesday afternoon, April 20, 1988

Walker pushed his cuff back discreetly and checked the time. He'd stopped wearing the sling and he was happy to have his right arm free. Seven minutes to go in yet another interminable AA meeting, this one sparsely attended, which made his unwillingness to share all the more conspicuous. Some of the regulars were there: an old geezer named Fritz, who was missing half his teeth; a woman who called herself Phoebe though he could have sworn he'd been introduced to her at the club by another name. The only person in the room under forty was a young dark-haired girl, thin as a snake, her eyes lined in kohl. Her nails were clipped short and painted dark red. She smoked and said nothing, which he personally applauded as he intended to do the same. She looked like she was barely old enough to drink and he wondered what had brought her to this sorry place. No sign of Avis Jent, which was a relief. He was nine days sober, a miracle in itself. In the past, when he'd claimed he'd quit drinking, he'd never actually gone more than two days without alcohol of *some* kind.

When the meeting ended he bypassed the bad coffee and headed for the side door, trying not to appear too thrilled to escape. The girl was a few steps in front of him and he flirted with the idea of making an offhand comment, something tongue-in-cheek to establish rapport. It would be nice to compare notes with someone in the same boat. He was beginning to understand why nondrinkers hung out together—misery loves company.

Outside the afternoon sun was brighter than he expected and he raised a hand to shade his eyes. It was close to three, coming up on the treacherous five-hour stretch between happy hour and lights out. This was the period in which his desire for a drink chafed and his resolve wore thin. He could live without mimosas and Bloody Marys, though he remembered with fondness the many mornings when he was on vacation or invited to a brunch or out on someone's boat. On those occasions drinking before noon was not only acceptable, but gleefully encouraged. He didn't mind doing without beer or wine with lunch. Those were pleasures he'd sacrifice in a heartbeat if he could just have a cocktail or two in the late afternoon. Every day he played the same little game. Technically . . . in truth . . . and if you wanted to get right down to it . . . he was free to drink if he wanted. He hadn't signed an *oath*. He wasn't under doctor's orders, forbidden to imbibe because of some dire medical condition. He hadn't been admonished by the court, though he knew if he were picked up for any reason while inebriated, things would go badly. Still, he had a choice. He could choose. He could drink if he wanted to, especially if no one found out. For nine days in a row, he'd behaved himself, and he felt good about that. Now the next cocktail hour glimmered on the horizon, and with it came the debate. Should he or shouldn't he? Would he or wouldn't he?

He scanned the parking lot for Brent, who preferred picking him up there instead of out on the street. He'd taken to running errands while Walker was tied up, timing his return so he could swing through just as Walker came out. The girl had paused, apparently waiting for a lift. A turquoise MG pulled to a stop and she got in on the passenger side, where an enormous golden retriever had taken up residence. He watched her wrestle with the dog, which had a prior claim on the seat. The dog rearranged itself, settling in the girl's lap with an attitude of entitlement.

Walker watched idly, smiling to himself. The car didn't move and he realized the driver, a kid, was staring at him through the windshield. He caught only a quick glimpse, but in that instant, he knew who it was: Michael Sutton, whose face was indelibly imprinted on his mind's eye. Incredible that all these years later, something as ephemeral as the slant of his cheek, the shape of his chin, could spark such a recollection. He'd last seen Michael when he was six and then only briefly. Walker had expected to run into him long before now, but it still came as a jolt.

He redirected his gaze and walked through the parking lot, feigning a casualness he didn't feel. He knew he had to put distance between himself and the kid. He glanced back and saw that Michael had turned his head, his gaze still fixed on him. The girl had turned to stare at him as well, probably wondering what Michael found so fascinating. Looking to his left, Walker saw Brent pull into the lot. Relieved, he moved forward as the car slowed. He opened the left rear door and slid into the backseat. "Hey, how's it going," he said to Brent as he closed the door.

Brent made eye contact by way of the rearview mirror. "Fine. How are things with you?"

"Good." Walker kept his face averted as Brent turned into the next aisle, passing Michael's MG. He pictured Michael's head doing a slow swivel as Brent's Toyota made the right onto Santa Teresa Street. Walker half turned in his seat and watched the exit. The turquoise MG nosed into view at an unhurried pace and fell into line behind them. Shit.

Walker put a hand on the seat back in front of him. "I'm late for a meeting, so let's get a move on. Take a right on Court and go the back way."

"The freeway's quicker."

"The back way's fine. Let's just do it, okay?"

Walker saw the shift in Brent's expression, one of those "You're the boss" looks. He turned the corner as instructed. Two blocks farther on, Walker took another quick look to see if the MG was still there. No sign of it. Walker wondered if he'd been mistaken. Maybe the kid hadn't recognized him after all. Maybe it was a situation where someone looks familiar and you can't quite place them. Thus the long stare. As Brent slowed for a four-way stop, Walker spotted the MG approaching from the right.

Brent said, "What's the deal? Do you know that guy?"

"He threatened me once."

"What was that about?"

"Too complicated to go into. The guy's a nut."

"You want me to lose him?"

"If you can, but keep it low-key. I don't want him to think I give a shit."

Brent pushed the accelerator, increasing his speed by degrees, four miles an hour, then five. Unfortunately the surface streets presented a constant run of stoplights and stop signs, which allowed the MG to stay close.

Brent said, "The guy's climbing up my tailpipe. If I spot a black-and-white, you want me to flag him down?"

"No, don't do that. We get to the bank, drive on past and drop me around the corner on Center Road. I'll walk back from there and maybe shake him that way."

"Does he know where you work?"

"I doubt it, but I'd just as soon not tip him off."

Brent cruised into Montebello and turned onto the main street. The MG was hung up briefly. Traffic at the intersection was regulated by a four-way stop sign and cars obligingly took turns. Brent sped up for the next three blocks and made a left turn onto Center, then pulled into the driveway of a small gym. Hastily Walker got out and waved Brent on. The Pelican was right there on the corner, one driveway down. He started to cross the motel parking lot, thinking to skirt the rear of the building, which at least shielded him from view. At the last minute, however, he changed his mind and took Redbird Road, an ancillary road that ran for one long block parallel to Old Coast.

Walker put his hands in his pockets and covered the distance as quickly as he could. The kid had nothing on him. A chance encounter twenty-one years before and what would that prove? Walker couldn't imagine why the police had been digging in the woods. Kinsey Millhone had somehow drawn a bead on his dad, using god knows what reasoning, but there was no real link between Walker and the dead dog. Maybe she'd talked to a number of veterinarians who'd been in practice at the time, and his dad was simply one.

He turned left on Monarch Lane, the side street that intersected Old Coast Road. The bank was on the corner and his office was located at the far end of the building. He traversed the parking lot, making a covert visual sweep as he pushed through the glass door into the reception area. When he paused to look back, he spotted the MG passing on the street. The girl was staring in his direction and he saw her reach over and grab Michael Sutton's arm to get his attention. The MG slowed and Michael peered past her at the front of the bank. Walker stepped away from the glass and then pivoted and took the side corridor to his office, where he closed the door.

At 6:00 he left the bank and walked the two blocks to his motel. He'd intended to eat dinner at the bar and grill off the Pelican parking lot, but he couldn't bring himself to walk in. He'd halted at the door, struck by the smell of whiskey and beer. The cigarette smoke didn't bother him as much as the clatter of flatware, diners bending over their plates, sawing away at steaks and pork chops. Nine days sober and he felt the old quickening, the automatic spark of excitement when he knew a drink was in the offing. Not tonight. Rather than order a meal, steeling himself against the old associations of red meat and red wine, he turned on his heel and returned to his room. He watched TV for a while, flipping from channel to channel.

At 9:15 he left his room again, crossed the street to the twenty-four-hour gas station, and shut himself into a public phone booth with a bifold door. He put a couple of coins in the slot and dialed Jon Corso's number. On the street a car slowed, turned in, and stopped in front of the pumps. Walker lowered his head, obscuring his face. He was behaving like a fugitive.

After four rings Jon picked up, sounding brusque. He was probably working on a new book, irritated at the interruption. "Hello?"

"We need to talk."

There was a pause of four seconds. "About what?"

"I'd rather not say on the phone."

"And why is that?"

"Shit, Jon. You're the one who's paranoid. I'm taking my cue from you."

"Where are you?"

"At the gas station across the street from the bank. I'm using a pay phone."

"I'll pick you up in half an hour," Jon said, and hung up.

Walker checked his watch, unsure what to do with himself until Jon arrived. He went into the minimart adjacent to the service bays, which were dark now. The place was empty except for a clerk who sat at the register reading a comic book. Walker ambled up and down the aisles, looking at the gaudy array of potato chips, Fritos, Cheetos, tortilla chips, sun-baked chips, and pretzels, along with nasty-looking jars of salsa and a cheese product as viscous as glue. Crackers, cookies, candy bars, Twinkies, packaged cupcakes covered in coconut. The refrigerated coolers were stocked with cheap beer, canned and bottled sodas, and a row of jug wines. He came to an ordered row of sandwiches and read the labels. Tuna salad, ham and cheese, a bologna with mayonnaise on wheat bread. He selected a bologna sandwich, which he hadn't eaten in years. At the counter he added four candy bars and paid for the lot. The clerk put everything in a bag for him, which he tucked under his arm. He went outside again and crossed to the half-wall at the far end of the paved area. He sat down, wishing he'd bought a soft drink, but too lazy to go back.

He opened the sandwich and took a bite. He chewed slowly, savoring the mild flavor of bologna, the sweet tang of mayonnaise. Montebello Bank and Trust was just across the street. He could see a light on, a low-tech burglar deterrent. Traffic was scanty, though he was certain that farther up the block, where bars and restaurants were clustered, the valet car parkers would be hustling back and forth.

Jon's black Jaguar finally tooled into sight at a leisurely speed. Walker was guessing he'd bypassed the freeway, opting to drive along the beach. It would be like him to take his time, leaving Walker to loiter on the corner like a bum. Jon pulled over and Walker opened the door on the passenger side, sliding into the seat.

Walker said, "Shit, this feels like we're having an affair."

"I didn't think you did things like that."

"Once for two months. Miserable experience. I swore off."

"Carolyn catch you at it?"

"She knew something was going on, but she never figured it out."

"Good for you. So where to?"

"You pick. I'm sick of being cooped up."

Jon made a leisurely U-turn and headed for the entrance to the northbound 101. The car was silent and the ride was smooth. There was no conversation. Walker slouched in his seat and closed his eyes, so relaxed he nearly fell asleep. Nights at the Pelican were a bad mix—headlights turning into the parking lot at odd hours, pipes thumping. Walker would wake to the tap and scratch of footsteps passing along the walkway outside his door. The place wasn't cheap, located as it was in the heart of Montebello, but the builder had cut corners. The shower was fiberglass and the bathroom vanity looked like something purchased from a cut-rate catalog. The kitchenette consisted of a hot plate, a toaster oven, and a tiny under-the-counter refrigerator too small to hold a pizza box.

Jon took an off-ramp and Walker raised an eyelid long enough to see that they were on Little Pony Road. Moments later Walker felt the car slow, turn left, and stop. Jon got out of the car, leaving the engine running. Walker roused himself from his reverie and looked out. He knew the place well, a pocket park once known as Passion Peak. Jon removed a chain stretched between two posts, barring vehicles. He returned to the car and took the road up and around two big bends until he reached the parking lot, where he pulled in, nose against the retaining wall. He shut down the engine. The two got out and began climbing the hill. They were well above the town, and once they reached the crest, the town would lie beneath them like a jewel. Walker carried his paper bag as they ascended from the parking lot to the small grassy meadow at the top, where six picnic tables were laid out.

Jon sat on a bench. Walker perched on the table, his legs dangling. A mist hovered at ground level, airy drifts of white. Trees sheltered the spot on three sides and the fourth was open to the view. The blackened remains of the bandstand hunkered in the dark behind them. In high school, this was the spot where the two of them had brought girls, more times than he cared to remember. He usually got the pretty one while

Jon got stuck with the homely best friend. Walker opened his bag and removed the four candy bars. He offered Jon a Three Musketeers bar and kept the other three for himself.

Jon said, "I didn't know you had a sweet tooth."

"It's weird. Now that I'm off alcohol, I crave sugar."

Jon pulled the paper off his candy bar and bit in. "So what's the big emergency?"

"I saw Michael Sutton this afternoon and he saw me. I came out of an AA meeting and he was there in the parking lot, picking up a girl. When Brent drove me back to the office, he followed."

"So?"

"So why's he tailing me? What if he goes to the police?"

"And says what? Two decades ago, we dug a hole. Big deal."

"I don't like it."

"Oh, for god's sake. You haul me out in the dead of night for this? You could have told me on the phone. The kid's a punk. Nobody's going to take him seriously. Besides, I can get to him anytime I want. He's not a problem."

"*Get* to him? What's that supposed to mean?"

"I know where he lives. I've kept an eye on him for years, following his illustrious career path. He's not a threat. He's a loser and a wimp. He's what we call 'malleable.' You can talk him into or out of anything. Everyone knows that."

"There's something else," Walker said. He was silent for a moment. "I think I might turn myself in."

The sentence hung in the air between them.

Walker couldn't believe he'd said it, but once the words were out of his mouth, he knew the idea had been hovering at the back of his mind for weeks.

Jon's expression was neutral. "What brought this on?"

Walker shook his head. "I've been having panic attacks and they're wearing me down. I'm tired of feeling tired. The damn anxiety's tearing me apart. It didn't bother me so much when I was drinking, but now . . ."

"So talk to your doctor about a sedative. Better living through chemistry."

"Wouldn't help. I mean, look at me. My life's in the toilet. Carolyn's kicked me out. I hardly see my kids. I killed a girl, for Christ's sake. I can't live this way."

Bemused, Jon said, "Which step is this?"

"What?"

"AA's famous twelve steps. Which one is this? Your 'fearless moral inventory,' am I right?"

"You know what, Jon? I don't need your snide fucking comments. I'm serious about this."

"I have no doubt. And what do you propose?"

"I don't know yet. You should have seen me today, skulking around on side streets so Michael Sutton wouldn't spot me and figure out where I work. It's all catching up with us. And here's the irony: for years, I drank to wipe out the guilt and all I managed to do was turn around and kill someone else."

Jon shook his head. "Jesus, Walker. You're deluding yourself. You don't drink because you feel guilty. You drink because you're a drunk. Get a clue. Confessing won't change anything."

"You're wrong. I know I'm a drunk and I'll deal with it. This is something else. I want to be square with life. I want to make amends. You've found a way to live with what we did. I can't. I want it off my chest."

"Good for you. Perfect. But your so-called amends will put my ass in a sling."

"That doesn't necessarily follow," Walker said.

"You're full of shit. How can you admit what you did without implicating me?"

"I'll handle it. This is not about you."

Jon seemed amused. "What are you picturing? You go to the cops and turn yourself in. You tell 'em what you did; you're now so very sorry and you want to make it right?" He stopped and studied Walker, waiting for a response. "You're never going to make it right. There's no way. We fucked up big time. That little girl is dead."

Walker said, "It would have helped if you'd read the label."

"Would you get off that shit? I did. I told you a thousand times. Everybody takes Valium. Ten-milligram tabs are no big deal."

"Guess again."

"Fine. You can make that part of your pitch."

"I will."

"So what exactly do you hope to accomplish in your feverish eagerness to unburden your soul?"

"I need to find a way to live with myself. That's all I'm saying. I want to clean up the mess we made."

"Live with yourself? Well, that won't last long. You're talking about felony murder, for which you'll get the death penalty. Is that what you want?"

"Of course not. If there were any other way out, don't you think I'd jump at it?"

"How the fuck do you expect to go up against the cops? They'll grill your sorry ass from here to next Tuesday until you tell 'em what went down. It doesn't take a genius to figure out you didn't act alone. They'll want you to name names, and mine's the only one on the list."

"I already told you this isn't about you."

"Yes, it is, you asshole. It's about me the minute you open your damn mouth, which I'm telling you not to do."

"Maybe I can make a deal. I tell 'em what I know as long as I don't have to talk about anyone else. Just my part."

"Great. That's swell. I can see it now. 'Gosh, Mr. FBI Agent, I'm willing to incriminate myself, but I want to be fair to the other guy.' That's not how it happens. Not with those guys. You've got no leverage. I'm the only thing you have to trade. Once you give yourself up, you'll turn around and give me up, too."

Walker's tone shifted. "You're forgetting it was your idea."

"My idea? Bullshit. It was Destiny's dumb-ass plan."

"But she didn't act on it and neither did Creed. You were the one who figured all the angles—"

"While you were doing what?"

"I did what you told me. You were always the man in charge. It was your show from the get-go. Now there's a price to pay. This isn't easy for me, you know? I have a wife and kids. What do you think is going to happen to them if I come forward?"

"Correction. You *had* a wife and kids. Now you got shit. You're living in a crappy motel, dining on candy bars. Carolyn tossed you out on your ass." He gestured impatiently. "Oh, skip that. Who cares? How much does she know, or do I dare inquire?"

"Nothing. I've never breathed a word to her."

"Well, that's a comfort. Walker, listen to me. I'm begging you to think about this and think hard. You're in a righteous lather because you want to cleanse your own soul, but the first time you speak up, you'll fall into a pile of shit from which you'll never extract yourself. You can't put me in the line of fire in the name of conscience."

"It's going to look better if I own up to my part before Michael Sutton rats us out. I've got that private eye breathing down my neck. She's already put part of it together, the business about the dead dog. I didn't think she could make the connection, but now it seems pretty fuckin' obvious that I'm it."

"So you're linked to a dead dog? Why would that inspire your running to the cops? It's not like that shit our parents laid on us when we were kids. 'All you have to do, son, is tell the truth. As long as you're honest, there won't be any punishment.' "

Walker shook his head. "It's only a matter of time before this whole thing blows. I can feel it in my bones."

"If you quit worrying and keep your mouth shut, we'll be fine."

"I don't think I can."

"Maybe I haven't made myself clear. I love the life I lead. I'm fond of my own ass. I don't want to die. I'm a respectable member of the community and I won't go down without a fight."

"Then you better come up with an alternative. I'm giving you fair warning. That's the best I can do."

# 30

## Wednesday evening, April 20, 1988

When I got home from work, I tossed the mail on the kitchen counter, turned on the lights, and sat down at my desk. I needed to organize my thoughts. With the investigation in tatters, it seemed imperative to catalog what I knew, consigning the details to index cards. There had to be a pattern, an overview into which all the little pieces would fit. Like an optical illusion, I was waiting for the shift, one image flipping over to its counterpart.

In both junior high and high school, I had trouble staying focused in classes where I was doing poorly, math being my weakest subject. Faced with a "thought" problem, my mind inevitably wandered to other matters. The math whizzes grasped the setup on sight. Not only could they divine the crux of the matter, but they'd start licking their pencil points and scribble the solution while I was still squirming in my seat. I wasn't stupid by any stretch. I was easily distracted and my attention would shift to details that turned out to be irrelevant.

*A train leaves Chicago for Boston traveling sixty miles an hour, while a second train leaves Boston, speeding toward Chicago at eighty miles an hour. A bird flies back and forth between the two . . .*

And that's as far as I'd get. I'd start wondering why the

bird was behaving so erratically, positing a virus affecting the bird's internal gyroscope. I'd daydream about who was on the train and why they were going from Chicago to Boston. Then I'd fret about what was happening in Boston that residents had crowded into the fastest train out. I'd never been to Boston and now I was forced to scratch it off my list.

What I experienced jotting down my notes was just another version of the same. I couldn't "get" the big picture. I couldn't grasp what was going on, so I found myself attending to issues that probably had nothing to do with anything. For instance, I wondered what they'd added to Rain's lemonade that knocked her out. Probably some over-the-counter sleep aid, though the proper dosage must have been a trick. I thought about the kidnapper dressed as Saint Nick, curious how he'd come up with a Santa Claus suit in early July. Short of working in a department store at Christmas or standing outside a supermarket ringing a Salvation Army bell, it couldn't be an easy outfit to rent in the middle of summer. There was no point in checking local costume shops to see if there were records going back that far. I could do it, but after twenty-one years, I'd be spinning my wheels, staying busy for the sake of it instead of canvassing with any hope of success.

I tossed my pen aside. This was pointless. Usually I surrender to the process, letting my thoughts idle while my attention is otherwise occupied. Recording minutiae is a form of play, temporarily derailing the analytical side of my brain. At the moment, frustration was jamming my circuits. There was something distinctly unpleasant about pondering the same disjointed facts when nothing new was coming in. I could fiddle the story any way I liked and the bottom line was the same. Michael Sutton was wrong. He'd made a mistake. Everything that rested on his basic premise was out the window.

Irritably I gathered the cards, secured them with a rubber band, and stuck them in a drawer. Enough of this. I needed Henry's company and his counsel. I opened the front door and peered across to Henry's kitchen. All his lights were out. I picked up my jacket and shoulder bag, locked my front door, and made a beeline for Rosie's. I spotted him the moment I walked in. I pulled out a chair and sat down, peering at the plate Rosie had just put in front of him.

To her, he said, "Thank you, dear. It looks lovely." He smiled, watching her depart.

"Is that the special of the day?"

He shook his head. "Oh no, you'll want to steer clear of that." He peered over his shoulder to make sure she wasn't in eavesdropping range. By then she was at the bar chatting with William while she kept a close eye on us.

Henry put a hand to his mouth, in case she'd recently learned to read lips. "She's serving calf's-liver pudding with anchovy sauce. It comes with a cup of souse's soup, made with sauerkraut." He paused for a moment while he crossed his eyes and then pointed to his plate. "This dish is stuffed cabbage and it's not half bad."

"Got it," I said.

He paused to study me. "How are you doing? I haven't seen you for days."

"Go on with your dinner. Let me grab a glass of wine and I'll fill you in."

"I can wait," he said.

By the time I reached the bar, Rosie had disappeared and William had poured me a glass of bad wine. I said, "Thanks. Would you ask Rosie if I could have the stuffed cabbage? It looks fabulous."

"Sure thing."

I returned to the table, wineglass in hand. Moments later Rosie appeared with my dinner plate. Henry and I spent the next five minutes in companionable silence while we ate. When it comes to food, neither of us fools around. As a reward for cleaning our plates, Rosie brought us each a slice of chocolate–poppy seed torte that reduced us to a state of moaning satisfaction.

Henry said, "Now, tell me what's going on. When you walked in, your expression was so dark I didn't dare ask. Is the misery about family or work?"

"Work."

"So skip that and bring me up to date on the family saga."

"I can't remember what was going on when we last spoke. Did I tell you I had dinner here with Tasha? This was a week ago."

"News to me."

"Wow, you really are behind."

"Matters not," he said mildly. "What'd she want?"

"Nothing. Surprise, surprise. She handed over a batch of letters she came across when she was cleaning out Grandfather Kinsey's files. Some were letters Grand wrote to Aunt Gin and some she sent me. I haven't read all of them. I mostly skipped around, but I picked up enough to know she was doing her best to maneuver Aunt Gin into surrendering custody. You can imagine how well that went down. Aunt Gin apparently read the first and sent the rest back unopened. Grand retaliated by hiring a private detective to spy on us." I paused, correcting myself. "Well, 'retaliated' might be too strong a word. She wanted proof that Gin wasn't a fit guardian."

"By fair means or foul?"

"That's about it. Her hunch was that Aunt Gin was gay and she figured if she could prove it, she'd have enough leverage to bring her to heel. Didn't work out that way."

"This was all in the letters? I can't believe she'd spell it out."

"She was too clever to do that. Among other things, Tasha came across invoices from the PI Grand hired. I drove to Lompoc yesterday and talked to him. He's a nice guy though not inclined to confide. Dang. I had to pry the information out of him, but he finally told me what she was up to. He persuaded Grand that Aunt Gin was straight, which was always my perception. Grand dropped the matter and that was the end of that." I lifted a finger. "I do harbor a tiny flicker of doubt. On a hunch, I asked him if he'd lie about it. I was curious if he was fudging for my sake, trying to make Aunt Gin sound better than she was. He deflected the question and responded with something else. I'm not saying he lied, but there was *something* he wasn't saying. It may not mean anything, but I'm not a hundred percent convinced."

"Not much in life is a hundred percent."

"You have a point."

"So now what? I'm assuming this precludes your going to the big family do at the end of May."

"Probably. I haven't decided yet."

Rosie appeared at the table to collect our dessert plates, and we set the subject aside until she'd gone off to the kitchen with her tray.

"Now tell me about work. Last I heard, you were asking William for a bar rag to clean off a dog tag that smelled like dead rat."

"Oh, man, you're really out of date and I apologize. Not to put too fine a point on it, but to all intents and purposes, I've reached a dead end."

I started with Diana and Ryan's revelation about Michael Sutton's birthday celebration at Disneyland and then went back in time and talked about my drive to Peephole and the conversation I'd had with P. F. Sanchez, who'd eventually given me the information about the veterinarian who'd put his dog down. I went into some detail about the shed at the rear of the clinic where euthanized animals were left for pickup by animal control. I also told Henry about Deborah Unruh and the four-year-old, Rain, who'd served as the "practice child." I went on to fill him in on Greg and Shelly, and my interview with her son, Shawn, who'd assured me the two of them weren't involved in the kidnapping scheme because they'd left the state by then and were working their way north to Canada. The recitation took the better part of fifteen minutes, but I felt I'd summed it up admirably, even if I do say so myself.

Listening to the story as I relayed it to him, I could still see a certain logic in play. My prime assumption had been wrong, but there were pieces that still intrigued me, even at this late date. Ulf, the wolfdog. The similarities between the two crimes. The ransom demands that totaled forty grand. I couldn't see the links, but they had to be there.

Henry seemed to take it all in, though I have no idea how he managed to keep the players straight. Once in a while he'd stop me with a question, but in the main, he seemed to follow the narrative. When I finished he thought about it briefly and then said, "Let's go back to the conversation you had with Stacey Oliphant. What makes him so sure the kidnappers were amateurs?"

"Because they asked for chump change, to use Dolan's words. Both thought it was odd to ask for fifteen grand when they could have asked for more. Stacey figured if they'd been professionals, they'd have ramped up the demand."

"Must not have been chump change to them. If they were rookies, fifteen thousand might have seemed like a fortune."

"Not that the money did them any good. Patrick photo-copied the bills and then marked them . . ."

Henry frowned. "How?"

"Some kind of fluorescent pen he used in the export side of his clothing business. Deborah says the marks would have popped out under a black light, which a lot of kids had back then. She also says none of the money ever surfaced, at least as far as she's heard."

"They must have figured it out."

"That'd be my guess."

"Which is probably why they tried again," he said. "If they discovered the bills were marked, they couldn't risk putting the cash in circulation so they got rid of what they had and tried again. Only this time they snatched Mary Claire instead of Rain."

"Oh, shit. I hope that's not true. That would mean Patrick set the second kidnap in motion. If the money had been clean, they might have been satisfied with what they netted the first time and let it go at that."

Henry said, "I'll tell you something else that just occurred to me. Suppose when Sutton stumbled into the clearing, the two weren't digging the hole to bury a child. What if their intent was to bury the tainted money?"

I stared at him. "And they buried the dog instead? How'd they manage *that*?"

"Simple. One stays in the woods to keep an eye on the site. The other goes off, steals the dog's corpse, and brings it back. They drop the mutt in that hole and hide the money somewhere else."

"How'd they know about the dead dog?"

"Beats me," he said. "You told me yourself that a couple of hundred people could have known about the shed and the pickup routine."

"All this because they were worried the little kid would blab?"

"Why not? I'm just brainstorming here, but it makes sense to me. Didn't you tell me Patrick packed the money in a gym bag he tossed on the side of the road?"

"Right."

"So picture this. They leave Rain asleep in the park.

They've counted the money so they know it's all there. Once they get home they discover the bills are lighting up like neon. Either they meant to dump the cash or their intention was to get it out of sight until they felt it was safe to spend. Once the little kid appeared, they decided it was too dangerous to leave the money in that spot."

"The dead dog's a bit melodramatic, don't you think? Why not just fill in the hole?"

"They were setting up a cover story to explain what they were doing in the first place. Sure enough, the police exhume the dog and that's the end of it. No big mystery. Someone's buried a pet. Might have taken twenty-one years, but it shows you how wily these guys were."

"'Were'? Nice idea. Like maybe they're dead or in prison."

"One can only hope," he said.


When I got home I decided to let Henry's suggestions percolate overnight. I'd been overthinking the whole subject and it had only served to confuse instead of enlighten me. Meanwhile, something else had occurred to me. I realized I might have a way to find out if Hale Brandenberg was being honest about Aunt Gin's sexual orientation. It didn't matter one way or the other, but I'm a stickler for the truth (unless I'm busy lying to someone at any given moment). There might be evidence at hand.

I went up the spiral stairs to the loft. I have an old trunk at the foot of the bed that I use for storage. I cleared the top and opened the lid, removing neatly folded piles of winter clothing I'd packed away in mothballs. From the bottom I hauled out a shoe box of old photographs that I dumped on the bed. If Aunt Gin had a "special friend" whose existence Hale was trying to conceal, I might find glimpses of her in pictures taken at the time. Aunt Gin had socialized with a number of married couples, but she also had gal pals.

Snapshots tell a story, not always in obvious ways but taken as a whole. Faces appear and disappear. Relationships form and fall apart. Our social history is recorded in photographic images. Maybe someone had captured a moment that would speak to the issue. I sat on the bed and picked through the pictures, smiling at the photos of people I recognized. Some I could still name. Stanley, Edgar, and Mildred. I blanked on Stanley's wife's name, but I knew the five of them played card games—canasta and pinochle. The kitchen table would be littered with ashtrays and highball glasses, and they'd all be laughing raucously.

I found shots of two single women I remembered—Delpha Prager and one named Prinny Rose Something-or-other. I knew Aunt Gin had worked with Delpha at California Fidelity Insurance. I wasn't sure where she'd met Prinny Rose. I studied their photos, with Aunt Gin and without, in groups where one or the other appeared. If there were secret smiles between them, surreptitious glances that might have been picked up on camera, I couldn't see the signs. I suppose I'd imagined arms thrown over one another's shoulders, hands slightly too close together on a tabletop, an intimate look or gesture neither was aware she'd revealed. I didn't see anything even remotely suggestive. In point of fact, there wasn't a single view of Aunt Gin making physical contact with anyone, which was confirmation of a different kind. She was not a touchy-feely person.

I did marvel at how young she looked. While I was growing up, she was passing through her thirties and forties. Now I could see she was pretty in a way I hadn't seen before. She was slender. She favored glasses with wire frames and she wore her hair pulled up in a bun that should have looked old-fashioned, but was stylish instead. She had high cheekbones, good teeth, and warmth in her eyes. I'd thought of her as schoolmarmish, but there was no evidence of it here.

I came to an envelope sealed with tape so old and yellow it had lost its sticking power. On the outside she'd written MIS-CELLANEOUS 1955 in the bold cursive I recognized. My interest picked up. I withdrew an assortment of snapshots. I appeared in the first few photographs, age five, my expression bleak. I was small for my age, all bony arms and legs. My hair was long, bunched up on the sides where bobby pins held the strands back. I wore droopy skirts and brown shoes with white socks that sagged. By that Christmas I'd been living with her for six months or so, and apparently I'd found nothing to smile about.

The next photograph I came to generated an exclamation that expressed my surprise and disbelief. There was Aunt Gin enclosed in the arms of a man I recognized on sight, though he was thirty years younger. Hale Brandenberg. She had her back up against his body, her face turned slightly as she smiled. His face was tilted toward hers. The next five pictures were of the two of them, mostly horsing around. In one they played miniature golf, clowning for a photographer who might have been me since the tops of their heads were missing and I could see the blur of a finger inadvertently covering a portion of the aperture. Another photograph had been taken in the gazebo in the hilltop park so popular with my high school classmates. There were two snapshots of the three of us, me sitting on Hale's knee with a snaggletoothed grin. I was probably six by then, in first grade, losing my baby teeth. My hair had been chopped short, probably because Aunt Gin got annoyed having to fiddle with it. Hale looked like a cowboy movie star, clean-shaven, tall, and muscular, in a flannel shirt, blue jeans, and boots. I didn't remember his being in our lives, but there he was. No wonder he'd seemed familiar when I first laid eyes on him. Furthermore, it occurred to me that Aunt Gin had been just about my age, thirty-eight, when this late romance blossomed.

I understood why he was so sure about her sexuality and why he was so well acquainted with her parenting skills. I had a hundred questions about the two of them, but now was not the time to ask. Maybe at a later date, I'd take him out for a drink and tell him what I'd discovered. For the moment, I returned the snapshots to the tattered envelope, which I set to one side while I put the remainder in the shoe box and repacked the trunk. I hardly knew what to think about my discovery. Hale might have been a stand-in father to me if he and Aunt Gin had stayed together. She didn't set much store by marriage and she probably wasn't suited for a long-term relationship. But she'd been happy for a while, and in those few images, I could see that I'd been happy as well.

# 31

## JON CORSO

### Summer 1967

The whole of the affair with Destiny lasted three and a half weeks, and ended abruptly when Jon least expected it. She was a gift he wasn't sure he deserved. His attraction to her was so strong and so compelling he assumed it would be with him the rest of his days. She was voluptuous, bawdy, and uninhibited. Her two pregnancies had left their marks, but she was completely unapologetic. Freckles, moles, scars, the small drooping breasts, the softly bulging abdomen, and saddlebag thighs—none of it mattered. She threw herself into sex with joy and abandonment. He would sleep with countless women afterward whose bodies were close to perfect, but most were embarrassed and self-conscious, unhappy with the size of their breasts or the shape of their asses, pointing out shortcomings that meant nothing to him. To him, they were beautiful, but they required constant reassurances about these imaginary flaws.

With Destiny, he was dazzled, a novice whose enthusiasm matched hers. Despite her claims about the open relationship, she had with Creed, there was no question of their meeting at the Unruhs', where Creed and Shawn popped in and out of the school bus. In the main house, Deborah was a constant presence. Rain had playdates, swimming lessons, and gymnastics.

Cars were always coming and going; kids being picked up, kids being dropped off. Their only choice was for her to come to his place as often as she could manage it. For transportation, she borrowed the Unruhs' Buick.

While Walker was away on vacation, Jon maintained a strict neutrality when he was in the company of Creed and Destiny, making sure no hint of their altered relationship emerged. Destiny, by nature, would have played the situation for high drama. She enjoyed creating conflict, and what better instance of it than two men vying for the same woman, especially if it was her. It was the substance of myth. Competition between them would endow her with status. She was the prize for which they would battle until one or the other was felled. Jon was having none of it. He had no respect for Creed, but he didn't see why he should suffer humiliation to satisfy Destiny's love of histrionics.

Waiting for her at his place, he felt suspended, counting the minutes. He woke early, lingering in bed, remembering what they'd done, fantasizing what they'd do next. He never knew when she'd arrive or whether she'd make it at all. He had no idea what excuses she gave for her absences and he didn't care to ask. Without warning, she'd knock on the door at the bottom of the stairs. At the top there was a second door, and by the time he opened it, she'd be taking the stairs two at a time. She'd fling herself at him, laughing and out of breath. They'd hole up in his room, making love at a frantic pace, all noise and sweat. She taught him about pleasure and excess, all the appetites of the flesh. Between bouts of sex they'd share a joint. His studio was a haze of weed and cigarette smoke. At intervals they'd trail down the stairs, often naked, and wander into the main house, where they raided Lionel's wine cellar, working their way through his high-end Chardonnay. Dope made them hungry and they devoured everything in sight, most of it junk since Jon didn't have the money to buy much else. Doughnuts, chips, candy bars, cookies, peanut butter and crackers—their makeshift feasts as intense as the sex.

In order to make time for the long runs he loved, he dragged himself out of bed at 8:00. His weight lifting was halfhearted and many days he skipped. He saw Destiny on random afternoons and after she left, he'd nap, forage for dinner, and then sit down at his desk, which he usually reached by 9:00. He worked into the wee hours, shorting himself on sleep. There was no other way around it. The dope, fatigue, and alcohol took their toll, fogging his brain and breaking up his concentration. This was a problem when Friday rolled around and Mr. Snow was expecting his work. The second week, his deadline came up on him before he knew it, and he was forced to pull an all-nighter, writing feverishly until the sky turned light.

He'd come up with a cool idea about a kid who ran with a pack of wild dogs; this in the Deep South—Georgia, Alabama, someplace like that. He pictured the kid living under the porch of a ramshackle shotgun house, feasting on scraps. Jon could smell the dirt and the animal scent of the boy. He wrote about the hot summer nights when the wind was still and the dogs howled from afar, calling to the kid. He didn't have a clue where he was going with the story, but he made a good start, fifteen double-spaced pages.

He handed in what he'd done, and sat, as he always did, feigning nonchalance while he waited for Mr. Snow's response. This time he read several of the pages twice and then flipped through the whole of it, frowning.

Jon said, "You don't like it."

"It's not that. I don't know what to say. I mean, there's nothing really *wrong* here. The prose is serviceable. You lean toward the melodramatic, but it doesn't play because the setup is manufactured. You think the setting is stark, but it comes off as syrupy instead. Do you know anything about the South? Have you ever even *been* there?"

"I was using my imagination. Isn't that the point?"

"But why this? You're talking about five or six dogs and I can't tell one from the other. Okay, one has yellow eyes and another one has a rough coat. You're giving me characteristics, not characters. Even if you write about dogs you have to differentiate. That's where conflict comes from. Then you have this kid with no personality at all, which is a tough proposition given the situation you've put him in. Where's Jon Corso in this? As far as I know, what you describe here bears no relation to your life or your problems or your hopes or your dreams. Wait, maybe I should ask this first. Have you ever *run* with a pack of dogs?"

"Not recently," he said, trying to be flip. The criticism stung. Mr. Snow was blunt and he didn't pull his punches. Jon felt himself shrink, but Mr. Snow wasn't done.

"You're writing out of your head. There's no heart. You understand what I'm saying? This is verbiage, empty sentences. Blah, blah, blah doesn't mean anything to you and it sure as shit doesn't mean anything to me."

"Is there a way to fix it?"

"Sure. Here's a quick fix. Toss it out and start somewhere else. You keep your reader at arm's length when you should be writing from your gut. That's the point of fiction, the connection between reader and writer. This is crap. You manage to make it look like a story, but you're just going through the motions. I want to see the world as you see it. Otherwise, a monkey could sit down and bang this stuff out."

"Well, that's bullshit. You said I could write anything I want and then you tear it apart."

Mr. Snow hung his head. "Okay. Good point. My fault. Let's skip the issue of content and talk about process. You're hiding. You're not giving me anything of you. You're waving your hands, hoping to distract the reader from noticing how much you withhold. You have to make yourself visible. You have to open up and *feel.* Mad, sad, glad, bad. Take your pick. I'm not saying you have to write your autobiography, but your life and your experiences are the wellspring. You want to write, you have to tell me how the world looks from your perspective. You have to absorb and deconstruct reality and then reassemble it from the inside out."

"I have no idea what you're talking about."

"Haven't you ever hated anyone? Haven't you ever been out of your mind with jealousy or fear? Your little doggie dies and you can hardly get to your room fast enough before you burst into tears?"

Jon considered and then shrugged. "I don't feel that strongly about things."

"Sure you do. You're eighteen—all hormones and emotion, testosterone and angst. The only thing worse than a teenaged guy is a teenaged girl. I don't want you coming from here," he said, tapping his head. He put the flat of his hand on his chest.

"I want you coming from here. Writing's hard. It's a skill you attain by practicing. You don't just dash off good work in your off-hours. You can't be halfhearted. It takes time. You want to be a concert pianist, you don't slog your way through *Five Easy Pieces* and expect to be booked into Carnegie Hall. You have to sit down and write. As much as you can. Every day of your life. Does any of this make sense?"

Jon smiled. "Not much."

"Well, it will." Mr. Snow flapped the pages at him. "I'll give you this much. Clumsy as this is, I can see just the wee tiniest spark buried in the muck. You can do this. You have something. The trick is to get out of your own way and let the light shine through. Now get out of here. I'll see you next week, okay?"

"Okay."

"You have to write every day, Jon. I mean it. No faking, no farting around, and no shorting me on time."


Walker came back from Hawaii and the first time the four of them convened at the bus, he took one look at Jon and knew what was going on. For a change, Destiny was cool. She kept her distance, her manner strictly matter-of-fact. Jon and Creed and Walker smoked dope and shot the shit while she sat cross-legged in the grass, reading Tarot cards. Jon thought they'd pretty much pulled it off, but when he and Walker left and were barely out of earshot, Walker turned to him with dismay. "What the fuck are you doing, man? Are you out of your mind?"

"I don't remember asking for your opinion."

"Well, here it is anyway. She's a slut and she's stupid on top of that."

"I notice you're not all that picky about the girls you screw."

"Because they're nice and they're *clean*. She's disgusting."

"I don't want to hear about it, okay?"

"What if you get caught? How can you try pulling this shit right under his nose?"

"They have an open relationship."

"Oh, right. You believe that, you're a horse's ass." Walker shook his head. "You're going to regret it, buddy boy. I'm telling you right now, this won't end well."

"Thanks. I'm touched by your concern."

Saturdays belonged to him and the freedom was a relief. Destiny, Creed, and Sky Dancer went off early to the farmer's market in town and spent the rest of the day in family pursuits. Destiny wanted to learn to tie-dye so she'd gone to Sears and shoplifted half a dozen three-packs of white T-shirts, which she intended to dye in batches and then sell at the beach. Jon was grateful for the long stretch of hours he could call his own. Friday night he slept well, and when he got up he threw on a T-shirt and cutoffs. He made a fresh pot of coffee and carried a cup to his desk. He reread his story about the boy who ran with wild dogs, this time cringing at turns of phrase that before had seemed lyrical. "Soaring" was what he thought to himself when he was crafting sentences. He went through line by line, X-ing out anything clumsy or pretentious. In the end there was maybe half a paragraph worth salvaging. He took Mr. Snow's advice and tossed the rest of it in the trash.

For a while he sipped coffee, stared out the window, and thought about Mr. Snow's rant. When he'd talked about jealousy and rage, when he'd asked if there was anyone Jon hated, his mind had gone blank. The same thing with grief. What the fuck did he know about shit like that? He could see where the loss of a beloved animal might generate emotion, but he'd never actually owned one. Growing up, his mother's asthma had precluded house pets. The only bright moment he remembered in contemplating Mona's arrival in his life was when he thought that maybe he could have a pet, a hope that was quickly dashed, along with just about every other hope he had. Mona was allergic to cats and she thought dogs were too much work. Mona ruled. The rest of them were there to obey.

The Amazing Mona. He did have things to say about her and none of them were nice.

He abandoned his typewriter, took a pad of yellow legal paper, and made himself comfortable on his unmade bed, pillows propped up behind him. The sheets smelled of two-day-old sex, a scent not as evocative as he'd found it on previous occasions. He thought about Mona, tapping his pen against his lower lip. He couldn't think where to start. As much as he hated her, he knew he couldn't write about her without jeopardizing his relationship with his dad, and more important, getting his butt kicked out of the house. He wouldn't show anyone his work, but it would be entirely like her to wait until he was gone and come into his apartment so she could go rooting through his things.

He heard a pounding on the downstairs door. Annoyed at the interruption, he set aside pen and paper. If it was Walker, he'd send him on his way. He opened the door just as Destiny reached the top of the stairs. She was exuberant, all hugs and smiles, rattling out a laughing account of her leaving Creed and Sky tending dye kettles in the yard. She'd told them she was going out to snag more T-shirts so she had only an hour. She was busily hauling off her clothes when she picked up Jon's mood. "Is something wrong?"

"This is my day to write. I've been kicking around a couple of ideas and I need the time to myself."

"I'm not going to be here long. You can write when I'm gone. I thought you'd be excited to see me."

"I am. I just, you know, had my head into something else."

Having stripped, she pressed up against him, running her hands along the front of his pants. He was already hard, a conditioned response. She slid his shorts down over his hips. She kissed him, lips soft and open, and then sank down to her knees and took him in her mouth. He grabbed her by the arms and pulled her up, kissing her with the same intensity she always called out of him. Smiling, she put her bare feet on the tops of his and he walked her to the bed.

The sex was good. It was always good, but this time his inclination was to be done with it and get her out of the way. She was a distraction. Her intensity was like a mass of hot, wet rags pressed over his face. He could hardly breathe. She must have sensed his distance because she clung to him like an octopus, all arms and legs and sucking. She wanted his full attention and she was doing what she could to arouse him for another round.

He pushed her hand away. "Enough. I'm bushed."

"Don't be such a shit. You never turned me down before."

"I didn't turn you down. What do you want from me? We just made love."

She settled on her side, her head propped on one hand. "You know what? We belong together. We're a good fit."

"How do you figure that?"

"It's the feeling I had the first time we met. Like we were together in another life."

"Yeah, right."

"No, I'm serious. It's like I remember you."

"What about Creed? How many reincarnations have you shared with him?"

"Don't make fun. He's boring. All mopey and glum. I'm sick to death of him and his parents and this whole stupid town. I'm this close to taking off, just getting the hell out."

"I thought the bus belonged to him."

"Who said anything about the bus? That's what thumbs are for. I hitchhiked all over the country before I hooked up with him. Pregnant, babe in arms. There's always a guy who slows down and offers you a ride. You go where the wind blows you."

"Go and god bless, but leave me out of it."

"Where's your sense of adventure? Don't you want to live on the wing?"

"Not particularly. What about your kid? He might not appreciate being dragged all over just to satisfy your whims."

"I'll leave him with Creed. Sky's crazy about Deborah. He'd be happy as a clam."

"You can't do that. You told me he's not even Greg's kid."

"What, you think kids are possessions? Mine, yours, and his? Sky's a child of the universe. He'll find his own path in life. He doesn't need me for that."

"He's eleven. You can't just dump the kid and run off."

"I'm not *dumping* him. I'm thinking about what's best for him. Deborah thinks I'm a crappy mother anyway and maybe she's right. At least with her he'd have a normal life, whatever that's worth. We'd have a blast, the two of us. We could go anywhere. Nova Scotia. Have you ever been to Nova Scotia? I love the sound of it. *Nova* means 'new,' but what's a scotia?" She put her head on his chest and wrapped her leg over his.

Her flesh was hot and the weight of her leg made him tense. He could feel her pubic hair against his thigh like a Brillo pad. "Nice idea, but it won't work."

"Why not?"

"Here's some late-breaking news. I'm eighteen. I live at home. In two months, I start college. I don't even have a job."

"Neither do I. Who needs a job when you can panhandle? You ought to see 'em in the Haight. Tourists stand around gawking at all the hippie freaks. For them, it's like being at the zoo. Hold your hand out, they'll give you cash. They're scared to death of us."

"I don't want to be a beggar when I grow up."

She hooked an arm over his shoulder and shook him playfully. "Come on. You old sourpuss. This is the Summer of Love. We're missing all the fun."

He stared at the ceiling, wondering how long he'd have to put up with her before reclaiming his day.

She kissed his neck, making a low sound in her throat like she was turned on. "I love you."

"Stop."

"I mean it." She licked his neck. She nibbled on his shoulder while she rubbed against him, amorous despite his failure to respond.

"Cut it out."

"So uptight. Such a grouch. Don't you even love me a little bit?" She put her lips to his ear and ran her tongue around the rim.

"Goddamn it. Get off." He loosened her arms and rolled out of her embrace. He found his shorts and pulled them on. He ran his hands through his hair, smoothing it.

She sat up, agitated. "What's wrong with you? Ever since I got here, you've treated me like shit."

"I told you. I have work to do."

"That is such a lie. You don't have *work*. That's ridiculous. Writing stuff down is not *work*."

"What do you know? You barely made it out of ninth grade."

"You're a real asshole, you know that?"

"Fine. I'm an asshole. So what?"

She pulled her legs up under her and got on her hands and knees, crawling across the bed. "What if Creed finds out about us? You think he won't come after you?"

"You said you had an open relationship."

She reached for him, her tone of voice teasing. "But you don't know if it's true or not. I might have made it up."

Abruptly, he sat. "Jesus, don't say that."

She smiled. "Why, are you nervous what he'll do if I tell?" She held him from behind, her arms around his neck. He tried to shrug her off and she laughed, grasping him tightly as though prepared to ride piggyback. He pushed himself up, using the bed for leverage. She locked her legs around his waist and the weight of her pulled him off balance. He stumbled sideways and they tumbled to the floor. Anger fanned up in him like a gas fire. She hung on like a demon, nails cutting into his chest. He elbowed her sharply, trying to break her grip. In retaliation, she grabbed his hair and yanked so hard his head snapped back. He turned over and shoved upward, dragging her with him. He managed to make it to his feet. She had his head in the crook of her elbow and he was choking for air. He leaned forward, trying to toss her off. She grunted and tucked a leg around his. His knee buckled and he fell again. He was far stronger than she, but she had the advantage of tenacity and the clumsiness of her hold. He couldn't get purchase and she used his momentary faltering to seize him anew. He heaved himself sideways, shaking her off, and then she was on the floor under him and he had his hands around her throat. He choked her, not even aware of what he was doing until he saw the look on her face. There was triumph in her eyes. She was an adrenaline junkie and she'd tripped him into a rage as inflammatory as desire. He felt her shudder and he released her. She turned on her side, hands at her throat. Both of them were breathing hard. She moaned once and it dawned on him she'd reached orgasm.

He stared at her for a moment, fascinated. What kind of creature was she that violence served as an aphrodisiac? Killing her would be the ultimate turn-on from her point of view, and what did that make him? Not another word passed between them. She dressed quickly. She wept and her hands shook as she struggled to fasten her skirt. He sat on the bed stupefied, his head in his hands.

When she was gone he sat down at his desk, where he rolled a sheet of paper into his typewriter. He wrote for four hours, took a break, and then wrote for another two. Words poured out of him. He could feel sentences form in his head, almost faster than he could type. It was like taking dictation. Paragraphs lined up and passed through his body onto the paper in front of him. No thought. No analysis. No hesitation. He wrote about Mona. He wrote about his mother's death. He wrote about his weak father and his own loneliness. He wrote about what it felt like to be shut away upstairs while the rest of the family enjoyed the comforts of home. He wrote about being a fat boy and what it felt like to run seven miles in the rain. He wrote without once thinking of Mr. Snow.

At 10:00 he stopped. He went downstairs and out into the chill night air. The property overlooked the ocean and he could see the sheen of moonlight on water as far as the is-lands. He was exhausted and energized. He thought he'd never sleep again, but he did. In the morning he read what he'd done. Some of it was awkward and inadvertently comical. Some of it was mawkish and maudlin. It mattered not. He knew what it felt like to work from the heart and he was hooked. Even if it took him years to get back to that flow, he knew it was worth every failed attempt and every misbegotten word.

At eight, he brushed his teeth, showered, dressed, and rode his scooter to Walker's house, taking the bridle paths that wound up the hill. He had to cross a public road only once, and even then there was no traffic. Walker had just gotten up and he was sitting in his kitchen in his boxer shorts, hair rumpled, his face embossed with wrinkles from his bedsheet.

Jon let himself in as he usually did. He poured himself a cup of coffee and sat down. "I have to get out of the house before the Amazing Mona returns with her merry band in tow. She sucks all the oxygen out of the air and I can't take it any-more. I thought we could get a place together near UCST or close to City College, whichever you'd prefer."

Walker said, "I'm up for that. How do we pay the rent, rob a bank?"

"I've been thinking we'd borrow Rain—fun and games for a day or two—and then we exchange her for a bag of cash. Easy does it. No rough stuff and nothing scary. We get a kitten and she can play with it. She gets to drink pink lemonade laced with tranquilizers. Mona has a big stash, fifty-two by my count. She won't miss a few. You have folks, so we keep the little girl at my place while everyone's gone. I have a new hot-water heater going in and we can use the box to make a house for her. As long as she naps, she won't make a fuss, which should give us time to negotiate."

Walker was attentive. "I'm with you so far."

"The only snag is the threesome in the yellow school bus. We have to find a way to get them out of there."

Walker's smile was slow. "Funny you should mention that. I've been mulling the selfsame subject . . . on your behalf, of course. You may be in the woman's thrall, but she's bad news. Consider yourself lucky if you haven't picked up crabs or a dose of the clap. I'm not passing judgment, Jon. I'm stating a fact. You want her gone, I can make it happen, the other two as well, unless I greatly miscalculate. Say the word and it'll be done by noon today."

"How?"

"First, I call the draft board and tell them where to find our friend, Greg. Then I stop by the bus and drop a hint to him. I figure fifteen minutes max we'll see them tearing out of there. Your idea about Rain we can implement once we get the kinks worked out. What do you think?"

"Far out. You're a genius. I take back every bad word I ever said about you. No offense."

"None taken."

# 32

## Thursday, April 21, 1988

I arrived at the office at 8:00, hoping to get a jump on the day. As I unlocked the door I could smell scorched coffee and realized with a flash of annoyance that I'd forgotten to turn off the coffeemaker when I'd left Wednesday afternoon. I scurried down the corridor to the kitchenette and flipped off the machine. I removed the carafe from the unit and set it on a folded towel to cool. The glass bottom had a ring of black sludge that would probably never come off.

I hauled out my trusty Smith-Corona, popped off the hard cover, and placed it on my desk. I spread out my index cards and typed a report for Sutton's file, covering what I'd done to this point. I included Henry's speculation about the sequence of events, which added a little ray of sunshine. When I finished I put the report in his file. I put a rubber band around the cards, dropped them in the same file, and closed the drawer. I'd gone as far as I could go and I needed a break. Over the weekend I'd reshuffle the facts and hope to spot something I'd missed. In the meantime, it was a perfect April morning, clear and sunny, still cool but with the promise of a warming trend. Surely, that boded well.

I stashed the typewriter under the desk again and caught

sight of the light on my answering machine, which was blinking merrily. I swiveled once in my chair and pressed Play.

I could hear background noise.

"Kinsey? This is Michael Sutton. I gotta talk to you as soon as possible. After I left you, I went to get Madaline at her AA meeting and saw the same guy I spotted at the dig. He has two black eyes and his face is banged up, which is why I noticed him in the first place. We followed him to that Montebello Bank and Trust at Monarch and Old Coast Road. I'm calling from the gas station across the street. We've waited half an hour and he hasn't come out so maybe he works there. Thing is, Madaline's antsy to get home so I was hoping you could spell me while I run her back to the house. I guess not, huh. Anyway, when you get the message, could you call? If I'm not home, I'll be here unless the bank closes in the meantime. Gotta go. Thanks."

I wasn't sure when the call had come in because the date and time function on my answering machine has been horsed up for months, claiming it's perpetually noon on January 1. He must have called sometime after I'd talked to Joanne Fitzhugh because I left the same time she did and I'd run errands until it was reasonable to go home. I picked through the papers on my desk until I found the yellow legal pad where he'd jotted his contact information. I called his home number and counted fifteen rings before I hung up. I couldn't see the point in driving to his house if no one was answering the phone. On the other hand, there was an undertone of panic in his voice I didn't dare ignore.

I locked the office, fired up the Mustang, and drove the twelve blocks to Hermosa Street in a matter of minutes. I pulled into his drive, slammed the car door behind me, and scooted up his porch steps. I knocked, then crossed to the front window and peered in. Lights were off in the living room and there were no signs of life in the areas beyond. I pulled out my notebook and scribbled a hasty message, indicating the time I'd been there and asking him to call. I jotted down both my home and office numbers, then stuck the note between the front door and the screen. I stood indecisively, looking out at the street. As though by magic, Madaline walked into view, Goldie Hawn ahead of her, tugging at the leash. I waited.

As she turned up the walk, she said, "Where's Michael?"

My, my. The little lady seemed cross and out of sorts. I said, "I have no idea. That's what I came to ask you."

"He left the house this morning to go meet some guy. He didn't say a word about what time he'd be back."

"He didn't mention the guy's name?"

"Nuh-uh. He was in a rush and all goofy. He said maybe now people would believe he was telling the truth."

I pondered the implications, knowing it would be a waste of time to press her further. Madaline would be no help. She was too wrapped up in herself. I said, "I left a note for him stuck in the door. If you see him before I do, tell him I stopped by."

"Oh great. Now I'm stranded. He's got the car and I have to be someplace."

"Really."

"Yes, *really*," she said. "I have a job interview downtown. It's, like, completely critical to be there on time. Michael promised me a ride and now what?"

"Guess you'll have to walk."

"In *heels?* By the time I get there, I'll be all sweaty and out of breath."

I looked at my watch. "When's your appointment?"

"Ten-thirty."

"So start now and walk slowly. You have plenty of time."

"Fuck you."

Smiling, I returned to my car and backed out of the drive. I was still hoping to catch Sutton on his way back to the house. No such luck. I drove one block up and three blocks over, picking up the southbound freeway on-ramp. If his meeting was over, he might have returned to his one-man surveillance at the bank. I was taking the chance I'd spot his car in the vicinity. I got off the 101 at Old Coast Road and cruised past Montebello Bank and Trust, searching for Sutton's turquoise MG. No sign of him in the bank parking lot or the service station across the street. Twice I drove the length of the main drag without results. Finally, I pulled into the narrow parking strip in front of the bank, taking up the vigil myself.

I got out of my car and went to the double-glass doors. I pushed and found the door locked, then realized the place wouldn't open until ten, forty-five minutes hence. I locked my car and walked to a coffee shop I'd passed two blocks down. I paused at the entrance beside a row of coin-operated vending machines. I plunked a quarter in one and pulled out the local newspaper. I bought a big container of coffee and doused it liberally with milk. If the coffee didn't cause my bladder to swell to twice its normal size, I could make it last until the bank opened. I reconsidered and added sugar in case the coffee turned out to be lunch as well.

I walked back to the bank, cup in hand, and sat in the parking lot. I read the paper, keeping an eye open for Michael Sutton or any of the various and sundry bank officers who should be arriving for work. The paper didn't offer much in the way of news, only column after column of items pulled off the wire, most of which I'd read the day before in the *L.A. Times*. I skipped the funnies but pored over the obituaries. The people who'd died in the last few days were in their eighties and nineties. I made a mental note of the names in case William had overlooked a hot one in his search for a funeral to attend.

At 9:54 a petite, dark-haired woman approached the bank, dressed smartly in a suit, panty hose, and heels. She looked like a sympathetic person, and I wished I was in the market for a loan so I could borrow money from her. She unlocked the glass door and punched in the code for the alarm system on a panel to the right. She disappeared from sight. Five minutes later a second woman crossed the lot, passing my car before she went into the bank. If Michael was right and the guy was a bank employee, surely he'd be showing up soon.

As though on cue, I heard heels tapping on the pavement behind me and turned to watch a balding, heavyset fellow lumber past my car. He walked like a man who hurt. He glanced at me idly and I registered a bouquet of fading bruises on his right cheek, purple, yellow, and green—quite the dashing assortment. I hadn't caught a full-on view of his face so I couldn't make a judgment about his sporting black eyes. Seemed reasonable to assume that whatever door he'd walked into would have rendered sufficient damage for blackened eyes along with the puffy cheek. I waited until he'd gone in and then folded the paper and put the lid on my coffee cup, which I stashed on the passenger-side floor.

I went into the bank. There were two half-walls in front of

me with a wide aisle between. A corridor opened off each side
of the reception area. I counted five doors down one hallway
and two down the other. There was no sound, not even bad
music being piped in. No employees in sight. Clearly, they
were in their cubbyholes, gearing up for the day, unprepared
for the early arrival of customers or bank robbers, whichever
came first. I was at leisure to case the joint, but it didn't look
like a place that carried cash. I'd have paid a hundred dollars
for a ladies' room.

Finally, the petite, dark-haired woman appeared on my
right. "Oh, sorry. I didn't know anyone was out here. Can I
help you?"

"A man with bruises on his face came in here a few minutes
ago and I think he may work here. You have any idea who I'm
talking about?"

"Sure. That's Walker McNally, the VP of New Client
Relations. He has meetings all morning, but if you want to
talk to him, I can see if he has a minute."

"No need. He looked familiar, but the name doesn't ring a
bell so I must have mistaken him for someone else."

"Are you sure?"

"Positive."

I did not actually gallop back to the car, but I proceeded
with all due speed, heart thumping. I didn't want Walker
McNally to catch sight of me. Not to flatter myself, but I still
looked much as I had in high school while he'd been trans-
formed into a middle-aged man. I unlocked the car door, slid
into the driver's seat, turned the key in the ignition, and pulled
out. I turned the corner onto the side street and parked. Shit.
Walker McNally. A critical piece of the puzzle had just fallen
into place. Walker had had access to animals galore through
his father's veterinary practice. Our senior year in high school,
rumor had it he was dealing dope, which meant he might have
supplied weed to Creed and Destiny at the Unruhs', where
they'd parked the bus. That was a stretch, but not beyond possible. If Walker was one of the two pirates, I even had a can-
didate for his sidekick. He and Jon Corso had been joined at
the hip. What a pair. Eighteen years old, arrogant, privileged,
stoned, and bored. It didn't take a leap to imagine them coming up with a scheme to net them some bucks. I couldn't imag-

ine why either one would be hard up for cash, but maybe their respective parents were parsimonious.

I returned to the office and called Michael's house again. No answer. Where the heck was he? Madaline had probably already left on her trek downtown. She'd been on the verge of hitting me up for taxi money or a lift, no doubt hoping to inveigle me into waiting while she showered and did her hair.

It was time to talk to Cheney Phillips and I wanted Michael at my side to fill in his part of the story. Again. Sutton's word was suspect, but what else did we have?

Not one to remain idle, I hoisted my shoulder bag and went out to my car. I drove to the parking structure adjacent to the public library and wound my way upward to the roof, where I found the only spot left. I reached under the passenger seat and hauled out the *Thomas Guide to Santa Teresa and Perdido Counties*. I toted it with me while I trotted down three flights of stairs and crossed the access lane between the parking lot and the entrance to the library.

I went to the reference department. My personal table had been rudely preempted by someone other than me so I settled at another table. I dumped my bag in the chair and then crossed to the section where the Polk and Haines directories were shelved. I pulled volumes for 1966 and 1967, then loaded the city directories for the same years on top. I added the current telephone book and carried the stack to the table. I sat down and arranged the references in front of me, keeping them in easy reach while I leafed through the *Thomas Guide* to the pages devoted to Horton Ravine. I looked up the name Corso in both the Polk and the Haines for 1966 and 1967. There was only one Corso listed, that being Lionel M. on Ocean Way. I made a note of the address and then checked the current telephone book. Lionel Corso was still listed at that address. I was under the impression he'd died. I had a dim recollection of running across his name in the obits, but it was possible his widow, if he had one, still owned the house.

I looked up Walter McNally's old address in the same two criss-cross directories. In 1967 McNally senior had owned a home on Bergstrom Hill, just outside Horton Ravine and connected by a street called Crescent Road, in easy range of the Corsos' place. Walter must have sold the family home when he moved to Number 17 Juniper Lane in the Valley Oaks Senior Settlement. I pulled out a pencil and made discreet black dots in the *Thomas Guide,* designating the 1967 addresses for the Kirkendalls on Ramona Road, the Unruhs on Alita Lane, the Fitzhughs on Via Dulcinea, the McNallys on Bergstrom Hill Road, and the Corsos on Ocean. I didn't care about the Suttons, who'd lived on the western edge of the Ravine. On the day in question, Michael had been dropped off at the Kirkendalls', whose lot touched the Unruhs' at the bottom of the hill.

I returned the reference materials to the shelves, and left the library and drove into Horton Ravine to the Home Owner's Association. There I appealed to the two kind women working in the office, who gave me a dandy map of all the bridle trails through the Ravine. I sat in my car, map open and propped up against the steering wheel, while I studied the warren of trails linking the properties of all the principals. If I affixed the trail map to the wall and used a pushpin for each of the relevant locations, a string running around the lot of them would form a crude circle.

Now all I had to do was persuade Cheney Phillips I was on the right track. I went back to the office and called.

"Lieutenant Phillips."

"Hey, Cheney. This is Kinsey. Are you tied up at the moment?"

"I'm here at my desk for another twenty minutes. What's up?"

"You mind if I scoot in? I have something I want to run past you."

"Can't wait," he said.

"See you shortly."

My office was two blocks from the police department so I walked, maps in tow. Anxiety stirred in my gut. When it came right down to it, I was selling air and sunshine, a theory with nothing concrete to back it up. This put me in the same position Michael Sutton had been in, on the same shaky ground. The pieces fit together, but where was the glue? Michael's claims had been shot out from under him, and now here I was, reconfiguring the facts without a shred of proof.

I went into the lobby at the station and waited for Cheney to come out and accompany me to his cubicle. He looked especially handsome that day—expensive loafers, dark slacks, and a white dress shirt with the sleeves rolled up. On anyone else it would have been standard office attire, but Cheney came from money and I knew what he paid for clothes.

He sat me down and since his time was limited, I had no choice but to launch into my pitch. I wasn't even halfway through the spiel and I could tell by his expression he wasn't buying it. He heard me out, but I was losing confidence with every passing breath. Nothing like telling a story with passion and conviction while the guy on the receiving end is so clearly skeptical.

"Interesting," he said. "I can see where you're coming from, but what am I supposed to do?"

"I don't know, Cheney. Think about it, I guess. I went to high school with these guys . . ."

He held a hand up. "I'm not saying you're wrong. What I'm saying is there's not enough to act on. I can't bring either one of those guys in for a chat. Based on what? Speculation and guesswork and all of it circumstantial. Is there any reason to think Corso or McNally even *knew* the Fitzhughs or the Unruhs?"

"Deborah Unruh says Greg and Shelly smoked grass constantly. She knows there were at least two dopers who hung out with them. She never actually saw them, but someone supplied the weed and Walker was a dealer, or so I heard."

"So were half the kids in town. What about Greg and Shelly? Could they corroborate? Last I heard, they took off and haven't been heard from since."

"Both are dead. Tuesday, I talked to Shelly's son and he says Greg died of an overdose in Canada and his mother died of AIDS," I said. "It's possible Shawn could identify the pair. He was just a kid at the time, but he's a smart guy and a face is a face."

"It doesn't make a whit of difference if Walker sold dope to Shawn's parents."

"But Michael Sutton identified Walker as one of the two guys he saw digging. What if he picked Jon Corso out of a lineup—"

"A lineup?" he said.

"Okay, not a lineup, but there's gotta be a way. I can't drop

Corso's name on him out of a clear blue sky. Sutton's easily influenced, and I'd be corrupting his testimony if it ever comes to that."

"You better hope it doesn't. He's the worst possible eyewitness. Even if he points a finger, it doesn't get you anywhere."

"What if he and Shawn both identify the two?"

"As what? You're grasping at straws. Two kids loiter at a friend's house. Big deal. How do you get from them to the guys who kidnapped two little girls? Where's the link? As far as I can see, there's nothing that ties either one of them to the crime."

"The Fitzhughs and the Unruhs were all members of the Horton Ravine Country Club. If the Corsos or McNallys belonged, they might have crossed paths there."

"Thin and too iffy."

"What about the fingerprint on the ransom note?"

"Give it up. We've never had a hit on that in twenty-one years."

"Maybe the last time you ran it, Walker hadn't been picked up on his first DUI. He's in the system now. I don't know that Corso has a criminal history, but he might have been printed in the past few years. It's worth a try."

"Maybe." Cheney looked at his watch. "I'll get somebody on it when I can, but it'll take time. Don't get your hopes up."

"What hopes?" I said.

His phone rang and he picked up the handset. "Lieutenant Phillips."

I could hear someone talking. Cheney shot me a quick look and then said, "Let me call you back. I have someone here." He hung up. "You'll have to excuse me."

"Sure. You want me to leave?"

"That's not necessary. Sit tight."

He left the cubicle and went into the one next door. He placed the call and though he was in earshot, I couldn't hear what he was saying. Damn. I had to content myself with a survey of his office. The guy was disappointingly neat at work. At his house there was always stuff lying around, most of it connected to the various home projects he launched but never seemed to finish. Nosy as I am, I'd never dream of snooping through his desk. For all I knew, there were teeny-tiny little cameras hidden everywhere and I'd be caught in the act. I'll admit that during our brief romance, I familiarized myself with all the drawers and closets at his place.

I folded my map of the bridle trails and tucked it into the *Thomas Guide*. I was so bored I was about to start cleaning out my purse when I heard him winding down his end of the conversation. I looked at the door in anticipation of his return.

A moment later he appeared, his expression oddly unreadable. "Michael Sutton's dead."

*"What?"*

"He was shot sitting in his car in the lot at Seashore Park."

I was speechless, staring at him with disbelief.

Cheney went on, probably hoping to soften the impact. "The officer at the scene says a woman walking her dog heard the shot and saw a black sports car pull out of the lot. She only caught a flash, and apparently she doesn't know a Corvette from a Sherman tank. The 'black' she's pretty sure about unless the car was dark blue. I shouldn't be telling you this much, but you're a good friend and I trust you to keep your mouth shut."

I sat there, unable to absorb the news.

He put a hand on my arm and squeezed. "We're heading out to the scene and I don't want you there. We can talk about it later when I know more."

# 33

## Thursday, April 21, 1988

Jon pulled his car into the driveway, removed the handgun from under the seat, and got out. He walked around the main house to the back door, gun carried loosely at his side. He let himself in. The liquor supply was kept in the butler's pantry between the kitchen and the dining room. He set the gun on the counter, opened the cabinet, and took out a bottle of Cutty Sark. He found a highball glass and poured himself a stiff drink that he downed neat. He put the glass on the counter and held out his hands. He'd expected to be shaking, but his hands were steady. His heartbeat was slightly elevated, but otherwise he felt fine.

How naive he'd been about the act of shooting a man to death. In his most recent thriller, he'd described a character's shooting of a vagrant. The killing was random—no motive, no weapon left at the scene, and nothing that tied the killer to his victim. The fictional police investigation had gone nowhere and it should have been written off as the perfect crime. Naturally, a mistake was made, a minor matter. In the end, the killer wasn't caught, but he endured a nasty fate of the sort only a novelist could cook up. Jon realized now how completely he'd misunderstood the act of taking another man's life. It was simple, of no consequence. The only surprise had been the sound Michael Sutton made when he realized what was going on. Jon would have to struggle to erase the quick cry.

He tucked the gun in his waistband, poured another scotch, and carried it with him to the garage, where he climbed the steps to his studio. He had a few things to pack yet. Other than that, he was ready to rock and roll. Over the past two years, he'd gradually moved all his money to an offshore account, starting with the ten grand his father had left him. Lionel had unwittingly bequeathed him more than he intended. During the confusion in the days following his father's fatal heart attack, Jon had had the foresight to remove Lionel's passport from the jumble in his desk drawer. Mona never even noticed it was gone. He'd held on to it until it was due to expire and then filled out an application for renewal, which he'd submitted with two small photographs of himself. He'd donned his father's glasses so the resemblance was close enough. Jon took a certain satisfaction in appropriating his father's identity.

As a boy, he'd worshiped his dad, proud that he was a college professor. Many times he'd sat in on his father's classes and marveled at how knowledgeable he was. Students were enraptured, laughing at his droll observations, scribbling down his witticisms, as well as the dense bits of information embedded in his lectures. His father had written two books published by a well-known university press. At cocktail parties, when Jon was a kid, he'd linger on the periphery of those gathered, listening to his dad tell anecdotes about famous literary figures.

After Jon's mother died and Lionel and Mona married, his father's output had leveled off. He'd written two more books, which hadn't sold well, and a third he'd been forced to publish himself. For years he was still sought after on the lecture circuit, and he was paid well for his appearances, but Jon had heard the same talk, with the same wry pauses to allow for the polite laughter at the mildly amusing jokes. By the time Lionel died, Jon saw him as shrunken and weak. Mona had sucked the light right out of him.

Meticulously, he went back over his preparations. He had almost a hundred thousand dollars, in hundreds, packed in two body wallets that scarcely showed under his sport coat. For two thousand dollars he'd bought an airline ticket, one-way, first class, to Caracas, Venezuela. Once there he'd purchase another ID—driver's license, passport, and birth certificate—and retire both the Jon Corso and Lionel Corso identities. After he found a place to settle, he'd write his next book and submit it to a New York literary agent, under a fictitious name. He knew whom he'd approach, a woman who'd turned him down when he was desperate for an agent early in his career. She'd jump at the chance to take on a Jon Corso–style writer, having forfeited a fortune by rejecting the original.

He shrugged into a windbreaker and slid the gun in his right pocket. How nice that an item he'd stolen from a neighbor twenty-one years before had now set him free. By the time the police put it all together, if they ever managed it, he'd be long gone and, he hoped, impossible to trace. He folded and packed his favorite sport coat, his raincoat, and six shirts just back from the cleaner's. He went into the bathroom, added a few toiletries to his Dopp kit, and tucked it in the suitcase as well. His second bag was already closed and waiting downstairs near the front door. He sat down at his desk and called Walker at work.

As soon as Walker picked up, Jon said, "Michael Sutton just called. He wants to meet."

"*Meet* with us? Why?"

"How do I know? Maybe he wants to make a deal. We pay up and he keeps his mouth shut."

"A shakedown?"

Jon kept his tone matter-of-fact. "Now that he knows where you work, it doesn't seem out of the question."

"Shit. I told you he was trouble."

"We don't know that. Maybe we can come to an agreement."

"A deal? How long would that last? We give him money now, it's only a matter of time before he comes around for more."

"True, but you're talking about turning yourself in anyway so I can't see what difference it makes. By the time he comes back with his hand out, you'll be in jail."

"I told you I was *thinking* about turning myself in. I haven't done anything about it."

"Oh, sorry. You seemed pretty sure of yourself when we last spoke."

"Because I couldn't see an alternative."

Jon said, "The way I look at it, a payoff now might buy us a couple of months, during which you might change your mind. I should probably point out that your confession will lose its impact if he gets to the cops before you do."

"So why talk to him at all?"

"I'd like to hear what he has in mind."

Walker was quiet for a moment, mulling over the idea. "Where does he want to meet?"

"He mentioned the coffee shop down the street from the bank. I guess he thinks he'll be safe out in public."

"Suppose he comes wired? Then anything we discuss, we're both screwed. I thought the whole point was to find a way I could go to the cops without jeopardizing you."

"That was before this came up."

"I don't like it."

"I don't either, Walker. We turn him down, he'll go to the police for sure."

"You told me he didn't have anything on us. We were just two guys burying a dog. Didn't you say that?"

"Suppose he has an ace up his sleeve? That's what worries me. I don't like surprises. We're better off knowing what it is."

"Shit."

"I don't see a way around it," Jon went on. "I mean, maybe the guy's harmless, in which case, lucky us."

"I don't think we should be seen together. These days, every other business has security cameras. We don't want that on film, the three of us huddled together in a coffee shop. It won't look good."

"I can always call him back and suggest someplace else if you can think of one."

"What about Passion Peak? We're the only ones who go up there. If you're worried about a wire, all you have to do is pat him down."

"You were the one worried about a wire, but it's not a bad idea, a quick body search. If he's clean, he won't object."

"When does he want to meet?"

"Well, that's just it. He says soon. He sounds a bit anxious for my taste so the sooner the better. Would you have a problem cutting out of there for an hour?"

"Probably not. I'd have to reschedule a couple of things."

"Why don't you do that? I'll call Michael and tell him I'm swinging by to get you and then we'll meet."

"Does he know about the park?"

"If not, I'll give him directions. You cool with this?"

"I don't know. Something doesn't feel right. I mean, how'd he get your name? I'm the one he saw."

"That's something we'll have to ask him. Clearly, he knows more than we thought."

"I don't know about this."

"Fine. Say the word and I'll tell him it's a no-go."

"We should probably hear him out."

"Agreed. That's my point. If there's a problem about the place, I'll call you back. See you shortly."


I walked back to the office in a state of suspended animation. Sutton's death seemed incomprehensible. For the moment, I didn't feel sorrow, I felt dismay. He'd gone off to meet someone and ended up dead. Unbelievable. Walker McNally couldn't have done it. I'd seen him at the bank at 10:00. He had a morning full of meetings. It was 11:30 now. I didn't see how he could have slipped away, driven up to Seashore, shot Sutton, and scurried back again. I assumed his license had been yanked because of his accident and he surely wouldn't have hired a taxi or bummed a ride. Of course, killers probably aren't that fussy about obeying traffic laws.

At the same time, if I was correct about Jon Corso and Walker being in cahoots, Jon could have been the shooter. He lived near the back entrance to the Ravine. Seashore Park wasn't far from his house, three miles at best. He could have driven to the park, killed Sutton, and returned home, and who would be the wiser? I opened my *Thomas Guide* and checked his house number, tempted to cruise by and see if he was there. I had no intention of knocking on his door, but it wouldn't hurt to look.

I went out to the Mustang and fired up the engine, plotting my route as I pulled away from the curb. The shortest path was to cut the two blocks over to Capillo and drive up the hill to the intersection where Capillo and Palisade crossed. I'd spent quite a bit of time in that area on a case I'd worked earlier in the year. If I turned left on Palisade and drove a mile, I'd be at Seashore; a right turn would take me past Little Pony Road, and then up another hill and into Horton Ravine.

Traffic was slowed by road construction and it took longer than I'd anticipated before I reached Horton Ravine and passed between the stone pillars. My Grabber Blue 1970 Mustang was conspicuous under ordinary circumstances, even more so in this upscale neighborhood where most vehicles (except those of the hired help) were late-model luxury cars.

As I passed Corso's house I was startled to see him emerge from the front door, a suitcase in each hand. The car sitting in his driveway was a sleek black Jaguar. I resisted the urge to stare, directing my attention instead to the road ahead. At the next corner I turned right and drove as far as the first estate entrance, where I did a quick turn and crept back toward Ocean. Jon had gone back for a briefcase. On the porch he took a moment to lock up and then returned to the car, where he arranged his bags. When he slid under the wheel, I was close enough to hear the faint slamming of his car door and the engine begin humming. He pulled out of the drive and headed right, toward Harley's Beach, back along Palisade. I gave him a twenty-second head start and pulled out after him.

When he reached the intersection of Capillo and Palisade, I thought he'd turn right, but he continued on past City College, neatly avoiding Seashore Park. He caught the southbound freeway and I tucked in behind him, easing off the gas to allow another car between us. By the time he reached the Old Coast Road off-ramp, there were two cars between us and I felt I was sufficiently protected to avoid notice. He made a sedate left-hand turn and came up on the far side of the underpass. He had to be heading for the bank. I couldn't guess his purpose unless Walker emerged with suitcases in hand, in which case I'd assume both were preparing to flee. Corso pulled into the bank parking lot and I drove by, making a mental note of his license plate:

I made a quick turn onto Center Road, reversed in a motel parking lot, and cut back, passing the bank again just as Walker ducked into the car. Corso pulled out of the lot. I kept him in sight as he crossed the intersection and eased from Old Coast Road onto the freeway, driving north. I wondered what they were up to. Did Walker know Michael Sutton was dead? Was that the arrangement they'd made? Corso would strike while Walker established an ironclad alibi? What about the risk to Jon, whose car had been spotted at the scene? It seemed clear Walker wasn't leaving town, at least in the next half-hour, so perhaps the purpose of the meeting was to bring Walker up to speed before Jon disappeared on his own.

It all seemed so pointless. If Henry was right about the burial of the marked bills, I didn't see how either one of them could feel endangered. The only trump out against them was the shaky report of a six-year-old boy, who'd seen nothing incriminating. If word of my queries had leaked back to Walker, he might have wondered about my interest, but it hardly merited radical action. Shooting Michael Sutton was a miscalculation, overkill, as it were. Perhaps they didn't realize Sutton had no credibility and was therefore harmless.

My current course was set and I was stuck with it. If I hadn't decided to cruise by Corso's house, I wouldn't be tailing the two of them now, engaging in all this endless speculation about why they were together and where they intended to go. Guess I'd find out. Ahead of me, Jon took the off-ramp at Little Pony Road and turned left. At the top of the rise, he was caught by a red light. I was three cars behind. If he'd spotted me, he gave no indication. His driving was circumspect as he turned left through the intersection and drove toward the beach.

Were they looking for a private spot? That was the only thing I could figure, given their route. Why did they need privacy at all when they could have chatted by phone? Surely they didn't imagine the lines were tapped. How paranoid would that be? I saw the Jaguar slow and turn left again into an unmarked side road I knew from times past. They were heading for Passion Peak, the pocket park that had been closed for two years, after a wildfire swept through it.

Here's what occurred to me: What if Jon was doing a quick

mop-up campaign, eliminating anyone who posed a threat
to him? He was set for an imminent departure, destination
unknown. Now that Sutton was out of the way, was Walker
next?

I pulled over to the shoulder of the road and got out, leaving my car running while I moved cautiously to the turnoff.
A mass of bougainvillea obscured the entrance to the park. I
lifted on my toes and peered. There was no sign of the Jaguar.
The chain that had been strung across the road was now down,
trailing from the post on the left. I returned to my car and
waited. The road up to the parking area was barely two lanes
wide, with sufficient turns to slow any vehicle winding up the
hill. I couldn't afford to round a bend and find myself smack
up against Jon's bumper. If the two intended to spend time up
there, I had to give them the ten minutes it would take to park
at the midpoint and climb the rest of the way to the top. If Jon
intended to pop Walker in the head, I was the only one even
remotely aware of it. I took advantage of the wait to open the
trunk of my car and remove the Heckler & Koch from my
locked briefcase.


Walker climbed the hill a few steps behind Jon. He'd wakened
early, finding himself at peace for the first time in weeks. He
felt good. He had energy and optimism. He'd suddenly turned
a corner. He had no idea why or when the shift had occurred.
When he'd opened his eyes that morning at the Pelican Motel,
a sight that should have been depressing was actually all right.
He'd have preferred to be home with his wife and kids, but
for now, he could do this. It dawned on him that being clean
and sober felt better than the best moment of being drunk. He
didn't want to live as he had, from happy hour to happy hour,
drink to drink, from one hangover to the next. It was as if a
heavy set of chains had fallen away. His demons had loosened
their hold and he was light as air. The battle wasn't over. Come
5:00, he'd probably still have the urge to drink. But he knew
now all he had to do was what he'd been doing for the past
ten days. Just not drink. Just not succumb. Just think of something else until the urge went away. Being clean and sober for
ten days hadn't killed him. The *alcohol* had been killing him.

The absence of alcohol was to be celebrated—and not with a drink or a cigarette or a pill or anything else that might come between him and his own soul. If he could attribute the sense of well-being to anything, it was his decision to turn himself in. In his conversation with Jon, he'd implied that he was still on the fence, but it wasn't true, He wondered if this was the euphoria experienced by someone bent on suicide. Turning himself in would be the end of life as he knew it, and that was okay with him. He'd brave it, all of itóthe shame, the humiliation, the public castigation. That was the deal he'd made twenty-one years earlier. There was no escaping his fate, and he accepted that now. Drinking created the illusion he'd gotten away with something, but he couldn't obliterate the burden in his soul. Owning up would do it, taking responsibility.

At the crest of the hill he paused to absorb the view. Southern California was at its best in April. Wildflowers had sprung up in the meadow and the long grass rustled in the wind. It was quiet up here, even against the faint noise of traffic that rose from the town below. Jon moved over to a table, where he stood, arms crossed, his hip resting against the edge. In early March, a storm had blown in with hard rain and high winds that had downed trees and torn off branches that now littered the area. Walker bent and picked up a stick. He flung it like a boomerang, though it whipped off without returning.

"I guess we better talk while we can," Jon said.

Walker sat on a picnic bench, elbows on his knees, fingers laced together loosely. "I was thinking about it on the way over. This business with Sutton won't work. I don't want to be on the hook to him, you know? Waiting around for his next appearance. Fuck that. The whole point in coming clean is we don't have to sweat this stuff. It's over and done."

"For you. We still have the problem of how I come out of it unscathed."

"We already went through this—"

"I know we did. I was hoping you'd come up with a solution. So far, I haven't heard one. Get me out of the line of fire. That's all I ask."

"I'm still racking my brain." Walker looked at his watch. "What time did you tell him? Shouldn't he be here by now?"

"I told him half an hour."

"Well, where is the little shit? You called me at noon."

"That was twenty-five minutes ago. You're avoiding the subject."

"Which is what, how you keep out of the line of fire?"

"Right. I'd like to hear your thoughts."

"Yeah, well, my thoughts are to stay clean and sober. To do that, I gotta get square, and I'm cool with that."

"So you said. Have you any concern whatsoever about what this will do to me? I looked it up. The deal is, you make amends unless doing so would injure others. You don't think I'll be 'injured' if you blow the whistle on me?"

"I don't think the admonition applies when there's a serious crime involved," Walker said. "I feel bad, Jon. I do. We were good friends, the best. Then this came between us, and I've regretted it. We can't socialize. We can't acknowledge one another in public. I can't even talk to you by phone."

"That's more your rule than mine," Jon said, mildly.

"Bullshit. That was your dictate from the beginning. I only ever called you twice in the last twenty-one years, and that was in the past few weeks. And you blew me off."

"Water under the bridge. I'm asking for protection. You owe me that."

"I can't protect you. With Michael Sutton on his way? Are you nuts? We'll be at his mercy. The first dollar changes hands and he'll have us for life. I can't believe you'd even entertain an offer."

"You must have been open to the idea or you wouldn't be here."

"I came because you talked me into it. I don't want to meet the kid at all and I certainly don't want to pay him money. Jon, this can all be so simple. If I go to the police we can put an end to it right here. He'll have nothing on us."

"He's got nothing on us now."

"Then why are we sitting up here waiting for him?"

"We're not. He's actually not going to join us. He's been unavoidably delayed."

"I don't understand."

"I reconsidered and you're right. Doing business with him is a bad idea. I changed my mind. I'm here asking you if you've changed yours."

"About turning myself in? That's nonnegotiable. I wish I could help you, but you're on your own. Do whatever you want."

Jon made a face. "Like fuckin' what?"

"Why not take off? Disappear into thin air. Isn't that what the bad guy did in your last book?"

"Book before last. And thanks for assigning me the part of 'the bad guy.' I've already thought about taking off, as a matter of fact. You go all holier-than-thou with this confession of yours, I have no choice. I gotta get out before the shit hits the fan. I'm offering you one more chance . . . just one . . . to do something other than what you've proposed."

"You want me to keep my mouth shut."

"Now you got it. Otherwise, I take control, which is not going to be good for either one of us."

Walker shook his head. "Can't do. Won't. I'm sorry if that creates a problem for you."

"My problem . . . and this is a tough one, Walker . . . it really is . . . I can't afford the tab. Your purging your conscience is going to cost more than I want to pay. You go to the cops, you know the story you'll tell? You'll make me the fall guy. How can you resist? You already said it was my idea, that I was the instigator while you followed orders. What kind of horseshit is that? How does it make me look? What wiggle room does it give my defense attorney if the law ever catches up with me? You'll rat me out and you'll be a hero while I take the rap. I mean, does that seem right? Think about it. You were in it the same as I was—every step of the way. You never once spoke up. You never expressed any reservations at all—until now."

"Times change, Jon. I've changed."

"But I haven't." He held his hand out. "Look at this. Steady as she goes. No wavering on my part. No ambivalence, no getting all weepy-minded. You're the fly in the ointment, if you'll excuse the cliché."

Walker recoiled in mock horror. "So what are you going to do, rub *me out*?"

"Pretty much."

Walker offered up a flickering smile. "You can't be serious. You think silencing me will protect you?"

"I don't see why not."

"What about Sutton?"

Jon stared at him.

Walker blanched. "Oh, shit, what did you do?"

"Shot him," I said, raising my voice. I'd reached the top of the hill, which was utterly without cover. They couldn't fail to notice my arrival so I figured I might as well speak up. In a heartbeat, Walker realized who I was. Jon was slower on the uptake. He looked at Walker. "Who's this?"

I crossed the grass. "Kinsey Millhone. I'm an old high school classmate. You probably don't remember me, but I remember you."

I had my gun in hand. I wasn't pointing it at anybody, but I thought it would be effective nonetheless.

Jon said, "This doesn't concern you."

"Yes, it does. Michael Sutton was a friend of mine."

He noticed my gun for the first time and nodded. "Is that thing loaded?"

"Well, I could end up looking foolish if it weren't."

Casually, he removed a gun from his windbreaker pocket and pointed it at me. "I'm telling you to get the fuck off this hill before I shoot you."

I made a face I hoped conveyed humility and regret. "Sorry to make a fuss about it, but here's my view. I'll bet Sutton was the one and only guy you ever killed in cold blood. I, on the other hand, have killed more than once. I can't give you the count. I try not to keep track because it makes me look like a vigilante, which I'm not."

"Up yours."

"I don't want to sound racist about this, but what we have here is what's called a Mexican standoff."

He smiled. "Right, the question being which of us will fire first."

"Exactly." I fired a shot, hitting his right hand. The gun popped up and landed in the grass. Walker jumped while Jon yelped in pain and dropped where he stood. I must have looked like a sharpshooter, but in truth he was fewer than fifteen feet away so it didn't require any tricks. Point and pull the trigger, easy does it.

"Jesus Christ," Walker said. "You fuckin' *shot* the guy!"

"He's the one who talked about firing first," I said.

I removed a hankie from my shoulder bag and bent down to retrieve Jon's gun, wrapping it daintily to preserve his fingerprints. Jon had rolled over and risen to his knees. He leaned forward, head almost touching the ground as he gripped his shattered right hand in his left. He watched himself bleed, his face ashen, his breathing ragged.

"You're fine," I said to him, and then turned to Walker. "Give me your tie and I'll make a tourniquet."

Walker was so rattled his hands shook as he pulled the knot on his tie and passed it to me. Except for the whimpering, Jon offered no resistance as I made a slipknot and secured the tie around his forearm. It's only in the movies the bad guys keep firing. In real life, they sit down and behave.

"I can't believe you did that," Walker said, distressed.

"Neither can he."

"We can't just leave him here without help."

"Of course not." I handed him my car keys. "My Mustang's parked down below. Take it to the nearest service station, call the cops, and tell 'em where we are. You better ask for an ambulance while you're at it. I'll wait here with your pal until you get back."

He took the keys, pausing to stare at me. "Did you just save my life?"

"More or less," I said. "So how's it going down with the clean-and-sober shit? That's a tough one. You gonna make it?"

Disconcerted, he said, "Good. It's great. I got a lock on it. Ten days."

I reached over and gave his arm a squeeze. "Good for you!"

# EPILOGUE

As of the writing of this report, Jon Corso's hired a criminal attorney with a five-star reputation who's busy preparing his case, filing motions left and right, trumpeting to the press his client's eagerness to lay the facts before the court in the interest of clearing his name. Fat chance. When the case comes to trial, he'll doubtless accuse Walker of being the mastermind, claiming he offered to testify purely to save his own ass. The case will drag on for years. The trial will take weeks and cost the taxpayers a bundle. And who knows, maybe subjected to sufficient obfuscation and sleight of hand, the jury will find for the defense. Happens all the time.

As for Walker, the fingerprint on the ransom note was his. Herschel Rhodes is working on a deal whereby he'll plead guilty to kidnapping for ransom and second-degree murder, with assorted other charges tacked on. In exchange for his testimony, the death-penalty allegation will likely be dropped. Still, once you factor in his guilty plea for felony vehicular manslaughter, drunken driving, and leaving the scene of an accident in the death of the coed, Julie Riordan, the terms of his sentence are bound to be stiff—twenty-five years to life, but with the possibility of parole . . . perhaps.

Walker said he never knew where Jon had buried Mary

Claire, and Jon, of course, refused to admit to anything. Three weeks after the incident in the park, a judge issued a search warrant. Sergeant Pettigrew, the K-9 officer, took his dog, Belle, to Jon's property. Nose to the ground, she sniffed her way back and forth across the grass, up and around the house, finally settling near the water heater at the back of the garage. The heater was mounted on a concrete pad, surrounded by a weathered trellis with a hinged door. A sticker on the side of the heater bore the name of the plumber and the date the appliance was installed. July 23, 1967. When officers jackhammered up the concrete pad and dug under it, they found Mary Claire's body five feet down, curled in her final sleep. With her, Jon had buried the fifteen thousand dollars in marked bills, still in the gym bag. Over the years, moisture in the soil had reduced the money to pulp.

Half of the Santa Teresa townsfolk turned out for Mary Claire's funeral, including Henry and me.

As for the Kinsey family gathering Memorial Day, I attended that, too, keeping Henry at my side for moral support. Grand was in a wheelchair at the head of the receiving line. Even from a distance I could see how frail she was. She was old, not in the way Henry and his siblings were old, but feeble and shrunken, as light and bony as an old cat.

I waited my turn, and when I reached her, her rheumy blue eyes widened with surprise and her mouth formed a perfect O and then turned up in a smile. She gestured impatiently, and my cousins, Tasha and Liza, helped her out of her wheelchair. She stood shakily and took in the sight of me, tears filling her eyes. She stretched a tentative hand and patted my cheek. "Oh Rita, dear angel, thank you for being here. I've been waiting all these years, praying you'd come back. I was so frightened I'd die without ever laying eyes on you again."

She touched my hair. "Look at you, just as beautiful as ever, but what have you done to your lovely hair?"

I smiled. "It was a nuisance so I cut it off."

She patted my hand. "Well, it's becoming and I'm glad you did. You wanted to cut it for your coming-out party and oh what a fight we had. Do you remember that?"

I shook my head. "Not a bit of it."

"Doesn't matter now. You're perfect as you are."

She held on to me as she searched, confused, among the guests nearby. "I don't see your little girl. What happened to her?"

"Kinsey? She's all grown up now," I said.

"I imagine so. What a little slip of a thing she was. I've saved some trinkets of yours I want her to have. Do you think she'd ever come visit me? It would make me so happy."

I put my hand over hers. "It wouldn't surprise me if she did."